In the Shadows of Enigma

A Novel

In the Shadows of Enigma

A Novel

Alex Rosenberg

**TOP HAT
BOOKS**

Winchester, UK
Washington, USA

JOHN HUNT PUBLISHING

First published by Top Hat Books, 2021
Top Hat Books is an imprint of John Hunt Publishing Ltd., No. 3 East St., Alresford,
Hampshire SO24 9EE, UK
office@jhpbooks.com
www.johnhuntpublishing.com
www.tophat-books.com

For distributor details and how to order please visit the 'Ordering' section on our website.

ISBN: 978 1 78904 666 3
978 1 78904 667 0 (ebook)
Library of Congress Control Number: 2020939164

A CIP catalogue record for this book is available from the British Library.

Design: Stuart Davies

UK: Printed and bound by CPI Group (UK) Ltd, Croydon, CR0 4YY
Printed in North America by CPI GPS partners

We operate a distinctive and ethical publishing philosophy in
all areas of our business, from our global network of authors to
production and worldwide distribution.

Contents

Preface

During the 1930s Polish mathematicians succeeded in breaking into coded signals the German military was sending on their *Enigma* cypher machines. A month before the German attack on Poland that began the Second World War, Polish intelligence passed on to the British and French their techniques and the hardware they had devised to break the German codes.

Developing this work, the British began to successfully decrypt first the radio traffic of the German *Luftwaffe*, then the *Wehrmacht*, and intermittently the German naval radio traffic. Much of this work was carried out at Bletchley Park, an estate in Buckinghamshire requisitioned during the war. As the Germans improved their coding techniques, Alan Turing, working at Bletchley Park, developed the first digitally programmable computers to continue to provide decrypts to the Allied military command.

By 1945, some 10,000 persons, of whom 8,000 were women, worked in Bletchley Park deciphering coded German military signals. When the war ended in that year all 10,000 participants in this work were enjoined to secrecy, on pain of prosecution under the British Official Secrets Act, with a maximum sentence of fourteen years for each violation.

Over the next twenty-nine years, until the matter was disclosed in 1974, not one of these 10,000 participants in the work divulged the secret. By contrast almost from the moment the war ended every other classified matter important to the conduct of military operations was leaked, disclosed to the public, or revealed to potential adversaries by espionage, including nuclear weapon design, ballistic missiles, jet engines, ground and airborne radar, the Norden bombsight, the proximity fuze, and submarine technology.

The only secret the western Allies' managed to keep was the

successful decoding of *Enigma*. That secret was kept for thirty years after the war. When it was finally revealed in 1974, much of what had been written about the Second World War had to be substantially revised, including all the official histories published by the combatant nations.

It's remarkable that this secret was kept for so long by the Allied governments—Britain, The United States, Canada, Australia, and New Zealand. A more interesting question is why they wanted to keep this secret for almost a further thirty years?

Portent

Otto Schulke hadn't really had such a bad war, nothing compared to the able-bodied men who'd served the fatherland in the *Wehrmacht* on the eastern front. Even his immediate post-war hadn't been nearly as bad as it might have been. Many of those who'd survived the eastern front were now in prison camps across the Soviet Union. Some of them would still be there until 1955, a decade after the war ended. Schulke hadn't really even suffered what POWs in the west had experienced, a year to eighteen months in a stockade on the same rations day after day, taunted and ridiculed by men half their worth as soldiers.

But he had been forced to undergo the process of de-Nazification in the glare of suspicious Amis—US Army intelligence officers, some of them native German speakers, escapees from the Reich, probably Jews. It took months, and certificates from friends and relations and a dozen interrogations to convince them he'd just been a simple policeman, a *muss-Nazi* with no choice but to join in order to save his job.

In the days after the occupation of Mannheim, Schulke had been worried enough to begin destroying everything he had that might identify him as an *SS-Untersturmführer*. But then he was sat down by his boss, the *Kriminalsekretar*.

"Otto, calm down. You'll only draw suspicion on yourself. Besides, you can't cover your tracks. There are records everywhere." Then he smiled. "But, don't worry. They're not going to treat a policeman as a war criminal, not even if he was a *Sturmscharführer* like me."

Schulke was doubtful. "What should I do, *Sturmscharführer?*"

"You can start by calling me sergeant-major, that's the old police rank before they *forced* us to join the SS, corporal." Schulke nodded, but his governor, the station's chief, couldn't tell whether he had really grasped the extra emphasis in the word 'forced.' The *Kriminalsekretar* had joined the party even earlier than Schulke had, and had eagerly accepted a transfer from the ordinary police force to the *Gestapo*. Almost everyone in the regular force had. The benefits were obvious, the alternative unpalatable. But if everyone had joined up, well, they had to, didn't they? You couldn't condemn every policeman as a war criminal, could you? "Since we didn't do anything more than our duty, and even that grudgingly when it came to our Jewish friends still in Germany when the war began..." He could see that Otto was not following. "Schulke, how many Jews did you personally arrest from the time you became a cop in '41?"

"A few, mainly some older people we caught trading on the black market, and those two women back last winter, the ones you made me let go." He recalled them with anger he could not show. It was an arrest that would have made his career. But the *Sturmscharführer* had ordered him to release them.

"And lucky for you I did! It would have been just the thing to get you in real trouble, leaving your fingerprints on a couple of victims of Fascism that late in the war. The others, the black marketers? Well, you were just doing your job, nothing to worry about."

Pretend to like them just to enjoy the brief luxury of a Camel or a tin of Spam.

Four years of living hand-to-mouth had reshaped Otto Schulke. Approaching thirty, he'd long lost the baby fat, replaced by the sag of a middle-aged jowl, the crew cut became first unnecessary and then impossible as his head went prematurely bald while the hair on his face grew relentlessly. Schulke needed a daily shave just to look respectable for whatever indoor job he could find.

Otto Schulke never thought he'd be grateful to Konrad Adenauer. The man had started out as the Allies' stooge, tool, puppet. But within a year of becoming the first Chancellor of the new Germany—the western two thirds of the Reich—he'd ended de-Nazification. Then the man had begun to welcome back into the civil service people he needed to govern a country sensibly, even former policemen who could prove they had been merely *Minderbelastete*—small fry, cogs in the Nazi machinery of state. Thank heaven Schulke had followed the old *Sturmscharführer's*, or rather the *Kriminalesekretar's*, advice. By 1951 he was back in the police and a paid-up member of the CDU—the Christian Democratic Union, the party of Adenauer, democracy, peace and freedom.

Then came the offer to join Adenauer's new intelligence agency, the BfV—*Bundesamt für Verfassungsschutz*. Like so much else in post-war Germany it had the least threatening, most innocent-sounding name: *the Federal Office for the Protection of the Constitution*. But Schulke knew exactly what its business would be: sniffing out the red turncoats and spies from East Germany while protecting those who had merely followed orders and were now, finally, being allowed to carry on their service to the state.

Keeping his nose clean and his head down, punctilious about constitutional and legal niceties, never making the same misstep twice, Otto Schulke should have made his way quickly up the promotional ladder in the BfV. He'd never even fiddled his expenses, not once. If he forgot to get a receipt he just wouldn't claim the reimbursement, ever. It should have meant something, along with the fact that his wartime credentials were impeccable, especially when so many others proved to be unreliable— former draft dodgers, exiles from the Third Reich, along with a large number of *Stasi* agents from the east it was pretty easy to uncover. By ten years after the war, there were plenty of men in the BfV whose *Nazionalsocialistische* pedigrees were no better than Schulke's. Some of these backgrounds were rumored to be far worse, and the rumors were always tinged with admiration. These men were all now well ahead of Schulke. He was still on the lower rungs of the ladder, wearing out shoe leather, or ordering a handful of other men to do so, with no chance to do something important.

He thought he knew why. He'd never cracked a case, never landed anything worth noticing. That was because they'd never given him a chance to do more than follow orders.

Schulke had nearly found his chance to shine, to do something really important, to become someone. It was back in the winter of '44. He'd begun to uncover something serious enough to carry him instantly up the *Gestapo* ranks, right to *SS-Standartenfurher*—captain in the security police. And then he'd been stopped cold by his super. The *Kriminalsekretar* had made him release his suspects, put an end to his inquiries, ordered Schulke to do nothing further. Schulke had always suspected his gov of being insufficiently ardent, of really being *muss-Nazi*, of defeatism—a hanging offence, even in the last days of the Third Reich. By the time Schulke was certain of it, the war really was lost. It was too late.

But this case, this missed chance...it ate into Schulke's conscience, it fed his resentment, endlessly obsessed his waking hours, until his anger faded into an inchoate sense of suffering that scudded along above his life, making every day bitter. He'd kept the case file though, all through the hungry years, and even after he'd been called back to his vocation, reading and rereading it to renew the grievance of a thwarted life.

* * *

Life in Bonn was a boring, pointless routine. Until it wasn't.

Charged with managing local surveillance, Schulke was running three or four teams of faceless, featureless men following low level embassy officials from Western countries—spinster secretaries, alcoholic chauffeurs, disgruntled clerks. Each of his teams knew what they were watching for—telltale signs of contact with *Stasi* agents or *KGB* rezidents eager to humor their grievances and fill their needs—carnal, monetary, moral. Every time it happened, the matter was swiftly taken from his desk, moved to other, presumably more capable, more knowing hands. The *Stasi*—East German's *Ministerium für Staatsicherheit*— was the BfV's special enemy, honey-combing every office in West Germany's Federal Republic with enemy agents almost impossible to detect just because they were as German as the West Germans.

Along with all the embassy work, there was one team Schulke had been tasked to run with no reason given and none he could discern. The watching assignment had already been in place when Schulke took over. His job was to keep the men at it, without asking why. This team was larger than others, sometimes he had to keep four men on the job, watching men and a few women, coming to and going from an old two-story government building near the Bonn cathedral. Schulke was told nothing about them—who they were, what they did, nothing at all. Week in, week out, he'd file a report, never more than half a page. His team's targets met no one, never varied from their routines, were punctual, regular, completely conventional in clothes, demeanor. Sometimes Schulke would even take a turn watching, following, in the hope he might learn what this assignment was all about. No luck.

Without rhyme or reason it was hard to keep men at the work, seven days a week, sitting in a parked car, or lurking in a vestibule. Month after month, the routine of starting in the morning gloom of a Bonn winter, and finishing well after dark, was breaking the watchers' spirits. The monotony of the work finally got to a couple of his agents. They'd both been caught skiving off, staying warm and dry, leaving their quarry unwatched hours at a time. There was a message to call headquarters in Cologne, the office of the *Vizepräsident* of the BfV for counterintelligence. The whole team—all of them—was to be replaced and sacked. Schulke was to present himself at BfV headquarters in Cologne for an inquiry. *How did they find out?* As his train rattled along, Schulke kept asking this question to himself, all the way from Bonn to Cologne. The answer came as he stepped onto the platform. *The job is important enough that they've got people inside that building watching us.*

He was standing at the desk of the assistant to the *Vizepräsident* of the BfV for counterintelligence, a class A flunky named Horst Schelling. Schulke had explained for the third time his duties, his methods and his excuses for this lapse.

The man's look was so plain, his expression so guarded, at first Schulke could read nothing of his fate. The face, Schulke realized, was the kind he hated—unlined, unweathered, unmarked by the Third Reich, the war or its austere half-decade-long aftermath. This was the new Germany, with clean hands, he had now to answer to. The face of the faceless Schelling was looking up into Schulke's face, evidently studying it carefully. Briefly it flashed a dubious smirk. Schulke knew why. *I'm going to be sacked.*

"Well, Herr Schulke, if we send you back to Bonn, can you do this job right?

"*Jawohl, mein Herr.*" The words stuck in Schulke's craw. "But I need people who obey orders, experienced men." *Men like me. Men who understand discipline.* He almost said it out loud.

"You'll get what we can give you. It will be up to you to keep them at the work."

Schulke wanted not to fail. He couldn't fail. He knew what he had to demand from Schelling. "Mein Herr, you have to speak to the *Vizepräsident* for me. I know I can discharge this watching mission, and keep anyone under me at it." He stopped for a moment, gathering his thoughts. "But the men doing the work, they must have an idea of what they are doing, what they are looking for, why the job is important."

The *Vizepräsident*'s adjutant shook his head. "Impossible. Most tightly guarded secret in the…" Was he going to say Reich?

No. This man had broken the habit. "In the Federal Republic."
"Then I can't do the job, sir, and anyone else you get will
eventually fail the same way"—he'd take the responsibility—
"the same way I did." The man behind the desk was mute. "Look,
sir, the people in that building my men were watching never put
a foot wrong the whole time we watched. There was nothing
to report on any of them. That's what made the job pointless.
You've got to give me a reason, something, anything, to make
men do this job."

The officer removed his glasses, put two fingers to the crease
between his eyebrows. Then he spoke. "Report back tomorrow
at 9:00 in the morning."

* * *

When he arrived at the assistant's office, the man rose. "Follow
me." He turned and walked through the door to the office of
the BfV–*Vizepräsident* for counterintelligence. It was a threshold
Schulke had never expected to cross.

The *Vizepräsident* was sitting at a large wooden desk before a
large bookcase of matching wood, filled with tomes of Roman
law in leather bindings. He was large, well fed and sleek in a
suit that fit tightly over a blindingly white shirt and a narrow
black tie.

The assistant announced, "Officer Schulke, Herr Schrübbers."

There were two seats before the desk, but he did not invite
either his assistant or Schulke to sit. The *Vizepräsident* sighed.
Then he spoke, in an undertone, as though he were afraid others
might hear. "Schulke, I am going to tell you something, because
you need to know." He grimaced in a way that suggested he was
acting against his better judgment. "But you will have to find a lie
for your men." Schulke nodded wordlessly. "In the war we had
a radio cypher code. The Army High Command, the Luftwaffe,
the Kriegsmarine, we all used it. Thought it was unbreakable

9

and used it right to the end." He paused. "But it wasn't, only we never found out." He kept using the word 'we.' What did that word mean to him, Schulke wondered? But he remained silent. "Neither did the Russians, because the western Allies never even told them they'd cracked our code." He paused again. Schulke wondered, was the *Vizepräsident* thinking the same thing he was, *That's why we lost the war.*

Schulke broke the silence. "And of course the Ruskies took the machines and the code, like everything else they wanted, and started using it themselves."

"Exactly." Schrübbers frowned. "They'd been trying to break the Enigma all through the war without success. When they crashed into Berlin at the end, there were a dozen machines in the Reich Chancellery and enough willing…" Was he going to say traitors, Schulke wondered? But he didn't. "…enough low-level code clerks to explain it all to them." Then Schrübbers smiled slightly. "And of course they never learned it had been cracked. They still think the code's unbreakable! That means the Brits, the Amis are decoding and reading Soviet military signals every day…and we're getting all the *Stasi and KGB* intelligence traffic too!"

Schulke raised his eyebrows. "Everything, every day?"

The *Vizepräsident* smiled more broadly. "And where is all this decoding getting done? In Bonn, in that building you've been watching people come and go from. The volume of decrypts is so heavy we have a half-dozen ex-Wehrmacht cypher clerks working every day, all day in that building." Then he frowned. "Schulke, if just one of them passed on to the Soviets or any agent from the East Bloc what they are doing…Well, we lost the war because we didn't know. And the East Bloc is losing this… cold war, because it doesn't know." He paused. "Your work is just part of a coordinated system for protecting this secret."

And suddenly Otto Schulke realized he knew something no one else knew, something so important it would be the making of him, it would vindicate the blighted life he'd been forced to lead for a dozen years. "Sir, one question, if I may?" The sleek man behind the desk nodded, inviting him to speak with a gesture of his hand.

It was a moment to relish and Schulke took it. "Sir, this secret code the Reich employed during the war, was it called Enigma?"

"Yes. That's not much of a secret. It was named after the machine we"—he corrected the slip—"they used. The crucial secret is that the Enigma code was broken. The Russians don't know that."

Schulke smiled. The smile was slightly surly and he saw immediately it was unwelcome, but he couldn't wipe it off his beefy face. "Sir, you have a much more serious problem than you realize. The secret that the code itself was broken during the war, that secret is almost certainly already known...known by at least one person, perhaps others, if she's told them."

"She?" Both the *Vizepräsident* and his adjutant reacted to the pronoun.

He didn't answer the question in their inflection. Instead, Schulke looked behind him and saw the chair. Without seeking permission, he dropped into it, leaned back and made himself comfortable. The other two were visibly taken aback by this unwonted act, almost one of insubordination. The *Vizepräsident* snapped, "Explain," but he didn't order Schulke back to his feet.

Schulke felt he was in command...for the first time, ever. He would even dispense with the *Mein Herr*. "In December 1944 I arrested a young woman, a Jewess, on false identity, in Mannheim. I'd already suspected her and had sent to Berlin for information."

He paused, but the *Vizepräsident* wasn't interested in dramatic effect. "Get on with it, man."

"This woman had a paper trail that went all the way back to the *RSHA*." This was the Reich Main Security Headquarters, *Reichsführer-SS* Himmler's very office. "Reports from Berlin police, from Krakow in occupied Poland, petty theft in Warsaw, and then at the bottom of the file, there was a signal from Berlin." He'd read and reread the signal so many times, Schulke had no difficulty repeating it word for word. "'Report immediately to *Generalmajor* Friedrich von Richter, *Wehrmacht Abwehr*'" — Army Intelligence Service — "'if and when apprehended.'"

The adjutant was still standing before the *Vizepräsident*'s desk. Schelling spoke. "What does this have to do with the Enigma code?" He added a "Please."

"There was one more item in the file from Berlin on this woman. A notation that she'd been living with a mathematician in the ghetto of a town in the *Generalgouvernement*." This was the part of Poland to be emptied of peasants and Jews and filled with *Volksdeutsche*. "The file said that this man, Klein, may have worked on the Enigma code. He certainly knew people who were trying to break it. But before they could find this Klein, he was sent to be gassed when the ghetto was liquidated." Schulke's tone was matter-of-fact. "The *Abwehr*" — military intelligence — "needed to know if the Poles had succeeded in breaking the Enigma code. If Klein had passed on the secret, this woman was probably the only one who could possibly tell them." Then Schulke added an obvious thought. "Living together, they were probably lovers."

"And you didn't report to Berlin? You let her go?" The *Vizepräsident* had raised his voice in spite of himself.

"It was an order, sir. The war was ending. We didn't know…"

Schrübbers thought for a moment. Then looked towards his adjutant. "The Americans took all the RSHA records after the war. But they gave them back in '51. Horst, get on the secure phone to Archives Administration in Bonn. Find out what they've got on…" He turned to Schulke. "The name, man, the name. Do you remember it?"

Schulke nodded. He knew every detail of this file. It had burned into his memory over a decade as he obsessed about his missed chance. "There were two names for her: Rita Guildenstern and Margarita Trushenko." Schelling wrote both down. The *Vizepräsident* was peremptory. "Come back again tomorrow, Schulke." He looked at an appointment diary. "Same time. Now, leave us." He turned to Schelling. "Sit." It was an order.

Twenty-four hours later Otto Schulke was standing before the *Vizepräsident* again, exulting in his importance to the organization. He was not invited to sit. The *Vizepräsident* had two copies of a one-page memo before him. He signed both, looked up at Schulke, then passed the papers to Schelling to initial. "New duties, Schulke. You're reassigned here. You're to find what became of this woman and...if by any chance she's still alive, we need to know, *sofort!*" In German it meant more than *right away*. It was an order. Schelling passed Schulke one of the signed copies.

Otto Schulke couldn't help himself.

He clicked his heels and almost shouted, *"Zu Befehl"* —Yes, sir. And he thought to himself, *Finally.*

Part I

In Transit

Chapter One

Salzburg has no right to look so beautiful. The thought repeated itself once, twice, a third time, as Rita stood, leaning against the rail of the balcony on the top floor of the best block of flats in the city. Everything she could see, looking south towards the cathedral dome—the archbishop's palace, the grand white sepulchral castle dominating the skyline above the city—was golden light and purple shadow, sculpted by the sun setting in an alpine sky. All calmly announced the town's purity, its serenity, its innocence. The rest of Europe was still a shambles. But here the cream colors of the buildings showed no burn marks from bombing, the trees along the boulevards had not given up their branches for winter firewood, the paving of the Max Ott Platz below hadn't ever been broken up by a single tank tread. She looked up at the ring of mountains in which the city nestled, protecting it from reality. *The good burghers of Salzburg can pretend their hands are clean.*

"I'm sorry, Gil, I was distracted by the scenery. What were you saying?"

Her husband's tone combined surprise and gentle reproof. "Distracted by the scenery? Rita, you've been living in this flat, looking at that view, for three years." They'd been given the apartment by the US Army, the occupying power, in late 1945, soon after they'd arrived. Gil had agreed to serve as the medical officer for a half-dozen displaced persons camps that were permitted to function, not in the city itself, but just outside of its precincts.

She turned, giving him her full attention. "Please repeat what you said."

"I said"—he paused for the importance of what would follow—"there will be another war...and soon." Rita nodded, inviting him to continue. "This airlift won't work. The Amis and

Brits won't give up Berlin without a fight." In late June, Stalin had closed the land routes to Berlin through Russian-occupied East Germany. For almost two months now the Americans and the British had been flying a continuous sequence of transport planes into Berlin, feeding the population of their two-thirds of the city. The slightest interference with the precarious airlift would force them to confront the Russians on the ground. That would mean war, atomic war, Gil just knew.

"How can you be sure it will come to that?" Rita had a good idea why he was sure. She'd heard him on the subject before.

"Rita, I'm unerring in these matters. It's how I survived the war, remember. I could always tell which way the tide was running and when it changed."

She didn't agree. Like hers, his skin had been saved by immense good fortune, not by Gil's opportunism, masquerading as foresight. The suggestion that it was chance, not wisdom or knowledge, had more than once provoked the worst arguments in their three years together.

Rita did have to admit that Gil had been lucky through six years of war—no, nine, if you count the Spanish Civil War. Perhaps his luck was holding out. Or maybe he really did have an instinct for how to save his skin. She would not be drawn into another debate about his world-historical discernment. "So, what do you think we should do, dear?"

"Get out. Leave. Emigrate. Now." He joined her at the balcony rail. They both stared out at the quiet streets six stories below. Gil broke the silence first. "We'll have to leave eventually anyway. The DP camps won't stay open forever. Every month there are fewer and fewer people. Besides, at some point the Americans will stop funding the UNRRA." This was the United Nations Relief and Rehabilitation Administration that they both worked for.

"But surely they'll need doctors here after the camps close." She looked at her husband. He was skilled and had a good bedside manner, especially with women. It wouldn't be hard to establish a practice, if he wanted to.

Gil shook his head. He'd already looked into it. Qualifying in Austria might be tricky. There was the problem of his French medical certificates in another name, Tadeusz Sommermann, a name from before the war, a victim's name, a name he'd buried in Spain ten years ago now. Then there were the exams to sit, an indignity from which an experienced medical man approaching middle age should be excused. More important, he just knew there was a war coming. He had escaped two already and he wasn't going to be trapped this time either. "You're not listening. We can't stay. Do you want to live with the Russians again?"

Rita shuddered slightly. Instantly she had recalled the pointless regimentation, the unstinting homogenization, the feeling of just being a cog that the twenty months of Soviet rule had imposed on her town in eastern Poland. If it hadn't been for what had happened afterwards, when the Nazis had driven the Reds out, those months would have seemed unendurable in retrospect. "Not again, ever." It was all she said.

"Besides, we can't stay here even if we wanted to. We're not Austrians. The children are stateless. We're certainly not going back to Poland." He made the last observation with finality. They'd smuggled themselves out of Poland, through Czechoslovakia, and then beyond the Soviet zone of occupied Austria, at considerable cost in border-guard bribes. There was nothing for them back there.

"I agree." She sighed. "We must leave." Gil was right. They had to get away. But her reasons were much more powerful than the ones he'd given: Rita had to leave because she was frightened, afraid that what had happened once would happen again. She knew she wouldn't have the strength the second time to do what she had done the first. That second time, if it came, would destroy a life she cared about more than her own. The only way to prevent it, to prevent it for sure, was to leave, not just Salzburg, or Austria, but Europe.

In the ghetto Rita had given up her child to someone who could smuggle the three-year-old boy, Stefan, to safety. He would be taken to her parents living in the west of pre-war Poland. It was the region absorbed into the German Reich and so not subject to the fatal triage of the Karpathyn ghetto. There, only those who worked were fed—not enough to work. The rest starved even faster, waiting to be herded to the extermination camp at Belzec.

Word had come back to the ghetto that her parents had been caught in an *Aktion*—a roundup—but there was nothing about a child with them. As the Karpathyn ghetto was torched and its last inmates disposed of, Rita had secured a new identity and escaped. Constantly endangered, she had searched in vain for her child, even bribing her way into the Warsaw ghetto just before its destruction. Then, on a summer day in 1947, watching her toddler twins play in the Mirabelle Gardens, she'd found Stefan, a happy seven-year-old with the very woman who'd taken him from the ghetto. Her moment of joy was overwhelmed when she saw that by claiming him, her boy would suddenly lose his mother for the second time in his life. Sitting in the park with the woman—his mother now, watching him and her twins—Rita found the strength to say nothing, do nothing, let him go.

Now every day she went back to that park in fear that she would see him again. She knew she'd never be able to do what she'd done the first time. She knew it in two wholly different but equally certain ways. First there was the astonishing emotion she'd overmastered just the once. And then later there was reflection on how strong that emotion had to be, an insight laid down in the two vast tomes she'd spent six months with in a Polish ghetto garret. With nothing to do, day after day, over and over she'd read Darwin, *The Origin of Species* and *The Descent of Man*, the only two books in the room, until she understood everything they explained about her nature, and everyone else's. Rita was the product of millions of years of relentless natural selection for the very emotions that demanded she never surrender her child to anyone. But knowing that was not going to enable her to resist their urgency. Not if she saw him again. She couldn't stay, she had to leave, tie herself to the mast of a departing ship. She needed one that was going as far away as possible.

With an audible sigh, she spoke. "Where shall we go?" But she knew the answer already.

Gil didn't notice the sigh. He was two steps ahead in the conversation, already making his own choice among the alternatives he was about to give her. "There are three choices, as I see it." She waited. "America, Israel or Australia."

Rita spoke quietly. "I think we can both rule Israel out, don't you, Gil?"

He nodded. Both of them knew the many different reasons why, some they shared, others quite different, none voiced. It wasn't just that neither of them were Zionists. They never had been, right through the '30s in Poland when the movement was sweeping the field. They'd been patriots—Poles, not Jews. And when their country had turned against them, even before the war, both Gil and Rita had sometimes secretly and shamefacedly blamed their own, or at least other Jews—the religious and the Zionists—for bringing it on themselves.

"Yes." He agreed. There was nothing in the struggle to create a country out of the desert that appealed to him. Not needing to admit it was a bit of a relief.

Rita saw no reason to wring it out of him. It was not a place where Gil's talents would thrive.

"I don't think I'd be happy in America," she said. "Would you?"

"Why ever not?" Was Rita going to make things difficult? The USA seemed the obvious choice to Gil.

"I had a taste of it, when I worked for the Amis in Heidelberg." Rita had spent long enough in a US Army canteen to become almost fluent in American English, including the swear words. "In the end I didn't like it." It was ground they'd covered before—invincibly ignorant superiority, the blatantly commercial attitudes, the racial tension that pervaded the unit, inevitable in a caste system that compelled menial servitude on anyone with a black skin.

Gil didn't feel the same way. He thought of the Amis as bumptious but well-meaning children. "I hardly think an American army unit in the middle of Germany is a fair sample of life in the USA."

"Yes. It could be even worse. At least the soldiers saw the horrors. People in America will have no idea of what went on here the last six years. They won't believe it."

"It would be the same in Australia, no?"

"Maybe not. The English we've seen since the war ended are certainly very different from the Americans. We're both more comfortable with them. Won't the Aussies be more like Brits?"

The South Pacific sun warming a colony of cultivated Englishmen...the image attracted Gil. With most stateless refugees wanting to go to the States, the wait for visas to Australia would be shorter, and once they got there, Gil knew he'd be more...more what? More interesting, more exotic a commodity, stand out a bit, be different, instead of just another of the two or three hundred thousand victims the USA would take in from the aftermath of the European war. He wouldn't be a victim. "Very well. Shall I look into it?" He was already sounding a bit like a Brit to himself.

Rita nodded and rose. She'd managed it quite nicely. Now she wanted to check on the twins.

So glad I was able to convince her, Gil thought. Remarkable how easily a life-altering decision can be made.

* * *

Rita was standing at the open door of the nursery, watching her twins sleep in the twilight of a summer evening still lit by a sun occluded behind the surrounding mountains but not yet set. At almost two, the boys were really too old for the cribs, threatening to climb out of them and crash to the floor every morning before Marta, the nanny, could lift them out. Marta was a local girl, as tall as Rita, plainer, with brown plaits and a clean dirndl every morning. She was more than happy to work for the small sums they could afford, the warm servant's room off the kitchen and the much more valuable bounty of the American PX that Dr. Romero had access to. She'd been indispensable in the first months after the twins were born. They were large, active babies, never going asleep or waking together, always demanding to be fed at the same time, and there was no one else, certainly no family, to help. Marta had been a godsend. She was wonderful with the boys, more an aunt than a nanny. How would they take to losing her?

Rita looked from Tomas to Erich. Fraternal twins, they were already very different. Tomas, blond, active, eager to please, with his mother's sunny disposition; Eric, older by a few minutes, took after his father—dark-haired, with a temper. Always slightly later to each milestone than his brother, he had been ill as a baby, and his parents had attributed the differences between them to this. Both had begun to speak early and were restless in their stroller, wriggling to go walk-about. For the moment both slept soundly.

Tomas and Erich—what might become of those names in an English country? Thomas, 'Tom,' and Eric, not much different give or take an unvoiced 'h.' Gil and she might have chosen well. Each had named one, with a veto by the other. By unspoken agreement they would not honor the custom of naming a child after a deceased relative, still less allow any ritual maiming. There were too many dead in their families to honor anyone. And they shared that unvoiced resentment of the traditions that had separated Jews from the rest of humanity. So, Gil had honored his favorite writer, Thomas Mann, and Rita her favorite, Erich Maria Remarque. They laughed, realizing each child had been named for a German. But it wasn't a novelist Rita honored. She had never told Gil about Erich Klein, the mathematician who'd lived with her, chastely, then saved her life as the Gestapo cleared the ghetto of Karpathyn. Nor had she mentioned the secret Klein had confided to her, to convince her the Germans would lose the war and she would survive it. In fact she hadn't even thought of it in years.

The boys wouldn't have to be Tom Romero and Erich Romero, she knew. They could grow up with her surname, as Tom and Erich Feuerstahl. What is there, really, in a name? She'd taken Gil's, but that was just convenience, to forestall awkward questions. Gil and Rita were not married. In the post-war turmoil these niceties hardly mattered. There had been no time before their escape from Poland. What did a piece of paper matter anyway? Besides, Rita had a husband, Urs Guildenstern, still living and undivorced, albeit in a country behind what everyone was now calling the Iron Curtain. It was nothing to her that he was with another woman, and their child. That his marriage was bigamy signified no more to Rita than the irregularity of her own situation. She'd been glad enough to find Urs alive after a war in which she had forced him to escape knowing he'd just be a burden to her. She had been equally glad to find that he had no expectation of resuming their marriage, one that had already been unhappy to both even before the war that had separated them.

Satisfied that the twins were snug, Rita closed the door behind her and returned to the sitting room. "Gil, I have an early shift tomorrow morning." For the better part of four years, even before the war was finally over, Rita had sat at a desk or stood across a counter from thousands of destitute, displaced, increasingly desperate wanderers, moving from city to city, still searching for one another as the rest of an indifferent Europe rebuilt itself. Speaking four languages fluently made Rita invaluable at the tracing service.

Gil frowned slightly. He was happy his wife had a calling, something that was important to her. He didn't want to be her sole preoccupation. "Well, I have a clinic and two inspections tomorrow. There's a jeep coming for me at 9:30." He certainly didn't want to be needed for domestic matters. Fortunately there was the girl to help.

"That's fine. I've already warned Marta. She'll keep the kids out of your hair." Gil was a good father, except in the hours immediately after he rose. Then he was grumpy and short with everyone.

Rita slumped down on the sofa, facing the windows still open to the terrace. Beyond it was the twinkling light of the first stars above the band of mountains. Below them in the silhouetted buildings a random pattern of windows were becoming visible as lights were turned on.

Gil reached for a cigarette box, took one, lit it and then offered the box to her. Wordlessly she declined. Then he spoke. "It's such a shame we have to leave. They've treated us very well, haven't they?"

"You'd hardly believe they were Nazis."

"Not all of them surely?"

Rita ignored the response. "We've made it easy for them... haven't we?"

"Easy for them? What do you mean?"

"Absolution for their sins — of omission and commission." She gestured towards the balcony and the city beyond. "The good burghers of Salzburg couldn't have the vermin from the camps tottering up and down their streets, importuning, begging, stealing. But they can feel good about how they treat that nice refugee couple, the Romeros."

He knew exactly what she meant. Dr Guillermo Romero,

and his obviously German Jewish, rather beautiful and well-educated wife, Rita, were welcomed everywhere.

She was tall, her husband's height, and thin—a feature everyone attributed to willpower, not the privation of forced labor. The blond shoulder-length hair needed no help to curve in a way that accentuated the strong cheekbones. Bearing twins and the demands they made didn't seem to burden her. It was as though she was naturally maternal, knew what to expect and how to cope. No one knew these were not her first, nor how many spoiled children she'd had to nursemaid as a domestic servant in the war.

Her husband was very different. His hair was dark and short, the face a bit stern. With the mustache it put some people in mind of Melvin Douglas or William Powell, the pre-war American movie stars. The intense black irises in his small eyes were hard to read. His dress was a bit dapper. Dr Romero wasn't aloof exactly or unapproachable. He had a certain dignity, a formality the Austrians liked. But he was a good physician, decisive and almost unerring in diagnoses. He was sometimes imperious with staff, but reassuring to patients. Everyone recognized his ferocious intelligence, even as they admired his wife's openness.

Gil asked, "Can't we give the Austrians some credit for being sincere? They've allowed six DP camps to be built."

"If they'd made any trouble about those camps, Eisenhower would have forced the city fathers to visit Dachau." The American commander had done this routinely in the first year after the war, personally escorting German civilians through the concentration camps, as they protested their ignorance. "It's just a morning's train ride away."

* * *

Rita reflected, did Gil really want to leave this lovely city in its magnificent setting before he absolutely had to? It didn't seem like him.

They'd both been overwhelmed by its beauty as their westbound train from Vienna pulled in through the deep mountain valley. It was a brief station-stop on the line to Munich. With no particular destination, they'd immediately agreed that this was a place untouched by the century's horrors. Salzburg was utterly different from anything they'd seen in a murderous decade. At least it stood a chance of banishing the somber vision they shared. After almost three years it hadn't done so, at least not for Rita.

Perhaps Gil's talk about leaving was talk, trying on an idea, thinking out loud, not a serous proposal. She would find out. The next day she wrote to the Australian embassy in Vienna.

Chapter Two

A week later Rita came home to find a fat, brown buff envelope in the post on the side table at the door. The return address was the Australian embassy in Vienna. She opened the envelope carefully, then scanned each page, working out the English, and then turned to the forms enclosed. The documents didn't ask for much. Apparently the barriers to entering Australia were low. If approved there would be subsidized transport, free initial accommodation, resettlement, and temporary financial support. The only thing prospective emigrants really had to document was that they weren't Germans. That would be easy. There was a branch of the International Refugee Organization in Salzburg. Rita worked for the office three days a week. They'd provide all the documentation Gil, Rita and the boys would need to secure Australian visas. The local bureau was run by Americans and she knew that even the much more coveted visas to the USA could be hers for the asking.

Rita sat down at the dining room table. The flat was quiet. Marta probably had the boys playing in the Mirabel Gardens. It was a good time to think things through a little more dispassionately. *Really, what are the chances you'd ever see Stefan again?* The memory of that moment she'd seen him in the park burned in her mind daily. *Are you holding your family hostage to your fears?* She began to work things out. *No, it's much more than that.* There really was no future in Salzburg, in Austria, or perhaps even the whole of Western Europe, not for her, not for her children either. The Germans were defeated. But they were unrepentant, especially the Austrians, who had rapturously joined the Third Reich in 1938, and now pretended to have been the first victims of Hitler's aggression. Losing the war, they had made the unilateral German *Anschluss* — absorption of their country — before the war began into a badge of innocence and injury. But Rita could see in their eyes the unspoken resentment of a child whose vile deeds are known but must go unmentioned, just because they were beyond forgiveness. In their sullenness they would admit nothing, allow nothing, to those who had witnessed their crimes in silent horror. Rita was such a witness. Her children were already being treated that way too. Born in Austria, they were nevertheless stateless—no documents, no rights. How long could they expect to survive on sufferance? Rita didn't know, but she didn't expect much more than that, not from the good burghers of Salzburg. There were more than enough reasons to leave.

* * *

Rita was still sitting with the envelope in her lap when Gil returned from one of his camp inspections. She raised the envelope. "I wrote to the Australian embassy." She was pleased to see a genuine smile on his face. "The forms will be easy to fill out." She handed him the envelope.

Without looking at it he replied "So, you agree with me, it's dangerous to stay."

"I think we need to leave." There was no point thrashing out the reasons why. There were enough.

Now she'd agreed, Gil was tempted to extract more. "Shall we apply to the Yanks too? See whose visas come sooner?"

Rita shook her head slowly. "I'm sorry, Gil. I'm just not cut out for it." She didn't want to tell him that he wasn't either. "Americans think everything can be bought, or at least paid for after the harm is done. All those GIs I knew in Frankfurt at the end of the war, all they cared about was getting rich, going into business, doing better than everyone else. The officers were the same, maybe worse, because they were educated." She stopped. "We're not like that, are we?" Gil, she knew, was even less suited to life in the USA than she was. He'd stand on his dignity at the wrong times, resent demands he prove his worth, spurn hard competition, even for outsized rewards. Rightly or not, he'd feel superior to them, and he'd show it.

He had to admit, at least to himself, that she was right. "Very well, Australia it is." Gil tried a winning smile. He picked up the forms, riffled through them and looked up. "Do you understand enough English to fill them out?"

"I think so. But you will need to learn English soon. You can't practice medicine without it in Australia."

Again he smiled, reached down to where she was still sitting and grasped her hand. "Can you start to teach now?" Gently he pulled her in the direction of the bedroom. Rita smiled, not shyly. Making love was still the best part of their relationship.

"Repeat after me!" she enjoined in English as they fell across the bed. "My name is Dr Romero, so very pleased to meet you, I am sure."

Gil was a good mimic, so the sounds he made were those of a German speaking a stilted and over-formal English. Rita laughed, only now realizing it was the way she sounded. Meanwhile Gil had reverted to the French they often used when making love.

Once the paperwork was gone, Rita began feeling the threat of the Berlin blockade. Month after month the fragile airlift was all that was keeping war away. When it collapsed, the Americans and the Brits would have to force their way through the eastern part of occupied Germany to Berlin. Then the ground war would start, Gil told her. Meanwhile the gears were grinding too slowly in Vienna, or wherever decisions were being made about their visas. Both tried to be patient, but daily their minds would turn to the rock and the hard place—the coming war and the stolid bureaucracy—they seemed to stand motionless between.

Finally, in early December, a letter came from the embassy in Vienna. *Too thin to be four visas.* Rita voiced her fear. "Have we been denied?" Gil's hand trembled slightly enough trying to open it that Rita grabbed it away. "You can't read English anyway."

Her hands too were unsteady as she pulled the onionskin sheet out from the envelope. Opening it, she read the English and smiled. "They say that visas will be issued, and travel arranged. But there are special opportunities for physicians. You have to bring medical certificates and references."

Gil took the translucent sheet of paper, and tried to make something of the English he couldn't understand. Then he dropped it to his side. "I suppose I'll have to write for my record to the *faculté de* médecine at the Sorbonne...and get a residency-statement from my director at the Woman's Lying In Hospital in Barcelona." But he was thinking something else. *Complications, Gil, complications.* The French certificates were in the name he'd buried twelve years before, in Barcelona, during the Spanish Civil War—Tadeusz Sommermann.

Rita was still cheerful. "What about the polyclinic in Katowice?" It was the town in Poland where Gil had been practicing medicine when they had met again after the war. "Or the Krupskaya in Moscow." This was the most important maternity hospital in the Soviet Union, and Gil had been indispensable there when Moscow had been threatened and many doctors had fled east. "Surely you can get a wonderful reference from them?"

"Perhaps. But that's not the right foot to start on in Australia, dear. See how suspicious the English and the Amis are of the Ruskies. It'll be the same in Australia. If I arrive with sponsorship like that no one will trust me. Fact is, I am going to have to hide that whole chapter of my life, Rita. I was an officer in the Red Army, remember." It was just for six months, and with his Spanish papers he'd wriggled out of the medial corps long before the war ended. But there were things Gil had done in the Soviet Union he wanted no one to learn about—terminations for the indiscreet wives of officers at the front, connivance with Spanish Republicans in exile, and then his participation in the forced winter-time removal of 240,000 Tartars, mostly women and children, from Crimea to the empty barrens of central Asia. Half died along the way or in the first year—a war crime, even if their menfolk had taken up German arms against the Soviet Union. These things he hadn't even told Rita about.

He was reluctant to uncover tracks he'd been carefully hiding since the moment he had arrived back in the fluid space between military occupation and civilian rule in Poland. He didn't think they'd want to get him back, but it would be best if no one learned where he'd gone. "You know how the Soviets have been since the war. They're demanding every former Soviet citizen be returned, no matter whether they want to or not. They certainly won't be happy about the IRO helping their nationals escape." As a UN agency the International Refugee Organization had to maintain a strict neutrality.

Suddenly Rita saw a new threat. "Vienna is in the Russian zone. Will the Australians have to tell the Soviets about whom they are issuing visas?" The thought froze her. Immediately after the war Rita had seen the terrible scenes of forced repatriations from Germany to the east. There had been suicides rather than return, even among those who had been brought to the Reich as slave labor. She sought to reassure herself. "But you're not Soviet. You're not even a Pole, with your Catalan name and your Spanish passport."

"Don't fool yourself. We both became Soviet persons the moment they absorbed eastern Poland in '39. You're at risk too. As for me—two names, three passports, a 'reputation' back in Moscow. I wouldn't stand a chance."

That evening Gil wrote his letters out by hand, French and Catalan, suppressing the inscrutable handwriting every physician seemed to affect. In the morning Rita took them to the Displaced Persons Tracing Service where she could use a typewriter. The French was easy, though she had to add accents and circumflexes by hand, and avoid the German characters on the keyboard. The Catalan was much harder. She had to peck out keys one by one in an order that made little sense to her. Rita was struck by the absence of cognates or other words she might recognize. Carefully, she added the diacritical marks Gil had made. She was not confident when she'd finished and she brought both products home without posting them.

Gil scanned each. With a peremptory wave of the hand he declared them satisfactory. Forgetting for moment that the typist was his wife, he snapped the words "Put them in the mail." Rita glared, thinking of her hours of work unappreciated. Catching her look, he added with a smile, "Please," and reached for a sheet of stamps to affix to the envelopes.

By the late summer much had been put in train. All their friends, Rita's fellow workers, the nurses and administrators of the six DP camps, knew that the Romeros were leaving. One or two of the latter might perhaps have already been contemplating their soon-to-be vacant flat. The visas arrived, photos affixed, covered with stamps from a half-dozen different offices and agencies, along with baggage tags for the one steamer trunk they'd be allowed, and steamer tickets, on an American troop ship, the *S.S General Heintzelman* — funny name for an American ship, Rita mused — from Bremerhaven, on the Baltic, towards the end of October.

But still no replies from Barcelona or Paris about Gil's medical credentials. Using the carbons she'd made, Rita carefully retyped and re-dated the letters, marked them urgent and posted them registered, delivery signature required. Back came the confirmation of receipt only days later. Daily for the next week, Gil waited for the first delivery of the morning, and then the second later in the day.

One afternoon Rita came out of the lift, the boys rushing ahead in a race to reach the door first, only to find it ajar. She could hear them greet their father, surprised to find him at home. He was in the bedroom, standing before a two-strap ersatz leather valise open on the bed. He had already folded a few pieces of clothing into the bag. As Rita entered he began to explain. "I've got to go to Paris, and probably Barcelona. Without those documents I've got nothing to convince them to allow me to practice medicine."

"Isn't there some way to qualify, exams you could sit?"

"I don't know. But I am not a schoolboy. I've been practicing medicine for ten years. I won't jump through hoops just to show them I can."

Not for the first time Rita was unwilling to talk him out of something. "How long will you be gone?"

"Not sure. Won't be problem getting to Paris. But I can't use my Spanish Republican papers and they won't recognize a Nansen passport, even a genuine one." These were documents given to stateless persons before the war by the League of Nations. No one examined them very closely anymore and Gil had purchased a forgery in Czechoslovakia. "I'll have to find a way to slip into Spain, across the Pyrenees."

" The way you came out in '38?" Rita recalled Gil's account of his escape from the turmoil of Barcelona at the end of the Spanish Civil War. He nodded. "But it's only a month 'til our sailing, Gil. The *Heintzelman* leaves Bremerhaven on the 19th of October." The troop ship would carry a thousand refugees to Sydney.

"That's more than a month from now. Plenty of time."

"Unless there's a bottleneck somewhere." Refugees were still moving across every frontier. There'd be some guard at every border ready to hold those without papers hostage to a bribe. Gil would have to buy himself out of trouble.

"That won't be a problem. I've still got a fair number of the gold coins I took out of Russia." He'd passed on more than one to ease their way across the borders between Poland and the American zone of Austria.

The thought of them gave Rita a frisson. She never wanted to see or touch a Louis Napoleon gold coin again, ever. Suddenly she was reliving the struggle to hold on to or hide away just such coins, and the danger of exchanging them, in the German occupation. There had been a score of such coins left for her by her husband as he escaped the German invasion of Soviet occupied Poland in '41.

Rita looked at the suitcase and then mechanically began taking Gil's shirts and socks out of the bureau, folding them and placing them neatly across the bottom of the bag. The sooner he was packed the sooner he'd come back.

Gil looked at her, seeking reassurance. "Will you be alright?"

She smiled and nodded. "Of course. I've got Marta to help me with the boys." *What if he doesn't get back before we leave?* "But, look Gil, we've got to be on that ship next month. We can't afford to miss our chance." She paused while her statement sank in. "If you're right, the longer we stay here, the greater the danger of war. Everything is drifting that way." The Americans and the Brits were still supplying Berlin by air, a year after the blockade had begun. The Western powers had unified their occupation zones into a single West Germany and absorbed it into a new military alliance, NATO.

"You're right. But don't worry. I won't be gone longer than a week or so."

* * *

Finally, Rita saw, they had to leave. Everything that happened just made for haunting, tragic memories. This time the trigger was Gil's departure at the Salzburg *Hauptbahnhof*. Waiting on the platform for the Munich train to come in from the east, all she could think of was that summer day back in '41, the last hour at the Karpathyn station, waiting to send her husband Urs off to the east before the German *Wehrmacht* arrived. She'd known she couldn't cope with both his ineffectiveness and the German occupiers. Now, she was sending off a man she still wanted, the father her boys needed. She had to have him back.

Rita held up each boy for a kiss as Gil leaned out of the compartment. Then the carriage began silently to slide along the platform. She sent him off with a brief wave of her arm and a confident smile she didn't feel.

* * *

Guillermo Romero too was remembering, as the train gathered speed and the pine groves began to rush past. But Gil was savoring memories, letting one image recover another to recapture the very moods, emotions, appetites of a long past Paris.

The passengers from Vienna were agog at the scenery as the railway car rattled down a narrow ravine cut through the mountain boundary between Austria and Bavaria. It was running along steep granite walls and fallen boulders, through which churned the foam of a mountain stream closely paralleling the track. Gil should have been enjoying the beauty of the scene, like the other passengers in his compartment. But Gil's thoughts were already recovering detail after detail of his Paris life, before the wars, in all its heedlessness of past and future.

Three days after Gil left for Paris, a letter arrived for him from Paris, and another from Spain. As Rita studied the second of these she saw it was the letter she had sent to Barcelona, now returned and marked in hand *Fatal retorn al remittent*. She had an idea what this meant but turned to Gil's small Catalan-German dictionary. Her guess was right: *Deceased Return to Sender*. So, Gil's mentor in Barcelona had died. The return address on the other envelope was the *Ecole de Médecine* in Paris. Rita hesitated and then opened it.

Cher M. Sommermann,

I write in response to your request for duplicate medical certificates.

As you completed your studies at the University of Marseilles and took your final examinations in that city, all records pertaining to your qualifications will have been retained there. You must apply at

Marseilles for duplicate certificates.
Please accept my most distinguished sentiments.
The Registrar of Records

Was Gil's trip to Paris pointless? Was there a way to reach him?

Chapter Three

Holding one hand on the rail and the other on the double pram, Rita scanned the length of the dock. They stood on the lifeboat deck beneath the davits that held one of the very large, barge-like crafts above their heads. Here there were no passengers at the handrail and she had an unobstructed view down to the dock sixty feet below. Both of the boys were leaning out of the pram, looking too, through the handrails, across the broken skyline of reconstructing dockyards and gantry cranes. They were wrapped in almost every inch of clothing they had against the North Sea gusts that persisted through the intermittent spells of blue sky and sunlight breaking the patchwork of cloud. The boys were agog at the sights. But Rita had eyes only for the small figures still moving on the quay almost six stories below. She watched as the passenger ramp was lifted off the quay into midships. Then the narrower fore and aft gangplanks were cleared. After that it was the turn of the vast bow and stern hawsers, and finally the last sheets tenuously holding the ship to the shore, lines so thin a single man could haul them off the turnbuckles. Now at last she gave up hope of seeing Gil.

And then she saw someone, a man, run out of the quayside warehouse, carrying a suitcase in one hand and gesticulating wildly with papers in the other. He was stopped by someone in uniform, an American soldier, an officer with a clipboard. Even a hundred feet away she could see the officer vigorously shaking his head. It was too late. He pointed to the increasing gap between ship and wharf. The man would have to jump the quickly widening gap, and then there was nothing but a blank wall of smooth gray steel. The civilian put down his case, looked at the water, then up at the passengers on the rail and shouted. Whatever he was shouting was completely swamped as the ship's foghorn went off, frightening both the children, who began to bawl. Ignoring them for the moment, Rita continued to try to gain the man's attention, shouting in the lowest register she could muster. Finally, he looked up, but only briefly, then turned back to the officer and shrugged. She watched him as he turned and slowly walked off the long pier. Was it Gil? Had some other male passenger missed the sailing by moments? *You could ask around.* Then she realized she'd look pathetic if she did.

Rocking the stroller to warn the children they were about to move, Rita turned from the rail, entered the ship's superstructure and began to search for their berths. She had a mimeographed diagram in her hand and a piece of oak tag attached to a single key, assigning her a compartment for four. At first glad to escape the chill wind of the boat deck, in a few moments she was lost in passageways made too warm by large overhead pipes hissing steam. She reached a bulkhead and was struggling to move the pram over it when a white-coated steward approached.

"May I be of assistance, Memsaab?" It was an accent she'd never heard and it took a moment to understand. The man was tall, thin, young, about twenty she judged, and Indian. The smile was broad, natural and somehow reassuring. Deftly he pushed the pram's handle down, until the springs compressed and the front wheels rose. Then he rolled the pram up to the barrier and pulled up the handle to lift the rear wheels over. Rita watched the operation with admiration. She would have to learn to execute it herself.

It would be a month-long voyage. Built to carry 3000 American Army troops, the *Heintzelman* had been converted to transport about a third the number of refugees, mostly in families. The crew, Rita noticed, was all civilian, and remarkably international—Italians, Latin Americans, Indians, Malays. But their language was English and the ship was still owned by and leased from the American Army, not the US Navy.

The passengers were also a mixed lot of nationalities, Rita

found, but quite different a mixture. They were mainly Latvians and Lithuanians, along with *Volksdeutsche* from as far as Crimea and the Volga, people who had come to the Reich during the war or fled west before the invading Red Army. She was often herself taken for one, addressed in German by these passengers. They were eager to share their *Volkische* solidarity, their consuming hatred of the Russians and whispered loyalty to the Third Reich, and their racial superiority to the other refugees on board— Italians and Slavs from a half-dozen countries Germany had devastated. What there were none of were holocaust survivors, or any Jews at all for that matter. Still, Rita thought, she shouldn't be surprised. Jews went to Israel, or America, not Australia. She could not know that the Australian government was actively discouraging the resettlement of Jews. Neither she nor Gil realized that they owed their visas to the refusal to identify themselves as anything but Poles on the forms they had filled out.

Shipboard life was a routine that changed only gradually as, the *Heintzelman's* course took them to ever-warmer climes. After the rough passage and general seasickness of the North Sea and the Bay of Biscay, everyone aboard had their sea legs by the time they passed the Straits of Gibraltar. In the Mediterranean it was wonderfully warm for November and only became truly oppressive below deck when they had passed though the Suez Canal into the Red Sea. At 10 knots and a breeze traveling south along with them, the air was still even at the bow. At first the warmth brought everyone out on the decks. Then as the air began to bake, people retreated again, perspiring and queuing for the insufficient number of showers and the miserly stream of tepid water that emerged from their salt-crusted heads.

To make the time pass Rita tried to lie-in every morning and keep the boys sleeping as long as she could. But in a ship crowded with people separated only by plywood partitions, the noise level was too great to sleep very late each morning.

After a week or two of starchy but unlimited ship's fare, many of the passengers looked less gaunt and less lethargic. But the food was not to Rita's taste, reminding her rather of what there was to eat in Germany during the last months of the war—boiled vegetables and plentiful potatoes. The boys, however, ate with relish, daily growing chubbier.

As the *Heintzelman* moved sedately through the Suez Canal, there had been little to see but the high banks, ships going the other way and the occasional Dhow. Once it reached the wider Gulf of Suez, now free from risk of collision, the big ship's speed increased and soon she was plowing a furrow through the calm of the Red Sea at nearly 17 knots. There was a bulletin board on deck amidships. On it speed, heading, weather and next landfall were posted, and updated daily in English. Not many passengers seemed interested in coming up to scan it, especially as a following wind kept the air still and the heat off the desert shores imposed an ever-increasing lethargy. Then, the ship passed Djibouti and entered the Gulf of Aden, where it caught the breeze of the Indian Ocean. As the day cooled down passengers rose from their cots to mill on deck at twilight.

Once her children had adapted to shipboard life Rita found she had time, time to read, to think, to wonder why Gil had missed the departure. The matter came back to her again and again. Was that forlorn figure on the quay her man? Had something happened to Gil in France, or worse, in Spain? Had he decided to stay after convincing her to leave? Briefly she worried, *Has he gone to America?* Impossible. No visa, no money. The questions gave way to deeper reflections. What if she had to do without him altogether? Rita found that working that prospect out was less disturbing than she expected. She'd have the boys to cope with, and to love. They'd all manage…if they had to. She didn't want to be without him. Two children without a father, a mother without a husband; there'd be questions, she knew, questions that would make it harder on the boys. No, they needed Gil. She needed him too. Gil still held strong memories for her—their love affair before the war, the way he'd banished the nightmares when they'd found each other again in '45. *Perhaps it's his skill and imaginativeness as a lover—something you don't talk about, or even want to admit to yourself.* All right: the sex was a part of what kept her with him. *How much does it count with him,* she wondered?

* * *

It was only months later, in a New South Wales refugee resettlement center, that Rita found the time, the need and the distance from those years in the war to write, to put it all, or as much as she could remember, down on paper. It was now five years since her war had ended. She could tell that her memories were blurring. The visceral, felt experience of some events was completely gone, leaving only a recollection that they had happened, without her being able to recreate any of the details. If she didn't write down what she could recall now, it would surely evaporate. The same increasing vagueness also made it feasible, tolerable to record the truth without entirely reliving the torture all over again. And Rita also had the time. In the resettlement village, days of waiting stretched into empty weeks and idle months that drove Rita, indeed most people in the camp, to indifference and depression. Most of the inmates didn't know what sort of a life they were waiting for.

The refugee resettlement center at Bathurst was a day's train ride west of Sydney, through the Blue Mountains, which couldn't impress Rita after the Austrian Alps. The five hundred or so refugees, all from the *Heintzelman*, were driven from dock to railway station in a relay of coaches, and from the rural station to the camp in another convoy of them. It was well after dark on a summer evening when the coaches disgorged their last passenger on the open space—a drill field it seemed—before the administrator's long, low building. Looking round, the new arrivals could see little beyond barrack-like structures, arrayed in rows that would have recalled a German concentration camp's layout to any among them who had survived one—or more likely had been a guard at one, Rita later reflected.

There'd been some difficulty about Rita's papers. She had no husband and no marriage certificate to prove one was expected, and she was about to be placed in an open barrack when she began speaking English. Surprised, the intake interviewer switched from good German to an Aussie twang. "Why didn't you say you spoke Pommy?" He was another soldier, like all the Australians she'd met so far, but with sergeant's chevrons on his sleeve.

"You didn't ask." She smiled, hoping to win him over. "But your German is very good and my English not so good." She allowed a German accent to be a little more pronounced. She pointed behind her. "These are my boys. They're almost four. My husband missed the ship. He will come in the next one he can find."

"Well, normally we need documentation. But I'll take your word for it." He tore up her accommodation order and began to type out another one.

Perhaps her English could secure some further advantage. "He's a doctor, my husband. Do you need doctors here at this camp?"

"Got plenty of 'em, ma'am. Aussie quacks too. What we need are people like you, who already speak pom, uh...English. Where did you learn?"

"US Army."

"Wot?"

"I worked for the American army in Germany. Where did you learn German?"

"In Germany. Escaped with my family when I was five." Rita did a quick calculation. "So, you're a Jew?"

The man looked round, evidently to see whether anyone had

heard her. He nodded with a slight grimace. Rita could see this was not a subject to pursue. All she said was, "Me too."

The sergeant nodded and continued filling in the form. "We don't get many." Then he looked up at her. "Name is Mond." This, Rita recognized, was a giveaway Jewish name in Germany and Poland. Evidently not here. Perhaps this Mond didn't know that about his name, or if he did, liked it that way. He handed Rita two pieces of paper. "This chit is for a private billet for you and the children. Room for your husband when he gets here." She nodded with gratitude. "The other one is a note to the camp schools officer, telling him you speak English. If you like they'll give you a job teaching these foreigners." She was already being treated as an Aussie.

A private billet turned out to be cubicle of corrugated metal, from the tar-papered roof of which hung a single dim electric light with a pull chain, four cots with olive green blankets—entirely superfluous in the summer heat—but no sheets, a canvas washbasin, one metal filing cabinet for clothes, and two small screened translucent windows, glass broken and taped. *We left Salzburg for this?* Rita slumped onto a bed and gathered her boys to her so they would not see her tears. Then she rose and pushed the stroller, now loaded with their baggage, up over the step into the cell.

The next morning in the cool early light of a sun rising above the Blue Mountains, casting long shadows across the scrub, the landscape revealed a spare beauty Rita immediately began to enjoy. *It won't be bad here, being what they call a New Australian.* She had to convince herself.

Chapter Four

It was two days or so before Rita discovered the school and found a class for her two boys. It was a large US Army tent, on a plywood platform, familiar to her from her USO days in Heidelberg after the war. The tent walls were rolled up but the shade did little to reduce the heat of an Australian summer in the "outback" — the first word she learned in the Aussie's lingo.

Tomas took to the class immediately, but Erich hung back a bit, repeatedly returning to his mother's side as the young Australian teacher tried to introduce the boys to the rest of the class. Then she tried to involve them in the group's play. It was a simple game of Simon Says, designed to teach the children body parts — Simon says hands on ears, Simon says touch your toes, touch your nose. You lose, and she named three or four of the children who had touched their noses. Having lost, Erich wanted no part in the game, returned to his mother, buried his head in her lap and couldn't be induced to play again. Tomas however began to listen, learned quickly and was soon teacher's pet. The class ran most of the morning and Rita remained. She was not the only mother to do so, but the others spoke Estonian and Latvian among themselves, languages Rita did not have. She smiled at them, but got nothing in return. If they spoke German they gave no sign of it, as though the language of the defeated were the mark of Cain. Most looked older than Rita, rather careworn. They appeared slightly suspicious of arrangements in the school, as though its relaxed informality were somehow improper.

Class for the children over for the day, Rita approached the young teacher. "My children enjoyed the class today. They are very eager to learn English."

"Well," the teacher replied, "they can learn at home. Your English's bottlin'." Rita's perplexity showed in her face. The

45

woman translated: "Bloody good, your English, first rate. It's Aussie, don't mind it."

"I'm afraid my children don't want to learn from me. They are already making fun of my German accent." It was the tyranny of conformity. The boys could hear the difference between their mother's English and everyone else's. "They are desperate to sound Australian." Then Rita proffered the chit from Sergeant Mond. "I was told to give this to the person in charge of the school."

The woman looked at the chit and then replied, "Not me. Go across to the next tent and see the captain in charge." She looked at the boys. "I'll entertain these two with a game or something." She took the boys' hands from Rita and led them to a low shelf. Erich saw the chess set immediately and pulled it down. They'd learned from an Indian steward onboard ship. Almost their first words of English. Soon both boys were sitting on the floor setting up the pieces. Tomas proceeded to hold up each piece and tell the teacher the English name of each.

* * *

An army private sitting at a typewriter stand near the opening of the next tent looked at her paper and grunted, pointing her further inside. There, speaking on a field telephone, was an officer with three pips she'd learned to recognize in British Army uniforms. The man did not put down the telephone but held out his hand for the paper. She gave it to him. He scanned it as he continued to nod and speak into the phone. Then he dropped the receiver into the base and spoke. "Camp needs someone to teach these foreigners"—he waved his hand dismissively towards the tent's exit—"how to speak white."

Rita was perplexed. "White? I can't speak that language."

"Don't be daft, ducky. English, what white folks speak hereabouts." She nodded. "Classes are for adults. Can you teach 'em?" Before she could answer he went on. "Had to sack the last teacher. Ex-Nazi, he was, not very ex." He sized Rita up. "You one?"

She shook her head. "No. They killed my family."

The captain frowned. "Commie, then?"

"Not one of those either." She didn't explain. Somehow she'd realized the less said the better.

"We'll give you a run, Miss..." He looked down at the paper on the desk.

She corrected him. "Mrs...Romero."

* * *

Teaching adults English turned out to be fun, for Rita and for the people she taught. For them, it was a surcease from the monotony of processing, queuing, waiting to be released by the authorities. But it was more than that for Rita. Almost immediately the problems it raised interested her. She began to puzzle through the differences between other languages she knew and English—a simple grammar with almost no conjugations but vastly more words. Then there were the differences between the English she'd learned from Yanks in Germany and the language of Aussies. She couldn't stop thinking about how to render them into German, French, Polish or Russian. Probably more important than all this were the acquaintances her lessons made for her across the 2000 immigrants in the camp, especially among people who needed documents translated, forms filled out, letters written in English. Most of these requests came with gifts, small payments, and reciprocal kindnesses. Together with payment for the classes she gave, they enabled Rita to make the cubicle more comfortable.

Teaching adults conversational English meant exchanging stories, first in English broken by phrases in Estonian, Latvian, Polish and German, then in broken English. After a few weeks their stories became more fluent but still employed a children's vocabulary. As most of her students had children ardent, like her own, to learn English quickly, they were well satisfied with the elementary expression of their narratives. The stories of hardship, dislocation, violence, death, escape, but also humor, ingenuity, survival and pathos, began to humanize people Rita had only been able to look upon with suspicion during the long voyage and the first weeks in the camp.

But somehow she couldn't, wouldn't, almost felt she shouldn't add her story to theirs. It was too different, too accusatory, too personal. There was still too much rage against people like these *Volksdeutsche* refugees. Who could say whether even in this camp in the Australian outback there were not people who stood by, who took a hand in, or at least relished the suffering she had endured or the much worse fate of vastly many?

Too often, as she listened, questioned, corrected conversations and narratives, memories would intrude so sharply she'd momentarily lose the thread, have to push the memories back into oblivion, force herself into the present. The simplest thing would set her mind down one of these tracks—a word spoken, the smell of smoke, the coarse laundry soap she had to use, the heft of a mop—any one of them would suddenly carry her back to Heidelberg or Krakow or, worst of all, the ghetto at Karpathyn. Pushing these thoughts away by acts of will, she would find them back, intruding on her mind, as she walked home, or stood in the line at the mess hall, showered at the communal baths, told the boys a bedtime story. Worst of all was when they haunted her attempts to get to sleep at night. She had to do something about these intrusions into her life, both to exorcise them and to record them.

One night she found herself in a camp chair, under the glow of a small lamp, its cord rose up to plug into the overhead socket hanging from the central tent pole, the cubicle's only source of electricity. The overhead light was off, but the boys had asked that the dim table lamp remain lit.

On the deal table next to her was a box of onion-skin paper, taken from supplies for the class, and a fountain pen, the recent gift of a family whose paperwork she'd written out in English. Rita lifted it and suddenly the simple thing was freighted with recollection. She remembered the weeks she'd worked behind the fountain pen counter in the Warsaw department store. Then came her face, the vicious girl who'd worked beside her, relishing the fate of co-workers whose false identities had been uncovered, watching them being taken away by the Gestapo, hoping for advancement into their better posts in the store. *What was her name, damn it! It was seven years ago...Yes: Lotte. Lotte.* Remembering the name rewarded the obsessive memory search. Rita reached for the pad. The thought came to her, *Write them down, write out your memories, your history, now. In English.* It would unburden her of the need to keep it all in memory, where, uncontrolled, it threatened to rear up at the slightest stimulus, pitching her into an unendurable past. She spoke at herself, *Try it. It may help you let go, forget, move beyond, stop obsessing every time some incident catalyzes a memory.*

The fountain pen was poised over the paper. She was about to begin. Then she put down her arm. No, it's too hard both to remember and to force it into her still quite imperfect, ungrammatical, stilted, adjective- and adverb-poor English. If she was going to do this, she had to write everything out in Polish, the language of her thoughts. Then, later, when she'd mastered English, she might think about a translation. Translation? She was writing for no one but herself. It was only to herself that she could tell the truth, all of it. There was no one else to understand, accept, forgive.

Rita picked up the pen and began to transcribe the Polish thoughts.

I came to Krakow in the fall of 1935, to study the law. I was Rita Feuerstahl. But in the years after that it became Mrs Urs Guildenstern and then it was Fraulein Margarita Trushenko.

Then she crossed out everything but the first sentence. She'd tell the story in the way it happened, all of it. She put the pen to the paper again. By the time she'd stopped writing that first night she had a dozen pages of closely written text spread out on the floor. She'd neglected to number the pages and now had to gather and sort them. Numbering them she realized they'd only taken her from her marriage to her meeting with Gil— Tadeusz Sommermann, as he was back then. This project, if she could carry it through, would take several weeks. *That's a good thing! Just what you need, waiting, not knowing what you're waiting for.* Rita found an oak tag folder, closed it over the papers and pushed the file under her clothes at the top of the metal cabinet. *See how you feel about it tomorrow, Rita,* she told herself.

The next evening she was almost eager for the boys to fall asleep so she could begin again, reliving the days before the war, when she had first met Gil. She wouldn't put on paper the sensuality, the wantonness, the freedom of her love affair with Gil. But as she wrote, hinting at it made the emotions return with a rush. When they subsided Rita began to wonder where he was, whether he'd really ever join them to face the hard slog of settling in this new country. She knew Gil better than he knew himself. It would be harder, much harder for him. *If he ever comes at all.* Rita stopped writing that night only when she had to record how her husband Urs had found out about her affair with Gil in the winter of 1938, his suicide attempt and her decision not to leave him for Gil.

In the nights that followed, only rarely did she fail to advance her narrative. A few times she told herself she was too tired. But she recognized each time that it really was an excuse to put off the most harrowing experiences—sending her son Stefan away to what she thought might be safety, smuggling herself through the charnel remains of the Warsaw ghetto in a crazed and vain search for him. Writing, reliving these moments were much worse than feeling again the twice-daily terror of passing through the main gate of the Karpathyn ghetto, or the RAF bombing raid she'd lived through in the Berlin Tiergarten. The hard work was trying to remember chronologies, incidents. She would sit in the glow of the small lamp, close her eyes, letting the sudden recollection of a small detail call up large events by a process she could neither control nor understand. Rita would run her mind over a remembered street or a room until she recalled something that triggered a stream of other memories. It became a trick, a device, a mnemonic that almost always worked for her.

She knew she could write endlessly about the people who touched her, loved her, saved her: Erich, the mathematician from Warsaw, her chaste companion in the ghetto, who made her survive, when everyone else was marched off to extermination, Erich — for whom she had silently named the boy now sleeping a few feet from her as she wrote. And there was Dani, the girl with whom she shared love in the ruin of their lives as forced labor, and who'd spurned her for a man when the war ended.

Writing endlessly about the pain of losing them was not the task she'd set herself. Sentiment and self-indulgence would not unburden her. She would not vainly ask the sort of questions she knew had no satisfactory answers. She wasn't going to demand why, why, why, still less give fatuous answers that worked only for gullible children. There was a trajectory to record, even though its narrative would not really explain why those things had happened.

Once she settled into the task Rita recognized that her work was not to excavate the emotions she had experienced, but the events that had triggered them. The feelings — of hopelessness, the emptiness of merely living another day, the humiliation, the purposelessness of continuing, the sudden relief at escape or wonder at spontaneous generosity, the outrage at crimes witnessed, the despair at inhumanity, these could repeat themselves a hundred times in her narrative, she knew. And even though she would be the only reader, the repetition couldn't but numb her, inure her to her own past self's suffering.

Rereading the first few nights' work Rita began to see that as dispassionate chronicle as she could produce was more powerful. It called up in her as its sole reader the very emotions that her narrative excluded. Before her, in the pages she was writing, were the triggers that would recreate the feelings, long into her future life, she suspected, when she wanted or needed to recall them, relive them, to overmaster them with a life that would now last long, with children she loved and would not lose, a life that, back then, in the war, she had no reason ever to expect to have, but was now hers to live.

By the time she'd written 258 pages, the American army had liberated her as it swept east to meet the Russians and end the German war. That meant she hadn't quite finished the story the morning Guillermo Romero sauntered into the camp and back into her and her boys' lives. Somehow she never got back to it.

Chapter Five

Gil reached the Bathurst migrant center one evening at the beginning of April. Summer had passed its peak, but the twilight still lingered and as usual Rita was having a hard time getting the boys to sleep. She'd read them the same story, their favorite, from one of the few children's books in the camp library. She noticed that both boys, but especially Tomas, were anticipating her words. Had they memorized the story, or were they already reading? The boys were demanding she repeat the story or read another when there was a light rap on the screen door. The solid door was not closed. Rita had propped it open, allowing the slight breeze off the flatlands surrounding the camp to cool off the baked heat still convecting off the metal walls of the barrack.

All three looked up, and saw in the dusk Gil's silhouette against the remaining brightness in the west. Then he stepped into the middle of the space and the boys jumped from either side of Rita and rushed to him. With a broad smile he opened his arms and hugged each to a thigh. Then Rita came to him. The arms unfolded from the boys and rose to crush her in as powerful a hug as he could deliver, holding her fast for a minute and then seeking her mouth with his own. She offered it eagerly, and both could feel unsated desire rising even as the boys interposed themselves between them. They separated, held each other for a moment, looking for changes, and then turned their attention to the clamoring boys.

Both began proudly to address their father in English, and both pulled faces when he replied first in a very limited English himself, and then in German. Erich and Tomas looked at each other. "We must teach him English." Rita noticed there was no trace of the German 'V' in their word "We." It was something she couldn't do.

Gil nodded firmly. "Yes, you must. I must to learn as quickly as possible."

He was immediately corrected by both boys simultaneously. Gil looked from them to Rita. "They will teach me."

"But you've learned some already," she said, impressed. He had resisted learning any before they left, insisting there would be time enough when they were settled in Australia. "Where did you pick it up?"

"When I missed the ship I had to go to Genoa for the next one." He was going to try to make his six-month sojourn as innocent as possible. "It wasn't going to leave till the middle of February. The British put me in a stockade full of people trying to avoid being sent back to Russia—men, women, families. I was the doctor and I reported to the camp commander, who only spoke English. In four months I may have learned as much English as the boys." He laughed when the boys began to make fun of his impossible 'th's.

Rita nodded, tousling one of the boy's heads. It had been half a year since she and the boys had left him forlorn on the dock at Bremerhaven. "Was it you on the dock waving and shouting as the ship pulled away from the dock?"

The hint of accusation in her voice made Gil decide to ignore the question.. In a cheerful tone he went on. "Would have been here sooner, but in Melbourne they sent me to the wrong camp. I passed a week in Bonegilla looking for you, wondering what could have happened, before they figured out where you were."

"We'll now you're here. Let's put these boys to bed." She said it in English, testing his language and pleasing her boys, who had by now formed an antipathy to German in their ardor to be Aussies. Each carried one child the few steps to their cots, laid them down, stroked their hair, kissed them once, and rose, quietly walking out. Gil made to turn off the light but Erich spoke from his bed in a German produced by a tremor of anxiety. *"Lassen-sie das Licht bitte an."*

Now Gil and Rita stood outside in the dark. Each lit a cigarette,

Rita not waiting and Gil not offering to light hers. They'd both been single now a long time. Both smiled at the shared thought. Rita put her hand on Gil's lapel, and that gesture was understood. They knew they had to wait for the boys to fall asleep, but each was hungry for the other's body. It dispelled for the moment questions and explanations, challenges and apologies. Rita was only just beginning to frame hers. Gil had his all worked out.

When after a few minutes they could hear the duet of rhythmic breathing inside the space, Rita led Gil in, quietly turned off the light and waited a few seconds for his remonstrance. He'd always preferred making love with a light on. When it did not come she turned and reached for him. He had already shed his shirt. Now he shucked his shoes and they bounded beneath the bed loudly enough to alarm Rita. Neither boy stirred. Gil had the presence of mind and self-control to hold her at arms' length, allowing her hands to unbutton the blouse with seductive deliberation. Then the skirt dropped, and the underclothes. Now she stood as he completed undressing and then reached back to unsnap her bra.

When later she tried to recall the next few minutes, Rita could really remember only surges of delight and relief, gladness that her body still responded and responded to his, pleasure that she had not lost the responsiveness that charged and recharged love.

Gil had been hungering for Rita from the moment he entered the door, seeing unchanged in face and form the woman he'd left in Salzburg. But he also needed reassurance that his long delay in arrival had not opened a breach with Rita. Was she ready to accept a version of what had happened that would provoke no recrimination? Allowing him unchallenged and immediate access was a sign she did not harbor resentments he'd need to assuage. It made him want to try to please her.

Another hour later they were both sitting on the steps out the door of their cubicle. The breeze blowing in the barren darkness stretching towards the western outback. Neither wanted sleep;

both were waiting for desire and arousal to stir them again. This time Rita accepted one of Gil's smokes and he lit it for her from a Zippo, something she'd seen often enough in the hands of Americans in Germany. She took it from him, hefted it and snapped it open in a gesture that had been familiar to her five years before. "Gil, tell me how you got that lighter. Tell me everything that happened."

Gil had rehearsed this narrative enough times in 150 days. Now it would have its debut. "Well, I managed to get most of what I needed in Paris. Had to wait endlessly. But then I was caught by the Spanish police crossing the Pyrenees. They found the Nansen passport on me and decided I was a spy. Kept me for weeks, interrogated me over and over, but I wouldn't tell them why I'd come. Had to protect the hospital director in Barcelona. That's why I missed the ship." Gil gulped. Silently, he contemplated what he'd been told. Had the man really been executed in '43, as the Spanish *Guardia* had said? Almost certainly. "Finally I used my Catalan and the dollars I had left to bribe my way out of jail. I was never able to get the documents I needed. All the money was gone, but I managed to get over the border. I got back to Salzburg with tickets from the Zionist agency in Paris paying transit costs to Israel. Told them that's where I was going."

Why is he lying to me? Rita could recall the letter from the *Ecole de Médecine* in Paris and the one returned from Spain with the handwritten notation *Deceased-Return to Sender*. She had them still. *If he got documents in Paris, they'll be forgeries. If they bear the name Romero, they'll be doubly forgeries.* Now she almost rose to demand the certificate and confront Gil. *No, not now. Perhaps later. He'll explain. It doesn't matter. He's here.* She would give him another chance. "At least you got the certificate you needed from Paris."

Gil brightened. "Yes, and in the right name too." He unsnapped the small valise that was his only luggage. "Here it is." Rita looked at the piece of paper and then back at Gil, inviting him to tell her how he'd managed to secure a forgery. All he did was beam at her.

Rita shrugged. "And the Zippo, where did you get that?" Gil took it out, thought of how he had come by it. The lie came easily. "It was from a Don Cossack, a bribe for giving him a medical certificate to put off forced repatriation to the Soviets." "Forced repatriation. Is that still going on? I thought all that finished in '48."

She could not see Gil reddened in the dark. *She's right, damn it. Caught in your first lie.* He bluffed: "One of the last. He'd been hiding in plain sight."

Then and there Rita decided she'd accept his stories without cross-questioning Gil, just as she had his account of how he'd survived the war. She would weigh them, scrutinize them, but she wouldn't challenge the discrepancies, inconsistencies, implausibilities, not out loud, not if she wanted their partnership to work.

Would he ask her anything? Did he want to know how she had managed things without him? Only if he asked, she decided. And she pretty well knew he wouldn't.

They ground their cigarettes into the dust. They rose. Hand against hand, Gil and Rita re-entered the compartment to resume, quietly but intensely, assuaging their needs for one another's bodies.

Afterwards neither could fall asleep, not immediately. They turned quietly from side to side in their cots, fearing to wake the other. Both finally realized sleep was not coming to either. Rita spoke first. "Brave of you, to protect your friend when the Spanish caught you."

"Yes, I was frightened I'd break down." Gil paused. "Worried about you and the boys. But I had to...protect him."

Rita wouldn't challenge him. She'd give him a chance to tell her something like the truth. That would be enough of what she wanted from Gil. "I think I know what you must have been feeling." She paused, but he said nothing. "Something like that happened to me once."

Rita's silence demanded an encouragement from Gil to go on. "What do you mean?"

"In the war, I thought I had a secret." This time Gil said nothing. *Does he want to know?* "In '42, when the Karpathyn ghetto was finally cleared, before I escaped, someone told me that the Polish intelligence service had broken the German radio cypher code and passed it on to the English. He was sure it would win the war for the Allies."

Rita could not see Gil's face, but his voice challenged. "I don't get it. That's not like keeping a secret under interrogation, the way I did."

"Oh, but when I was caught at the end of the war by a Gestapo detective...I was sure I'd blurt it if they interrogated me. I even looked for some way to kill myself before they could."

Gil rose in his cot, propped himself up by his elbow and sought her face in the gloom. "What happened?"

"They...just let me go. The war was lost. The two Gestapo men were already worried about covering up their crimes."

"I see..." There was something in what Rita said that still bothered Gil, a loose thread. *Ah, yes.* "Rita, you said you *thought* you had a secret. Did you?"

"I doubt it. A secret like that? It would have come out by now, wouldn't it?"

"Yes, surely." His reply was immediate, but then the student of politics and history in Gil took hold. What if the Poles had really broken the German code? What if they had given it to the western Allies? They'd never give anything to the Russians. Poles hate Russians more than they hate anyone, even German invaders. But surely the Russians would have figured out by now the secret that the German code had been broken, if it had been. They'd managed to steal so many other secrets, even the

Atom bomb.

But then what if they hadn't? Gil spun out the scenario for himself. *They'd be using it now, like everything else they could take from a prostrate Germany. And the Brits, the Americans..., they'd be listening in!* Gil almost laughed out loud at his deduction.

Now Gil was wide awake. He watched Rita turn onto her stomach, to make another attempt at sleep. Then he caught sight of the Zippo shining in the dim light on top of the white certificate from the *Ecole de Médecine*. He'd never be able to tell Rita about how he got either one. He had real secrets.

Chapter Six

The Paris of Gil's prewar wasn't there when he arrived in October of '48. This Paris was still shabby from occupation, hunched over against an early winter, another one of a succession of the worst winters of the century. Gil could even make out the German *fractur* print on the walls. Penetrating the slapdash whitewash over-painting, it was still directing the ghosts of Wehrmacht soldiers on their Paris-leave. Gil's shudder was involuntary.

He walked the streets away from the *Gare de L'Est*, hoping to feel that he knew where he was, seeking the aromas he remembered more vividly than anything else—the bread smell from the *boulangeries*, the waft from starched bedsheets hanging in the *blachisseur*, most of all the waft of an *express* on a bar's zinc counter in the morning. Instead, along the *grandes boulevards* he found the plane trees cropped to their trunks, haunted and haggard. In the narrow streets there were no smells but the occasional odor of urine. At 8:00 shopkeepers were watering the pavement. But the flotsam and detritus in the curb was too heavy to be moved by their feeble sprays. The few women already out shopping were drab, elderly and too familiar to him from life in Moscow. Where was the Paris of his memory? He pushed his way into a café and suddenly found reassurance in the waft of tobacco smoke from the *Gitanes* and *Gallois* of the men at the zinc. Only then did he realize he'd forgotten to change money at the *Gare*. Without a *sou*, he could order nothing. "Rube," he muttered to himself and began to walk back in the direction he'd come.

Armed with a wad of francs, Gil descended to the *metro*, bought a *carnet* of ten tickets and joined the moving throngs to the platform. He had only to glance at the entry map to remember the direction on the *Clignancourt-Porte d'Orléans* line for the Left Bank, the *Boul Mich* and the streets surrounding the

Ecole de Médecine. At *Odéon* station he was steps from the *Ecole.* He had only to wait till the secretariat opened for business in an hour or so. But he wanted badly not to complete his business immediately. He needed a day or so, enough at least try to find the rhythm of this Paris. He began to mount Rue Monsieur le Prince to the rather rundown *Hôtel Modern* he knew from his earliest days in the city. Twenty minutes later, the contents of his valise were already unpacked into a rickety bureau.

Now Gil was ready to be a *flâneur,* letting his feet carry him where they willed, down towards the *bouquinistes* along the Seine embankment. He sauntered along the river to the pedestrian *Pont des Arts,* crossed and, seeking warmth, entered the Louvre. It was no warmer inside, along the grand gallery, almost deserted but for a guard every hundred meters. At last he recognized some old friends—Gericault's *Raft of the Medusa,* and David's *Napoleon Crossing the Alps.*

Sitting at an easel before the David, carefully copying Bonaparte's face, was a woman, about thirty, dark and thin, with brown hair, cut short to the nape of her neck, her face fixed in concentration. Her beige smock was drawn tight and she wore a sleeveless lambskin vest over it. He walked up to the easel, looked back and forth between original and copy. The movement elicited a look from the copyist—just what Gil hoped for, as if to say, "What do you think?" Gil's smile showed warm appreciation. The woman smiled briefly, but before he could speak she had returned to her work, face again concentrated. Slightly disappointed at her reticence, Gil moved on.

Forty minutes later, he saw the woman again, in front of him, no longer wearing the smock but still wrapped in the sleeveless sheepskin vest, descending the vast marble stairway beneath the *Nike of Samothrace.* Gil decided to follow her discreetly. He pulled the wedding band off his ring finger and pocketed it. Rita and Gil wore them as a concession to respectability. *Why wear it here? You're not really married, legally, after all.*

By the time Gil left the building she was leaning up against it, one foot behind her against the wall, looking skywards as she smoked. He pulled out a packet of *Gitanes*, put a cigarette to his lips and sauntered over to the woman, patting his pockets. "Got a light?"

She nodded, and still wordlessly handed him a silver American Zippo.

He looked at it, handed it back and spoke. "*Américaine?*"

She shook her head. "Got it off a G.I. in '45. No one's managed to steal it from me yet."

Gil lit his smoke and pretended to pocket the lighter. She laughed and he handed it back. "On a break?" Gil drew on the cigarette and waited for an answer. There was none. He'd try once more and then give up. Looking towards the Left Bank he said. "Buy you a coffee?"

She pushed off the wall she'd been leaning against. "Why not?" By unspoken agreement they chose a path through the crushed white gravel towards the *Pont du Carousel*. Before them the trees were branchless and the little Arc de Triomphe forlorn without a halo of hedges. There wasn't a nurse with a perambulator as far as the eye could see, all the way down to the *Place de la Concorde*. The Paris day was too cold, too grim.

Still no small talk, no conversation, no inquiry from the woman. Gil would have to do all the work. "*Parisienne?*" he asked.

"No. I came with the Germans." No trace of German, her accent was faultlessly native to Gil's ear. Surely she was teasing him, testing him.

He had to show he saw through this confession. "What do you mean?"

"I was an art student in Lyon. I knew Germans would covet the art. Thought there was going to be a market for copyists. Didn't realize they'd just steal the stuff. You're Polish, no?"

"No." It was almost the truth. "I'm Catalan, but you have a

good ear. I lived in Poland for a while after the war." He looked at the paint on her ungloved hands. "Is there a living in copying?"

"Yes, for a few of us. There's a shop in the 5th *arrondissement*, up behind the *Senat*, that specializes in them. Sometimes I paint for them on assignment, sometimes on spec for myself...sell them off the easel."

They'd gone in from the Seine a street or two up the rue Jacob in search of a café. "Not worried about leaving your rig, are you?" Gil asked as the distance back to the museum lengthened.

"No. The guard will watch things."

When the waiter came to their table inside the café they'd settled upon, she asked for *un express* and a *Marc*, the strong liquor made from remains of the grape—the skin and the seeds. It was something Gil had never seen a woman order in his Paris-years before the war. She mistook his look of surprise. "Don't worry. I'll pay for the booze. Need to warm up."

He spoke to the waiter. "Same for me." Offering her one of his cigarettes, Gil took out his matches. This earned a shrug and a smile. Then she took out her Zippo and he reddened, remembering how he'd struck up this acquaintance.

"I'm Guillermo Romero, but people call me Gil. You?

"Citrine. Citrine Calvaud." She let the smoke emerge from her nostrils. "Been here long?"

"Lived here before the war. Studied medicine. Now I'm back to get my medical certificates." He didn't volunteer why. No point telling an attractive woman you just met that you are leaving forever.

But Citrine made an intelligent guess. "Why'd you need them? Going somewhere? Not back to Spain, I'd guess."

"Don't know. Certainly not Spain. Might stay in Paris a while." Why had he said that? Was it what she might want to hear?

She shrugged. "Have to get back to work. If you like, you can meet me at the shop this afternoon. Show you some more stuff

I've done." She rose and Gil did too.

"I'd like that."

"I'll be there round 5:30. It's on the rue de Condé, just where the tank battle was during the liberation."

"Didn't know about that. What's the street number?

"Just look for the *vitrine*— shop window—with the grand masters for sale."

"Fine. Dinner afterward? I know a place nearby."

She was already on her way to the café door. Turning, she spoke above the noise. "O.K., but not the damn Polydor." It was the very place he'd had in mind, round the corner from his hotel. Now he'd have to think of somewhere different and probably pricier.

* * *

There was certainly enough time to visit the secretariat of the *Ecole De Médecine* and get the papers he'd come to Paris for. As he walked back down the *Boulevard Saint-Germaine* he began to try to work out the problem of changing the name of whatever certificates they gave him from Tadeusz Sommermann to Guillermo Romero. He'd been Romero ever since he'd sloughed off the skin of the Polish Jew-boy Sommermann when he'd arrived in Barcelona from Paris in '36.

It was the same shabby waiting room he remembered from fifteen years before. The rows of benches facing a set of brass-grilled windows looked more like a municipal pawnshop than a university's credential office. One or two were marked *Ferme*. Before each of the others a man stood, dealing with a clerk through the grill. The wooden benches were crowded with men of various ages, in threadbare suits, some wearing detachable collars. The cellulose collars were too loose for these haggard men, and the ring of grime was visible inside each as Gil walked past them. Despite the chill, body odor drifted across the room in waves. There were no women. Each man on the benches clutched a small bit of paper. Gil watched as the man who'd entered just before him went to a machine in the corner and pulled off a numbered ticket. Above the grillwork windows there was an indicator board, displaying the number currently being served. It said 19. Gil advanced to the machine, pulled a ticket and examined it. 51. He took a seat. A quarter of an hour later, the number on the indicator had not changed and no one new had been called to any of the windows.

Gil looked to his right and left. On one side a man was absorbed in a racing paper. *Le gars*—the guy—on the other side was staring into space, folding and refolding his ticket.

Gil turned to him. "How long will it take, do you think?"

"No idea. I got here at 7:30 this morning. There were already 23 people outside lined up." He held out his ticket to show the number 24.

"But it's 3:45."

"Yup, and they close spot on 5:00. I don't fancy my chances today. Have to come back earlier tomorrow if I can."

"But at least with your ticket you won't have long to wait in the morning." Gil spoke hopefully, trying to cheer up the downcast fellow.

"But tomorrow I'll have to get a new ticket. They start over every morning."

"Why's the process so slow? I don't understand." Gil was beginning to worry.

"A hundred reasons, my friend. First of all, these clerks, they won't be rushed. They won't be worked too hard either. They take an hour and a half for lunch every day. But none of us leaves, of course. We'd lose our places. Most of the records are in disarray, and they are very scrupulous." He smiled grimly. "And then, they are just plain *méchant*." The word meant naughty and mean at the same time.

"What do you mean, *méchant*?"

"Look round, most of these guys waiting are forty or more. They qualified long before the war. So their records are hard to find, and they're probably refugees, people who had to escape the Germans, people who lost their papers one way or another." He paused again. Then he spoke one word quietly. "Jews." It was self-explanatory.

"I can't sit here endlessly. Isn't there any way round the problem?"

"Well, you could try bribing a clerk at the window, but these guys are watching." He looked at the benches full of men. "If they saw anything like that they'd tear the culprit limb from limb and then go for the clerk."

"Thanks for the lowdown, friend." Gil rose, dropped his ticket to the floor and moved to the door, surveying the others, motionless in their patience. What was he to do? Queue up at dawn? And then there was the name change problem. He was hoping to slip some banknotes across the counter. But that might not work, if he ever got to the counter.

Chapter Seven

Daunted by his problem, Gil returned to the Hôtel Moderne, trudged up the stairs, and decided to take a nap. He drew the overcoat up over the thin blanket and fell into a light sleep. It was dark when he awoke and suddenly he felt the fear of a missed rendezvous. Pulling his watch from the nightstand he saw he had five minutes. The shop, he knew, was only that far away, the other side of the *Théâtre Odéon*. He stared at himself in the mirror briefly and drew a comb across his hair. He had hoped to shave. Now he'd be late. Would she wait? A little test. He unbuttoned his shirt and pulled a tube of shaving cream from his kit bag.

* * *

Through the window he could see Citrine in vigorous debate with a paunchy older man, who looked every inch the shop's patron. Gil paused, surveyed the familiar pictures through the glass and waited to see if either would notice him. Neither did till he opened the door, thereby ringing a bell attached to its top corner. Citrine and the older man looked up. The patron's instant smile, slightly unctuous, already contemplated a sale.

Citrine spoke. "This is my friend…" She paused long enough for Gil to see she'd forgotten his name.

He quickly volunteered it, proffering his hand. The man's smile disappeared. He took Gil's fingers up to the second knuckle and pumped them exactly once, limply. "M. Jansen."

Citrine turned to the back wall. "That's one of mine." It was a copy of Manet's Olympia. "No surprise, there's a steady market for it—Germans, Americans, Englishmen. There should be a Goya too. I was in the Prado last summer."

67

M. Jansen intervened. "*La Maja Desnuda*? Sold this afternoon."

"Do you only paint nudes?" Gil smiled at her.

"Was Napoleon naked crossing the Alps, this morning?"

"Point taken."

Citrine grabbed a bag and slung it over her shoulder. "Shall we go?" She took Gil's forearm and pulled him out the door. He enjoyed being dragged off by her. She turned to him and announced, "We're going to the *Procope*. Ever eaten there?" It was the oldest continually open restaurant in Paris, arguably in the world, straight down the street and across from the *Place de Odeon*.

"Never ate there when I was a student before the war. Couldn't afford it. But I'd like to try it tonight."

The restaurant was a long, gilded room with leather banquettes. Under a dark ceiling each table was lit by the glow of a sconce reflected in nearby mirrors. It was crowded. But Citrine was recognized at the door as a familiar, and shown to a quiet table away from the cold of the entryway. The waiter took Gil's overcoat and her sheepskin. Gil noticed that she was wearing a maroon dress, open to a V between breasts that showed no cleavage. The dress wrapped tight across her body. It was cut like a robe without any buttons and held by a belt at the waist. She didn't appear to notice his survey of her body. "We'll have to drink for a while." She took up a drinks menu from the table. "Too early for the kitchen."

"Willingly."

The waiter returned. Citrine looked up at him. "Two champagne cocktails."

"Rather tame for a girl who drinks marc, no?"

"Let's stay sober enough to taste our meals." She put her hand on his in a way that seemed slightly motherly.

"Is copying all you do? Do you have time for your own art?" Gil really wanted to know. Besides, he wanted to make himself interested in her work.

"Abstract expression. You know what it is?"

Gil did indeed. "Ah yes. In the Soviet Union it was the kind of art you could get sent to Siberia for producing." He'd had a few friends who did it secretly in Moscow. "Here you can only go to the poorhouse for doing it. That's why I copy."

"But the skills are so different, careful drafting as opposed to wild improvisation."

"No one ever arrived at expressionist painting except by getting tired of studying academy style, Gil." Finally she'd used his name.

Perhaps he'd said something worth taking seriously. "Can I see some of it?"

"That stuff of mine is not in any gallery. You want to see it, buy me dinner." She picked up the menu.

* * *

Two hours later, Citrine was leading Gil up a narrow little street called the rue Larrey. It was one Gil had never ventured down in all the years he'd been in Paris during the '30s. Citrine pushed open a wide but unlocked door and they mounted a steep set of stairs in the dark. From a pocket in her sheepskin she withdrew a long single-toothed key, turned it once in a lock and slid a door as tall as it was wide along the rail from which it was suspended. Only then did she turn on the industrial lighting. "Keep your coat on. There's no heat." Around walls of the drafty open space leaned a dozen canvases, some black and white, others a riot of primary colors, still others heavy with palette brush-loads of pigment. A few were so washed out it was like looking through a fog. Citrine was still searching for a technique.

Gil walked round the walls, looking and then looking again at each picture, while she brought a coal scuttle out from a corner, drove it into a bin and then emptied it into a stove that she then poked at several times. Only then did she join him. Silently they surveyed the canvases together. She did not ask for his opinion, and he did not offer one. Instead he lit two cigarettes and put one in her mouth. She drew on it appreciatively. Seeking the warmth of the coal stove, Gil saw a double bed, bureau and a desk. So, she lived here among her canvases.

Standing next to the coal stove they took off their coats. Citrine turned towards Gil, and took his coat by its lapels. "Thanks for the meal." Then reaching her arms behind his neck she brought his face down to hers and opened her mouth. At the same time their mouths met he pulled the knot on the belt holding the wrap dress closed. The dress open, her body wriggled away from him and dove onto the bed, pulling the duvet over her. Suddenly he saw her head poke from the coverlet like a turtle's. Then her tights and brief *slip* came flying at him. "Kill the lights and come here," she commanded.

Citrine woke up in an ardent, indeed, demanding mood. She pulled him towards her and set to work arousing him. It took only a touch or two and the thrust, to his mouth, of her breast, somewhat pendulous on a meager frame. As the night before, Gil took his time, teasing her body with his lips, hands and sex. He was applying lessons he'd perfected since first learning them from a young Trotskyite named Lena seventeen years before and not two kilometers from where they now lay. Ten minutes after his tentative first strokes, confident that she would climax, he entered her swiftly. Matters came to a well-orchestrated conclusion. They separated and sprawled across the mattress, catching their breaths. Only then did they begin to feel the cold and pull the duvet over them. Citrine spoke first. "Took you to bed last night to recompense the dinner. But I had you wrong. You were worth keeping in bed a while longer."

He looked at his watch. 8:30. Was it too late to bother queuing up at the *Ecole du Médecine*? Probably. He'd leave it to the next day.

Citrine noticed the glance at his watch. "You're right. It's late. I need to get to work." She looked round on the floor beside the bed, found the tights she'd thrown at him the night before.

Gil turned to allow for any modesty and began seeking his clothes, wondering how he'd pass the day. *Might as well check in on the secretariat at the Ecole du Médecine.* Then he walked over to the large window above a gutted courtyard of packing cases and empty coal sacks. In a wan morning light the sheen of wet paving stones was pockmarked by the splash of raindrops. Gil shuddered from the image of cold, wet discomfort the view presented.

A quarter of an hour later Citrine and Gil were gulping down *cafés au lait* at a bar opposite the *Place Monge Metro* station, feeling their wet feet, as they watched people cross the boulevard and descend, shaking the rainwater from their umbrellas. She licked the line of milk foam edging her cup, put it down with finality, and said, "Well, I'm off. Come back tonight if you want. I'll get a couple of *merguez* on my way home." These were Algerian lamb sausages favored in the Latin Quarter for their pungency and cheapness. Then she was gone.

Gil was left to contemplate his night. One thing he knew. He'd be there for the *merguez* that evening. A second thing, almost as clear to him, was the feeling of self-satisfaction. He might be fifteen years older than the kid who had come to Paris in 1932, but he could still keep a woman's interest.

Of course, Rita would have been furious. But she was a thousand kilometers away and would never know. So, she wasn't harmed by the pleasure he'd taken last night, and would take again tonight if offered—no, when offered, he was confident. It was just a bit of fun. Meant nothing. Besides, what right did Rita really have to be censorious? After all, hadn't things started with her the same way all those years ago, in Karpathyn, before the war? She'd been a married woman when she'd seduced him, almost the first time they'd met, in her own home.

He ordered *un express*, pulled out his *Gitanes* and lit up. He let the images of the previous night run through his head, along with scenarios of the next few, knowing full well he wasn't going to resist. Why should he? He'd allow himself to be swept along by Citrine's availability, willingness, interest, while it lasted. When he had his documents and was ready to leave, he'd go and there would be the end of it, leaving just a memory, something for him to savor, silently, from time to time. But something that would never make any difference between him and Rita.

Gil stubbed out his fag and made for the metro station. It wasn't far to the *Ecole du Médecine*, but the ride would keep him out of the rain.

* * *

Pointless. He could see it even before pulling a numbered ticket from the machine. There indeed in the first row, front and center, still waiting, was the same guy he'd spoken with yesterday, smiling briefly at him like a co-conspirator. He turned and walked out. How to pass the day waiting for Citrine? It was no weather for a *flaneur*. He'd get a paper from the kiosk at the place de l'Odéon and find a cinema. He wanted a *Figaro*, but he didn't want to be seen reading it, or even carrying it—too *haut bourgeois*. *Le Monde* was the right image but it carried no film adverts. So he bought a *Parisien* and walked back past the École de Médecine to his hotel. He couldn't decide between *Jour de fête*, the comedy by Tati, or the historical drama, *Le Secret de Mayerling*. Everyone knew the story, how the heir to the Austrian throne killed himself over a woman. It would be interesting to see how the French treated it. The theaters where on the left bank, close together. He'd see both.

* * *

That evening and night, Thursday night, was everything Gil hoped and expected it to be. Two *merguez* and a baguette didn't satisfy his hunger but everything else did. He could neither complain nor rouse himself any earlier than the previous morning. In fact he'd slept so soundly and so long, Citrine was gone. There was a note on the mirror hanging from a wire above the industrial sink.

Gone to the Louvre. Left a key. Lock up when you leave. Come with me to a party tonight?

But now it was Friday and the bureau of the *Ecole de Médecine* would be closed over the weekend. He'd let nearly a week slip by with nothing to show for it. Well, not quite. But Citrine's company wasn't what he'd come to Paris for. It was at the party that Gil's problem was solved, a little late but better than never.

It was already late, nearly 11:00 in the evening, when they emerged from the metro station at *Dugommiers*, a stop Gil hadn't even known about, on the Rive Droite, somewhere in the 12th *arrondissement*. Citrine led him through a long dark passage, wet from rain and smelling like a refuse tip, littered with rotting wooden vegetable crates. They came out into the open space defined by the looming tenements that walled it in. There stood a low corrugated iron shed, doors thrown open, spilling bright light into the courtyard. Jazz music in a thumping beat and cigarette smoke, an iridescent blue, emerged from the entrance.

Inside were several dozen people clumped into groups of drinkers, dancers, debaters. The listeners were ranged round a raised dais on which a trio of men and a woman were quietly playing a piano, double bass, snare drum and a clarinet in the spotlight. There were enough bodies moving inside to make the space warm and Citrine and Gil dropped their coats on a pile at the entrance. Then they moved towards the music. Standing beyond the penumbra of light, they began to listen. It was the last number in a set. When the applause tailed off Gil turned to where Citrine had been standing. She was no longer there, but on the other side of the space, in a dark corner sharing a smoke with another woman. Instead of Citrine he was looking at the lined, leathery face of an older man, white-haired, but more carefully dressed than others. The man smiled with Gil in mutual appreciation of the quartet. Something in the man's face put Gil at ease. The man too must have seen some kindred spirit in Gil for he moved a bit closer. When a brace of chairs between where they stood and the stage came free, they both sat by unspoken agreement.

The older man spoke first. "I'm Gravé. You came with Citrine?" Gil nodded. "Artist?"

"No, I'm a doctor actually. Name is Romero, Gil Romero." They shook hands. It was a solid hold of the whole hand Gravé gave him, not the fishy finger-holding one-pump of most Frenchmen. He liked this man more and more. "What do you do?"

"Like the name says, I'm an engraver, wood cuts, etching, dry point."

"Quite a coincidence, the name and your work?"

"Not really. Got the name in the Resistance. It stuck."

By now Citrine had returned. Cigarette in her mouth, she put a hand on each of their shoulders. "So, you two have met?" They both smiled up at her standing between their chairs. "Gravé saved a lot of lives in the war. Kept us from starvation more than once."

The older man waved her remark away but Gil asked, "How's that?"

"Best forger in Paris, that's how. *Faux papier*, ration cards, German *Ausweis*, you name it. You know, maybe Gravé can solve your problem, Gil."

"What's that?" The old man searched Gil's face.

Gil lowered his voice, as though German occupiers might be listening. "I need a copy of my medical school credentials. But the wait for them is interminable and they might not even find them." He frowned at Gravé. "Do you think you could help? I can pay."

"*Sorbonne*? *Ecole de Medicine*? Standard certificate, or a specialty?" He seemed to be thinking aloud.

Gil broke in hastily. "Quite standard."

"I suppose I could whip something up. Might not pass the closest scrutiny. They've changed forms since the war…my fault, really. They knew I had been doing them, getting med students off the STO." This was the *Service de Travaille Obligatoire* that sent hundreds of thousands of young Frenchmen to Germany for forced labor during the war. "How soon do you need it?"

"Right away, actually." Gil did not disguise the urgency and Citrine failed to suppress a look of surprise.

"Have you a *pièce d'identité* with you—anything, driver's permit, passport?" Gravé put out his hand. Gil withdrew his Nansen passport from his jacket and the older man opened it, running his fingers over the page. "Nice work. Where did you get it?"

Gil was impressed. "In Prague."

"Well, I wouldn't use it anywhere they look carefully. May I borrow it ?" Gil looked at him in perplexity.

Gravé understood immediately. "I'll need it to prepare the certificate. When did you matriculate?"

"32. But I left for Marseilles in '35. Finished there, actually. I was going to head there next if I had to."

"No need. I'll prepare a complete certificate for you if you like." He looked at Gil. "Tuesday soon enough for you?"

Gil was overwhelmed by gratitude: almost all his problems solved at one go: the document, the name 'Romero' on it, not the one he'd come to Paris with—Tadeusz Sommermann—and no need to go to Marseille at all. He'd be almost back on schedule. He dared to ask. "How much?"

Gravé looked at Citrine and then back to Gil. "Real friend

of yours?" She nodded. "No charge." Gil pumped his hand so vigorously the forger might have feared losing its use. Gravé handed Gil a business card with his address. "Come by about 11:00 on Tuesday." Then he kissed Citrine on each cheek and strode out.

Chapter Eight

Sunday evening at Citrine's studio things came crashing down for Gil, owing to the most trivial incident. They were getting ready for bed. Citrine was already nude. It was the way she slept. She was lying on her stomach across the bed, head propped up by her forearms. Gil had taken off his trousers. Bending down, he picked them up by the cuffs, letting all the coins fall out. Some ran off under the bed, others towards the stove. As Citrine dropped her head over the bed looking for the coins, she found his wedding band. Holding it up, she looked at him. "What's this?" Gil pretended not to understand. "You didn't tell me you were married."

He wanted to say "I'm not" and explain that he wasn't legally married to Rita. But that might make matters worse. He could say "You never asked," but it was pretty clear that by his actions and conversation he'd intimated that he had no attachments elsewhere. It was safest, he thought, to appeal to her contempt for bourgeois values. "Does it matter?" He wanted to add, "We've been having a nice time."

But her response cut him off. "No, it doesn't matter you're married. What matters is you didn't tell me. You're the one who cared whether I knew. You're the *petite bourgeois*, chasing skirts in Paris while your wife is…where is she, exactly? Lille, Amiens, Metz?" She ticked off a list of middle-class industrial towns. There was complete disdain in her face. Without bothering to cover herself she rose, pointed at the sliding warehouse door and said, "Get out." When after a moment he hadn't moved, Citrine picked up her Zippo from the floor and threw it at him. It missed and bounced off the entry door.

There was nothing for it but to dress and leave. She was right. He was the one ashamed, embarrassed, watched, as he dressed, by a naked woman who would have nothing to do with him, so contemptuous she couldn't even bother covering herself.

At the door, almost without thinking, Gil picked up the Zippo and pocketed it.

* * *

Monday Gil went to the Gare D'Austerlitz for a ticket on the Tuesday night express to Bordeaux. There he'd have to change for a local train to Pau, 200 kilometers south in the Pyrenees. It was the best place to find someone who could smuggle him into Spain.

There'd be no way for him to enter Spain legally. The old Nansen passport would have made Guillermo Romero suspect as a Catalonian exile even if it had been genuine; detected as fake, it would have resulted in instant arrest by Franco's *Guardia Civil*. He certainly couldn't use the Republican one he'd been issued in '37. Gil's Polish passport in the name Tadeusz Sommermann was almost twenty years old. It had long ago expired and wouldn't pass muster at the Spanish border. No, he'd have to find Republican exiles in a border town like Pau, in the Pyrenees. They'd know the by-ways in and out of Spain, smuggling Allied airmen from occupied France.

* * *

Tuesday morning well before 11:00 he presented himself at the address Gravé had given him. It was a flat in a block not far from Citrine's loft. The old man came to the door, opened it and without a smile or a word led Gil back to a room with a drafting table, a couple of steel filing cabinets and draftsman's tools hanging from a pegboard. He turned to Gil, handed him the Nansen passport and held up a plain manila envelope. "That'll be 3000 francs."

Gil's mouth opened. "But, you said…"

Gravé raised his hand, palm out. "I said, for a friend of Citrine's." He let the words fill the space between them.

"But..." Gil had no idea what to say in his defense. Why should he even have to defend himself to this man?

The look on Gravé's face was implacable. "You are fortunate I've already put the work in."

Gil withdrew his billfold, took out one of the $100 notes he'd received for a half-dozen gold coins before leaving Salzburg. They both knew its value in Francs to the sou: a hundred or so francs more than Gravé had demanded. "It's all I've got."

"It'll do," said the older man as he seized it while dropping the envelope to the floor for Gil to retrieve. When Gil had done so, the man gestured down the hall, forcefully turned Gil around and marched him towards the door.

At the threshold Gil turned. He couldn't understand Gravé's rage. It had been a natural enough little lie he'd told Citrine. Surely another man would understand. "Why are you so angry, sir?"

"I don't like men who trifle with my daughter."

* * *

Gil packed up and left his hotel for the *Gare D'Austerlitz* that evening, but not before putting everything he had in the identity of Guillermo Romero into a large envelope, along with the forged medical certificate, one of the $100 notes, and the Zippo. He deposited it all with his hotel's proprietress. In Franco's Spain it would be dangerous to be caught out in all the lies that identity told the world.

Sitting in the metro to the *Gare*, he took out his ancient Polish passport in the name of Tadeusz Sommermann and began thumbing through it, looking for the Spanish border entry stamp it had to carry, somewhere in its pages—July 1936. Careful inspection would find it. More careful inspection would reveal no exit stamp, nor one for re-entry into France, when he'd fled to escape the collapsing Spanish Republic in '38. But at least it was a genuine document and he had to have something if he were stopped on a street by an officious *Guardia Civil*.

* * *

It was not easy to sleep in a crowded second-class compartment, despite the gentle rocking as the wheels clicked like a metronome over the track joints. Once when he woke, Gil found his hand in his trouser pocket fingering the wedding ring. He pulled it out and slipped it on his ring finger. Now he began for the first time to realize that perhaps he owed Rita a letter or at least a postcard, telling her of his progress, and where he was headed next.

The days, no, the nights with Citrine, were already a delightful blur of sensations, smells, images. But for the silly accident of a discovered wedding ring, could it have been more, might it have lasted longer, changed his life? In the darkened 2nd class compartment, Gil smiled to himself. *That's how things started with Rita.* They'd carried on an intense affair for almost three months, back before the war, in Poland. It had begun in pure sensuality but then he'd fallen in love, for the first time in his life and very hard. In the months of that clandestine affair she'd seemed compliant, reliant, dependent on him, right up until the last words they'd exchanged. Then he'd been dumbfounded by how her husband Urs' attempted suicide had put an instant end to the affair. Compassion for Urs' weakness had driven every other emotion out of Rita. She'd refused to follow Gil, refused to put her wants first, refused to accept Gil's demands that she think of her own happiness.

That made Gil want her more, remember her always, and silently honor her for all the qualities, strengths, certainties, he knew he would never have.

When they met again, after the war and almost ten years after those brief months, she was just as beautiful to him. Perhaps she was more beautiful, mouth firmer, gaze more distant, eyes deeper set, haunted. The first evening they'd found one another brought back their carnal passion in vengeance against a past that had wrecked their lives. Soon enough each had recognized the survivor in the other, without asking too much about how they'd managed it. Gil was afraid to ask. It was enough to hold her when she awoke from the nightmares. He knew he couldn't really bear the details. He was glad for her continued reticence, even as it surprised him. *Don't women need to talk?* he'd ask himself. Rita too hadn't asked much about how Gil had managed to come through six years so un-scarred. This, he knew, was because she wouldn't judge, wouldn't weigh and balance the compromises anyone made to survive. She didn't ask so she wouldn't have to judge, not out loud at least. *Does she see through you, Gil?* The question recurred often. He didn't think so.

Did he still love her as he had four years before? Well, he admired her awfully.

He'd send her a card from Bordeaux. *Everything on schedule. Heading to Spain. Love to the boys. X X X Gil.* The boys—Tomas and Erich: it was the first time they'd even come into his head since he'd left Salzburg.

* * *

Gil would have missed the brief station stop at Pau and ended the day at Lourdes but for the conductor, tapping his shoulder to waken him a second time. *"Vous descendez a Pau, Monsieur."* It sounded like a command, not a question.

Gil dropped down the unexpected three feet from the train to the platform and almost sprawled across it, pulled down by the weight of his valise. He gathered himself together and walked across the track, through the ticket hall and into the still glaring October sun. There, rising 100 meters above him, was a promontory crowned by a grillwork walkway. At its base a funicular station awaited pedestrians and passengers who'd come off the train ahead of Gil. Five minutes later the surge of passengers carried him from the small crowded car. Gil found himself on the *Promenade des Pyrenees,* a boulevard flanked on one side by a stone barrier at the cliff edge and lined on the other with vast apartment blocks still reveling in their late nineteenth-century glory. Beyond the broad avenue the view swept thirty kilometers south to the snowcapped Pyrenees glaring in the sunshine. Gil was perspiring freely by the time he'd crossed the road and found a café. Instead of installing himself outside, Gil sought the *zinc,* not so much to save a few *sou,* but to make discreet inquiries of the barman. After the stark mid-morning sun, the dark, cool shade of the café was a relief.

After paying for a *café au lait,* he asked, with all the casualness he could muster, "Friend, is there a circle of *Anciens Combattants* of the Spanish Civil War, a café where they meet, somewhere a fellow veteran can find them?"

The man looked at him, up and down. "Where did you serve?" His French was foreign.

Gil was ready with a lie and spoke it in Catalan. "The Ebro in '38, XIth brigade." This was a Polish unit and would make sense of his passport, were he required to show it. Gil had to hope that none of its members were still living in Pau.

The barman looked round the nearly empty café, raised his right arm, closed fist, in the familiar salute. He was silent but smiled.

Gil spoke again, quietly. "I guess I was in luck, coming here."

"Most of the bars in this town you'll find a veteran or two. After all, we liberated this country from the Germans for the *Gabacho.*" It was the classic Spanish term of abuse for Frenchmen. Gil hadn't heard it for a decade. "The least they can do is offer us a crummy job." He wiped the counter as he spoke.

The man seemed to believe him without asking for any further *bona fides.* Gil decided to confide in him. "If a guy needed to get to Spain, is there anyone in town who could get him across?"

The barman's entire demeanor changed. He leaned over the bar and grabbed Gil's necktie. Then he spat out the words in his own native Catalan. "*Provocateur?* Fascist agent? Falange spy? Which one are you?"

"None, comrade! I swear." He put up his hands in a gesture of surrender. "Please, let me explain."

"Don't bother." Watching Gil, he moved to the pay phone on the other side of the bar, dropped a jetton in its slot, and dialed a number. Soon he was mumbling into the receiver. Then he turned to Gil. "Sit tight, 'comrade'." His tone remained harsh.

Chapter Nine

Five minutes later a haggard old man walked in. His gray double-breasted suit was shiny and many sizes too large, but displaying the rosette of the *Légion d'honneur*. He looked to the barman who nodded in Gil's direction. The old man gestured Gil to a table in the corner and sat down facing him. He badly needed a shave and a shower, but he exuded an authority Gil could feel across the table. The man was silent for a moment, evidently sizing up his prey. Then he introduced himself in a calm and methodical tone. "I am Gerard Foquet, chairman of the *anciens combattants* of the *FTP*." This was the Communist-organized, highly effective war-time resistance to the Germans. "Also secretary of the local Communist Party branch, head of the city's *CGT*" — this was the most militant of the trade unions — "and deputy chief inspector of police for Pau." He paused. "I mention this only to make it clear that you have no option but to answer my questions, completely and the first time I ask them. If not, you will be beaten severely and then sent back to Spain crated up in a baggage car. So, who are you, and what are you doing here?"

Gil had to be believed the first time. He would try not to lie and only shade things slightly. "Monsieur, my name is Guillermo Romero. I am a doctor. I have an expired Polish passport in the name of Tadeusz Sommermann." He touched his chest where the document sat in the breast pocket of his suit. Foquet put out his hand and Gil passed it across the table. He leafed through it quickly and laid it down. "Sommermann was my name before I came to Spain in '36. I changed it to Romero when I began working in the Hospital del Mar in Barceloneta. I escaped from Spain when the Civil War ended." He'd actually left well before then, escaping the roundup of Trotskyite dissidents required by the Russians who were actually running the Spanish Republican government. Gil knew this couldn't be checked now, not immediately, not easily. "I need to go back to get documents showing I qualified there, in the maternity wards, for two years." Foquet was shaking his head. He didn't believe this story. Gil had to do better. He had to lie. "After I left Spain I was in the Soviet Army for five years as a medical officer." Could they check this lie? He'd been in the army only six or seven months before finding his way out of the military and into a Moscow maternity hospital. But the lie might have worked. Foquet's demeanor changed.

"Any proof?"

"None. Not a good idea to travel round Western Europe these days with evidence you were in the Red Army."

"No shame in it hereabouts." Foquet finally smiled slightly. "So, what's so important about a certificate from a Spanish hospital that you'd risk your neck for, getting across the border or being caught by the police in Barcelona?"

"My family is leaving Europe, for Australia. I need proof that I can work in my medical specialty. Otherwise I'll have to start over when I get there. I'm too old to do that. But I can only get what I need in Barcelona. I thought it was worth the risk."

Foquet withdrew a small bound notebook from his coat, unscrewed a fountain pen and passed them to Gil. "Write down the name of the hospital in Barcelona, the address, the name of the director and the dates you worked there…not in Spanish, in Catalan." When Gil finished, he began to pass the notebook back. But Foquet held up a hand. His next words surprised Gil. "Pozhaluysta"—Russian for please. He continued in a native Russian Gil hadn't heard since his years in Moscow. "Now, write down your names, both of them, and the details of your military service, rank, units, campaigns." Then he added, "In Russian."

This man was clever, Gil decided. But it was reassuring. An agent of Franco might know Catalan; but Catalan *and* Russian, very unlikely. He smiled and set to work. Confidence growing,

Gil wondered if he should volunteer to write his details in Polish and Ukrainian. Wisely he decided not to bait the Frenchman. *Or was he a Frenchman?*

Foquet continued in Russian. "Now, wife's name, maiden name, children's names, ages."

Foquet looked at the page of his notebook Gil had filled out and back at Gil. Then he looked at a wristwatch. Reverting to French, he was peremptory. "Go out of the café, turn left, go through the Place Clemenceau to the prefecture. You'll see it. Tall wrought iron fence and gate. Check into the *Hotel de Commerce* opposite the prefecture, in the rue Joffre. Tell the clerk Foquet sent you." Then he rose, nodded again to the barman and walked out of the bar.

* * *

Gil sat there, contemplating what had happened. Why did an elderly Frenchman speak Russian like a Russian? *Because he spent the war in Russia, like a lot of French Communists*? But once he got beyond that conclusion, nothing else made much sense to him. Why did this man want all that information, even details about Rita, the boys? Would he check with the Russians and discover Gil's lies about how long he really had been in the Red Army, or exactly what he'd done in Moscow during the war, how he'd managed to get out? *Doesn't matter. You'll be long gone.* The thought gave Gil some relief from his disquiet.

* * *

That night Foquet handed the paper Gil had written out, along with a covering note, to the secretary of the local party cell for transmission to Paris. They would know how to pass both on to the Soviet embassy. It was probably of no importance, but that wasn't for Foquet to decide.

The local party secretary was a stalwart—a veteran of the Spanish war. Dutifully he put the piece of paper in the post to the Paris headquarters of the *Parti Communiste Français*. But not before he copied out Gil's Catalan details carefully and took it to the post office where it was sorted in time for the evening bus to Pamplona, Spain. He didn't really know why any more than Foquet did. Neither of them liked it much, either, playing footsy with Franco's *Falange* fascists. But it had been Moscow's standing orders, ever since the Hitler-Stalin pact of '39. The friend of Stalin's friend is my friend. So make nice with Franco. Maybe the KGB had just forgotten to rescind the order when the Germans attacked the Soviet Union. It remained standard operating procedure for unapproved, freelance border crossings.

* * *

Late in the afternoon several raps on Gil's hotel room door brought him to wakeful attention. It was the desk clerk. "Monsieur, I was told to bring this note to you." The man's hand was out and Gil fished a few coins from the pocket of the trousers he'd fallen asleep wearing. The clerk's appreciation was grudging as he withdrew his foot from the door. Gil locked the door and turned to the sunlight slanting but still streaming strongly into the room.

There is a Post bus for St Jean Pied de Port at 6:24 tomorrow morning. Be on it. Get off at the post-office and have a coffee in the bar across the street. Someone will find you. You will need to have a carton of cigarettes for the man. It is a signal and a bribe.

The note was unsigned.

* * *

Gil found himself up well before the rap on his door at 6:00. It signaled his watery café *au lait* and a still warm *croissant* on a tray at the foot of his door.

Twenty minutes later he was standing in the post-bus queue, shifting from foot to foot in the cold, along with the dozen others. Most looked like small-hold farmers in overalls, returning home to St Jean Pied de Port. A few carried the packs and staves of pilgrims on the way to Compostela. He studied the route posted with the schedule and saw his was the last stop, less than 100 kilometers but five hours away to the west on switchback roads. The town's name suggested it was at the base of a pass into Spain.

The big yellow bus pulled up and Gil climbed aboard along with the rest, paid the driver, passed along the seats to the back and settled himself in for a long ride. The bus would stop at every village and most of the crossroads on its way. But at least it would be beautiful—cultivated fields, giving way to vineyards, then open grazing land dotted with goats, sheep, and cows, now brought down from their summer ranges high in the uplands.

It was late in morning when the Post bus jostled and rumbled over the uneven cobblestones between the shuttered windows of what seemed like a deserted one-street village. Gil found his rendezvous, the beaded curtain in the only open doorway announcing that it was the town's one café. There were five small tables and a bar no more than two meters long.

Gil hadn't even ordered his coffee when a small but stocky farmer made his way into the bar, noticed the carton of fags at Gil's table and made straight for him. He did not offer his hand but he did look round to be certain the other patrons remained uninterested. Then put an open rucksack on the floor, sat down and swept the carton off the table into it. "You're Romero?" Gil nodded. "I'm Eduardo. Follow me. You've got about twenty-five kilometers to walk." He looked at Gil, sizing him up, then he rose and walked out of the café.

A few minutes later under a warming sun and waning wind

they were walking south out of the village. Gil tried to make conversation, but the man remained mute. An hour out of the town, Eduardo led Gil away from the paved road and onto a cart track down the middle of which patches of grass grew. When the track became rough and stony, they reached a small unoccupied farmhouse. Here Eduardo told Gil to wait, drew out a large key and opened the door. In a few minutes he returned with a dry sausage, and a length of rope. Evidently he'd been watching Gil shift his case from hand to hand as they walked. He handed Gil the sausage, took the bag, rapidly ran the rope round it and soon had constructed a harness that enabled Gil to carry it on his back. "This will be easier, señor." He used the Spanish. It was the first thing he had said since they'd left the cafe.

Gil was emboldened. "Where are we going from here?"

Eduardo pointed to the track. "It leads up to where the border makes a sharp turn. I'll show you where to stay for the night. A refuge we use in the summer when we graze up there." He pointed south. "Then in the morning you'll walk back to the main road south of the border checkpoint. Easy. Better eat that now." He pointed to the sausage in Gil's hand.

"Aren't you coming?" Gil asked with some anxiety.

"No need. I'll point out the track before I leave you. It will only take an hour or so to reach the paved road again. Then you're in Spain, and it's seven kilometers to Roncesvalles. There's a Post bus to Pamplona." Gil's face must've continued to show distress, because Eduardo added, "Look, anyone stops for you on the road, just tell them you're on your way to Compostela and you must do it by foot. Come on. It's getting dark."

It was very cold an hour later when they reached a squat stone structure. It stood by the side of a footpath that had been moonlit soon after they left the farmhouse. Gil chose to remain outside the refuge till Eduardo lit a fire and called him in. "Senor. You can rest there." He indicated a shelf wide enough to lie on along the back wall. "There's more wood in that corner."

He pointed into the dark. "Water in the stream down the ravine is clean this time of year. In the morning just follow the footpath till it becomes a track again. When you reach the main road go south. You know which way is south?" Gil nodded. Then he was gone.

Chapter Ten

Gil came down a beaten path in a cold but bright morning sun through barren brown hills, studded with boulders that could only have been left by an ice age. Beyond the last of these he could see a paved stretch. But there were no Compostela pilgrims on it that morning, nor another soul, all the way into Roncesvalles. When Gil reached it, he found it wasn't a town at all, but a series of formidable ecclesiastical buildings glowering at the few pilgrims wandering round them. With grinding gears and then the shriek of padless brakes, a yellow coach pulled into a place a hundred meters from where he stood surveying the buildings. Gil grabbed his case and ran to the bus. Catching his breath, he boarded, only to realize he had no *pesetas*, only *francs*. He offered a handful from which the driver pulled fewer than he expected and turned his ticket machine three times to generate a strip of paper that he handed to Gil. It was only then that Gil noticed the two *Guardia Civil* comfortably seated in the rear of the bus. They gave him a cursory glance and resumed their quiet conversation.

* * *

Gil hadn't been in a Spanish city for more than a decade. But if Pamplona was anything to go by, matters had deteriorated badly since he'd left an already beleaguered Barcelona in 1938. He walked from where the bus stopped before the post office to the vast central square in which the trees had all been cut to stumps, probably for firewood, Gil suspected. Crossing the river he noticed that there seemed to be hardly any motor traffic in the town. The streets were badly potholed and there were horse droppings everywhere, though Gil could see no horses. The tenements were dark with coal dust.

At every corner from the main post office to the railway station there were a brace of emaciated, blind or mutilated men in fatigue uniforms, selling quarter parts and eighth parts of whole lottery tickets. Between them scurried shoeless urchins searching for burning cigarette butts and even fag ends crushed into the curb. There were bakeries, and before every one snaked lines of black-clad women, mostly middle-aged but none looking any more well fed than the lottery sellers. The two *Guardia Civil*, Gil noticed, were headed in the same direction as he was, but apparently in no hurry. Gil stopped to examine a frayed poster advertising a bullfight. The words *Con Permiso Superior* in dark letters ran across alongside a silhouette that was clearly Generalissimo Franco's profile.

There was a *Cambio/Bureau de Change* at the train station, charging outrageous commissions even on dollars. Gil still had enough French francs for exchange to inconspicuously provide himself with enough Spanish currency for a meal, a packet of *Celtas*—cigarettes so strong he probably wouldn't be able to finish the pack—and a 2nd class ticket on the night train to Barcelona.

Seated in the station buffet, Gil turned from the menu to watch the leisurely passage of the few passengers coming and going through the station. There were the two *Guardia* again, apparently purchasing tickets at the same counter he had used. Then they too made for the buffet, where they sat well away from Gil, to his relief. Gil ate a tasteless meal of sliced pork and boiled potatoes as slowly as he could. Then he lit a fag and ordered a coffee. What the waiter brought and served with ceremony tasted of the chicory everyone had hoped to forget after the war.

Someone had left a newspaper on the next table. He reached for it, began to try to make it out and found the Spanish he hadn't used for a decade begin to come back. Gil would have to kill the best part of the day in the station buffet. He really couldn't afford to saunter through Pamplona, a target for any policeman who might want to see identification. He ordered an Orujo, the strange Spanish brandy he'd acquired a taste for soon after he'd arrived in Barcelona. Then he ordered a second one and began carefully to nurse it through a long afternoon of waiting. Every little while he watched the shafts of light beaming though broken panes of the grimy glass ceiling. They made stately progress across the dusty floor

At 6:15 the destination board began to show his train. After paying his bill and finding a few magazines and another Spanish newspaper, more for camouflage than distraction, Gil walked slowly down the quay to a carriage marked *Barcelona*. A few early birds had already taken seats but there were unoccupied compartments and Gil chose one. *It's going to be fine. As usual, you've figured things out.* He watched as a six-wheel steam engine came into the track opposite and made out the plaque below the engineer's cabin—*Stuttgart 1922*.

At 7:06 Gil felt a lurch as the engine connected to the cars, and a few minutes later another lurch as it began to pull them away from the station. It was only then that the two *Guardias Civil* entered his compartment.

"Stand up." The older one spoke in peremptory Catalan. "Hands behind your back." Before Gil could say a word, the younger, beefier Guardia had spun him round and was securing his arms so he could be handcuffed and patted down for a weapon. "Sit" came the command, in Catalan behind him. Gil did so as the shades were drawn on the corridor side of his compartment. The two police did not search Gil, nor speak to him. They merely sat opposite him, their patent leather hats on the baggage rack above them, their collars loosened, watching him, smoking the same strong brand he had purchased, occasionally picking a tobacco leaf off their lips, or spitting one away. It was the Catalan in which he was addressed, exclusively, that frightened Gil the most. Did they know he understood it? They must have, or they would have spoken to him in Castilian instead.

The train stopped only once the whole night. It was still dark when the older *Guardia* shook Gil awake and pulled up the shade. The train had reached the Barcelona station. He was surprised he'd slept at all, but could feel the tingle in his hands bound tightly behind him.

At the end of the platform Gil was turned forcefully to a side exit of the station and hustled into the rear of a windowless Black Maria. Ten minutes later he was standing before the grillwork of a cell, deprived of his wallet, wristwatch, belt, tie, shoelaces and his expired Polish passport, all bravura long gone. A guard passed the corridor, took one look at him, and said in Spanish, not Catalan, "Might as well sit down. You'll be in here a long time." There was no seat, no cot, not even a bucket. Gil took a step back to the wall, and slid down into the dust. He was well past wondering where he'd gone wrong, what mistake had led him here. All he wanted to do was weep. So he did. Drained, hollow, an empty vessel, Gil leaned over on the floor and fell asleep.

When he woke in the early morning gloom of light from the small window, Gil needed badly to relieve himself. He called and called, but the echo told him that his corridor was closed off. After a quarter of an hour trying to get attention, he had no recourse but to find a corner and urinate into it. The liquid pooled, began to trickle along the uneven floor and to smell unpleasantly. It must have been an hour or more later that a guard came by, immediately understood what Gil had done and returned with a mop and pail, ordering him to clean up the mess.

Now the hunger rose in his body and there was no distraction from it. *How long have I been here? Is it one night? No, it's two...and a day in between.* He slid down, drew up his knees and began to whimper again.

There was a noise. Raising his head from his knees, he looked up at a jailer with a ring of keys, opening his cell, motioning him to rise. The guard evidently regarded Gil as no threat at all, turning his back while motioning him to follow. The man led him through a warren of corridors without windows and then locked him in the blackness of a windowless room.

A light came on and he could see he was in an interrogation room, with two chairs opposite each other at a small table. He sat at one, feeling the seat under him as a small mercy after two days standing, leaning, crouching, sprawling.

The door opened, and a man stood at the entrance. He was dark, thin, in an ill-fitting suit, with a scar down his cheek, a pencil moustache, and file under his arm.

Gil wanted to say *Please, some food.* But somehow this man didn't look like he'd comply with any request. The man sat, opened the folder, looked once in a cursory way and began to speak in a non-native Catalan. "So, your Stalinist friends across the border sold you out without a qualm, Romero...if that's your name."

Gil nodded. "It's my name. What have I done?"

The man smiled. "Not much. It's what you came to do that interests us." He passed a sheet to Gil, who read from it the details he'd given the French man, Foquet, that afternoon at the bar in Pau in what now felt like a century ago. "What's the real reason you came?"

"It's just as I told whoever you got this information from. I came to get a certificate, a letter, some kind of document from the Hospital del Mar in Barcelona, from Doctor Felipe Marti, the director. That's all." It was too bad he'd had to reveal the name.

"Won't work." The man shook his head. "Marti is dead. Executed in '43. Your people knew that. He was hiding escapees from France, not just airmen, but your political, reds. Careless of them to give you that cover."

"It's no cover." A pang seized Gil. "Please, can I have something to eat?"

The interrogator smiled, responding to the plea. "As soon as you tell me something I can use...In Spain, we can't afford to feed useless mouths."

Was Gil going to faint from lightheadedness, he wondered? "I have nothing to tell. I only came for that document, no other reason. I wouldn't have come at all, if I had any other way..."

"What do you mean, any other way, any other way to do what?"

"Prove my credentials. I'm a doctor. I'm leaving Europe for Australia"—he calculated—"in less than two weeks. I needed something to show that I am qualified in my specialty."

"And for this you risked your life, Romero? Rubbish."

"I didn't think it was dangerous." He paused. "I thought it would be...an adventure."

"An adventure? Is that why you disguised yourself as a Pole, used an expired passport, got smuggled over the frontier, pretended you didn't understand Catalan?"

"Please, just ask about me at the hospital. Someone will remember me. Check out the name Guillermo Romero. You'll find he died at that hospital just after I arrived. Marti gave me that name to hide me from the Soviets running the war for the Republic."

"The Russians, they were looking for you? Why?" The interrogator sounded slightly interested. He didn't look it.

Gil didn't have the will to lie, even if the admission would be a labor-camp sentence. "I was supposed to join the International Brigades."

"And you didn't join them, why?"

Gil could only gulp. "Comfort?" He shrugged. "Cowardice?" Then he added, "I was better at delivering babies than removing bullets from limbs."

There was contempt in the man's eyes. He rose and turned for the door. When he knocked once it was opened. He glanced at the guard. "Put him in a general cell."

And there Gil languished. One day, a second, a third. There were others in the cell. He was fed, allowed a bit of exercise, the use of a toilet, but no shower. The others in the cell were mainly petty thieves, a series of drunks drying out, a sixteen-year-old car thief. No one talked with him beyond a few words. It was as though they had been warned off this foreigner. And none was there longer than a day or two. None but Gil. Days passed. Gil grew more and more indifferent to his plight, uninterested in the passage of time, the changing of his cellmates, any attempt at personal hygiene or cleanliness. He barely ate the food passed along to him, and was quite indifferent when other cellmates stole it. He knew that a kind of depression was settling over him, but the diagnosis had no therapeutic effect.

He'd been in the cell a week, though he had lost track, when he was taken from it and again found himself before his still nameless interrogator. The prospect of another interview neither filled Gil with any dread nor awoke any hope. He shuffled into the room, barely registering the other man's grimace as his nose was assailed by Gil's body odor, his eye by Gil's soiled linen. It was only when Gil noticed that his personal effects were spread before him on the table that he offered a small spark of interest. The man gestured him to the chair opposite.

"Well, your story checked out, Romero, or Sommermann, or whatever name you want to go by. You're a nobody." He pushed Gil's wallet, watch, passport, his belt, tie and shoelaces, back across the table. "Take them." Gil shrugged and began to pick up his belongings. The interrogator continued. "You're being expelled from Spain." He paused. "If you return you'll be in a labor camp for life, got that?"

Listlessly Gil opened the wallet. It was empty. Almost without interest he observed, "The money is gone. There must have been three $100 US bank notes."

"Call it a fine, or the cost of your incarceration, or perhaps it's a fee for the inquiries we had to undertake in your case. Can't expect the services of the state to be costless, can you?"

Faced with a reality that demanded he take some action, Gil

was stirring from his stupor. "How am I to get out of Spain if I have no money?"

"You'll have a ticket to Perpignan, third class." This was a large French town 200 kilometers north of Barcelona. The man rose. He was finished with this matter. The door remained open and the warder came in.

He spoke in a manner made friendly by Gil's impending release. "Follow me, señor." It was the first time Gil had been called that since he entered Spain.

* * *

Three hours later, dirty and disheveled Gil passed through French customs at Cerbère. His expired passport excited no interest whatever. Probably it was fortunate that he'd been in third. Herded through the checkpoint, he smelled and looked like a *clochard*—the sort of alcoholic beggar to be found at every public *pissoir* in France. The border guards wanted nothing to do with him. When he got back into the carriage, someone along his wooden bench passed him a hunk of coarse bread and a black sausage. They had seen the hunger in his eyes. Gil ate ravenously. Only then did he begin to contemplate his hopeless situation. He'd certainly missed the ship. Rita and the boys had sailed without him.

Gil shuffled off the train at the Perpignan terminal. Somehow, he had to find his way to Paris. There was money there, in Paris— documents, a change from the clothes he'd lived in for...how long? *You don't really know, do you?* Walking down the platform without enthusiasm he began to look at the freight wagons in the marshaling yards of the terminal.

"M. Romero?" Gil didn't hear him the first time. The man looked at him and said it louder. This time "Senor Romero?" It was a stick-thin middle-aged man, dressed in fatigues, looking rather like one of the down-at-the-heels lottery sellers he'd seen on every intersection in Pamplona. Gil looked at him, in slight amazement. The man smiled, and Gil was struck by the row of steel teeth visible in his mouth.

"*Si, Oui*, I'm Romero." Gil's tone was disconsolate, but the man didn't notice or didn't care. Still smiling, he held out a hand with an envelope. "What is it?"

"I only know I was told to meet you here and give this to you." Gil took the envelope and the man turned to leave. It was the steel teeth that made Gil call after him, "Blagodaryu vas." It was the Russian for thank you. The man paused and turned. Gil was right. The man had to understand Russian; only in Russia could you get steel teeth. Gil opened the envelope. It was a wad of French francs, enough for a third-class railway ticket to Paris and maybe a meal. The man was about to turn again when Gil asked, in Russian, "What's the date today, please?"

"It's October 16." Then he walked away, rather too quickly.

So Gil had lost track and then miscounted. He had exactly three days till the *Heintzelman* sailed. And there was $100 waiting for him in Paris. Rita and the boys would leave Salzburg for Bremerhaven on the 19th. Could he get back in time? He was suddenly so relieved, he found himself breathing deeply and smiling broadly. Everything would be all right after all. It didn't occur to him to wonder why he'd been met at the platform by a man with Russian steel teeth in his mouth. That small detail was completely obscured by the prospect of a life returned to its rightful owner.

* * *

Gil had to walk to the *Hotel Moderne* from the Gare D'Austerlitz before dawn. But there was a bit of a spring in his step. The money waiting for him would be enough to buy a change of clothes, and a ticket to Salzburg. But first a shower and a shave. He was already contriving the wonderful adventure story he would have to tell Rita.

Six months later, lying in a cot 12,000 miles from Paris, in the vastness of the Australian hinterland, Gil was able to savor every detail from the week in Paris that brought him pleasure. He had no trouble suppressing the Spanish unpleasantnesses almost completely. It was as though they'd happened to someone else, someone who could tell Gil the story but couldn't make him feel the shame, chagrin, and dishonor, certainly not any guilt. What had happened to Gil after Paris, the weeks he'd spent imprisoned in Barcelona—the utter guilelessness he'd shown, the degradation he'd been subjected to, his craven submission— these he had no trouble forgetting. He'd managed to submerge everything about Spain, except for one thing. Now, in the dark, the surprised look on the wizened face of the man with the steel teeth when Gil had spoken to him in Russian came back. It wasn't haunting him, it was warning him. *Someone has taken an interest in you. Spanish Republican veterans? No... Soviets then? You'll have to become invisible again.*

Part II

Down Under

Chapter Eleven

The morning after Gil's arrival in the resettlement camp the boys' excitement at the novelty of a father had not yet worn off. They woke Gil soon after they rose. Standing at a hot-plate making oatmeal, Rita could hear the strain of the slender wooden cot's frame taking their weight as they climbed in with him. They were reluctant to leave for school, and Gil had to promise them he'd still be in bed to play with them when they came back before lunch.

Rita returned from taking the boys to their lessons a few minutes after nine. She busied herself straightening blankets. There really weren't beds to make, just cloth cots without mattresses. Then she turned to Gil. "Give me your clothes. I'll sponge and iron them. Shave. Then we'll go see about getting out of here. I've been cooped up in this camp waiting for you too long." She smiled to make it clear there was no criticism in her words.

"It should not be a problem. I already have a job waiting for me." He rose from the cot smiling.

Rita absorbed the news, asking herself why he had not told her the night before. Then she began smiling too. "This is wonderful! Tell me."

"It's a mental hospital in Victoria State, in a small town a hundred miles west of Melbourne. They organized it for me before I left the Bonegilla camp to find you."

"A mental hospital? But your field is obstetrics. Do they need a woman's doctor in a mental hospital?"

"No. But they need doctors, any kind of doctors. I'll be able to begin to practice immediately, have a position, a salary. There will be a cottage for you and the boys. It's 'all found'."

"'All found'? What does that mean?"

"It means the house, food, everything is free, along with a

salary."

"But you don't have any training in psychiatry."

"Don't need any. All they care about is that I have a medical degree."

"Have they told you anything about what you'll be doing?"

"Medicine. I'll be a doctor."

"Yes, but..." She looked at him. "It'll be great to escape this place. But is this the right choice for you, dear? The first thing that comes along?"

Gil stopped. "Why are you asking these questions?"

"Back in Austria they told us what you had to do to qualify in Obstetrics — first an internship, then a residency, then medical board exams. You won't be able to do any of that in a mental hospital." She stopped, waiting for Gil to concur. When he didn't she went on. "If you can't qualify, you'll be stuck in dead end work forever."

"Look. I am too old to go back to school. I can't be bossed around by nurses or junior doctors. I won't sit a lot of tests asking me about things I don't need to know. I want my life back."

"But..." Then Rita understood. It was the war. She'd seen it in others. It had taken their ambition, their relish, their energy, their thirst to achieve. It had taught them the emptiness of effort. She was surprised to see that in the months they'd been separated Gil had learned this lesson. He'd decided he wouldn't make himself work hard anymore. She thought he would regret it. She knew she couldn't talk him out of it. She'd have to live with Gil that way.

* * *

An hour later, Gil was sitting before an Aussie captain, sweltering in his gray wool suit, a tie tightening the starched white collar around his neck. Rita sat beside him wearing her only suit and a nylon blouse also too warm for the climate.

He was the same officer who'd made her a language instructor two months before.

Rita began. "Captain, now my husband has arrived, we'd like to be discharged from the camp and begin our lives."

Seeing the man next to Rita, the officer turned to him and spoke. "Well, Mr Romero —"

Gil undiplomatically interrupted. "*Doctor* Romero." The captain didn't notice Rita's sharp glance at Gil. With a show of annoyance, he corrected himself. "Dr Romero. You've only just arrived. Is your English as good as your wife's?"

Gil had no trouble lying. "Naturally." He cleared his throat, but added nothing.

Gil was for once glad to let her continue for him. "Dear, show him your job offer." She pointed at the document resting on his lap.

"Ach..." It was not the right noise for an English speaker. "Ah, yes. Here." He handed it to the officer, who removed the flimsy sheet from the envelope and read.

"Well, I suppose that's all right then, Dr Romero." He looked at the paper again. "But this hospital" — he tapped the paper — "is in a small town a long way from anywhere...must be a hundred miles west of Melbourne. I hope you're prepared for it."

It was exactly what Gil wanted, what he needed. He had to become of no use to whoever had been interested enough to spring him, to save him from being ground to dust in the millstone of a Spanish labor camp. Years in a dead-end job nobody else wanted, invisible in the Australian Outback, might just do the trick. It wouldn't have to last forever.

* * *

Ararat was almost the Outback, but not quite. They would spend two years there. It was a nineteenth-century town founded on gold and the Chinese coolie labor that spent half a century extracting it. Once the gold had played out, no one would ever have known anything about the place had it not been for the Aradale Mental Hospital. This was a vast walled prison for a thousand troubled souls, held under conditions to which their illnesses made them largely indifferent. The Romero family lived on the grounds, and were soon accustomed, adapted, no longer distressed by the formidable meanness of their surroundings, right up to the interior moat that made the walls of the asylum insurmountable only from the inside.

For Rita and the boys there was free passage in and beyond these precincts, down a long, straight, gravel road that passed through empty fields to the tiny elementary school and a paltry library. There was not much else to the one-street town—a general store meeting sheep farmers' needs, a tavern for men only, and a mean little white clapboard church with a narrow steeple pointing at the sky. It was poised, Rita thought, to burst any thought the clouds might have of fun or frivolity. Beyond the town was a disused tumbledown racecourse, and east of the asylum was a small lake, surrounded by eucalyptus trees. On a summer evening in December, the lake could almost be beautiful. It was there that Rita taught her boys to swim.

But for the lake, the library and schoolhouse, there was no reason to leave the hospital grounds. The family lived in a small but comfortable house separated from the long arms of undetached wards. Looking through their gaunt, haunted windows when the sun was right, one might see a slowly moving human shape.

A truck trundled up to the house once a week and from it Rita could take what she needed to feed the boys, Gil and herself. There was more than one carefully cultivated garden allotment on the grounds, from which she would have the pick of fresh vegetables from inmates, patients eager to please someone, anyone, who was not their custodial warder. At the beginning Rita's chief concern was whether her boys might be endangered by any of the patients wandering the grounds. But within days she'd been reassured. These patients, mainly men, often veterans of the Pacific war against the Japanese, were no danger. Indeed they were all too often pathetically frightened of the bumptious, boisterous children that Tommy and Eric were becoming. The boys had insisted on the Aussie version of their names almost as soon as they'd heard the sounds of them. Neither boy showed much interest in how different their parents were, how European, how foreign. Both sought to be more Aussie than the Aussies. Rita didn't mind. Gil didn't really notice.

* * *

Gil soon fell into a routine, one in which patients would be lined up for the same examinations, the same treatment, day in and day out—insulin injections, sulfa and penicillin, treatments for bouts of malaria, especially among ex-servicemen, monitoring patients for tuberculosis. He soon realized there was no scope here for real psychiatry, even if there had been specialists to instruct him. The director, his immediate subordinates, the nursing staff looked upon their role mainly as sequestering their charges from a public their comportment would embarrass, protecting these troubled people from harming themselves, and otherwise leaving their recovery to unguided forces of nature.

* * *

Gil had been wrong about the Berlin airlift. The Brits and Americans had seemed to know exactly where the line between war and peace was located. Stalin had backed down without a direct confrontation. But now in 1951 Gil was more confident there'd be another world war, this time an atomic one, spilling over from the limited war on the Korean peninsula. The Americans were losing to a massive Chinese offensive. One late summer evening, sitting on the veranda of their cottage, the boys tucked up, Gil broached his new prediction. "The only way they can stop the Chinese is with A-bombs."

"But the Russians have them now." Rita spoke with anxiety.

Gil was preternaturally calm. "That's why there'll be a war. Glad we're here, well away from any battlefield."

Most of the medical staff at Aradale shared his opinion. Then the American president, Truman, fired his commander, MacArthur, for wanting to use nuclear weapons. The war ground to a stalemate no one had expected. Again, the Americans were behaving more intelligently than Gil gave them credit for. More than once he wondered why.

Almost from the first Gil began to regret he'd had to take this job. The Aradale hospital was a professional dead end. That of course was why they would take on any doctor, almost no matter his qualifications. The place had just barely graduated from being a hill station. Ararat, when he came to know it, was without interest, diversion, culture. It and its inhabitants were not for Gil, and he made this known too widely. As a result the Romero's social circle was even narrower than they wanted.

Gil had wanted to hide himself away. Arriving in Oz he was still haunted by the days he'd spent buried in a Spanish prison, and even more by the vision of those steel teeth in the mouth of a stranger seeking him out, handing him a wad of money on a train platform for no reason at all, or for a reason he knew too well—he was back in the maw of the Organs of the Soviet State. He'd have to escape again.

No one, Gil hoped, would find him in Ararat.

But after four months his unhappiness had overwhelmed his unspoken, secret caution. He'd wake mornings with no memory of the spectre in his dreams of steel teeth. He'd been unnecessarily anxious, he now concluded. He began scanning the medical news for jobs elsewhere, writing out letters of application Rita had to improve and type. These applications exaggerated his past experience and current duties right up to the point she might refuse to type. He began coming home middays just to check the mail, tearing thin envelopes open and discarding them. The fatter ones he opened more carefully, smoothing out the folds and pulling his fountain pen from his white clinical smock to fill out their forms, reaching into Rita's purse for stamps. In their first year in Ararat there were no encouraging replies to any of Gil's inquiries.

* * *

One day in the second winter after they arrived, Gil announced at breakfast that he would be gone for a few days, to attend the South Australia state medical society's annual conference in Adelaide. There was a gleam in his eye that made Rita slightly suspicious.

Late in the afternoon three days later Rita heard the crunch of gravel on the drive. It wasn't the time of day or even day of the week for the hospital supply truck to lumber up to their back door. She wiped her hands on the apron and pushed the screen door open.

Before her was a passenger car, a very large, very shiny, two-tone beige and brown, chrome-grilled four-door automobile. Behind the wheel was Gil, smiling sheepishly. He unrolled the window and beamed. "Do you like it?"

Rita began walking round the car towards the driver's side. "Did you buy this car...in Adelaide?"

"Yes. It's a Holden FJ. Wanted to surprise you."

"Well, you have." She appraised it. "How much did it cost?"

Gil got out of the car. The door closed with satisfying finality. The question hung in the air between them. "We can afford it, dear."

Rita wouldn't be fobbed off. "How much?"

"About a year's salary."

"Nine hundred pounds?" There was disbelief in her voice.

"A little less." He was waiting for Rita to remonstrate. When she didn't he had to explain. "We have nothing to spend the money on, my dear. Food, shelter we have free. The money was just piling up in the bank." He walked round the car and opened the passenger side door. Then he ushered her in with his arm. "We don't need to be stuck here month after month. Now we can go places whenever we want—Adelaide, Melbourne, Sydney…"

The money was spent, gone. You couldn't return a car for your money back. She'd just have to make the best of it. She shrugged. "I didn't know you could drive." Gil was relieved. Rita slid along the bench seat and touched the steering wheel. "Can you teach me?"

* * *

An afternoon weeks later, Rita was beside Gil on the front seat. They'd just passed a road sign reading 'Adelaide, 107 miles.' It seemed like the right time to broach a topic with Gil she'd been thinking about since he'd arrived at home with the Holden. "You know, Gil, with a car, you could open up a surgery of your own, become a general practitioner in Ararat or any other town that needs a doctor." When he didn't respond, she went on. "You'd be your own boss."

"No thank you, ma'am. Not staying here any longer than we must." He shook his head without taking his eyes off the road.

"But it doesn't have to be in Ararat. You could open up a medical practice anywhere."

"Not so simple."

"Why not?

"To begin with, we've no money to buy one." Rita looked round the car but remained silent. *Nine hundred pounds might have been enough.*

"Can you borrow from a bank?"

He ignored the question. Instead he painted a picture he hoped would be grim enough to close the subject. "Start a new practice in some godforsaken town in the Outback? The only doctor for miles round. Driving long distances in the middle of the night to diagnose heartburn, to deliver babies a local midwife can take care of, tell old people to prepare for the worst." Rita didn't interrupt. So Gil went on. "Reassure overly protective mothers that their precious will recover from the measles. Write prescriptions for piles. Treat the local aboriginals?" He grimaced at the thought. Suddenly Rita realized her husband didn't really want to be a doctor at all, not anymore. Perhaps he never had.

Chapter Twelve

It was another year before Gil finally managed to move the family to Sydney. The offer of a job came literally out of nowhere. Gil could not remember applying and Rita couldn't recall typing a letter of inquiry or filling a form. He'd applied for so many, and they'd not made carbons. But there it was, in black typescript on white with the letterhead of the Waterside Workers Federation in Sydney, New South Wales. Dr Romero's application for the post of union medical examiner had been approved and could he take up his duties as soon as convenient? The salary seemed to both Gil and Rita large enough to survive on in Sydney and matters were decided in less time than it took to light up two cigarettes and smoke them down. Gil would leave after the New Year of 1953. Rita and the boys would arrive in Sydney before the school year began in late January.

After two years in what he'd come to think of as his personal "Outback," Gil didn't really know what to expect from Sydney, or from his new post. He knew what he wanted, hoped for, intended. Soon enough, Gil discovered, Sydney, New South Wales wasn't Barcelona or Salzburg. It wasn't even Moscow. The drabness was petite bourgeois instead of proletarian, unremitted by Bourbon palaces or the grandiose ambition of Soviet Congress Halls. Sydney was Ararat all over again, only vaster, spread out on each side of a monster trestle bridge across the harbor. The sea lapping up on its sides was the edge of a vast barrier between Gil and the rest of the world.

Gil had served his time in rural purgatory, but was now disappointed by Sydney's utter provinciality. The country was too new, he thought. Its numbers too small, its aspirations too confined, to create a real city, even with a population almost large enough to sustain it. It would be hard to remain there forever. But he probably had to.

* * *

That first morning, Gil was in a deep slough of despond by the time he'd arrived at the Waterside Workers Medical Clinic. Despite a prodigious memory, he couldn't for the life of him remember enough about this job, exactly what its duties were going to be. He hadn't been willing to betray his ignorance, jeopardize the offer by impolitic questions, raise concerns about terms, conditions, salary, or anything else that might queer the pitch. He'd been offered the job, so he must have applied for it, amidst the welter of applications he'd filed. And it was the only one he'd been offered, a lifeline he'd grasped with both hands, unwilling even to ask anything much about what the lifeline was tied fast to.

It was up a flight of stairs in a two-story ramshackle clapboard building badly in need of paint. The place stood between two dark brick windowless warehouses on a gloomy, sooty stretch of Port Jackson harbor that Gil would come to know as Barangaroo. There had not been another private car in sight when he pulled up, set the hand brake and carefully locked the door.

Gil was expected. A formidable woman of early middle age was seated at a desk in a waiting room. She sat athwart a pebbled glass door that Gil assumed would open up to a consulting room—his domain. The woman rose from her guard post as he entered. "Dr Romero?" He nodded. "I am Nurse Winthrop." She offered her hand. It was a gesture Gil was unused to in a woman. He took her hand with a show of enthusiasm he didn't feel.

"So glad you've come. We've been without a full-time physician for almost a month." She thought for a moment. "No idea why he was discharged."

Gil didn't pursue the matter. "I am very glad to meet you."

"The Union secretary said you'd be coming today." His middle-European accent immediately flummoxed her: "My, but you don't sound Spanish. We were expecting a Spaniard. You are Dr. Romero?"

"Yes, yes. It has been a long time since I lived in Spain. I was taught English by a German." He was impressed that she'd even detected an accent at all. Australians often didn't, or didn't comment on it, at any rate. The nurse turned to a coat tree, pulled a white jacket from it and withdrew the stethoscope from its pocket. She handed both to Gil as though they were the badges of his rank, as she helped him off with his suit coat.

He slid the white coat on and re-pocketed the instrument. "Thank you."

Both stood silently, each waiting for the other to begin. She was a large woman, with auburn hair tucked under a white cap with wings that would have done justice to a nun. But she exuded a warmth he hadn't experienced since his days in the maternity wards of the Barcelonetta hospital. Fearing to set a foot wrong, Gil decided he would wait for her to speak. Finally Miss Winthrop did so. "Well, Dr Romero, have you known Mr Healy long?"

Gil was perplexed. "I am sorry, Mr Healy?"

Winthrop's face showed surprise. "Why, Mr James Healy, the union's general secretary, of course. T'was his office told us to expect you." Now Gil noticed that her accent was not Australian. Not English either. Scottish? Welsh?

"I am afraid I don't know him at all, Nurse..." He'd already forgotten her name.

She supplied it with a genial smile. "Winthrop."

Gil went on. "No, we haven't met. All my contact has been by post."

"Well, his office told us you'd be just the sort of doctor we need here in the clinic."

"And what kind of a doctor is that, exactly, Nurse Winthrop?"

Just then a knock on the clear glass of the clinic's waiting room announced their first patient of the day. It took only that patient for Gil to learn what sort of medicine the Waterside

Workers Federation expected him to practice.

A tall, well-tanned man of about thirty-five came in, shirtsleeves rolled up over powerful forearms, the seams on his shirt stretched taut by shoulder muscles. He pulled off a wide-brimmed hat and extracted a folded piece of paper that he handed to Gil. "You the new quack then?"

Gil nodded. It was an endearment familiar to him from Aradale Mental Hospital. He indicated a screen in the corner. "Please disrobe there. No need to remove undergarments." He turned to Winthrop, putting out a hand for a file. "Is there a history?"

The other man looked at the nurse briefly and then, still holding out the piece of paper, turned to Gil. "No need, Doc. Just came by for the signature."

Nurse Winthrop explained. "This is Mr"—she looked down at the register on the desk—"Haspell. We're meant to provide certification for his workman's injury payments."

Gil looked at the man standing before him. Taking the form, he asked the nurse, "What condition am I certifying?"

The reply came from his patient. "Same as before, Doc. T.B." Haspell put a hand to his mouth and manufactured a cough. Then he smiled.

Gil pulled the stethoscope from his white coat pocket. "Stand up. Unbutton your shirt." The man did both with a show of reluctance that turned to a look of menace. Gil placed the instrument above four different lobes and listened carefully.

"Well, Mr Haspell, you'll be glad to hear that you are cured."

"Cured? Look Doc, I only got this diagnosis two weeks ago. How do they expect me to get all those blacklegs off the ships—"

"Blacklegs?" It was another word new to Gil.

"Scabs, strike breakers, wogs the owners brought in when they locked out the union." Haspell was buttoning his shirt, making plain by the action that he would brook no further examination.

'Wog' was a word Gil had already learned the meaning of. He'd been taught it by orderlies and patients describing the few aboriginals who worked menial jobs at Aradale. He looked towards Winthrop. "What am I to do, please?"

Winthrop looked from Gil to Haspell and then back to Gil. "Doctor, surely Mr Healy or someone at the union told you what we do?"

"Yes, yes..." Gil feigned impatience. *Healy again. Who was this person?* Gil decided he needed to find out. Perhaps it would help him figure out how he got this job and what he was expected to do. It evidently wasn't just medicine he was expected to practice. He took the form from Haspell's fist and, plucking a pen from the desk, signed it. The man picked it up and without a word sauntered out.

Gil decided he would have to take command. "Who's next, nurse?"

"No one for an hour, Doctor."

"Very well." He pointed to the seat next to the desk. "We have time to become acquainted." *Perhaps you'll tell me whom this Healy is,* Gil thought. "You aren't an Aussie either, are you?"

"No, Doctor. I'm from Cardiff in Wales. Came out before the war. Mi dad was in the pits and what with the closures, the family couldn't afford to keep me. There was a scheme for sending kids to the white colonies before the war. '31 it was."

"And they trained you too?"

"No. In fact I had to go to work right away, as a char. Fourteen, I was. I learned nursing in Spain. Went as a volunteer during the civil war. That's how I met Mr Healy. He recruited me for the Republic in '37."

Gil nodded. "I was there, too, Miss Winthrop." "That must be why you got the job then, Doctor."

"I don't follow."

"Mr Healy is always lookin' out for old party members. He's keen to get them work on the docks, or in the union. Knows they'll be stalwart." She smiled and after a moment's hesitation, put her right arm up in the Republican salute.

Gil almost laughed out loud, so incongruous did the radical gesture seem for this middle-aged lady dressed in almost the habit of a nursing sister. Hesitantly, almost sheepishly, he too raised the arm. The gesture was enough to make him remember his exhilaration in Barcelona during the heady days of the Spanish Republic. Then he felt again the anger at his own Fascist jailors — was it already three years ago now? In an instant he had become again the militant he'd been twenty years before, in Paris. Could he find revenge on all those who had stolen his ardor, turned him into a calculating survivor, here in this medical clinic? Without premeditation he rose, hugged a very reluctant nurse Winthrop to his breast, then held her before him and whispered the words, "Comrade."

He wouldn't tell her the truth about himself, not all of it, in fact not even much of it. But Gil thought he could trust this woman at least to begin to answer some questions, to help him find his footing, perhaps even to tell him who this James Healy was, this man whom Winthrop just knew must have hired Gil for the clinic.

* * *

Soon enough Gil learned what most people on the docks already knew about Mr. Healy and his union. The Waterside Works Federation had been at war with the ship-owners along the Darling Harbour wharves for almost a century. The battleground had come to be called the "hungry mile" — first a path, then a street, now a road along the quays down which longshoremen had trudged, seeking work offered and withdrawn, pitted against one another by pier foremen. Queuing each morning before dawn just for the chance to be rehired another day, sacked on the spot when a back spasm or a hernia slumped a man over, paid a wage that wouldn't support themselves, let alone a family. The solidarity a union had finally created in the '30s, and then the threat from Japan in the '40s, made the class struggle along the hungry mile less one-sided. By the middle '50s it had become a war of inches and attrition. On the one side, wharf owners and shipping companies itching to displace men with containers and forklifts while the Waterside Workers Federation dug in to preserve the old way of break bulk cranes and stevedore's cargo hooks.

And this Mr. Healy, who must have hired Gil for the medical clinic, who was he? James Healy was the union's general secretary. He was a self-avowed, fully paid up member of the Communist Party of Australia, and he had the loyalty of his rank-and-file, ready at the slightest provocation to drop their cargo hooks and jam the winches, bringing the entire commerce of the country to a standstill. The clinic of the Waterside Workers was just an outpost along the stalemated battle lines of this conflict. Gil had been chosen to man this redoubt on the front. There was nothing in his conscious thought asking why they'd chosen him to do so. If the question lurked somewhere in his subconscious, it was steadily suppressed.

The work would not be arduous or even very demanding of his medical acumen. Gil's training, experience and his manner suited him to the treatment of women. Alas, here his patients were restricted to men only, and of these almost all had simple physical ailments. Gil tended to a steady stream of bone and muscle damage, broken limbs and herniated vertebra. Many of the men he saw throughout each day were not eager to be cured of anything or even treated for their ailments beyond the pain they suffered. To be successfully treated, and marked fit for work, was to lose benefits the union had fought to secure its members. Gil had to sympathize with them even as he sought avenues to exercise his professional abilities, to improve, to alleviate, to treat injuries and cure chronic illness. And he was ready enough to fall in with the needs of the union to secure, insure, enforce the interests of its members, even if this meant cutting some medical corners—embroidering a few diagnoses, altering some findings, or even falsifying a record or two. Through it he sought the warm feeling of being on the right side of history he had found sometimes in 1930s Paris, often afterwards in Barcelona, and even occasionally in wartime Russia.

To make things manageable Gil established a regimen for himself. He would leave every morning before the children breakfasted. Not for him the pre-dawn boisterous energy of nine-year-olds. He'd found a quiet teashop halfway to Darling Harbour that was too refined for workmen, where he could pass an hour with the Sydney papers before he had to arrive at his clinic. It was in their pages that Gil became more thoroughly acquainted with "Big Jim Healy"—Red menace and general secretary of the Waterside Workers Federation. He thought he knew enough to read between the lines of redbaiting to a character he would like if he ever met the man.

Once his English hit its stride he discovered in the café's newspaper rack the weekly airmailed *Economist* from London. It kept him in touch with the rest of the world. As he read it silently to himself in a British accent, his own began to lose its central European tone, without however becoming in the slightest Aussie. In fact he had decided to cultivate the very airs and graces of the English gentleman he had hoped to find lounging in a leather wingchair beneath the Southern Cross. That the airs of an Englishman would not sit well with a medical practice on the barricades of the Australian class struggle didn't really occur to Gil.

Most days he went to work in one of a brace of double-breasted suits he thought well cut, bought off a tailor from Singapore whose work Gil liked. He had his shirts laundered by another Chinaman, and would have had his shoes done by a bootblack if there had been one on his route to the docklands. Once he got to the clinic there was only Nurse Winthrop to admire his sartorial standards before he slid into his badge of authority—the white coat, now monogrammed with his title and name. But coming and going, Gil needed to be taken for a sophisticated European gentleman.

Chapter Thirteen

By the winter of that first year in Sydney, family life had assumed a pattern. By the next summer the pattern had taken the shape of a monotonous routine, at least to Rita. Five mornings a week Gil would leave the small two-story undetached brick house on George Street in Redfern, a working-class neighborhood a mile or so south of the city's center.

Gil would drive the Holden past the row of a dozen docks in Darling Harbour to the Longshoreman's Union headquarters on the Sydney waterfront. Rita would send the boys off to school, clear the breakfast dishes and then try to stretch out her reading of the Sydney *Morning Herald*'s pages as long as possible. She'd even begun to make herself read the endless sports reporting, trying to puzzle out cricket, Australian Rules football and rugger. Much of the background knowledge for doing so came from the boys, especially Eric, already versed in all three sports.

One morning in late January, having spent as much time on sport as she could bear, Rita turned to the business pages and the legal notices. There among the divorce notices, legal disclosures, and court proceedings was a box headed *Translators Required*. The Australian government was seeking speakers of German, Polish, and Russian. Appointments would be by competitive examination. Rita began to read the fine print with increasing interest till she came to the requirement of a degree from a recognized university. *That's too bad. I could do that. I might even like it. But without a degree...* Then the thought came, *What do you have to do today? Here's a way to fill time.*

She rose, went to the bedroom, found as sober a suit and blouse as she owned, and was soon striding down to the Cleveland Street streetcar. It would be a half an hour ride to the University of Sydney.

* * *

It wasn't only her attractive looks and cosmopolitan accent that brought Rita to the attention of the Professor of Slavonic and Germanic languages, an Englishman—a Scotsman actually, but Rita couldn't distinguish—well beyond middle age named McKay. It was also her ignorance of the authority signaled by the vast gothic quadrangle that charmed the elderly professor.

"Professor MacKay?" He nodded. Without leave, Rita entered his sanctum. "My name is Rita Romero."

Initially taken aback by her forwardness—knocking on his oak door without so much as a by your leave—the elderly man invited her to take a seat. He was small, a bit plump, bald, with a worldly look, neatly but very formally dressed and wearing an academic gown. He listened without interruption or comment to her request to be taken on as a student. Then he drew himself up. "I regret, Miss Romero…"

Rita had no intention of correcting him to Mrs. In fact, she reached her right hand over her left to cover the wedding band, only to realize that she had worn gloves in an extra token of formality. Wearing the ring had been a stupid oversight. She knew perfectly well that married women were expected to remain at home with their children.

MacKay was going on. "Without a first degree you can hardly be admitted for a master's, and an honors BA will take three years." He paused and shook his head. "Besides, term begins next week."

"I'm thirty-four years old, sir." Rita's German false identity had taken five years off her age and she had never given those years back. "I cannot start a first degree at my age. Besides, I have a law degree from Krakow." *Well, I could have had one if I'd stayed*, she told herself.

Professor McKay brightened. He was eager not to end this delightful conversation, she could tell. "Can you submit a certificate from Krakow?"

Instantly, Rita knew her tactic. "I lost all my documents in the war. I tried to get them but the University records were destroyed during the German occupation. Please, just give me a chance. I am fluent in four languages." She smiled as winningly as she could. The old man was shaking his head. She needed to give him a reason. She had to take a risk. "I am prepared to be examined, on the spot if necessary, to prove I'm qualified to study with you, sir."

"You are a very confident young lady." MacKay reached into a drawer, pulled out first one and then another bound sheaf of papers, looked through them briefly, pulled two from the first sheaf, one from the second, pinned them together and passed them to Rita. Then he handed her a pad of foolscap. "Do you have a pen?" She nodded. "Across the corridor, you'll find an empty classroom. Come back with as much as you can do in two hours." He pulled a pocket watch from his waistcoat and looked at it. "I'll be back from luncheon then."

Rita gulped, rose, pushed her chair back into the desk and walked out. Now she looked at her watch. The boys wouldn't be home till after three. Plenty of time. Standing in the corridor, she had to decide — flee, or dare? She looked down at the sheets. The first two pages were translations at sight, ten lines from Goethe, *Faust*, and a scene from Schiller's play, *Maria Stuart*. Then she turned to the last page and smiled the smile of the saved. It called for a translation of twenty lines of Mickiewicz's *Pan Tadeusz*, twenty lines she knew by heart, twenty lines of the great Polish epic poem she'd listened to, repeated in the silent speech of her thoughts, over and over in the Karpathyn ghetto, in Warsaw and Krakow, even in Germany.

Light was filtering into the classroom through a fine gauze that curtained the large mullioned windows. It was silent and cool. She pulled a heavy dark chair with arms from the table, sat down, placed her handbag at her feet and began. A literal translation of the lines from *Faust* was easy. When she finished she set herself to make it metrical verse, if not rhyme. The Schiller was easier, a dramatic confrontation between the English Queen Elizabeth and the henchmen she'd sent to kill her cousin Mary. Unlike the Goethe, Schiller's poetry lent itself to English verse. Then Rita turned to the Polish epoch. Satisfied with her translation, and thirty-five minutes to wait for the professor to return from lunch, Rita recalled from memory the next twenty lines or so, to the end of the verse, wrote them out in Polish and then translated them too. Suddenly she caught her breath. *You're doing it again, Rita. Will you never learn not to provoke? Are you going to prove to the old man he has nothing to teach you?* Then she separated the pages, and folded up the text she'd set herself and pushed it down into her purse.

At the stroke of 2:00 the door to the seminar room was opened slowly and a head peered in, turning from one end to the other. It was the elderly professor. His look showed genuine surprise. "You're still here, Miss…" The elderly man couldn't be expected to remember it.

Rita supplied the name again. "Romero." She rose and offered up the examination papers in one hand and the foolscap with her writing in the other.

The old man received her work with ceremony. He looked down at it long enough to see the pages were not blank. "Come back tomorrow morning…not too early. Shall we say 11:00?"

* * *

At a few minutes past 11 the next morning MacKay shuffled down the corridor to his study. Rita had been waiting a quarter of an hour. He brightened as he reached for his office latchkey. "Ah, Miss Romero, I'm glad you've come. There are a few points of translations on which we differ slightly." He turned the key, opened the door, pulled his academic robe off and hung it on a clothes tree in the corner. Then he ushered Rita back to the seat she'd occupied the day before and held up his hand to prevent her speaking. Dropping a leather case, he pulled out her translations—marked, she could see, in a few places—and laid the pieces of paper on the desk between them. "Now, about this line just before the prologue in heaven, why did you write 'so he goes to the narrow board room' instead of 'so he goes in the narrow board room'? And you circled the German there too? Why?"

Rita looked at the paper and thought back. "Ah, yes. Well, the German is 'an den'—to the, not 'in dem'—in the. And I circled 'an den' because it didn't look right in the German of the poem."

MacKay looked at Rita's translation, the text of the examination paper, and then turned to the bookshelf, reaching for a copy of Goethe's *Faust*. Quickly he flipped through pages until he found a passage. Then he put his hand to his forehead and shook it slowly.

Rita became anxious. "What is the matter, Professor? Are you ill?"

"Slightly, Miss Romero. It seems I made an error in transcribing the passage for last spring's final honors examinations and no one noticed it till you did yesterday."

"Is that bad, sir?"

"Bad? Yes, very bad. Bad for me, bad for the students who got firsts and perhaps should not have done. But not bad for you." He reached back into his briefcase. "I took the liberty of securing these forms from the bursar's office this morning. You must fill them out in order to enroll in the master's program."

Rita looked from his face to the forms. Perhaps she had not entirely absorbed the meaning of his words. She had to be sure. "I'm sorry, Professor MacKay, you mean I must fill them out to apply, not enroll."

"No, no, Miss Romero, I mean you are to enroll. All you need do is fill out the forms and pay the student fee. The tuition will be

paid by a vacant junior scholarship. Term begins in a fortnight."
He smiled, and so did Rita. "After reading your examination
paper I very much wonder whether I have anything to teach you.
But I am going to try." He cleared his throat. "Now, let's get on to
your translation from the Polish. There are some points of meter
I am interested in. I saw you preserved the Polish alexandrines
in your translation. Why didn't you try iambic pentameter? It's
what most translations use."

Rita warmed to him. "Ah, Professor, you will be able to teach
me something. What is it, this iambic pentameter?"

* * *

It would be a yearlong slog, balancing childcare and housekeeping
with two seminars a week, preparation, research papers and
then study for a master's examination. Rita was good at exams,
she knew. The challenge was her English—not yet fluent enough
to compose in that language. Perhaps it would never be. She
would have to sit an examination on which everything turned,
an examination to be set and marked anonymously by external
examiners who would know nothing of her or her preparation.

The morning of the first master's seminar of the term, there
were already two or three men in the room. They were in their
late twenties, trying hard to look like English academics—
tweed jackets, regimental ties, two with fags lit and the third
puffing on a pipe. Before entering, Rita remembered to remove
her wedding ring. She put her things down at the far end of the
table. When the three men looked up at her inquiringly, she took
it as an expectation that she should introduce herself. "I am Rita
Romero."

The pipe smoker nodded but didn't give his name. "Would
you bring us a cup of tea, Rita. There's a good girl." He turned
back to the newspaper he'd been reading.

Slightly taken aback, she replied, "Where can I get tea?"

He frowned in surprise at her question. "You must be new."
She nodded and smiled. "Yes, my first day."

"Well, then, just round the corner, in the middle common room." Before she could turn to the door, two others looked up from their newspapers and added their requests for tea as well. "Two lumps." "Just one for me, no milk."

She made four cups, poured some milk into a creamer and put a few sugar cubes on the saucer of each cup, added some spoons and brought the tray back in to the seminar room. By the time she re-entered there were eight in the room and Professor MacKay had arrived. He was taking papers out of his briefcase but he stopped and looked her up and down. "What are you doing, Miss Romero?" There was irritation on his face.

"Just bringing some tea for three of the other students and me."

"Why'd you do that, pray tell? Are you a student in this seminar or a scullery maid?" It was the surprised faces round the room that made things clear. He glared at the men. "Did you think Miss Romero here was the char?" He looked at the very man who'd demanded she get him a cup of tea. Evidently he was the leader. "Captain Mallory?" He waited in silence as the man relit his pipe, and puffed a few times to be certain it had lit.

"Isn't she, Prof?" Evidently the pipe smoker was a military officer, or perhaps had been. He was unable to suppress surprise at the question.

MacKay ignored the remark. "Hereafter, you're not to make tea for anyone but yourself, Miss Romero. These chaps are having you on." He indicated the others with a disdainful show of the back of his hand. "They've been toying with you." Then he spoke with formality. "May I introduce the new member of this seminar, gentlemen, Miss Rita Romero." He glared at each of them while Rita moved along the table to the place she'd left her books and bag. Then he spoke again. "No, no, Miss Romero. Not back there." MacKay drew a chair up at his right and offered it to her. She'd be teacher's pet. She walked back past the men, all now glowering at her with a mixture of envy and ill will. *Not the best reception, Rita,* she thought. *You'll pay for MacKay's preferment.*

* * *

Rita didn't know the expression 'to be sent to Coventry,' but she quickly learned what it was like. Following Captain Mallory, week after week the men made a display of pretending she wasn't even there. More than once some of them made a point of loudly beginning an off-color story, usually one they'd learned in the forces, when she entered, and finishing it with a hearty laugh as she flushed. This practice ended when Rita began conspicuously joining in the laughter. Evidently she didn't understand that the filthy stories were intended to offend her. If telling them couldn't make her feel excluded, there wasn't much point to a practice that would have otherwise made these civilized gentlemen feel slightly unclean. So, they took simply to falling silent when she arrived in their midst. The silence was palpable and oppressive. After a few weeks of this treatment she wanted to shout, *Why are you doing this?* But Rita could see this was exactly what they wanted her to do, so that they could display their indifference to her existence.

It wasn't the end of their raillery, their boyish fun. A few weeks into the course Rita began receiving a weekly, unwanted installment of a correspondence course in secretarial skills. When, anxious she would be billed, she called the school to have it stopped, she was informed it had already been fully paid. Then on two occasions there were deliveries in well-marked boxes of wildly vulgar woman's underwear. In the most garish scarlet, the garments' openings left nothing to the imagination about how they were to be employed. Someone was sparing no expense to "have her on". The next week the men in the seminar surveyed her in ways that made clear their speculation about whether she might be wearing them. This made an unwelcome change from their usual practice of completely ignoring Rita.

* * *

Too often she came into class with MacKay, after an hour or more in his office, speaking German or Polish, sometimes Russian. It was the old man's only chance to speak these languages he taught and thought about so much. Rita too enjoyed the conversations. Like MacKay, it was her only chance to use her languages in conversation. At home Rita and Gil could speak only English to the boys, who still resented their parents accents and made fun of their errors in grammar.

MacKay's preferment made the men in her course even more visibly resentful. But his attention and interest more than made up for being treated by the men as though she were invisible. MacKay hadn't noticed, or if he had, he affected not to. And the student of Darwin inside Rita's head understood the men's treatment of her perfectly well. Male dominance had been laid down in the animal kingdom long before the emergence of *Homo sapiens*. The patriarchy was a biological fact, not just a cultural one. Rita would simply have to deal with the threat to it that she posed.

Chapter Fourteen

Gil had never before found himself practicing medicine without supervision, tending to a perfectly manageable flow of cuts and bruises, minor matters, recalcitrant patients, perfunctory paperwork, and no one really to answer to at all. Every week he saw off all the cases that presented themselves, with time to spare, little need to keep clinical records, and a compliant subordinate. There was even the occasional expression of appreciation from satisfied patients.

But it was unremittingly monotonous. He certainly didn't want to return to the custodial duties of the vast asylum at Aradale he'd escaped. Sydney was a bland provincial town but there were paved streets, and a veneer of urban existence. On balance he knew his life was better than it had been. But it wasn't good enough. He didn't want to work harder, learn something new, earn more money, exercise power over others. He just wanted to be allowed to enjoy something suitable to his experience, sophistication, intelligence.

In Moscow during the war, how had he passed time agreeably? How had he employed his intelligence most fully? Where had he met people worth knowing? Playing bridge with that third secretary of the Ministry of Foreign Affairs...what was his name, Dalglashin? Playing chess with his great hero, the writer Ilya Ehrenburg. Why shouldn't he try to recreate such pleasures here Down Under? There had to be people his equal who shared his leisure and his tastes.

It didn't take much beyond studying a telephone directory to find such clubs. There was but one of each. Contemplating their names, Gil had been slightly worried that the Sydney Bridge Club and the Sydney Chess Club might be too English, too snooty, too establishment for him to be entirely comfortable. Perhaps he needed more time in this country to hone the graces that would be needed to shine suitably in such surroundings. Anxiety about making the right impression kept him away from seeking out either of these clubs until the routine of work and the fug of domesticity became unendurable.

Looking at a street map, Gil was surprised to find the Sydney Bridge Club was literally a stone's throw away, a five-minute walk from the Barangaroo docks, down the rather seedy Grosvenor Street. A long afternoon free of patients finally drove him there one Friday afternoon. Expecting to enter a sort of British club-world, Gil was disappointed. The rooms—for the club was just a flat in a two-story building—were rather down at their heels. And the members suited the place—scruffy, unkempt, even a bit raffish. Their appearance, the cigarette smoke smell, and the lack of any furniture but bridge tables and folding chairs seemed discouraging. At least they would have been to anyone not serious about the only matter important to the club's members—contract bridge. And, as Gil immediately saw, or rather heard, listening to the accents, it was sprinkled with foreigners, and even a few women. If Gil played well, he'd be accepted here as an equal. Despite the lack of amenities he might be distracted here.

There seemed to be no formalities. No one approached as he stood surveying the five tables of players in two connected rooms that had to have been the lounge and dining room of a middle-class apartment. After about three minutes however, a balding middle-aged man in shirtsleeves, rose, snapped his braces, pulled his suit coat off the chair behind him and in a loud voice announced, "I'm off." The others looked up in disappointment. "Can't be helped. Business." He turned and saw Gil. "Here, take my place. Keep these boys happy." The others nodded in agreement, raised their arms in welcome and made it impossible for Gil to refuse. This table was all Aussies, but with an evident relish for playing with a European, especially a Spaniard and a medical man. By the time he left early that Friday evening,

Gil was a fully paid up member of the club and the New South Wales Bridge Association.

* * *

Within a few weeks, another 'New Australian' had joined the club, an attractive Czech woman, who played well. It was natural for Gil to partner her. The woman was an émigré, seething about the Stalinist show trials that had taken place the previous year in Prague. More than once between rubbers she'd ask whether Gil had followed the charade of confession and recantation in her country.

Gill had to ask himself, is this a provocation, a test? Have the Organs of Soviet State Security been looking for me? Have they found me again? Or is this just a loud opinionated escapee from behind the Iron Curtain? He had to steel himself not to respond to her anti-Soviet tirades. "I'm from Spain," he observed. "I don't follow central European affairs." After a month or so the lady suddenly ceased to attend. Gil had only a little trouble convincing himself he was indulging a certain self-importance. *No one's keeping tabs on you.*

But partnering with a woman appealed to Gil. *Why not teach Rita the game?* The thought hadn't occurred to him before. Now there was a reason to do so. She was smart, she'd learn the game quickly. Then they could both play here, together, as a team, meet new people too, widen his set of acquaintances beyond Nurse Winthrop and her circle beyond those fellow students about whom Rita never spoke. Somehow he never got round to teaching her.

* * *

Gil had made no difficulties about Rita's course at university, once he'd found it would cost nothing and impose no burdens on him. The boys' reliability and resistance to supervision emptied out the house and left enough quiet most weeks for Rita to work at her studies. Besides, her harsh experiences in domestic labor during the war had provided her with the habits that made short work of its duties, enabled her to prepare meals quickly, and even contrive treats for her family—Apple Strudel above all, from a recipe that had saved her life more than once in the war. All in all, she felt, things were going smoothly. It was only Gil who began to be an unexpected burden to Rita.

His pay was enough, just barely, and the hours—9 to 5—were rare for a medical man. But the inability to exercise his skills, the steady diet of men and their complaints, the absence of interesting and attractive women, ether as nurses or as patients, all these annoyances Gil brought home to her. Almost every night at the evening meal, even before their young boys, Gil would repeat the same litany of frustrations. And each time Rita would try to commiserate, and to walk him through alternatives. The conversation repeated itself with minor variations.

"Why not apply for other jobs?"

"Not qualified, my dear." He would sigh. "Not certified in anything."

"But there's got to be a way for you to get back into Ob-Gyn?" She covered his hand and smiled. "You were so good at it."

He shook his head. "No time to study for the exams."

Rita resisted the frown that her face wanted to make. "You're at the bridge club three nights a week, Gil. Can't you use some of that time?"

Gil heard the observation as a complaint, a charge against him. She didn't know that he was also there on weekday afternoons too, in the frequent slack times at the clinic. *I'm not womanizing, or even gambling more than a few pounds a week. What does she want?* Bridge was the only pleasure he took, and she wanted him to give it up. For what? To mug up medical texts that would teach him nothing he hadn't learned by experience already?

Rita knew this was not a tack that could work. She needed to entice him somehow. "We could study together, Gil. The kitchen table is big enough for both of us." Between meals it was Rita's desk, where she studied, pecked out papers on an old typewriter, opening dictionaries in a half-dozen central European languages, puzzling out hypotheses about the origins and etymologies of their predecessors.

Gil thought about the matter for an instant. What if he worked at it and then failed? Just thinking about the loss of face was too much. "Rita, drop it. I've told you, I'm too old to be a schoolboy!" He didn't want to have this argument again. "Besides, even if I qualified, I'd have to start over in a hospital. It'd be two years of 16-hour days, 80-hour weeks, at the beck and call of some consultant half my age who doesn't know a quarter of what I do." He caught his breath and before Rita could reply, continued. "And besides, we can't afford it. The pay a medical resident gets wouldn't keep a roof over our heads."

Rita couldn't understand it. She could see how dissatisfied he was. Why wouldn't he try? "Look, Gil. I'm going to finish my course in a year. The kids are old enough now. They don't need me around all day. I'll be able to get a job in government, translating. It'll be enough together with what they'll pay you as a resident."

"We'll see…" It was a way to end the matter, he knew, at least for a time. If only Gil could wish away the obstacles. He really wanted to escape the boredom of the union clinic. He wanted the respect that came with being a specialist. He wanted the money, too, needed it if he was ever to make his existence really tolerable again.

* * *

It was only after the dock strike of November 1954 that Gil became fully reconciled to the comfortable monotony of his work at the union clinic.

Rita had seen the strike coming in the papers—failed negotiation, the rejection of arbitration, Red-baiting speeches by politicians and threats by Jim Healy, the Waterside Workers' leader, perfectly happy to be called a Red. Gil knew it was imminent from the chatter of workmen in the clinic. Most were looking forward to a bit of a change—picket lines on the quay instead of dank holds belowdecks, others worried about strike pay, a few eager to provoke police and black leg strike breakers.

It was an early afternoon a week before the strike deadline when Gil came home unexpectedly. He was quiet, taking a seat at the blue gray Formica dinette table between the kitchen and sitting room. Rita, peeling vegetables at the sink, did not hear him enter. She turned and gave a slight gasp of surprise, then saw his frown. "What is it?"

"They've closed the clinic." Gil paused but Rita made no immediately reply. She wanted to hear more before speaking. "Till further notice. They want to save as much as they can for strike pay, keep the men on the picket line."

Rita nodded. "Makes sense. No idea how long they'll keep you closed?"

"I asked. It'll be at least the duration of the strike, plus a few weeks to build up reserves again. Everybody's been put on the street till there's a settlement."

Rita thought for a moment. "But that's a month…"

"More like six weeks."

"We can't afford you're being off work that long, Gil." He did no more than nod. "Well, it's time you registered with the medical association as a…" She had to search her memory for the Latin word.

Before she could find it, Gil provided it. *"Locum?"* It was the word used everywhere, even back in Europe, for a temporary replacement physician, one who filled in for a regular when there was need—illness, holiday, heavier-than-usual caseloads.

Each month the New South Wales Medical Association placed a call for *Locum* doctors in its newsletter.

Rita turned from the sink and pulled on a kitchen cabinet drawer. There she rifled through some papers and pulled one out, passing it wordlessly to Gil. She smiled wanly, hoping he'd take the gesture as she meant it, a chance to find something better, something more fulfilling, and not a calculated move in an intermittent war of attrition. "Perhaps it's a blessing in disguise. You'll be able to try something new."

Looking at the page of medical vacancies, he understood immediately. She had been waiting for the right moment to raise the matter of his job again. What did she want—more money, a bigger house, more status, private school for the boys? No. She'd never asked for any of that. So, why was she prepared to vex him this way? And now there was really no way out for him. He really would have to do something, find some other work, at least till the clinic reopened.

Gil looked at his watch. "Very well." He rose, studied the list briefly, and reached for the hat and coat he'd deposited on the table. "I'll go now, there's still time." Rita smiled, trying hard not to look like she'd won a round. He looked at her, smiled himself. *I can probably get in a rubber or two at the club if I go now. She deserves it. I deserve it.*

* * *

But Gil did find a *locum* practice, in Rosebury, a suburb south of the city, one that made driving the Holden to work more convenient. The local physician had suffered from appendicitis and would be unable to work for exactly the six weeks that Gil could count on being without pay from the union. It was a fee-for-service practice and the local man would take only enough from the fees paid to cover the costs of the practice. Gil stood to make rather more doing this piecework, he realized, than he was used to at the clinic. It would be his little secret.

But it was all too much for Gil: the middle-class suburban housewives with their various afflictions and ailments, the sullen children wriggling beneath his hands making an examination inconclusive, the occasional male patient with urinary pain finally overwhelming prudery. The women were less guarded but garrulous. He found himself preferring the gruff, undemanding, inarticulate workmen at the union clinic. There were endless examination notes he had to keep up to date. The repeated clarifications of his handwriting the officious nurse demanded made her anathema. Gil realized how much he missed the solidarity, the complicity of Sister Winthrop at the clinic. Keeping the billing straight was a chore he disdained. It was for others to tote up his bills and charges. He was a doctor, for God's sake, not a bloody accountant. Worst of all were the hours—not just the three weekends over the six weeks that he had been on call. It began before 9:00 every morning, an hour too uncivilized for work, and often he couldn't extricate himself from the consulting room till after six in the evening.

Between the hours and being on call he'd hardly played a hand of bridge the entire month of November. Sitting by a telephone weekend evenings, Gil lamented his misfortune. Fortunately he hadn't been required to visit more than a handful of patients. One he had in fact rather enjoyed, if that was the right word. It had been a sudden and complicated delivery. No time to take the woman to a hospital, no assistance but a teenaged girl and a worried husband. He'd done things neatly and nimbly, relishing the interest, excitement, the deference, and even the limelight a little, after it was over. *If only this system would let me do what I'm really good at.*

The work was just too hard, not worth the nearly doubling in his earnings from the clinic. What was the money good for if he couldn't enjoy himself? What he really wanted, a chance to travel, back to Europe for example, was still hopelessly out of reach even at three times the salary he might earn. So, why bother working that hard.

When the regular physician came back, he was happy enough with Gil's work to offer him continuing employment, even part time. But by then the dock strike had been ended. It had been broken by the government, and Gil had already been called back to the clinic. Soon after Gil mentioned the offer to Mr. Healy's secretary at the Union, he found his pay raised. *I didn't ask. They must be pleased with my work.*

Chapter Fifteen

It was three months into the course when one of the men finally broke down, crossed the barrier of silence erected round Rita and broached a conversation. His name was Geoffrey St John. Everyone was addressed by surname, except Rita who was addressed only by MacKay and always as Miss. St John was called 'sin gin' by all, so for weeks Rita failed to connect the man so addressed with the name on the seminar attendance lists. '*St. John*,' *sin gin*? Then the penny dropped. *St for Saint. Sin gin* was some sort of Anglo-Saxon corruption of the French, *St Jean.* She smiled when she finally figured it out. *You've got a lot of English to learn, Rita.*

Geoffrey St John was thin, owl-faced, quiet-spoken, almost timorous, with wavy blond hair and clear-framed glasses that made him look even more featureless. He wore the same well-pressed but slightly threadbare gray suit every day. His accent was different, not Australian, Rita suspected, but it never came up.

That St John should have broken ranks surprised Rita. He seemed to be more under Captain Mallory's wing, or was it his thumb, than any of the others. And it was Mallory enforcing the ban on even diplomatic recognition of Rita Romero.

By May, winter was coming. It was a blustery morning outside and chilly in the unheated room. The seminar was coming to an end. Rita had been silent throughout its two hours, except when the Prof had called on her. This happened only when the other students were unable to respond to his questions. When Rita did, and did so easily and to MacKay's satisfaction, she could see the others stiffen in their seats. They would not look at her. She always felt a little rush of pleasure when this happened, but tried with good success not to show it. She didn't want to make bad matters worse, but she was not going to be coerced into silence. Why didn't any one of them answer? Was she smarter? Did she know more? Or was she simply a better student? It couldn't be the time she was able to put in. With the children and Gil to deal with, she had little enough chance actually to devote herself the way she wanted. Perhaps the others in the class knew the answers, but didn't want to curry favor, show off, stand out, like an Australian tall poppy. *Well, let them speak up if they don't want to hear my voice!*

MacKay looked down at his pocket watch ticking over at his place on the long table, closed his notebook with finality and rose. It was the signal that class was over. Rita pulled on her thin coat, a few of the others reached for trench coats on the coat tree. Soon she found herself gliding down the broad, shallow, sandstone stair treads in tandem with St John, both silent, staring straight ahead, refusing to acknowledge the presence of the other. This unacknowledged convoy persisted through the quad, and out into Fisher Road. With tension mounting at each step as their trajectories matched, each waited for the other to peel off and go in a different direction. When both turned right on City Road, they couldn't help looking at each other, silently speculating. If each was simply headed home, why hadn't this coincidence occurred before?

A low afternoon sun foretold the early winter darkness to come. Rita wondered briefly if St John was feeling an unexpected urge to accompany a solitary woman through darkening streets. Finally he broke the silence. "Going along to Cleveland Street for the street car?"

"Yes." She nodded evenly.

"So am I. Just moved to a place on Shepard and Vice." This was about halfway to Rita's home on George Street. "I say, you're awfully smart, Miss Romero."

"Call me Rita, please."

He ignored the invitation. "But why are you doing this?"

"Doing what, please...walking to the street car?"

He grimaced. She was toying with him. "No." He stopped. Looking at her, he blurted out his question. "Acting such a know-it-all in the seminar. Everyone hates you for it."

"What rubbish are you talking?" Rita started to walk on, but St John reached out for her arm.

"Half the men were hoping to win a lectureship that will open when MacKay retires at end of the year. Now you come along and scupper their chances."

Rita repeated the word "Scupper?" It was new to her.

St John didn't notice. "He's bound to offer you the job, even if you are a woman."

"And why is that?"

"Isn't it obvious?" He looked at her, annoyed at the false modesty. "You're more qualified...you've got the languages like a native. In fact, you are a native. He's practically made you his assistant already."

"I am not interested in such a post, Mr" — she decided to try the words — "Sin Jin."

"Please call me Geoffrey." He made it sound even more distantly formal than St John.

"Well, Geoffrey, I haven't the slightest interest in a lectureship."

"Why exactly are you in the course...Rita?" He hesitated on her name. Then he continued under his breath, "No place for a woman, really."

"I want the degree. I need it." She didn't wish to say more. "Do you want the lectureship?"

"Me, no. I'm in the foreign ministry. If I have the languages I could apply for a posting abroad. That's all."

"I see." Rita volunteered no more. They walked on in silence for a time.

St John began to speak again. "What do you mean, you need the degree? You're too pretty for a bluestocking,...Rita." He looked at her. "You can't be much more than thirty. Still young enough for a man and a family."

She was about to tell him how bad a judge of age he was but first she needed to know what a bluestocking was. She repeated the word with a quizzical intonation. "Bluestocking?"

"Means an over-educated woman not interested in men."

"In that case I want to be a bluestocking."

"Well, you are certainly going about it the right way, then. Every time MacKay stumps the class with examples of Grimm's law or Verner's law, you've got the right answer." These were arcana of German phonology that only Rita seemed to understand. "It's making you even more unpopular than you were the day Mallory had you fetch tea."

"Ah, Captain Mallory. Seems to be the leader…or should I say ringleader."

"Well, yes. Establishment Aussie, if there is such a thing. Had a good war. He was a kid pilot with Number 3 squadron. Shot down by the Italians in Africa. Rommel kept him as a 'pet' prisoner of war for a year. That's where he learned German. Escaped. Was decorated." Geoffrey pondered for a moment. "Steer clear of him, Rita."

"Why, please?"

Again silence. St John was deciding what to say. "Doesn't treat women well."

"It won't be a problem. Remember, I'm a bluestocking, or at least want to be. No interest in men."

He smiled, stopped and looked at her. "Look, Rita. I need some help in the course. I can't get the German historical philology because my German isn't good enough to read the texts. And Polish pronunciation is completely beyond me. I wonder if you could help me?"

"A little private tuition, Mr St John?" Rita smiled. "How much can you pay?"

"Actually, I was thinking of a trade. You need some help on translation to English. Your translations are too correct, too exact, too—"

"Too faithful to the original?" She knew it was a problem.

"Yes, the best translations are idiomatic. I can help you with them if you like."

* * *

So Rita and Geoffrey St John began meeting weekly, usually before class, at a teashop somewhere in Cleveland Street, before it intersected with City Road at Victoria Park. Afterwards they'd walk to the university, speaking German or Polish at St John's insistence. Rita would sometimes correct, especially the Polish, with a smile of gentle exasperation. Walking up Fisher Street to the university, they would part by mutual agreement, each taking one side of the street, careful not to be seen with each other. St John worried about violating the other men's continued hostility and Rita did not wish to compromise her only friend.

* * *

Once she had accustomed herself to Australian academic ways, Rita found the master's course untaxing. It was as though her past life were preparation for just the program of study it demanded.

What made the degree hard for the men was the challenge the languages presented. They would have to offer at least two for the examinations. And this they soon found was a good reason to resent Rita's presence among them. She already had not just two or three of the four languages each was struggling to learn. She had them all—German, Polish, Russian, even tolerable French. To be shown up by a woman who didn't even need the degree was intolerable. The Romero woman was able to devote herself to philology while they endured the mind-numbing tasks of memorizing irregular verbs, deciphering German *Fractur*, internalizing the Cyrillic alphabet, silently sounding out the relentless combination of unpronounceable Polish consonants. No wonder she was the star of the seminar.

In the late spring, all the members of MacKay's seminar began serious preparations for the end of course examinations, all to be written, all the same day. There would be three papers — sight translations in two languages, both directions, and an examination in English on Slavonic linguistics and philology. It was the last that caused Rita some concern, and one morning she shared it with St John. They were walking companionably along after an hour at their usual rendezvous, the teashop at the end of Cleveland Road.

"Geoffrey...I am worried about the examinations. I am going to make myself practice a few essays without a dictionary and grammar. Can you look at them?"

"I don't think you'll have any trouble. Your translations are pretty smooth now."

"But I do them with the dictionary, even a thesaurus...I don't have all the words I need."

"But you're translating archaic literature and academic scribbling. We all need our *Dudens* for that stuff" The *Duden*, in several volumes, was the official source for the German language.

"It's not the translations I am worried about. It's the linguistics and philology essays...in English." They knew that though MacKay would set the questions, the papers would be marked anonymously and by external examiners.

Her friend reassured her. "I'll be glad to look over your practice essays. Probably help me!" He hesitated for a moment. "I say, I'm not the only one who may want your help. Mallory asked if I knew where you lived last week."

"Captain Mallory? The one who's been enforcing the" — she sought the unfamiliar word — "keeping me in Coventry all the year?"

"The very one."

"Does he know you even talk to me, that we study together?"

"I didn't think so till he asked me."

"Did you tell him?" Rita was anxious, suddenly remembering St Johns' warning of months before that Mallory didn't treat women well.

"'Fraid I did. Had to...actually."

Rita didn't ask why. She thought she knew.

* * *

It was the first week of November 1955. Michaelmas term was coming to the end and the final examinations were fast approaching. Rita was working hard at mock essays, translations at sight, reading and rereading material that MacKay had set the seminar to work through. She was certain that it was from this material the examination questions would be drawn. She had to get a first. A second-class degree, even an upper second might not be enough to get her the sort of work she wanted. There would, she knew, be enough barriers to surmount. She was a woman, and a foreigner, a refugee, a Jew, and a mother with children at home. She had to be better than the competition. She had to be the best, and everyone had to know it, so there would be no excuse, no argument against her merit. And then she had to hope that there would be somewhere in the government where language was needed and merit would trump all the prejudices. Each week she had scanned the newspapers for work that needed languages. The only ones were in government, a thin but steady flow—trade and commerce, the foreign ministry, the military. She would try them all.

One afternoon, walking down from Cleveland Street Rita was on the lookout for her children, perhaps playing along the street near home. The freedom of their years in the small world of Ararat had made them fiercely independent urchins of Redfern. They knew its ins and outs better than their parents. Rita was hoping to collar them into coming home and doing their homework along with her at the kitchen table. The late spring warmth was making her regret the sweater and pleated wool skirt she had chosen that morning. It had been harder as the weather improved to get the boys to sit with her, doing their sums, spelling and geography. If she couldn't intercept them, at least the quiet in the house would make her own studying easier.

Suddenly she heard a voice, a plummy upper-class voice she recognized from the university. "Mrs Romero." Mrs? There she was 'Miss' Romero. She turned to see Captain Mallory, smiling as his long stride caught up with her. *Why is he following me? Why is he calling me that? Why is he smiling?* Rita stopped in mid-step, turned and frowned.

Mallory suddenly found himself looming over her. He took off his hat, moved back a pace, glanced at her, almost as if he were appreciating her as a woman for the first time. Then he looked each way and spoke. "Can we go somewhere? Off the street." The tone was as conspiratorial as the words.

"I am Miss Romero, not Mrs. Please tell me what you want," Rita said firmly.

"There's a tea shop back on Cleveland Street. Can we get a cup?" He added, "Miss Romero." The concession was enough for Rita and they both turned back. The two blocks to Cleveland Road were passed in complete silence between them.

Chapter Sixteen

They were sitting before two cups and a plate of non-descript biscuits when Mallory took some pages from his suit coat and laid them out between them. He did not turn them round and Rita was unable to decipher anything but the crest of the University of Sydney at the top of the first page. Then he spoke. "I need these translated by tomorrow." He spun them round and Rita began to read the first words on the top page. They were in English, instructions to candidates sitting the very examination for the MA in Slavonic Languages she was to take herself. Her eye moved down to the gothic *Fractur* print. It was a passage in German, identified as *Geschichte der Philosophie* by someone named Windelband. She scanned it quickly and turned the page. Beneath further instruction in English was a passage, unidentified, in Russian, from *War and Peace*—the characters speaking made Rita recognize it instantly. She turned the page once more, and laughed to herself. It was a passage in English to be translated into German, the very last page of Darwin's *Origin of Species*. She hadn't encountered it since the ghetto of Karpathyn. She'd been alone with this book's German translation, and nothing else to read, and reread it, for almost six months. Shut into a small room at the back of a rickety structure in the ghetto, while the men were gone each day to work, Rita had tended to her child and learned the German text almost by heart. Now she read its original English for the first time. She drew in a long breath. She wouldn't have to worry a moment about two thirds of her master's examination. *No, that's quite wrong, Rita.* She gulped. *Your worries just became much, much greater. You've seen the questions. If anyone finds out, you'll never get a degree at all.*

Rita stammered. "But where did you get...how did you get these?"

Mallory shrugged and smiled. "Doesn't matter. But you'll

be very well paid for an evening's work, Mrs Romero." *Mrs Romero*, again. *How did he know?* She studied Mallory but his gaze was fixed on the papers, like a stack of poker chips in the middle of a table, chips he was gambling to win. He didn't notice the consternation growing on Rita's face. Taking her silence as complicity, he continued. "Five hundred pounds."

She gulped. It was more than half what Gil made in a year at the clinic. Still she was silent.

Mallory reached for his hat, his transaction concluded. "Get me the translations by tomorrow at 6:00." He stopped to think. "Here…I'll be waiting here." He looked round the tea shop with disdain. "Don't be late."

She pushed the papers back at him. "I refuse." She rose.

"Not advisable, Mrs Romero." It was no slip. He continued to call her Mrs. As she picked up her purse and made to leave, Mallory grasped her wrist and with a painful wrench pulled her back into her seat. "If you refuse, I'll inform the Pro-vice chancellor's office." Rita didn't understand. He made the threat plainer. "I'll tell them how the clever Jewess in MacKay's class broke into his office, stole the examination papers, and then tried to sell them to me."

Rita was still defiant. "Why should they believe you when I tell about this meeting."

"I should think it's obvious." He looked up to the public telephone on the wall of the teashop. "I know the vice chancellor. I'll call the man now. He's probably at the club, my club."

Rita could only repeat herself. "Why should he believe you?" But she knew why.

"Because I'm Captain Robert Mallory, MC, RAAF, and you're Miss, or Mrs… Rita whatever your name really is…a lying, scheming stateless Jewess, that's why."

She had to stop him somehow. "Professor MacKay won't believe you. He knows me, he knows my work." Rita warmed to her argument. "He knows I don't need those papers."

"Ah yes, Professor MacKay. You're such a favorite of his. Perhaps he gave you the papers. Anyway, that's what I'll suggest to the Pro-vice chancellor's office when I hand them in tomorrow." Rita remained silent as Mallory warmed to this theme. "Yes, perhaps I'll worry aloud that you seduced the old man. Who knows what you two've got up to in his office every week or so all year." He smiled as another thought occurred to him. "And you tried to sell the papers to poor old St John as well. When he threatened to turn you in, you tried to seduce him for his silence."

"Seduce Geoffrey?" She lowered her voice. "He's not interested in women."

"You know it. I know it. But the world doesn't know it... yet. I promise you, St John will back me." They both knew why perfectly well. It wasn't just St John's job in the foreign office. Homosexuality was a criminal office in New South Wales.

"You would do that to a friend?"

"Not unless I had to." He pulled another envelope from his coat. "Look, here's 250 quid." He placed it on the table beside the examination papers. "Other half when you deliver...tomorrow." Then he rose. "One more thing, Miss Romero." He emphasized the *Miss* to cement their agreement. "Don't make it perfect, just good enough for a first class degree." Mallory drew a few coins from his pocket for the tea, dropped them on the Formica and walked out of the shop.

Sitting alone, staring at the envelope of cash, the papers beside it, Rita began to plumb the full dimensions of her predicament. She couldn't see a way out. She had to do as Mallory demanded. But it wasn't just that. To begin with, her own prospects for a First were gone, along with the doors to work it might have opened. She couldn't risk writing a paper better than what she'd have to prepare for Mallory. If it were too good her First could scuttle his. She'd have to be certain of no better than a second. She'd have the degree but it wasn't going to be the lever she needed to pry open the chances for a woman. Then there was this money, and more to come. What could she do with it? It was impossible to explain. If anyone were to discover its source, that would certainly be enough to convict her of writing Mallory's examination papers. The inevitable question formed itself in her thoughts. *What could possibly make a first class degree so valuable to Mallory he'd spend that kind of money on it? Will he really take down MacKay and Geoffrey St John if I refuse?*

She rose slowly from the table and made her way home. She saw Tom and Eric before the house, in the middle of the quiet street, playing a modified form of cricket with a tennis ball that could occupy them for hours. They merely waved as she passed by. She called to them with a smile, "Don't go far. I'll come out for you when it's dinner time." Gil she knew wouldn't be back till after 6:00. She had two hours. It was exactly the amount of time the examiners would allow.

* * *

Mallory was waiting when she arrived at the teashop. There was a pot and a cup before him along with a few dreary-looking scones. He looked up at her half-conspiratorially. But Rita would not meet his eye. As she approached the table Rita reached into a sack, the kind women often used for groceries. She withdrew a large buff-colored envelope, put it down and walked swiftly out of the restaurant.

Mallory opened the flap. immediately he saw, lying on top of the examination question paper, the white envelope of cash he'd given her the day before. Now anxious, he pulled the sheets from the larger envelope, rifling through them. Had she written the translations? He sighed. Yes. There they were. He had only to copy the sheets out enough times to memorize them. But first he had to get the question papers back in MacKay's desk before they were missed. He rose and left the teashop.

Chapter Sixteen

* * *

As in the previous hundred years or so, on the 23rd Monday after Trinity— Sunday, November 14, 1955—the University of Sydney examinations began. All the M.A. examinations were given in the same large room in Great Hall, a vast gothic pile. There were more than a hundred candidates, all dressed in a sub-fusc imitation of the Oxford final honors school uniform— evening clothes—in the middle of the morning.

Sitting before her examination paper, fountain pen poised, wearing a black suit and a short, equally black gown, Rita had an overwhelming sense of anticlimax. She knew all too well the examination paper about to be put before her, knew exactly what she had to do, what mistakes to make, what ink to blot. She had to be good enough for an upper Second, but not good enough for a First. With only a handful of candidates the examiners would probably award no more than one First. She was glad that MacKay was not to read the scripts. Her mistakes would surely give the game away to him. She couldn't afford even to be on the borderline and risk a *viva voce* in case MacKay were asked to participate and shown her exam script.

Looking left and right, she could see Mallory leaning back in a chair, twiddling an expensive-looking fountain pen, and Geoffrey St John, gown and black suit coat draped over the back of his chair, semicircles of perspiration spreading beneath his arms almost to braces so taut they seemed to be holding him down to his trousers, his feet crossing and recrossing, trying to find a comfortable place beneath the desk. Looking round, Rita couldn't see another woman anywhere near her in the examination room. The proctors passed down the rows of small tables, slapping a sealed and numbered examination book before each candidate. At the tolling of a large clock above the door, the white-haired chief invigilator solemnly intoned "Candidates may open their examination books."

Was there any chance she'd be surprised? Could the questions have been altered in a fortnight? Had old MacKay ever even had an inkling he'd been burgled? Rita realized it was more a wish than a fear. Suddenly it became a fear. If the questions were not what she and Mallory expected he would instantly suspect her of betraying him. She gulped. *Then what?* Suddenly in a hurry, Rita ran a finger underneath the seal and spread the booklet before her.

Relief bubbled up as she read the very passages she'd tried without success to forget after giving their translations to Mallory. She set to work. Within an hour she had finished the three translations, double-checking to make certain of the small errors that would bar her from a first. Then with a returning anxiety, she opened to the last page and the essay questions on the history of the Slavonic languages and their important literary milestones. There she found Professor MacKay's favoritism staring her in the face, favoritism so stark it forced itself on everyone else in that room, a dozen or so, who had spent the year in his seminar. The Polish question began with a dozen lines of poetry and required a thousand words, identifying the work, the author, the period and the cultural significance. But it was *Pan Tadeusz*, the Polish national epic. How many times would this work come back to save her, to haunt her, to turn her thoughts back to the war, the Ghetto of Karpathyn, her friend and lover, Dani, sitting over a factory work bench, declaiming the stanzas from memory. Rita really should have expected it. MacKay had made her translate ten lines of it the first morning she'd come to him and then he'd argued about the poetic meter the day he'd told her she could enroll for the MA. This examination question was a parting gift, a signal that he would do what he had to, to ensure she secured a first. And now she'd have to disappoint him.

With forty minutes to spare Rita rose and turned in her answer paper. The rest were still working at their scripts.

* * *

Examination results were posted publicly, by name, for all to see, and for the high flyers to be exalted, on the 1st of December, a warm summer's day that year. Rita rose and dressed without enthusiasm, only anxiety. Mallory had to have a first, she still didn't know why. She had to have no better than a second. She knew why only too well. The boys were already awake. She could hear them as she dressed. Gil rose, dressed and left for his café, to breakfast on the way to the clinic. He stopped at the door to say, "Good luck today, dear." He was certain she'd get her first, glad the course was over and Rita's distractions at an end. Perhaps now he could teach her bridge. The bridge club had become his main preoccupation in the time since they'd come to Sydney. He smiled at the thought, *How nice it would be, to be seen by the others, with his rather beautiful wife.* Rita took the smile for encouragement and tried to smile back.

The boys too knew it was results-day. School was out for the summer and they'd tried to sleep in without success. "Can we come along to the 'varsity', Mum?" Their accents were already resolutely Aussie. Eric and Tommy could still assume a heavy German accent, if only to mock their mother, gently but unmistakably. "There's nothing to do. Please can we come?"

Rita thought. Was there any reason not to take them? Would it help when she saw the results, force her to control herself, hide her regret, even if the standings were what she needed them to be? "Very well. Come along."

At the entry to the Great Hall, where the exams had been held, there was a crowd, milling round the tight scrum of men immediately before a glass case raised to eye level. The men— all men—were running their fingers down the lists beneath the glass. It was difficult owing to the reflections of a strong sun that made one squint hard. As individuals would turn and push their way out from the scrum, others would take their place, maintaining a constant semicircle round the notice board. Rita slowly worked her way through the crowd, trying to hold the hands of boys too old to want to be seen allowing their mother to do so. Well before she reached the lists Rita had given up the struggle to keep her boys with her. The worst that could happen to them was a porter's reproof for trespass of lawns reserved for faculty. Three rows from the glass Rita found herself rubbing elbows, forearms, even shoulders with Geoffrey St John. She was glad to see him. He would do better than her boys as a barrier against emotional display.

Waiting their turn, he spoke. "I saw you come into the quad."

"Have you been here long?"

"I came before they posted the marks. There was already a crowd. I decided to wait."

"Why?"

"I was waiting for you, hoping you'd come. I wanted to celebrate your first."

Rita turned her face from his. He wasn't to see her cringe. Turning back, she smiled. "Let's hope so."

"No fear, Rita. Those passages, those questions, they were made for you. Helped me immensely too, after six months of working with you." Invisibly he reached for her hand and gave it a squeeze. Finally they were there in the front row, running their index fingers over the lists, looking for their degree. St John knew what to look for and quickly found their results. He smiled and then frowned. Then he waited as her eye followed his finger. An upper second. Rita sighed with relief but St John didn't notice. He was still scanning the board. She watched his eyebrows rise. Then he turned and pulled her away to let others through. Neither spoke till they were ten feet beyond the swarm of bodies, walking slowly down the footpath in the direction of her boys wrestling on the grass.

Rita spoke first. "You've got your Second, Geoffrey, same as me. It's what you needed."

He nodded. "But you didn't get a First. What happened? Did you have a *viva*?" They both knew oral examinations were sometimes given to students on borderlines.

"No, no. I was overconfident. Didn't study hard enough. I even left the exam with time to spare. Got what I deserved."

St John could only nod. Then he remembered. "I say, I saw Mallory before you got here. He was more pleased than he wanted to show. Got his first. The only one in the course. I checked on the board." Rita said nothing. "He'll be relieved, bloody well relieved."

Bloody well? It was not something St John had ever said before. Did Geoffrey St John know anything about how Mallory had secured his result? She tried hard to sound indifferent as she replied. "Relieved? Why, was he expecting a first?"

"Don't know. But he needed one, needed it badly to banish the cloud hanging over his head."

Rita was suddenly avid. "What are you talking about, Geoffrey?"

"Thought most people knew, any rate, most people in his circle..." He looked at Rita. "But that's not...ours." Was he going to say 'yours,' she wondered, but remained silent. "Anyway, Mallory was a Rhodes Scholar, after the war. Read history at Oxford, or that's what he was supposed to do. Once told me it was three years of drunkenness and six weeks of swotting." Did she know what it was to swot? Rita's nod answered his unspoken question. "He was accused of cheating in the exams, something about getting the answer paper. Never proved. But he was sent down."

"'Sent down'?"

"That's Brit for tossed out. He denied it, made a fuss, but it was no good. Been under that cloud ever since. Just put everything else into the shade—his money, connections, rank. Always that little whisper in his set." Perhaps this was Geoffrey's set, too, Rita wondered. He went on: "Mallory's been trying to break into politics for a couple of years. Liberal Party wouldn't have him. Country Party wouldn't have him either." These were the Australian parliamentary parties on the political right. "A first in languages from Sydney may be just what Mallory needs to dispel the doubts."

Rita nodded. Her mystery was solved.

Chapter Seventeen

That summer Rita answered every call a government agency placed in the papers for language specialists—both of them. She made the rounds of every office, consulate, trade association, export/import business, anyone who might conceivably need someone with any two of her six languages. There was simply no call for these skills in Sydney. Rita was frustrated. Gil was annoyed.

"You spent a year and a fair amount of money on that degree, dear. Now there's no job you qualify for?"

"Gil, it was the only degree I could have gotten. They never would have let me in any other degree."

"But what's it worth, if it qualifies you for nothing? Can you teach? There are language schools, maybe a job in a high school?"

"I've tried that too." Tourists, she had learned, didn't want to learn German, let alone languages from behind the Iron Curtain. And French teachers, ones far more proficient than she, were a drug on every market—in the few language schools and the high schools. It wasn't even a question of her upper second. She'd never even gotten far enough in an interview to have to explain it. "Tomorrow, I'd like to go round to the Immigration office at Circular Quay...if you can drive me." It was the passenger ship terminal, a quarter of an hour walk across downtown Sydney from Bangangaroo docks, where the clinic stood. "I'm going to volunteer to meet the immigrant ships from Europe, help the refugees."

"You could have done that a year ago, without the degree."

"I suppose so." She sought an excuse. "But the boys weren't really old enough to leave completely alone." In her year as a student, Rita's schedule had coincided with the boys' school days. And sitting at the same kitchen table, when she could cajole them, had made a difference to their work. But now cajoling no longer worked. It wasn't necessary either. Neither boy was facing much difficulty in school. "I can't sit around, Gil."

"Are there still refugees coming from Europe?"

"Not like five years ago, but they're still arriving."

"They won't pay you to do anything if you offer to do it for nothing."

"I suppose not, but at least I can use my languages."

* * *

They were both wrong. The day Rita presented herself as a volunteer translator she was taken up on the offer. That morning there was a line of immigrants, mainly Germans displaced from the eastern part of pre-war Germany that had been given to Poland after 1945. These were farmers, mainly. Having tried and failed to find a life in West German cities, they had grasped at the straw, literally, that was offered to become farmers in Australia.

Standing on the quay, Rita surveyed them, forlorn from years in temporary accommodation. The men looked more defeated, the woman more hopeful, as they tried to make their children interested in the sights around them, finally on land after a month at sea. Then she went to the head of the queue they had formed, entered the building and asked a clerk if she could help.

Rita spent the afternoon on her feet, clipboard in hand, offering the strangers the familiar sounds of their language, reassuring those at the end of a long line that they would be helped, explaining the forms to be filled out, bringing new copies to replace those so easily torn or spoiled by the running ink of fountain pens on oak-tag. The whole experience seemed familiar, as if she'd done it before. *Of course you have, Rita. Those years at the displaced persons tracing service after the war.*

Before the office closed a woman approached her. She was in the uniform of the Immigration Service. The European immigrants responded to uniforms only too well, Rita noticed.

Perhaps that was why the immigration officers wore them. The woman held out her hand. "I'm Mrs Lowell, head of the Family Service Division."

Rita took the hand and gave it a firm Australian shake, the strongest one she could. "Rita Romero." She wanted to add MA, but she didn't think the woman would care.

"You've been out here doing good all afternoon. Can you come again tomorrow?"

"Are you expecting another boat tomorrow?"

"No, but we need someone to visit the migrant centers we're sending this lot to." She looked towards the buses taking on passengers.

"I can come, but I have no car to visit the camps. And they are so far away."

"Actually the migrant hostels are around town, much closer that the old camps. Were you in one?"

"Yes. Bathurst. Back in '50."

"Then you know the drill." Rita nodded. "Anyway, we'd provide transport, have you back here by 6:00, and pay you a *per diem*. Can you do it?"

Rita did not even ask how much. "I think so."

* * *

Six months later Rita was offered a job, a real job, a permanent one, as a translator for the Family Service, in the Sydney district office of the Department of Immigration. Mrs Lowell, the head of the unit, had called her in one afternoon when there was no passenger traffic in the port.

Rita arrived, slightly anxious. Had she put a step wrong somewhere? Had there been a complaint at one of the centers, of her work, her strong advocacy for some of the refugees she worked with, her recorded suspicions about others — wife-beaters, alcoholics, parents neglecting children, even a few war criminals?

Lowell was at her desk in a small office behind the reception area. She looked up from paperwork, smiled in a way that reassured Rita and pointed her at the only chair before the desk. Then she initialed a file, closed it and looked up. "Well, Mrs Romero. You've worked for Immigration on an *ad hoc* basis for some time. And you've handled the assignments very well. No complaints, not even from the arrivals, and they're surprisingly"—she looked for the right word, smiled when she found it—"outspoken."

Rita nodded. "Thank you."

She cleared her throat. "I'll get to the point. If your husband will permit it, we'd like to offer you a permanent job. As an official translator. Requires a degree. You have a degree, haven't you?"

Rita nodded again, but she was thinking, *If your husband agrees?* No, that wasn't it. *If he permits.* Was she serious? Did she need Gil's permission?

The other woman went on. "I'll have to file some papers and get the post approved, but it shouldn't be a problem." She looked down at the sheet before her. "878 pounds per annum. What do you say?"

"Of course I'd like the post. But why do I need my husband's consent?" Rita tried not to sound indignant.

"Oh, so sorry, I didn't mean that literally, Mrs Romero. But I would like to assure my boss. The department don't want to push a lot of papers for someone who won't stay long, may have children and decide to quit, might be moved when a husband changes jobs. We find when the husband disapproves, the wife's work suffers..." She tailed off, hoping that this was enough to make things clear. "So, do you think there will be any trouble?"

Poor woman is only doing her job, Rita. Don't be angry. "No. It will be all right. My husband approves, my children are old enough, and I am not going to have any more." She didn't add how glad her husband would be of the money. It would remove some of the pressure she'd been putting on Gil to find a better job, one that would be more challenging and pay better.

"Well, that's settled. I'm glad." Lowell looked at Rita in a companionable way. "You must call me Betty."

Rita smiled. "And I am Rita."

"I have a feeling, we've been through things together."

"I'm sorry. I don't see how?" Rita was mystified.

"What did you do in the war, dear?" The word seemed natural to Rita and she wanted to confide.

"I was in a ghetto until I escaped and then lived in Poland and Germany for some years, on false papers."

Betty Lowell nodded. "Thought it might be something like that." She stopped for a moment. "I was in Singapore when the Japanese attacked in '41. We were torpedoed escaping. Spent three years in a Japanese prisoner of war camp on Java." Rita gasped. "Lost my daughter." She said it as a matter of fact. "Beriberi, malaria."

Rita reached out a hand. "Me too. He was three."

"Same age as my child." Lowell held on to Rita's hand. "I escaped. Then I was on the run with the native resistance till the war ended."

The two women recognized that they were ready to break down a barrier both had spent years building up against the past. Betty and Rita spoke without inhibition long into the evening.

* * *

So Rita came to work at the quayside Immigrant Processing Bureau. Her first duty was translating regulations issued by the Department of Immigration into all the languages she knew. There was a backlog of requirements, prohibitions, rules and their exceptions. At first she enjoyed learning a new vocabulary of legal terms and juridical constructions. Even before translating she needed to grasp the complexity and logic of government regulations. Then she needed the vocabulary. It made the work difficult, demanding, interesting in a way she'd never experienced. Others in the department would look in on her, surrounded by reference works and binders that made her desk groan. They would tisk tisk in mock sympathy, and she would accept their expressions of concern, all the while secretly enjoying the work.

Soon enough Rita realized that refugees needed advice about what to expect at registration, not legal regulations governing their status. She began drafting pamphlets to hand out among immigrants, as they waited on line, in the languages they could understand. No one had ever thought of doing a thing like this. But no one in the office had ever been an immigrant themselves, without an idea of what to expect when they got to the head of the queue. Betty Lowell had warmed to Rita's proposal immediately and soon their hands were blackened with the ink of a mimeograph machine, churning out sheets in three languages to be stapled together and passed along the queues of immigrants waiting to be processed at the quayside. Rita even found help in the migrant centers, translating the pamphlet into three Baltic languages she didn't know at all. To the general surprise at the reception center, processing time dropped almost in half and some days lines never got very long at all, as people were processed faster than they could disembark their ships.

* * *

As the months of 1955 passed on into 1956 Rita could see the numbers of immigrants from Europe begin appreciably to dwindle. By that winter there was enough slack in the bureau on the quay for her to begin to worry about losing this job she had come to enjoy, not to mention the income that made a difference at home. But that Aussie spring had been a cold European autumn. The Hungarians had revolted against their Russian masters, who had sent tanks to occupy Budapest. Western sabre-rattling had again led Gil to predict war, but again it never came. But within months there was a tide of Hungarians flooding into Sydney, most of them close to fluent in German. All of them were as bewildered by their fate as any of the refugees who had preceded them. Suddenly Rita was out on the quayside again, receiving the arrivals, reassuring the parents, chatting up the children with the few words of the strange Hungarian she tried to pick up.

One morning in the spring of 1957 Betty Lowell appeared at Rita's desk with a letter. "Good day, Mrs Romero." She smiled. They'd remained at surnames during business hours for almost a year now. It was what the men did, though for women they added the Miss or Mrs to underscore the formality. Betty placed the sheet before Rita. "Thought you might be interested in this circular." Rita glanced at the sheet. It was a call for qualified government employees with any Eastern European language. Qualified candidates would be seconded to the Department of Foreign Affairs and Trade. Rita looked up from the sheet. "Thanks for thinking of me. But I'm not qualified, not a citizen." Then she added another reason. "I can't move to Canberra in any case...my husband's work."

Betty Lowell was shaking her head. "There's a branch of the foreign office three streets away, here in Sydney. And becoming a citizen is child's play. You've been here since '51, or was it 1950? You qualified by the time you'd lived in the country for a year. Been meaning to tell you to do that anyway, my dear." She turned and, leaving the paper, walked out of Rita's cubicle.

* * *

So in a matter of a month Rita, Gil and the boys all became Australian citizens, and British subjects, for that matter. The morning after the letter came, conferring citizenship, Rita found herself staring at the call for applicants from the Foreign Office, yellowed but still hanging from the edge of the corkboard on her office wall. She pulled the drawing pin and put the notice before her. Then she pushed a sheet down the typewriter before her and began to compose a letter of application.

A week later Betty Lowell came to the door and leaned into Rita's cubicle. "Foreign ministry called me about you. Told them about your splendid work here." She smiled. "We'll be sorry to lose you…"

Another week passed. Rita came into her cubicle to find a letter at her desk with a government frank instead of a postage stamp and a return address in Canberra, the Federal capital. She sat herself down, picked the letter up and carefully opened it. Inside was a rather cheaply reproduced facsimile of a letterheaded typescript. It was plainly a form letter Rita was receiving.

Dear Applicant:

We regret to inform you that your application for a post in the translation and interpretation office of the Department of Foreign Affairs and Trade has been unsuccessful.

There are a limited number of places and candidates may be declined employment for many different reasons.

Sincerely yours,

There followed a scrawled signature. Rita reread the letter and was about to crumple it when her eye was drawn back to the signature. Below it, in typescript, were the words. "On behalf of the Deputy Minister (Personnel), Captain Andrew C. Mallory, MC."

Well, that's put paid to any chance of a job in Foreign Affairs, Rita. The inner voice had a tone of finality. She sighed, put the letter down. Only then did she begin to worry. Could it be worse? Had her application gone all the way up to the deputy minister and been rejected by Mallory himself? *If he knows where I work, will he have me sacked here?* Thinking about it more, she decided she was probably safe. It was another ministry and Mallory would call too much attention to himself if he showed any interest in firing someone who'd done the same course he'd done. She tossed the letter into the trash. *What will you tell Lowell if she asks?* Betty Lowell never did.

Part III

The Past Recaptures

Chapter Eighteen

Stefan Sajac was almost nine when he and his mother arrived in Dortmund at the end of 1948. They were only two of 12 million ethnic Germans, driven from Poland after the boundary shifts the Russian victors had imposed on the Germans. Stalin had simply picked up the entire landmass of Poland and moved it hundreds of kilometers west, as though rearranging the furniture. Thus he compensated Poland for the slice of its territory Hitler had given him in 1939, land that Stalin wasn't giving back. Once in possession, the Poles had no qualms about forcing the formerly German population out. Along with them went thousands who knew they'd never be welcome in a Communist Poland. This included most of the patriots in the Polish Home Army, men and woman who had resisted the Germans. Among them Frania Sajac, Stefan's mother.

Stefan was old enough to understand why the Germans had to move, but also old enough to know he really wasn't one. He knew from the first he was different.

His mother didn't need to tell him much. It wasn't that Sajac was a Polish name, or that he had no father. Lots of kids lacked one. Others were still waiting for their fathers to return from the Russian POW camps. There were still 30,000 POWs in the Soviet Union by 1953.

Changing clothes for football, looking at his own body, he knew well enough he wasn't really a German at all. He didn't have a word for it, or understand it, but it made him different. He wouldn't talk about it with anyone, certainly not his mother. It only made him want more urgently to be like everyone else, go native, not stand out, be accepted as just another *knabe*—a German kid.

The German language came to him quickly after they'd arrived. He was willing enough to speak Polish at home, but he wouldn't respond to it, not ever, in the street. From the start he looked the part of a *knabe*—tall, tow-headed, thin like all the undernourished German kids of the immediate post-war. By the time he'd been in school a year he'd completely shaken off the Polish accent.

Frania Sajac remained enough of a proud Pole to speak only Polish at home, and insist on reading stories to her son in the language. When Stefan began to read the Latin letters of German, she kept his favorite Polish stories before him often enough to learn the unique Polish alphabet. Perfectly bilingual, even in the presence of other Polish speakers, Stefan would pretend he didn't understand. He would speak nothing but German. He would be a German and a patriot.

More patriotic than the other kids! By the time he was twelve or so, Stefan saw that he had a great advantage over them. He could be proud of being a German without a personally shameful past. He didn't need to excuse his parents, his family, himself from the responsibility of ever having made the *Hitlergruss*—the greeting—"Sieg Heil."

Patriotism for Stefan began by supporting the local eleven, Borussia Dortmund. Much later he could take pride in the football club's history of resistance to the Nazis, along with its championships. But to an eight-year-old, it was the entry-ticket to a tribe, a shared loyalty binding one to other boys. He needed to be proud of the country that had taken him in. He found it in its history, or at least in the stories it was made into by his teachers, and in the books about great men he'd borrow from the public library. He even found a few books for boys about the military heroes of 20th century Germany, generals like Erwin Rommel, whose complicity in attempts to assassinate Hitler dissolved some taint of Nazi guilt. There was something to admire in the discipline, skill, effectiveness and camaraderie of soldiers fighting out of loyalty to one another, even in a cause that deserved to lose.

Frania Sajac waited until her boy was old enough — 14 or 15 — to deal with the reality of the war that everyone in Germany pretended to have forgotten or misremembered. She began cautiously and tentatively to draw back the veil and reveal the horrors in their details. Stefan came to her with questions, ones inevitable to a boy absorbed by history that had gone blank after 1933. When he asked about her life in the war, she would sketch chapters of her own story of resistance and survival — the German attack and occupation of Poland, joining the resistance, courier for the underground Home Army, her capture by the *Gestapo* and release. He was too young to hear how they'd tortured her, taking a fingernail each night for ten days. To Stefan it was a harrowing adventure story that turned his mother into a heroine even before she told him very much about how she'd saved his life.

In fact, when it came to those details, Stefan was suddenly uncurious. His mother understood. She'd had first to lay out the senseless Nazi war against the Jews in Germany before their murderous assault on all Europe. He was at first secretly unbelieving when she told him of the genocidal atrocities of the *Einsatzcommandos* — the killing teams tasked simply to shoot a million people. She could see the doubt in his eyes and had to pull books off the shelves with brutal, grainy photos. Sent to the public library — the adult library now — he confirmed the unbelievable truth: how the Nazis had found the brutal efficiency of gassing when it turned out that bullets were too slow, too costly, and too harmful to the discipline, morale, and usefulness of the soldiers tasked with the work. Now he understood the reticence of adults, the silence of the radio, the absence from the school history textbooks of anything beyond the 1914-1918 world war.

Then, when she thought he was old enough, Frania told Stefan how as a courier, crisscrossing Poland with messages for the resistance, she'd been given the chance to save a three-year-old Jewish boy and took it. "That was you, my dear." She hugged him to her in a way that made him feel the warmth of his mother.

She was his mother, his real mother. Stefan had nothing in common with the powerless victims of the war. He was Frania Sajac's boy, the child of a soldier in the army of resistance to evil. He had to have a parent he admired. He could not be proud to be the sole survivor of a persecuted, enslaved, emaciated remnant, who offered no resistance, who feebly shuffled along to the killing pits and the gas chambers. So, he wouldn't ask his mother about himself, the details, what she might have been told, about who he had been, and where he was from, or anything else about him before he'd become Stefan Sajac.

The pride and the shame struggled against one another from the time Stefan entered puberty until nearly the end of secondary school. By then he had found a way to reconcile his nurture and his nature, to be comfortable with the peculiar mixture of history that had made him.

Everyone knew Stefan's final exam results would be very strong. Called the *Abitur*, the exam would be his passport to any university in the country. But Stefan couldn't face more years at a desk, in a library, working up material whose only use was to pass still more exams. His friends, the boys preparing for the *Abitur* in the *Gymnasium*, occasionally talked about which university they'd start at and which they'd move to. The German system allowed such free transfers and they were popular. But the academic high flyers like Stefan were all really preoccupied by the obligatory German one-year's military service and how to avoid or postpone it.

Unlike his friends, Stefan realized the *Bundeswehr*, the new German army, was in fact a solution to his problem. So, it wasn't patriotism alone that made him welcome the mandatory military service. What he felt wasn't just an abstract German sense of duty. He really owed something to this German state, trying so hard to be a civilized country. It had taken him and his mother in, offered them and millions of other refugees more than just survival. He could be an example of why the new Germany had done the right thing, He would do his part to help make it a new Germany. It was, he was old enough to know, going to need help. Forearmed by what his mother had taught him, he could detect the shadow of the Third Reich's Germany, still ravening, lurking in the memory of almost every middle aged man he knew. Where better to resist its re-emergence, at least for a few years, than in the army?

* * *

Stefan discovered that he liked the army, that its orderly life agreed with him, that he was good at being a soldier. Not all of it, of course. Like every professional soldier he lamented the wasted motion, the lock-step chain of command, the punctilious record keeping inseparable from the vast organization constantly in training for eventualities no one sought. And there certainly were a handful of men in the service who still, or perhaps again, secretly felt the exhilaration of Nazism. These he had to confront with a new German soldier, one with only the old virtues and none of their barbarity.

When his year in the ranks was over, Stefan extended his enlistment, and was sent to an officer-training course.

* * *

At 21 Stefan Sajac was a *Leutnant* in the *Bundeswehr*—the new German Army. He'd sworn his oath on the 20th of July, sixteen years to the day after officers of the old German army, the *Wehrmacht*, had attempted to assassinate Hitler. The date, all officer candidates were told, was not coincidental. The new German army had chosen it to make officers know that their duty was to the state, not its politicians, chancellors, *Führers*. But he knew just as well that most of the men who'd give him orders didn't think about the date the way he did, on the rare occasions they were forced to think about it all.

Stefan Sajac had stood there on the parade ground, looking exactly like every other candidate taking the oath. Motionless, matched in formation for height, every uniform exactly like every other one. Each cap visor was tilted so far down that the man's face was just a flesh-colored gap between the matching grays above and below it. The 243 candidates might as well have been toy soldiers taken from the box. But Stefan wasn't like all the others, or any of them. He looked the part well enough—above-average height, thin, wiry, a long face and rather deep-set blue eyes, hair just now cut so close and high above the ear no one could tell it was blond. He knew too that his formation, trajectory, his path to the parade ground set him apart from the other cadets.

So did the woman standing fifty meters away, across the cold, wet gravel of the barrack square, his mother. She too knew why he was there, why he had chosen to make the *Bundeswehr* his life. He'd been surprised and pleased by her acceptance, understanding, even gratification at his choice. She would be proud to watch him take the oath.

* * *

Frania Sajac detected her son's place in the ranks now, standing rigid in the front row. He was wearing the same field gray uniform and insignia of rank as the officer who had extracted every fingernail on both of her hands because she would tell him nothing about the Polish Home Army. She'd never forgotten every badge, every ribbon of service on her interrogator's tunic, its color and cut, the military stripe down the trousers, the polished jackboots. She had studied them day after day in that prison, desperate for distraction from the agony he was at pains slowly to bestow on her. That morning Stefan was to take the oath, she scrutinized her son's uniform. A chill crossed her face as she saw that only the death's head insignia of the SS was missing from his cap badge.

She had to blot out that image. Instead she tried to remember Stefan as a small boy in the long caravan of Germans that had carried her and Stefan to their exile. They had trudged along, both pushing a baby carriage sagging beneath its load—mainly blankets and food—sharing what they had and accepting from others what they didn't. No one was any longer asking for evidence of racial purity. When the German Federal Republic recognized her as a citizen, she hadn't forgiven what she'd suffered or from whom she'd done so. But she hadn't indicted a nation, only her own generation.

Like most patriotic Poles, Frania Sajac secreted and stored her real venom for the Russians. The Germans she knew, most of them, some of them anyway, had only been following orders. In '44 the fiercely well-armed Russian millions had stood at the Vistula, in the middle of her Poland, ready to break the German *Wehrmacht* like matchwood. Instead, they'd happily watched as the patriots of the Polish Home Army were crushed by German tanks, artillery, flamethrowers, machine guns. Then, when they'd won, the Soviets made their Polish stooges round up these heroes and put them in the very concentration camps the Germans had built. Somehow Frania had managed to escape the betrayal, and carry her child across the new Polish German frontier with the 12 million Germans made to pay Poland back for Nazi crimes and Soviet greed.

In this new country Frania had been pleased to accept an offer to make use of her knowledge, experience and even the links she still had back to Poland. Almost immediately after settling in Dortmund the Gehlen Organization had found her, sought her expertise, began supporting her. General Gehlen's hands weren't clean, but at least he wasn't a Nazi. His intelligence network in the east had survived the German defeat. By the early '50s its American CIA sponsors had turned it over to the West German government. It gave her work Frania Sajac wanted to do, work that made a difference, that somehow continued the struggle for a Poland she didn't know when she'd ever return to. Her son, Stefan, had become a German, a good one. So, she'd decided to allow him to take a hand in this fresh Germany. Once he'd decided on a career in the *Bundeswehr*—the new German Army—Frania thought there might a way to help him and help a cause she still embraced. She had a quiet word with someone in the middle of the chain of command of the new German Federal Intelligence Service, the *Bundesnachrichtendienst* that had succeeded Gehlen's office. Her old friend would be glad to arrange his secondment.

* * *

Once he'd finished the officer course, things had moved fast for Stefan. He'd chosen signals, cypher and communication school. It fit his aptitude for mathematics and his facility with languages—the Polish he'd learned at home and the English he'd been absorbed by in *Gymnasium*. The day his first furlough had ended, a letter arrived, offering him a posting to the BfV—the Federal German counterintelligence service. He hadn't applied. It must have been the Polish, the English, the mathematics, maybe even the cypher training. The post appealed. Within a month of active service in Wiesbaden he'd already begun slightly to tire of uniforms, leather belts, holsters and sidearms, toys that had attracted too many of his fellow cadets. The BfV would make a change from the pointless regulations he had to enforce against conscripts smart enough to seek ever more imaginative ways around them. This posting at least held out the prospect of a *Beruf*—a calling, a vocation.

Stefan knew well enough he'd have to start out at the bottom of the intelligence bureaucracy.

The bureaucracy knew that too. Where might it start him off in this career? What he needed first was a desk job, one where he could be looked over, measured for suitability, for discipline, for loyalty to the rules, the code, the lines of authority in the BfV. His cypher training meant at least he knew the importance of code security. And it also meant he had a security clearance, a high one. The solution was obvious. Stefan was assigned to the *Vizepräsident* for counterintelligence, and handed over as an assistant to Otto Schulke, who was given the authority to brief his new subordinate on the Enigma problem.

Chapter Nineteen

"Two gentlemen to see you, Dr Romero." Nurse Winthrop spoke from the door of the consulting room.

Gil was filling out a form for a workman sitting before him. "Show them in when Mr" — he looked up at the patient and then down at the form, seeking the name — "Mr. O'Brien leaves."

The two men ushered into his consulting room were very different. One was a large Australian, evidently uncomfortable in coat and tie, wearing a felt hat he removed only when he saw the other do so. "Good day" in a strong Aussie accent were the only two words the larger man spoke as he shook Gil's hand companionably. The other man was small, dapper, well dressed down to a stick pin in his tie, and doffed his homburg politely as he put out his hand. The grip was, Gil couldn't help noticing, distinctly European. "My name is Macintosh," the man said in so strong a central European accent as to make Gil laugh out loud at the name. He smiled and shrugged his shoulders, sharing the disbelief with Gil. "This is my...associate, Mr Armstrong." The hesitation suggested that Macintosh, or whoever he really was, didn't really want to divulge their actual relationship.

"What can I do for you gentlemen? Evidently you didn't come for a medical consultation."

"No, indeed, Dr Romero. We've come to offer you an interesting opportunity." Again the sheepish smile. "But before we get into it, we need to make some things clear, Dr. Romero." The repetition of his title sounded slightly ominous to Gil. He remained silent. "We know a good deal about you, Dr...Romero." There was an overtone of disbelief clear in his use of the name. He held up a hand in case Gil had any idea of interrupting. "For example, we know that your French medical certificate is a forgery...that you spent a fortnight in a Spanish jail after trying to enter that country illegally in 1949. We know that before all that you were a Soviet army medical officer and a doctor in Moscow for three years during the war. We presume that none of this appeared in your application for immigration to this country or your citizenship file." Macintosh put his hand down, inviting Gil to respond if he wished. It would, Gil realized, be as pointless to confirm these claims as it would be to deny them. "I mention this only to ensure your discretion."

Gil nodded. "My…silence?" Meanwhile, he could feel the perspiration rising from his body up and breaking out on his forehead.

Both men nodded. Now Macintosh went on. "We have no intention of using that information." He reached out across the desk to pat Gil's hand as if to reassure a child. "In fact we wish to offer you an opportunity to travel…to take some sea voyages, back to Europe. We can't be sure how many, but perhaps as many as three or four over the next few years."

Gil's heart stopped racing for a moment and then began again. This time it was not an oppressive weight in his chest, but a quiet thrill. *What's the catch, gentlemen?* The unvoiced thought came immediately. Travel, especially back to Europe, was what Gil craved most, what his work made impossible, and the family couldn't afford. He was slightly frightened by their knowledge, but avid to hear more. Instead, he replied with solemnity, "Gentlemen, I don't see how I can help you. This job prevents me from traveling, and it supports my family."

"It's not a problem, Dr Romero." Macintosh could already see no hard sell would be necessary. "We've had a quiet word with Mr Healy." This was Big Jim Healy, the head of the Waterside Workers union. "You'll have the time off, your salary will continue to be paid, and your job will be protected."

Gil wanted to hear more. He remained silent.

"So, here is how it will work, Dr Romero." He paused, waiting for Gil to object that he had not yet agreed. Hearing no objection, he went on. "We'll send you a steamship ticket, cabin class, with a bill marked paid. You'll have enough notice to cancel appointments and be gone for about a month. Someone will deliver a small sachet to you just before sailing. You will transport it in your shaving kit. You will deliver it to someone where the ship docks in a Mediterranean port. You will have a nice holiday wherever you choose in Europe and return. Your paychecks will continue and be sent to your home. Think you can manage that?"

"Do I really have a choice?" He wanted them to decide for him. It would be easier that way.

"I am afraid not. Don't you agree, Mr Armstrong?" Macintosh looked at the other man. He shook his head but did not speak.

Armstrong? Strong-arm more likely, Gil said to himself. "Very well, but I don't really want to know anything more, Mr... Macintosh." Gil was still amused by the name for this man whose accent had to be Ukrainian, Russian or Polish.

"I am afraid you will have to know one more thing, Doctor." Macintosh was frowning. "You can't take the sachet anywhere near photographic film."

Gil thought for a moment, then he volunteered, "Or a Geiger counter?"

For a moment Macintosh looked angry. Then he rose. "I don't know what a Geiger counter is, Dr. Romero. And neither do you." Macintosh rose, looked at his companion. Then he turned to Gil. "We will be in touch." Without another word both men walked out of the consulting room.

Gil sat in his consulting room, putting the pieces together. It wasn't difficult. *Someone is testing atomic weapons, maybe even hydrogen bombs, in Australia...Can't be the Americans, not in Australia, they have the whole of the Pacific. Must be the Brits. The Russians have got wind. They want to know as much as they can about the tests. But whatever it is they want to get back to Moscow, almost certainly radioactive samples, they can't use a diplomatic bag to carry it. Subject to photographic plate screenings, that would alert the*

Australians, wouldn't it? Of course it would. Gil knew well enough how much could be learned from fallout after the American Pacific tests back in '54 that had gone badly wrong — an H-bomb blast twice as large as expected, with fallout across an area wide enough to sicken observers, inhabitants of nearby islands, even men on a Japanese fishing boat a thousand miles from the detonation. An English scientist — Polish émigré, actually — had managed to calculate the three-stage design of the bomb from the radioactive fingerprint. Despite American denial, it was all there in a medical journal the clinic took. It was obvious why the Russians would want samples from a test in the Australian desert.

Won't it poison you? Gil answered his question immediately: *Probably no worse than the agents who pass it to me. Probably tiny amounts — how much can they actually smuggle out of a test site?* His mind turned to another anxiety. *What if you are caught?* He'd already tempted fate this way once before. Back in Moscow during the war, he'd been forced to keep secrets from the Soviet government for the Spanish Republican exiles. Suddenly he laughed as the thought came to him, *At least the Aussies won't kill me if I'm discovered!*

Why had they come to you? Wrong question, he realized. *They had you all along.* This was why the job offer in Sydney came out of nowhere, a job offer he couldn't remember applying for. This was why he was hired by Jim Healy and the Waterside Workers. It was all at the behest of the Soviets. They'd dropped a line, dangling a lure, reeled him in and then kept him on ice. They'd been keeping tabs on him since…how long? Suddenly he knew. It all came back, weeks of a life Gil had successfully forgotten. *For how long, Gil? Seven years?* Now he couldn't get the scenes out of his thoughts and every moment he relived made him wretched, made him hate himself. Every misstep, every miscalculation had handed him over to these forces he'd never be able to control, forces he thought he'd escaped forever.

Sitting in the half-light of an empty consulting room in a shabby clinic on the Sydney docks, he was half a world and almost a decade away from those weeks in Spain. But only now Gil finally saw what had really been happening to him from the moment he'd sought out the *ancien résistants* in Pau. They must have sent word along through the French Communist party, who gave him to Moscow. Then the Russians had sold him to the Spanish, and bought him back, even paid his way back to Paris. *Remember that poor man with the Soviet steel teeth who responded to your Russian word of thanks on the railway platform in Perpignan?* They'd put him in their pocket back in '48, then checked on him from time to time—Gil recalled the provocative Czech woman at the Sydney Bridge Club, who came and went, but not before trolling for anti-Soviet sentiments. They were just waiting for the right task to put him to work. *You're just one of those useful idiots Lenin talked about, Gil.*

Really what choice did he have? He wanted, he needed to have the answer, *None.* It wasn't hard to convince himself he was already too deep in the quicksand to wriggle out.

Almost relieved, Gil began thinking about the voyage, the ships, the pleasures, small and large—on board, the prospect of docking in Italian or French ports, landing in Genoa or Venice, Nice, Marseilles, weekends in Paris or Rome. The hard question was how much to tell Rita, and what to tell the boys about why he was taking an ocean voyage by himself. He'd have to tell her something, or contrive a tissue of lies. *What sort of lies might work?* A cruise he won at a bridge tournament? A gift from someone in the club who couldn't use the ticket? Even if that worked, what about the time off from work, and paid time off at that? Why insist on going alone? Because someone had to stay home with the boys? And of course she had a job she couldn't take time off either...Could he be ill, get time off from work, and need a sea voyage? Didn't physicians sometimes prescribe sea voyages for their rich, ailing patients?

Not any longer, and you're not rich, Gil.

He couldn't tell her the truth, not without admitting things he'd never told her about Paris or Spain. Something would occur to him.

* * *

Gil heard nothing until the middle of November, a few days after the Soviets had finally crushed the uprising in Budapest. He'd wondered why the Americans hadn't forced NATO to intervene against the Russian tanks to save the Hungarians. Did they think it would start the war Gil kept predicting?

A uniformed commissionaire came into the clinic, insisting on speaking to Gil and handing him an envelope personally. Opening it he found instructions, a wad of Australian currency, a steamer ticket to Trieste on the Adriatic, a few baggage tags, and an Australian passport in his name. It seemed entirely genuine, down to his photo. He recognized it as the one he'd given with his citizenship application. Had they applied for his passport? How considerate. He slipped everything into his desk. Now he had to dream up something convincing.

* * *

"Rita, I've had an interesting offer."

She was lying across the sofa, feet up, reading. Rita looked up from her book. Her thought immediately turned to the offer of a better job, something that would satisfy Gil, employ his talents. "Oh yes. Tell me." She tried not to sound avid. It would provoke.

"One of the shipping lines has a passenger route to Italy. They need a medical officer on board. It's temporary, just for one trip. It pays the same, and the union will let me go…" He trailed off, waiting for Rita's reaction. She was silent, evidently thinking the matter through. He continued, with an eagerness he could not suppress. "There and back, I'd only be gone a month. What do you think?"

"Why would the Waterside Workers Federation let you go?"

"The ship is the *Roma*. I think Healy, the union boss, must be friends with the ship's purser. Something like that." Gil was pleased with his fabrication.

"It's the summer holidays. You'll miss time with the boys." So, she was going to allow him to go...

"I need the holiday, Rita. The work will be more interesting. It's the only way I'll get back to Europe any time soon. And I might meet people who could help us when I get back." Gil rose and went to his suit coat, hanging over a chair in the dining nook. He pulled the wad of notes from an inside pocket and brought it to Rita. "They've given me an advance." He pushed it into her hands.

Rita looked at him with confusion. "Is this a bribe, dear? To let you go?" Before he could respond, she went on. "You should go. The boys and I will soldier on, dear." Then she took up her book and began to read again. At least she pretended to. But she was trying to work through what had just happened and what she really felt about it. Gil was perfectly prepared to take himself on a nice holiday. He wouldn't miss her or the children, at least not enough to prefer staying. And it didn't make her angry, not in the slightest. In fact, Rita found herself equally indifferent about whether he went or stayed. She'd lack adult company, that was true, and there was the weekly sex that made her feel wanted, attractive, young. But his being gone wouldn't otherwise matter much to her. Just thinking about the domestic duties he imposed—cooking, cleaning, laundry, seeing to the children—on his schedule, up to his standard, to suit his moods, she was actually quite happy to see him go. *It will be a nice holiday for you, too, Rita.*

Gil slumped into the armchair. It had been easy. Too easy. There was no objection, no fuss, not even an expression of regret that he'd be gone a month or more. The need to sell this idea to Rita was instantaneously and insidiously replaced by anxiety. Did she want to be rid of him? Did she care what he would get up to in a brace of ocean voyages, there and back? Was he so surplus to her needs that he could easily be done without? He knew that he could still be jealous of the attention of other men towards Rita. But now he had to worry that she no longer seemed to be jealous for him.

* * *

He thought he'd be gone a little more than a month. But Gil hadn't reckoned with world events. He'd boarded ship in mid-October just after the Hungarian uprising was crushed. The ship's daily news-sheet carried stories each day. But then, a day after the *Roma* had passed through the Suez Canal, a war broke out between Egypt and Israel. Within days Britain and France had "intervened" to separate the belligerents, but not before the Suez Canal was closed. The return voyage to Australia took Gil an extra ten days, via Cape Town in South Africa, from which an airmail postcard announced the delay in his return.

There had also been three postcards from Rome—the Forum in black and white, the "Wedding Cake" monument to Victor Emmanuel, the Italian king, and a garish card from the Vatican, covered with papal stamps. The one from the Cape of Good Hope warned that the return voyage would be longer, but expressed no concern for Gil's job, or the family for that matter.

And then almost two months later, Gil was back, with a gold locket for Rita and two pair of football boots for the boys. They were many sizes too small, but at least it showed he'd thought of them.

His mission had been discharged so efficiently and so discreetly that he could pretend it had been no part of the holiday at all. A small leather case handed to him by a longshoreman as he stepped onto the gangway, taken from him with a wordless but knowing nod by an Italian customs official inspecting his bag on arrival. *Why did they need me at all,* he thought?

No seaboard romances, alas. But it had been delightful to dress for dinner, take attractive Australian women for turns on the dance floor under the watchful eye of husbands who couldn't, wouldn't dance. He ate well and sampled the red wines of Tuscany. Gil had been heavily in demand, almost from the first day, at the bridge tables, even met one or two good players from a social class that would never set foot in the Sydney Bridge Club.

Warmly enough welcomed home, Gil returned to his routine at the Waterside Workers clinic, refreshed and reconciled to the *ennui* of the work, his appetite for serious bridge playing renewed by the weeks on board enduring duffers, appreciative of the order and convenience of domestic arrangements that had resumed almost as though he'd never left.

Rita noticed that Gil was back. Suddenly there was more to do, the time was no longer her own, there was that friction generated when the untidy boisterousness of boys rubs against the demand for order and tranquility that was the breadwinner's right. She'd six weeks surcease from Gil's self-indulgence, his self-importance, the overbearing demands, short temper with his boys, fastidiousness and double standards. She and the boys had rubbed along very well enough without him, going for days without remarking on his absence.

* * *

Rita had done a lot of thinking while Gil was away, thinking about Gil.

To begin with, she'd never understood his reluctance, his refusal, even to try to make as much of his medical skills, training, and talent as he could. It was a mystery that couldn't be explained by anything she knew about him. He was smart, he was affable, when he wanted to be. He liked the things that more money could have bought them. He didn't much like where they lived, what they did, and what they couldn't do. Gil was dissatisfied in a way Rita wasn't. But he wouldn't do anything about it. Why? What didn't she know that would make sense of his self-blighted life?

Is there some secret I don't know about? One evening after the boys were in bed she even set to work rummaging round the drawers in desks, and the few boxes storing papers. She didn't know what she was looking for and soon enough gave up. It was silly. If Gil had things to hide from her they were in his head.

She thought back on a string of events that didn't add up, or at least never had any very satisfying explanations—the missed departure from Bremerhaven, consigning himself to rusticate in Ararat, then the job in Sydney that came out of the blue. She knew full well she'd never typed out a letter of application, nor even seen an advert for it in the Medical Association bulletin. His refusal to try to qualify, even after she began earning enough money to make it painless. He'd been offered a perfectly good situation—a private practice near home paying good money— and declined it, without even a discussion with his wife. Now there was this cruise back to Europe, so conveniently organized. *What don't you get, Rita?* It didn't add up. There wasn't another woman, or even a casual affair or two. He's not incapacitated by depression or anxiety. He hasn't tried and failed. Gil's life choices just didn't add up. After ten years of marriage her husband was more of a mystery to her than when they'd met again after the war.

What about the secrets I do know about, the ones he's hidden from me since we got here? He'd lied about the certificates he'd secured in Paris. They had to be forgeries. Was he worried that they'd be spotted if he applied to practice a specialty? *Maybe, but if he only told me I'd get off his back about it, wouldn't I?* He'd lied about

Spain too, about how he'd protected his former chief, when she knew the man was already dead. *Why? What had really happened in Spain?* It gnawed at her, but only a little, she realized, a sort of mild curiosity, not the burning need to know of a jealous lover.

He's rather shut you out of his life, hasn't he? She couldn't think of why, unless there was something more he didn't want her to know, or unless he didn't really care about her enough to share his real life with her, his inner life. Rita tried out an idea. *He doesn't love you anymore...if he ever did.* She paused in her thoughts, weighing the possibility. *No. He did, once,* Rita was sure. It hadn't been just lust. He'd been besotted, before the war certainly, and in the first years after it, perhaps even till they had decided they had to leave Salzburg. But in the years since? Ardor, she knew, decayed, for both partners in a marriage. And when it was gone, what was left? Well, there wasn't much ardor anymore. As for the companionship that might take up the void it left, Rita could see that her husband didn't want it from her, sought it elsewhere, or didn't need it at all.

What about you, Rita? Still love him? It had become obvious to her, even before his weeks away, that she could live without him. Now it was also clear that her boys were old enough not to even notice he was gone. *Even the puzzle he presents to you isn't more than a curiosity, Rita. Solving it isn't really very important. You don't much care about it, do you?* She had to admit that not understanding Gil wouldn't keep her up worrying at night. What did that mean? *No, you don't love him anymore, need him anymore, even miss him, now he's gone.*

Chapter Twenty

Almost exactly a year later, at the beginning of October 1957, Mr Macintosh came to see Gil at the clinic once more. This time he was alone. There was, he had rightly surmised, no need to bring along Mr Strong Arm. He made the same request of Gil, this time without the prefatory menace that his past might be disclosed to anyone. Gil was only too pleased to fall in with Macintosh's proposal—another round trip to Trieste, expenses paid, salary paid, responsibilities minimal. It would only be a question of securing Rita's agreement. They shook hands on it.

* * *

In the early evening of the same day, Rita was sitting on the chesterfield reading the book that had gripped almost everyone in the country old enough to read. It was *On the Beach*, a novel that described how the last people on Earth, Australians, dealt with a lethal nuclear fallout cloud, drifting relentlessly towards them from a cataclysmic exchange between the nuclear powers in the northern hemisphere. *Why wouldn't humankind go extinct? Most species in the history of the planet had done so.* Then Rita reflected, *We'd be the first to do it to ourselves, wouldn't we?*

The phone rang. She turned to the boys reading comic books on the rug at the foot of the chesterfield. "Will one of you answer that?"

Eric answered, covered the receiver and spoke. "It's someone named 'Sinjin' for you, Mum."

She smiled at the reminder of her ancient mistake. "St John, dear, pronounced *sin jin*. It's a corruption from the French." Rita reached for a kitchen towel, wiped her hands and crossed to the telephone.

"Geoffrey, how nice to hear from you. I had no idea you were back."

"Rita, so glad I found you. Been back a few weeks." He paused. "I need your help, badly. I've an offer for you." There was a 'No' in her exhaled breath. Before she could speak he stopped her. "Hear me out, please."

* * *

Geoffrey St John had returned from two years in the European embassies. He had been posted to supervision of credentials and visas for the Eastern European diplomats accredited to Australia. He faced a constant flow of paperwork from embassies and back to them as their personnel turned over. Everyone in the office knew why. The churn of people powerful enough to get out of East Germany, Poland, Russia, even for a few months or a year, constantly spilled paperwork onto desks in the diplomatic service of every Western capital, even provincial backwaters like Canberra.

Most of the credentials and documents submitted were in their native languages and working them out had been laborious. The office's backlog, already sizable when St John arrived, kept growing. It was then he thought of Rita. While he'd been away in Europe they'd exchanged brief notes and he'd sent the occasional picture postcard from a place in Germany or Poland he thought she'd recognize.

Before picking up his telephone to make the trunk call, St John had sat with a legal pad, putting his arguments down so that he wouldn't forget any. Could he convince her to leave Sydney for Canberra, a town he needed to escape each weekend for Sydney? That, it turned out, wasn't the problem.

* * *

St John hadn't finished his sales pitch—interesting work, more money, a nice place to raise children, even the need for doctors in a growing town, when Rita stopped him. "Geoffrey, very convincing, very nice of you to think of me, but it won't work."

"What's the obstacle, Rita? It would be grand to work together." She could feel his smile through the phone line. He was genuinely enthusiastic, quite out of character, she thought. But she had to stop him. How much could she tell him about why it wouldn't work. "I've applied for these jobs before. I'm not qualified."

"Who told you that? You not qualified?"

"The letters of rejection." There had been only the one, signed for Andrew Mallory, as deputy minister. She hadn't reapplied.

"Rita, this post reports to me and I can pick whoever I want, provided they can do the job."

There was only one way to put an end to this discussion. "Look, Geoffrey, you'd have to get my appointment past Andrew Mallory. And he doesn't want me working anywhere near him." She paused, waiting for him to ask why. He didn't. Did he have any idea?

At the end of a silence, St John cleared his throat. "Mallory won't be a problem, Rita. He's been posted to the High Commission in London and left last week. Be there at least two years. When he comes back he'll probably stand for Parliament. We'll both be far below his radar." There seemed to be some emphasis in the 'we.'

"Very well, Geoffrey, you win. If I can convince my husband to move."

"Shouldn't be a problem for a doctor. Lots of good jobs here."

* * *

Gil came through the door thirty minutes later. The weight of his day, the boredom of his routine was not visible on his face. Had he stopped at the bridge club, Rita wondered? She wanted to sit him down and discuss St John's offer.

Before she said a word, his coat barely off, Gil began to speak. "Rita, I've been asked to take on another cruise by the same shipping line that asked me last year, next month probably. What do you say. Shall I accept?" He was ready to cajole, to marshal arguments, but somehow he felt it might not be necessary.

"Next month?" she pretended to think it through. "That's fine." She hoped immediate agreement would smooth the way for her proposal. "But, when you come back, I want to move the family to Canberra."

Gil's mouth opened, apparently to catch his breath. "You want to do what?" The voice was loud, too loud.

"To move, to Canberra. I've been offered a good job there. It pays more than I make here, more than you make." She put her hand up. "And there are plenty of posts for doctors there, I'm told."

Gil sat heavily. They'd been over this ground so many times before. She was going to try to rearrange his life, to make it better. But he just couldn't face the demands of a harder job, the constant drum beat to learn new things he didn't need to know, the risk of failing in front of others. He couldn't tolerate the indignity of being an underling, a subordinate, not anymore, not at his age. "We're not going, Rita. You can simply put it out of your thoughts. That's final." Her look made it evident he had not convinced her. "Besides, Canberra? How could I...uh, we live in Canberra? There's nothing to do there, no culture, no life..."

"Would that be so different from Sydney? What is it you do besides your bloody bridge club?"

He rose from the table. "I'm not moving to Canberra. That's absurd." He almost laughed. An ersatz creation halfway between Melbourne and Sydney, not yet forty years old, and famously the most boring city in the country, if it was really a city at all.

Rita was calm. But she knew her mind. "If that's your last word." He nodded vigorously to end the discussion. It failed.

"Then the boys and I will have to go without you."

Gil smiled. *She's bluffing. She has to be.* "You want a divorce? Is that it? What have I done?" He knew he could play the innocent husband well enough. The last time he'd really deceived her was when he had reached Australia back in '50. The lies about his first cruise to Italy, and this new one didn't count. They didn't harm her or the boys, did they? High dudgeon gripped him. "Which is it Rita, do you want me to move to Canberra or do you want a divorce?"

Rita spoke quietly. "I don't actually need a divorce from you. We never married." She reached her hand out and pulled him back into his chair at the table. "Look, Gil, for a long time after the war, we needed each other. Anyway, I needed you. But the last few years. Well...we've been ships saluting each other as we passed, not even slowing down to sail together in the same direction. I didn't really notice till you were gone last year and I didn't miss you. Now you want to go again. I don't know why or what's driving you, but I don't think you're getting much out of this marriage either."

Suddenly what she was saying made sense to him. Was it just inertia keeping Gil with Rita, legally or not? Could he imagine himself alone, single again? For the moment he wouldn't let himself. He had to mount more resistance, just to prove to himself that he wasn't the one breaking up this family, she was. "But the boys, they need a father."

"For what? For show? You pay no attention to them, not really. Except when they disturb your routine." She stopped to think for a moment. "You've never stayed home with one of them when they've been ill. I cannot even get you to come with me to see their teachers. I've never been able to keep you here for a kid's birthday party. When was the last time you went to one of Tommy's afternoon violin recitals?" She didn't mention that Gil had banned violin practice when he was home. "It's too late for you to worry about being their father. They've managed very nicely without you for twelve years now. The boys'll be quite alright."

Instead of a reply he began to wonder, if she left him, what would she want? Money? Would he have to support the boys if they weren't really married to begin with? The questions flitted through his mind till he forced himself to banish them as unworthy. But they revealed to him that he was already thinking ahead to a life without her or the children. "All the years, Rita. You're prepared to forget them, to count them for nothing?"

"All the years? Gil, we only ever really shared anything deep those few weeks in '38. Then the war wiped all that out. Do you realize we never talked about what we did, what really happened to us in the war? It's been a conspiracy of silence we both agreed to." He made no reply. Gil was not about to begin unburdening himself now. And he knew he couldn't bear to hear of the atrocities Rita must have seen, lived, survived. He was silent. "You don't know this, but back in the resettlement camp, before you got there, I wrote a memoir of everything that happened to me in the war." She rose and walked into the bedroom. A moment later she was back, with the file in her hand. Evidently she had known exactly where it was. Why had he never come across it? She put it on the table before him. "I had to write it. I was beginning to forget. But I've never had to take it out, to refresh my memory telling you what happened. Because you never asked. Not once."

Now Gil was floundering, confused. What should he do? How should he react? Open it and start to read? He couldn't. He wouldn't be able to bear it. She was right. He looked up from the file, willing himself not to push it away in his fear of what it might contain. He had to work his way back to high dudgeon again. "And you? You were never interested in my life in those years—the Red Army, Moscow during the war, how I survived and got out." He thought again of how prescient he'd been, always one step ahead of history. *But then your streak broke.*

Coming to Australia was a mistake, wasn't it, Gil, a terrible mistake?
The war in Europe he'd foreseen, that drove him to the other side
of the world, had never come, even as his certainty of it washed
him up on a distant shore.

Rita was going on. "I listened to your stories about the war,
Gil, but I never thought I was getting the truth, not the real
truth, just some smoothed down, highly polished, very neat and
orderly version of it, one in which you came out of every scrape
unscathed, always one step ahead of history." In fact she'd
been unable to avoid putting together ten years or more of idle
conversation, tangential remarks, chronological inconsistencies,
into a pattern of half-truths, innocent fibs and outright lies. It
hadn't mattered. They were just history, the dead past. The
white lies, convenient fictions, tactical omissions had never
really mattered, not enough, she realized. Even the grand lies,
about what had really happened in Paris and Spain, just didn't
matter to her anymore, not even enough to bring up now, to win
the argument.

Gil could see that Rita really knew him after all, understood
him. But then why had she never revealed her clear grasp on the
kind of person he really was?

She spoke. "We all make compromises to survive. I know I
did. You must have made them too. But you wouldn't tell me
about yours, and you never wanted to really understand mine."

He knew she was right. But he'd really only done it for her
sake. There was so much he'd kept secret, not just the war or
before the war, but so much that had happened afterwards.
All these things, they would just sour the relationship, make
for resentment, recrimination, pointless argument. She didn't
need to know them. How much had she managed to guess at?
Everything, most of it, much of it, some of it, any of it? It couldn't
be much. But Gil didn't want to find out what she knew. "It's
really too late now, isn't it, Rita?" He pushed her manuscript
away from him.

She picked it up and went back into the bedroom. Then she returned and sat down again. "Yes it is, Gil. It's far too late." He knew she was right. He wanted her to be right.

Chapter Twenty-One

Canberra was dull. Everyone said it made dishwater look exciting. Rita could cycle from one end of town to the other, at nine o'clock in the evening, without her headlamp on, and not see a car, another cyclist, not even so much as a dog walker. But Rita didn't think this would bother her. Life in Sydney hadn't been roaring. The schools might be better in the capital, more demanding and sophisticated, catering to the demands of the country's ruling elite and its cohort of permanent civil servants. Her boys would continue to roam free after school, as they had in Sydney—spend Saturdays haunting the War Memorial, playing cricket in the road, pedal round the vast artificial lake in the center of town. The boys would do it every weekend, even without her, when she had too much to do. And it turned out she had a great deal to do.

There was the work, of course, a great deal of it, enough to take home at night in the panniers of her cycle—translations to do in all four of her languages, in both directions. None of them secret, some of them confidential, most of them interesting. There were the one-to-one meetings St John needed her for. She would sit slightly behind him, to have his ear, telling him when there was a willful misinterpretation of what he'd said by the Soviet or Polish or occasionally even East German translator. Even more interesting were the larger meetings he brought her to, meetings with diplomats who spoke English to him but one of her languages to each other, not realizing there was a nearly native speaker listening. This sort of eavesdropping could not last long, Rita and her boss knew. Word filtered round the embassies about the rather striking woman of a certain age, clearly European from her accent, whom St John took with him from meeting to meeting, even where language was no apparent barrier.

Canberra, it turned out, made Sydney seem like Paris. There was almost no social life in the capital. Each weekend, summer and winter, anyone who could would beat a path to Sydney or Melbourne. Even Rita went from time to time with the boys, to spend a day with their father. Often they'd ride the ferry under the great black bridge on its stolid stone pilings, down the Sydney harbor to Manley. Then they'd tramp to the beaches behind the town and spend the afternoon there before taking the ferry back and camping out in Gil's flat.

It was an uneventful, orderly life and Rita tried hard every day to like it that way. She had her boys, her work and no surprises. Some days she couldn't make herself like it entirely. But there was still Gil in Sydney. He had receded to a manageable, companionable part of that life. Neither demanded much of each other, both were politely interested in one another's comings and goings. At least one day a month she'd bring the boys to the bigger city. Gil and Rita could even spend an agreeable afternoon together indoors while the boys, now fourteen or so, enjoyed the bustle of a Sydney park.

* * *

It was there, back in Sydney for a weekend in the fall of 1960, on the far end of Manley Beach, that everything began to come apart in Rita Romero's well-organized existence. She and Gil and the boys had crossed the town from the ferry wharf to Manley Beach and then headed for the Queenscliff rock pool at the far end of the beach. It was a long swimming pool, filled by the tide, and much more suitable to swimming than the Pacific surf pounding up on the beach. The boys loved it particularly.

As they approached, Rita could see silhouetted against the sun the black shape of a couple walking hand in hand ahead of them. As she got closer it became plain that it was not a couple, but two men, thinking themselves far enough away from anyone who might notice them holding hands. *Two men can be a couple, Rita*, she upbraided herself. As the distance closed between them and Rita, Gil, Eric and Tom, she pulled her family on a course that led far enough away from the two men to give them the privacy they thought they had. But then, a dozen strides in front of them and fifty feet to the seaward side, she casually turned to look at the men. There, scowling back at her, was Geoffrey St John — thin, pale, almost naked in a skimpy bathing suit, a look of chagrin, then embarrassment and finally anger passing across his face. Quickly Rita turned round, hoping she hadn't been recognized, knowing she had been. The next time she dared to look, the men had veered off and were striding in the other direction down the beach, no longer holding hands.

Back in Canberra, thrown together every day the following week, neither spoke of their chance encounter. Rita was eager to efface any registration of its occurrence on her memory and she was certain St John would make no mention of it. Everyone knew, quite without saying, that nothing made a man in the Foreign Service more vulnerable to blackmail and more immediately subject to dismissal than what Rita had discovered about her boss. She was unaccustomed to the days of frosty formality that suddenly arose between them. As they lengthened, Rita began to think whether she should reassure St John that he had nothing to fear from her.

One morning there was a note on her desk when she arrived. *Please see me when you arrive.*
GSJ

Strange, Rita thought. *I'm always here before Geoffrey. Not today evidently.* She put down her briefcase, automatically checked herself in the small mirror behind her door, and marched across the hall. This wasn't the way they did their business. It was much too formal. *Is he going to threaten me? Fire me? Swear me to secrecy?* How can I convince him I've known for years and kept his secret? Then she remembered she wasn't alone in having guessed. Mallory had hinted he knew four years before, when he had forced her to write his exam answers.

St John was waiting for her, his desk cleared, nervously drumming a pencil against the desk blotter. He pointed to the chair facing him. She'd sat in it many times, without being formally bidden. Rita was silent. St John coughed, clearing his throat, plainly anxious about how to begin. "Miss Romero." He coughed again, perhaps realizing how silly it sounded between them. "Rita," he began again, "I'm recommending you for a posting abroad, in fact, a post with the United Nations in New York, as a translator/interpreter." Rita drew a breath. *He really does want to be rid of me.* Before she could reply he went on. "Along with our contribution to the UN budget we get a certain number of places in the international civil servant. Just now there's a need for people with your languages. We've got to fill these jobs or they'll go to people we can't completely trust."

Rita understood his meaning—Eastern Europeans, with at best dual loyalties. But she couldn't let the charade continue. "Geoffrey, that's not why you're recommending me." She left unvoiced the reason they both knew perfectly well.

"Rita, let me finish." He was determined not to stray from his prepared speech. "The pay is much higher, and you get housing allowance in New York. There's a UN passport, and diplomatic status in the USA. And the work is much more interesting than pushing paper here for embassies and consulates." He tried to smile. "What do you say?"

"What I say is that you have nothing to fear from me. Besides, I'm not qualified for the job. And your recommendation wouldn't be enough even if I wanted it." *Do you want it, Rita?* In the silence before St John could reply she asked herself the question. The surprising answer came back, quietly but unmistakably, *yes*. It set her to thinking about why she did. Meanwhile she had to reassure her boss, her friend. "Look, Geoffrey. I've known, or at least suspected, since our year at Uni. I've never said a word, and I never will. This secret of yours is quite safe with me."

Under his breath, as if afraid that someone was listening, he replied. "Rita, do you know that until a few years ago, *it* was a capital offence in New South Wales?" Even the pronoun was almost too much for St John to admit. "Just your knowing is dangerous for us. We...I...can't risk it."

"What exactly are you afraid of, Geoffrey? Is someone going to use torture to get the truth out of me?" She had to convince him she was no threat. "Look, in the war, I lived with a..." The word *homosexual* was too clinical for Erich Klein, the man she'd almost fallen in love with, back in the Karpathyn ghetto, before he'd told her the truth about himself. She began again. "I lived with someone like you. He saved my life. I named one of my boys for him." She knew she could say still more, but admitting that she'd once loved a woman *that way* was too intimate, and too painful. "I couldn't...tell..." The memories drove Rita close to tears. She blinked once or twice. Then she continued. "Besides, I'm not qualified for secondment to the UN. Surely there's someone with a stronger record, someone in the department with a first in languages, who deserves the job, who'll get it over me."

Rita watched St John relax slightly. He smiled as if he'd won, or at least had won the first round. It was, she realized, the tense of her reply, the future tense—she was going to apply and not get the job. He smiled, as if he were holding a high trump card. "Rita, you're far better at the job than anyone with a first class degree. You speak the languages like a native. You are a native."

"It won't matter before a selection board, Geoffrey."

"Not if I know someone on that board."

"What do you mean?"

"Robert Mallory is back from the High Commission in London. He'll be on the selection board."

Rita was suddenly angry. She'd already begun wondering if there was any way for her to really get this job. Now the prospect was dashed. "Geoffrey, if Robert Mallory even finds out I'm working in the ministry, he'll have me sacked in an instant." She shook her head. "I think he was personally keeping me out of it for years before you hired me."

"But why, Rita? Why should a high flyer like him care about you?"

Without premeditation she plunged, the anger coming back to her in a torrent. "Because when we took our MA exams, he made me cheat to ensure that he got a first, and that I wouldn't." St John looked at Rita, mouth agape. "He'd got part of the exam, the unseen-translation texts. Threatened to tell old Prof MacKay I'd stolen them if I didn't write them out for him beforehand." She paused to let it sink in. "I didn't understand why till you told me about what he'd been accused of in Oxford." Then she frowned at St John. "It's worse, Geoffrey. At any rate worse for you. He knows about you, too. Something he said when he forced me to write out the translations for him."

St John's almost involuntary wave of the hand told her that this was not a concern. It was enough to put her in the picture. Mallory and St John must have had a "past" together that both needed to hide. Now he thought a moment. "Rita, have you proof?"

"What do you mean, proof? Witnesses, something in writing from him? No." She shook her head. Then she remembered the encounter in the teashop. "Actually, I might, now I think of it."

"What is it?"

"Well, after I wrote out the translations for him, I copied them over for myself, so I could contrive to make the mistakes I needed to cover my tracks. If we'd turned in the same translations, word for word, we'd have both been ploughed... worse, in fact."

"Do you still have them?"

"Don't know. I might. Why?"

"They keep those examination scripts for years. Your copies could be compared to Mallory's. If they're word for word the same…well, it might not be enough for a court, perhaps. But given his record, it would be enough to scare him." Rita remembered instantly, the way Mallory's First had blotted out the charge of cheating at his examinations in Oxford.

"But what if I can't find the papers?"

"Then we'll have to bluff. The threat may be enough." He smiled.

* * *

Rita left the office with a knot in her stomach. She knew she wanted this new challenge, knew she'd had rather enough of the quiet of Canberra, and the provincialism of Australia. It had been a refuge, free of reminders of what had haunted her. These ghosts had faded. Now she knew that there was a long life before her. During all those war years the odds had been against her. Her life could have been ended a dozen times by the sudden violence of a German Luger, at least once by a whiff of Zyklon-B, most likely of all by the grinding annihilation of a concentration camp. But it hadn't happened. She'd been given a life to live. *You're still strong, even young.* Rita's face did not carry the scars of her experience and the rest of her was still years younger than her real age. Even her documents took five years off her real age. *You've got a chance to make so much of these years, Rita.*

But what would the boys want? They'd been troopers about the move to Canberra, claiming to be charmed from the first by the bucolic town, its green fields and its open spaces. Had they really become Aussies? Were they ready to leave? Would they see America as an adventure, an opportunity, or a wrenching departure from the life they'd known since they'd been babies? Pedaling along, among the other government workers bicycling home, Rita decided, *I'll leave it to the boys. If they want to go, I'll apply.* Would it matter that their father wasn't to come along? Would he want to? It didn't matter, he wasn't to be invited.

* * *

From both there was incredulity mixed with glee. Tom and Eric found themselves almost shouting the words "New York! America!" over and over. "Of course we want to go. Is there really a chance?"

Rita pulled them down on either side of her, sitting at the chesterfield, trying to calm them to a serious discussion. "It might be for a long time, boys, for years. You'll lose your friends. Your dad won't be coming."

Neither was listening anymore. Tom spoke the words "New York" in a tone that made it sound the center of the universe. At the same time, Eric said "It's New York." He looked at Tom. "We never agree on anything," he said, then turned to their mother. "But this time he's right!"

Suddenly Rita began to worry, the very opposite of what had concerned her the moment before she'd entered the house. *What if I don't get this post? They'll be crestfallen.*

Part IV

Metropolis

Chapter Twenty-Two

Walking the streets of Cologne under a perpetual winter gloom it was easy for Stefan Sajac to lose himself in thought. There was almost nothing to vary the scenery block after block. Featureless postwar reconstruction—three stories of mock sandstone facings, square windows with black wooden frames, sloping tiled roofs, all above the same sequence of tobacconists, chemists, food shops, men's clothing and woman's underclothing. Their stock yellowing in the window, none seeming to do any trade at all. The only storefronts before which people paused were the appliance dealers. There pedestrians stood, studying the Grundig stereos, the portable phonographs in their leather-look cases, and most of all the television sets, showing test patterns on their 33-centimetre screens. There was nothing to break into Stefan's funk, not even the occasional sunny winter's day. The BfV had been a mistake and he couldn't see a quick way out.

For months now, Stefan Sajac had been sitting at a desk in a windowless office on the Komodienstrasse, down from the Haupbahnhof, ten minutes past the cathedral. Running his finger down lists, endless lists of names, any lists he could call forth, from all over the country, and from the countries of friendly services. He'd had occasion to use his Polish, too, on documentation that had come to him, at some risk, from Warsaw, Krakow, even Lvov. He had long ago routinized this process, looking for two names—Guildenstern, Trushenko. He was deathly tired of the evidently pointless search, tired enough to allow himself rank insubordination. He'd been put to the task by his boss, *Oberamtsmeister* Otto Schulke, the day he'd arrived at BfV headquarters. Each time he found the name—man, woman or child—he had to begin to seek addresses, government records, police files, anything that might reveal whether this Trushenko or Guildenstern was the one they sought. It was the most tedious kind of policework.

Now Stefan knew he was going mad. He had to find a way out of the labyrinth Schulke had constructed for him.

* * *

It hadn't taken long for Stefan to discover why he was the target for despairing glances from the male clerks and sympathetic looks from the middle-aged typists as he passed along the cubicles and hallways of the BfV. His second day, the new boy in the cafeteria, he'd been shown the drill by an elderly lady: what to take and what to leave alone on the steam table. They were quickly joined at a long table by a pair of secretaries and another youngish man in an ill-fitting suit and very narrow tie clipped too high on his shirtfront. Somehow, they all knew to whom Stefan had been seconded.

Otto Schulke, it turned out, was a piece of work almost everyone in the Cologne BfV had an opinion about, at least as a character. He was the stereotype of the officious retread from the old order—the Reich. Schulke was someone who made them feel a little uncomfortable about what they were doing, reminding them of what they might have been doing twenty years before. No one at the table had any idea why Schulke had been given his own office, and a task no one was told about. But now apparently he'd been given an underling, a subordinate, a well-trained *Bundeswehr* officer, someone who should be ordering Schulke around. An *Oberamtsmeister* was not much more than a sergeant in the Army. How could he have been given this kind of autonomy? The whole thing seemed more than the usual bureaucratic black box. Apparently Stefan's lunch companions were hoping to assuage their curiosity about his work, and their sense of irregularity, in exchange for what they already knew and were prepared to tell Stefan about Schulke. About all they did know for sure was that the man was punctilious. He was never without his little black expense book, he kept every little receipt, filed for reimbursement weekly like clockwork. The woman from accounts ended the brief discussion of the matter. "But he never cheats. The only one who doesn't."

Even that second day, Stefan's resentment of his cartoonish boss was tempting him to join the banter. Already he couldn't stop his mind's eye from seeing Schulke's ogre-like face scratched into the steel of a George Grosz etching. On the sides of the globular head, red veins crisscrossing the bulbous cheeks that pushed up the folds beneath his eyes to make them narrow slits. There were errant tufts still on the head, which sat on a torso of the same shape, large enough to cast a shadow on his own lap, perpetually pushing shirttails out from trousers. These were suspended by braces visible beneath jackets with patterns too loud for a civil servant.

But Schulke wasn't the only stereotype of a holdover from the old days to be seen moving through the corridors of the BfV, or any other office of state in the new Germany. School, army, business management, government—by now Stefan was used to seeing it happen everywhere. Having tried to do without retreads from the Third Reich, Adenauer, the German chancellor, had given in to reality. Now every ministry was honeycombed by men with a past to dissimulate. But at least they could do their jobs. These men of forty and fifty weren't asked and they didn't tell. They simply did their jobs, correctly, punctiliously. They kept to themselves, made no show of their pasts and no one wanted them to do so either. It would only make everyone involved feel complicit.

Stefan would banter with the others in the canteen. But they were all too professional, and conscious of it, to talk about anything serious. He would certainly say nothing, not even hint at the mindless grind he'd already wearied of. For there was just the slight chance that Schulke was on to something very big and very dangerous. It was something so secret it had been known only to Schulke and the BfV *Vizepräsident* and his adjutant, Schelling. Now Stefan was the only other person entrusted with the knowledge.

The first morning he'd reported, Schulke had sat him down, sized him up, and decided on the spot that he was one of 'us'. 'Us' meant someone Schulke could trust, trust with the truth about the work, trust with the truth about Schulke's own checkered provenance. Looking at his file, Schulke had calculated that the young man would be a stalwart. He was just old enough to have been molded the right way by the war. Far too young to have been a *Hitler Youth*. But certainly he'd been old enough to remember the trek from the Communist east, toughened by the hardships of the late '40s. They'd understand each other, make common cause. They'd become *racial comrades*—words Schulke hadn't uttered since the end of the Reich.

Schulke had confided their mission to Stefan with the urgency, excitement and self-importance of a prisoner finally released from wrongful confinement. Schulke couldn't just explain Stefan's task and why he had been set to it. He insisted on a narrative, one that went back to the winter of 1944, and stigmatized everyone who had ever blocked, frustrated, overborne Schulke's advancement. He'd been on to something big, right from the start. Impugning motives, condemning post-war sloth and stupidity, until at last he announced that they were on the hunt for this woman who had harbored the secret that had lost the Third Reich its war. And now it was up to Schulke and Stefan Sajac to prevent her from divulging the same secret to the Third Reich's only real enemy, the victorious Soviet Union.

"How do you know…how do we know all this, Herr Schulke?

"Know what? About the code breaking? Because we're reading the signal traffic, along with the Brits and the Amis. It's practically our only tool for ferreting out the *Stasi* agents in our own government."

"No, sir, how do we know the woman has the secret?"

Schulke reached down to a drawer and pulled out a yellowed oaktag folder, crumbling at the edges, onion-skin flimsies overlapping the covers in three directions. "Read this." He pulled the sheaf of papers from the file and passed them along. Stefan began to work through the documents.

When he had finished Stefan spoke. "So, this woman, Guildenstern or Trushenko, whatever she's called, she may know…but she probably doesn't know that she knows?"

Schulke looked blank. "What do you mean?"

"If she knows, and she might not…but if she knows the code was cracked, she'd have to put that together with the fact that no one has revealed it was cracked, to figure out that the Russians might be using it and that we and the Amis and the Brits might be listening in…It's a lot of 'mights', Herr Schulke."

Schulke's face darkened. "Look, Sajac. It's enough for the BfV-*Vizepräsident* to have assigned you to the task of helping me find her."

Stefan had to admit there was a risk, a very serious one. If there was one chance in a hundred that Schulke was right, it had to be tracked down. With just the first secret the woman could figure things out, or tell someone else who would do it. And it could have happened any time since the war, could still happen, for all anyone knew. Shorn of the rancor, the callousness, the utter imperviousness to his role in the moral catastrophe of the Third Reich, Otto Schulke's narrative had been compelling. And now reading the file Stefan saw the task was undeniable in its importance. Almost a vindication of the man's obsession.

But then there was the reality of the work. Schulke had been able to think of only one way of proceeding: months filled with weeks, made of days, taking up hours, of just running one's finger down endless lists of names, looking for any sign of a Guildenstern or Trushenko, or the slightest misspelled variants on these two. Schulke could make himself do it. A brutal fetish drove his hunt through endless lists of names that came in every week. Finding this woman was a matter of personal vindication and thinly disguised hatred. It kept Schulke to the task. But Stefan had no such motive. It was, he thought, a pointless way to proceed.

"Herr Schulke" —Stefan thought he'd better sound respectful if he was going to challenge their standard operating procedure— "do you think they will let us use the census data?"

The other man looked up from his files. "Census data? Come again?"

He didn't know. Stefan would have to explain. "In '56, sir. There was a house-to-house enumeration of everyone in Germany, by name, with all their details." He paused. "Probably similar records in other countries. The USA does one every ten years. Can we get permission to use them?"

"Excellent idea, Sajac."

* * *

Schulke, Stefan saw, reveled in the importance of the work, and savored the priority that gave him a subordinate, a well-trained, highly intelligent, but thoroughly subservient one. It had been the only thing he'd demanded when he'd begun the work. Months later, Stefan had arrived. Schulke seemed satisfied with him. But Schulke's way of proceeding was pointless.

* * *

"Herr Schulke?" It had been three months and Stefan had not yet been invited to address him any other way. "There must be something else to go on besides the names Guildenstern and Trushenko?"

The monotony of running one's finger down every alphabetized list of names anyone could provide them was making every day unbearable. Stefan had devised a dozen tricks to play on himself, little rewards and games to keep his mind from wandering away from the task and then having to start over somewhere in a list he'd already let his fingers unthinkingly slip down. Every morning as he sat down he told himself how important it was to find this woman. Stefan would tell himself, *This is how policework is done!* But it didn't work. How had Schulke been able to force himself to do this, day after day, for years? Turning over the records of every department, every business, every institution in the Federal Republic, every telephone directory in every country on the continent. It was a tribute to Schulke's doggedness, his devotion, his stupidity!

Stefan had to find some other way to hunt for their target. Either that or get out altogether.

"Look, Boss"—a slight, perhaps involuntary smile crossed the older man's face—"we'll never find this woman passively, searching through lists of names that come in like so many adverts. We've got to take active steps. We've got to go out and demand lists, especially of emigrants. This woman wouldn't want to stay in the Reich...in Germany"—he made the slip purposely—"after the war. If I were her, what would I have done?" He paused to make the answer obvious. "I wouldn't have stayed in Germany. And I wouldn't have gone back to Poland... no family left, not welcome there anyway." Stefan thought about all the reasons his mother had taken him from Soviet-controlled Poland. "We can't find her because she's not anywhere we can look. She's in the US, Canada, Israel, or some other country that took refugees after the war."

"Don't you think I thought of that, Sajac?" Schulke glared. Stefan had lost the slight increase in good will he'd won by calling him *Boss*. "The first thing I did, combed through the lists we have from the emigrant lists—the Ami's *UNRRA*, the Jew's Joint Distribution Committee and the International Refugee Organization. No Guildenstern, no Trushenko. No one emigrated by those two names, not legally at least. "

"Can I see the file again, Boss?" Stefan riffled through the sheets. He picked out the Third Reich identity document, with its photo of a pretty young woman smiling brightly. He held it between two fingers, conscious that he was touching an SS document. "How widely has this picture been circulated?"

"*Vizepräsident*'s office wouldn't let me. Said the whole matter is too sensitive. Too many questions would be asked. The picture would get back to the *Stasi* and the KGB for sure. Then they'd begin to ask themselves why we were interested."

Stefan grimaced. "And if we asked permission to check with the Allied security services, they'd forbid it, too, for the same reason." Schulke nodded.

Now was the time to strike. Stefan cleared his throat. He was going to take a chance. "Sir, did they give you a budget—a spending limit on this project, travel warrant, even long distance telephone authority?"

"Didn't ask for any of that. Just for one assistant." He pointed across the desk. "You."

"Has it occurred to you, Herr Schulke, that the *Vizepräsident*'s office has never taken this matter seriously? That they've just put you to this job to keep you quiet, to stifle the whole inquiry?" Was this idea too hard for Schulke? Could he explain this possibility to him?

"What are you saying, Sajac?" The voice was angry.

"Sir, with respect. Here is one possibility. The BfV-*Vizepräsident*'s office doesn't believe there really is such a person to worry about.

There was fury in Schulke's eyes when he replied. "But there is, I know it. I had her in my hands. And she knows." The voice kept rising. "I've got to find her...take her out."

Stefan could see it was personal, not just professional. He had to calm him. "You know she's real, sir. But they can't be sure. Maybe they're allowing you to putter about in the records just in case. To protect themselves in case they're wrong. They'll be able to say, well, we put someone on it, but he didn't come up with anything. They could even make you take the blame." Stefan paused. "That's how things work sometimes." He stopped to gage the reaction.

Schulke began to lean over, bent double. Then, elbows on knees, he cradled his large, almost bald head between his hands. It was evidently all too much for him. Stefan should have begun to feel just a little sorry for the man. Finally, he looked up, with the face of a drowning man. "What am I to do, Sajac?"

"I suggest you tell them you've decided to shut down the whole project, sir. Then see what happens."

Perhaps this Sajac kid has something. Schulke was tired of the constant reporting, budget form filling, bureaucratic rigmarole. *What do they think I've been doing down here in this cubicle, day after day? Playing with myself?* It took little to convince himself that the conspiracy to ruin his life was still fully in force.

Chapter Twenty-Three

Rita slid into the comfortable chair, straightened out her Security Council agenda, and looked down through the tinted glass. There, beneath a vast mural was an equally massive table that inscribed almost a complete circle. Round it the names of the council member-states were placed. The presidency this month was the nation of Poland, and so Rita had been assigned main duty all week. It wasn't just because the chair, Ambassador Lewandowski, was Polish—his English was perfectly serviceable. Rita had been called upon because, as everyone knew, the demand for English and Russian simultaneous translation would be paramount. In two years on the team of interpreters she had become the unofficial star. Invisible to speakers and hearers, it was Rita who gave the speakers the one voice all shared. Her simultaneous translation bore none of the hesitation that betrayed the others as they sought to speak and listen at the same time. The crises of the early 60s—the Congo civil war, the confrontation between the American and Russian tanks at check point Charlie in Berlin, now the missiles sent to Cuba—they had all made her voice, but nothing else about her, almost famous.

No one was surprised when the director assigned her to the meeting of the Security Council that week. The United States had accused the Soviet Union of placing intermediate-range nuclear missiles at its doorstep, in Cuba. It had already imposed a blockade and people in both countries, including Rita and the boys, were locating their nearest fallout shelters. The threat of nuclear war was palpable.

The Americans had demanded an emergency session and the US Ambassador was already seated, working up a scowl as he waited for the session to be opened. He was as well known in the UN as he was in his own country. Adlai Stevenson, twice his party's candidate for president, had a certain reputation as an "egghead", with good, indeed mild manners. Eggheads were very smart but not very passionate. His scowl now belied the reputation.

Rita looked forward to interpreting his Midwestern American drawl, one she found easy to follow. The Russian, Valerian Zorin, would be harder.

Her task would be more interesting and much more challenging than mere translation. Simultaneous interpreters had to understand what they heard. But as they listened they had also to search out the best words that in another language would convey the emotional register of the speaker's words. It was like translating poetry on the fly, but for much higher stakes. The right word with the wrong intonation could provoke an international incident. Today it stood the chance of adding to the likelihood of a nuclear exchange between the superpowers.

* * *

She'd sent her fifteen year old boys off to their high schools, over their demand that they be allowed to accompany her and watch this potentially world-shaking confrontation from the interpreter's booths above the floor of the Security Council. When Rita told Eric no one was allowed in those precincts but UN staff, he announced that he was staying home to watch proceedings on TV. Pleased at his interest, nevertheless, she pushed him out the door, armed with a sack lunch, books, a loose-leaf binder stuffed with his homework. At the apartment door he searched his pocket for his subway pass. Finding it, he caught up with his brother at the elevator. They were in different schools but used the same subway stop at Lexington Avenue and 86th street.

Now Rita sat down with the *New York Times* and a stack of briefing papers, some in Russian, some in German, others in English. She'd review them just to have a grip on the nuanced differences in vocabulary that described the issues in three different languages.

By quarter to ten she was dressed—blue serge suit coat and skirt over a plain white blouse. No jewelry, a touch of lipstick but no other makeup. She was still mulling over the material she'd read as she slipped into a topcoat—something she hadn't needed in all the Australian years. Absorbed in her preparation, she was on automatic pilot all the way to the subway. It would be five stops on the Lex, as she'd learned to call it, and then a ten-minute walk to the UN Secretariat—the iconic high-rise beside the inverted-bowl-topped General Assembly Building. Behind it, invisible from First Avenue, facing the East River, was the Conference Building in which the Security Council met. She had to be in her place above the Council chamber by 11:00 that day. She looked at her watch. Time to spare.

Rita didn't notice the completely nondescript middle-aged man standing almost next to her on the platform. He'd followed her all the way from her doorstep, and saw in her absorption no need for precaution. The man was a freelance investigator, one who usually followed wives around midtown on behalf of suspicious husbands. Hired by the Soviet UN mission through three cutouts, he had no idea what he was looking for, or how long he'd have to tail this particular woman. His reports were to be made by phone at a set time once each day, from a payphone and to a payphone, as he discovered when he called back on one occasion.

It was, he thought, very peculiar. The man who'd offered him the job was evidently not an irate husband. When asked what he was to watch for, the man had replied, "I have no idea. Just see who she meets, what she does, where she goes."

"What do ya mean, no idea? What am I looking for? What do you suspect her of doing?"

The voice at the other end sounded equally frustrated. "I don't know exactly. If she does anything out of the ordinary, like making a lot of phone calls from phone booths, or changing subway cars suddenly, or looks around as if she suspects she's being followed. You know, suspicious stuff."

* * *

In fact, Dmitri Ivanoviotch Yakushkin, the new KGB rezident—its station chief—in the Soviet's UN mission, didn't know what he was looking for either. All he knew is that he'd been tasked to perform a service for the *DDR Stasi*—the ministry of state security of the German Democratic Republic. This was not unusual. The Stasi and the KGB were joined at the hip, worked so closely it would have been impossible to keep secrets from one another had they sought to. As the New York KGB *rezident*, Yakushkin was certainly senior enough to be told exactly what he was supposed to be looking for. The trouble was, no one knew—not in East Berlin, not in Moscow. All they knew, and all he was told, was that somebody in the West German B*v*F was turning over every file, scrutinizing every list that came into their possession, for a woman named Guildenstern or Trushenko, that he'd been doing so for years, that he'd got others working for him, and that why he was looking was as closely guarded a secret as the BfV ever had. The *Stasi* infiltrator in the BfV had tried hard to find out why, but the papers had been held too closely in the office of the *Vizepräsident* of the BfV for counterintelligence. And the irony of it all was that the KGB knew exactly who she was, where she was and what name she was going under. Only they had no idea what the German BfV wanted from her.

Sitting at his desk, Yakushkin was on the phone to Moscow. He needed to know more, but wasn't getting anything useful at all. "And how do we know where she is when the people who presumably know why they are looking for her don't know where she is?" He paused. The silence on the other end of the secure line to Moscow perplexed him. "This is a secure line, no?" He hoped so. Yakushkin didn't trust it. He sent everything really secret to Moscow Center in the secure code.

"Yes, Comrade. I'll have to ask for permission to discuss details. Can I call you back?"

Yakushkin slammed down the receiver to let the underling at the Lubyanka know how irritated he was. Then he got a grip. *Don't do that again, Dmitri Invanovitch,* he ordered himself. *Unprofessional. Poor man was only doing his duty.* The secure line rang again. "Da?" He made the 'yes' politely interrogatory, and heard a small sigh of relief at the other end of the line.

"Thanks for waiting, Comrade. Here is everything we know. The woman's name, Romero, came to us through East Berlin. They really don't know why the West German BfV wants her. But her common-law husband belongs to us." It was a euphemism for a possibly unwilling but compromised stooge. "Guillermo Romero, former Soviet person despite the Spanish name, was located crossing the Spanish frontier in 1949. We kept tabs on him. Went to Australia. Then worked for us as a willing courier, transporting samples from the English nuclear tests in Australia about five years ago. Nothing since."

"And the wife, the one the Westerners now want?"

"Well, KGB secured her name and background when we identified the husband on the Spanish border. But we never approached her. No need."

"Why haven't the West Germans found her already? She's operating in plain sight here at the UN as an interpreter."

"It's her name—Romero. They are looking for her under other names—Guildenstern and Trushenko, a name she used under false identity in the war."

"So, if we don't know why the West Germans want her, why should we think the matter is of any importance?"

"Two reasons, sir. The West Germans must think it's important. They've been looking for a couple of years, but looking passively. They haven't gone out and beat the bushes. It's as though they don't want to attract attention to the fact they're looking for her."

Yakushkin sighed. "Second reason?"

"Well, the West Germans share everything with the CIA. But not this. There were strict instructions on the file that it was not to be divulged to anyone in any other service. Looks like they're not taking a chance on leaks...anywhere."

"Thank you, Comrade. I will put some trusted persons on the job, following her." Slowly he put down the secure phone, already thinking about which cutout to employ for this task.

* * *

Yakushkin had been paying hard currency for a month, with no results, to American "gumshoes" — strange name for private detectives, why gumshoes? He'd even made it his own business to lay eyes on this Romero woman as she came and went to and from the interpreters' booths at the General Assembly and the Security Council. Now he looked at his watch. It was time for the session to begin. Yakushkin was confident she'd be translating into Russian today. He swiveled from his desk, rose and went to the television console across the room. He clicked it on and stood before it, waiting for the picture tube to expand from the single, bright, glowing spot in the center to fill the screen. He knew he'd have to adjust the rabbit ears to get the best reception. When the picture came on he spun through the dial past the six other channels to the only one that he knew would carry the whole session live, the new educational TV station that broadcast from Newark, New Jersey and had no advertising to lose. Then Yakushkin switched on the shortwave receiver tuned to Radio Moscow. When it warmed up, he lowered the volume. He would listen to both the TV and the radio, to monitor the interpretation. Then he returned to his chair, lit an American cigarette, and leaned back, as the springs beneath his chair creaked with the weight.

The screen showed the American ambassador's balding dome, reflecting the spotlights trained down on the arced table of the security council great hall. Adlai Stevenson, he could tell, was angry, papers quivering in his hand, eyeglasses pulled off his face. Yakushkin thought, *If only he'd shown such passion when he ran for president in '56.* Meanwhile, Rita's voice was even as she spoke the American ambassador's inflammatory words. "All right, sir, let me ask you one simple question: Do you, Ambassador Zorin, deny that the U.S.S.R. has placed and is placing medium- and intermediate-range missiles and sites in Cuba? Yes or no— don't wait for the translation—yes or no?" Stevenson paused, as though he was waiting. The camera panned slowly to Zorin, the Soviet ambassador, a man Yakushkin knew for his mild temper, measured tone and his fluent English. Zorin sat immobile, waiting while the official translation was provided. And now the Soviet ambassador's voice was heard, in Rita's even tone. "You will receive your answer in due course. This is not a court of law, I do not need to provide a yes or no answer..." Then she fell silent as Stevenson spoke again. "You can answer yes or no. You have denied they exist. I want to know if I understood you correctly. I am prepared to wait for my answer until hell freezes over, if that's your decision. And I am also prepared to present the evidence in this room." Then another voice spoke, naming the new speaker, the Polish ambassador, presiding over the meeting. "The chair recognizes the representative of Chile—" But now Rita's voice again spoke for Stevenson, interrupting. "I have not finished my statement. I asked you a question. I have had no reply to the question, and I will now proceed, if I may, to finish my statement."

The drama of the proceeding had now completely arrested Yakushkin's attention. He switched off the Russian feed from Moscow and went to the television, raising the volume. Behind Stevenson, men were placing an easel and putting large photographs on it. The Americans were going to put on a show about the Soviets' nuclear missile launch sites in Cuba.

Almost an hour later Yakushkin was again listening to Rita, as she faultlessly translated ambassador Zorin's Russian. He knew how word perfect she was, for Yakushkin had the text that had been prepared for Zorin before him as he listened to her simultaneous translation. Again almost in a monotone of evenhandedness she spoke the provocative answer to Stevenson's insolence. "Yesterday the United States, in fact, instituted a naval blockade of the Republic of Cuba, thus trampling underfoot the norms of international behavior and the principles enshrined in the Charter of the United Nations. The United States has appropriated to itself the right—and has stated so—to attack ships of other countries on the open seas, and this constitutes nothing other than undisguised piracy. At the same time, at the Guantanamo Base, a base located on the territory of Cuba, landings of additional troops have been effected and the armed forces of the United States brought to combat readiness. Such venturesome enterprises, together with the statements of the President of the United States to explain them, statements made yesterday on the radio and on television, give evidence of the fact that American imperialist circles will balk at nothing in their attempts to throttle a sovereign state, a Member of the United Nations, as that little country is. They are prepared, for the sake of this, to push the world to the brink of a military catastrophe." Rita's tone was carefully unperturbed.

Yakushkin laughed. This woman, Rita Romero, would have to continue in the spotlight, interpreting in that vein for some time, signaling her whereabouts to all the world, hidden in plain sight, while the Germans were looking for her everywhere, fruitlessly.

* * *

When the session finally ended, Rita rose, pulled off the

earphones, rubbed her ears a few times and began putting her things away. *Is the world going to end, just as I have finally found a life to live?* It was an irony to Rita that her personal world had finally sorted itself out into a wonderfully satisfying whole, just as the rest of the world was preparing to destroy itself. Her mood was valedictory as she walked slowly down the steps from the plinth of the UN buildings. A low sun setting in the west glared in the broad width of 42nd Street. It created a golden frame of the towering buildings, as they reflected its light in the miles of glass stretching west all the way to the Hudson. New York looked at its best on an afternoon most New Yorkers were contemplating never seeing a sunset again.

* * *

The city had surprised Rita, delighted her, enchanted her. New York was everything she still wanted from life and never expected to find. Rita knew it from the moment they'd arrived. If New York was America she'd been profoundly wrong about it back in '48 when she'd spurned the chance at US visas.

For her boys, too, it was very soon a never-ending cornucopia of the very experiences and opportunities that they had been brought up by Rita, and even by Gil, to thirst for. Almost from the first all three were breathing different air, listening to a cacophony of polyglot voices, sharing the palate of a hundred cuisines, moving to drumbeats they'd never heard before, finding their way through cultures that had never penetrated their lives. All three were participants in a life that only Rita had ever remembered having glimpses of, before the war and after. These glimpses she'd never allowed herself to absorb as real. Until now. It was living in Europe again, but unhaunted by an unbearable past. They were all three alive in another reality, but only Rita could know fully how wonderful it was, how wonderful the simplest everyday things were.

They'd found a comfortable apartment in Yorkville, the old German quarter of Manhattan. Now, fifteen years after the war, there was no trace of its sympathy for Nazi Germany, of the German American Bund that had paraded down its streets in the late '30s. The neighborhood was all *Gemutlichkeit*, protected by zoning and rent control from the well-defined Puerto Rican ghetto immediately to the north and the waspish Blue Stocking district below it on the east side of Central Park.

The boys had made the park their personal front yard, their bicycles crossing and re-crossing between the splendid Metropolitan Museum of Art on the east side and the massive American Museum of Natural History facing it across the park on the west side. Both were free and sources of endless fascination to her boys. Almost weekly they would dragoon their mother from one diorama to another, revealing their discoveries. Rita had never been to Paris. Now, living in New York, she felt as though she didn't have to go.

* * *

She reached the stairway descending to the subway. The thought came back to her: *And it's all going to end in the mutually assured destruction of the superpowers?*

The afternoon papers were already out on the stands as she walked along the 42nd Street subway platform. The *Post*, the *Journal-American*, the *World Telegram and Sun* were all screaming doomsday. Had the boys noticed on their way home from their schools? They'd have to take the subway, too, and stare at the 40-point typeface of the papers opened before them by riders wondering if there'd be another edition tomorrow.

It was a Friday evening. If it was going to be the last Friday evening of their lives, she wanted to spend it with Phil. She'd take the boys over to his place. It was a comfortable habit they'd fallen into. They'd cook dinner with him and his daughter, Alice.

Then the boys and Alice would curl up in front of the television in Phil Morton's living room, watch *The Twilight Zone* and argue about it among themselves for another hour.

* * *

Phil Morton was the other adventure, a quiet adventure, offered by Rita's life in New York. They'd passed one another in the corridors of the UN secretariat once or twice, both noticing the other. He was six feet tall, perhaps pushing fifty but remarkably fit, a leathery face over a somewhat wrinkled neck, but still a fine head of black hair, a square jaw and clear blue eyes. Phil Morton dressed quietly but well in suits that reminded Rita of the American president, Kennedy.

Then they'd seen each other emerging from the same subway station on 42nd Street, walking briskly to the East River. Neither spoke to the other on the first three or four occasions, neither wanting to appear forward, or even interested in complicating their lives. But then they found themselves in the hallway of a middle school in Yorkville, both attending meetings with a teacher about their children. Now Rita and this man realized that they both worked in the same building and lived in the same Upper East Side neighborhood, Yorkville, and had children in the same school. They had at least to exchange pleasantries.

"We've met, haven't we?" she asked, as they sat on a bench outside a classroom. "UN?"

Morton nodded. "We have, and we haven't." His laugh was shy. "I think we have kids in the same class." He inclined his head towards the door. "Both in a little trouble for talking too much?" Rita frowned slightly. Intuitively, he understood the question in her look. "My daughter mentioned it this afternoon." Why hadn't Rita known? She knew immediately. *Boys!*

Rita didn't ask why it wasn't his wife coming to meet the teacher. Again, he read her thoughts. and volunteered.

Chapter Twenty-Three

"Widower."

Suddenly it was her turn to answer the unspoken question. Something possessed her to reply, "Never married, " as a test. He didn't so much as turn a hair. *Impressive*, Rita thought. They exchanged names and shook hands formally.

He'd come to New York from Ottawa, five years before, seconded from a government department called "External Affairs," following the Canadian UN diplomat who'd won a Nobel Prize for separating the Egyptians and the Israelis in 1956. Phil Morton was from a town she'd never heard of in a province of Canada Rita couldn't pronounce. He'd served in a half-dozen Canadian embassies, legations, missions before taking charge of the documentation center at the UN, with a large staff that dealt with diplomatic documents, passports, visas, permissions, customs, removals—everything needed to uncoil the lines of an international civil service that were too frequently knotted up in the conflicting regulations of multiple countries. It was the very thing Rita had done in Canberra.

Phil was nothing like Rita's first husband, Urs, still less did he remind her of Gil. He wasn't reticent, and he wasn't voluble. He had opinions but didn't force them or even convey them unless asked. He knew a great deal, but made it manifest only on demand. Phil Morton was a calm presence. He asked questions and he listened. He didn't mind silences, either. He'd served in Europe during the war, seen enough there to understand immediately what had happened and who had survived. Her stories didn't frighten him away. It made her want to tell him more, more than she'd told anyone in years, since an afternoon on the Sydney docks with Betty Lowell. Phil was, Rita decided, wise. It was a trait she'd never found in a man before.

Rita and Phil Morton had seen enough no longer to ask for love. They gave each other something else, something that seemed more enduring.

Chapter Twenty-Four

The world did not after all come to an end those weeks in October, 1962. Dmitri Ivanovitch Yakushkin was well satisfied with the outcome—Soviet missiles withdrawn from Cuba in exchange for American ones withdrawn from Turkey. It would not be for another year that he would learn the party's official verdict on Khrushchev's adventurism was not so favorable. Meanwhile he pondered how it was the Americans were willing to risk so much in a blockade. How could they be so confident that the Soviet freighters loaded with intermediate range missiles would turn back? They'd fine-tuned their embargo, tailored their blockade perfectly. It wasn't like the ham-handed Americans. It was almost as if they were reading the Politburo's minds.

Meanwhile, the month of trailing the Romero woman had extended to six weeks, with nothing whatever to show for it. Repeated inquiries all secured the same reply from the Lubyanka. The matter had to be important. The Germans were still looking for her after two years, were no closer, and still no one knew why they were searching so assiduously. But for the New York *rezidentura* the whole matter seemed an expensive distraction. Yakushkin needed to get it off his desk. Then one morning in November he had a brainwave. It was 8:00, still early enough to call Moscow. He picked up the secure line. "Get me Sakharovsky." He put the receiver down on the cradle and waited.

Aleksandr Michaelovitch Sakharovsky was Yakushkin's boss, head of the KGB First Chief Directorate—foreign intelligence. They'd both grown up first in the service of the MGB, then its successor, the KGB. They knew each other well. They could talk, man to man, with no comebacks. Yakushkin gulped. *Can we, really?* Then he gave himself a sharp rebuke. *God damn it to hell, you can't be thinking this way. You'll never serve the state if you have to second-guess yourself like this. Besides, this isn't 1937.* Yakushkin could still marvel he'd survived the Great Terror before the war. Unlike so many others, he'd really been guilty of demonizing Stalin, silently, in his mind.

The phone rang. Soon he was talking, to an old friend. When he hung up, Yakushkin felt he'd at least gotten Moscow off square one. They had a plan.

* * *

"Well, what is it, Comrade? I am a busy man." Vladimir Yefimovich Semichastny, chairman of the committee for state security, the KGB, was so busy, he hadn't looked up from his desk at the older man, standing at attention before his desk, square-shouldered and pasty gray from his hair, to his skin and his suit. When he did glance up, the minister was surprised. It was his first directorate chief, a major general who looked the dour part even out of uniform. *This man must be thirty years my senior,* Semichastny thought. *Why is he standing before me like a recruit to the service?* Changing demeanor, he smiled, pointed at the leather seat before his desk. "Please sit, Aleksandr Michaelovitch"

"No, thank you, sir." He had schooled himself for five or six years now to take no liberties with the successors to Lavranti Beria, Stalin's psychopathic hatchet man. Sakharovsky was not going to relax, even if the younger man was not even out of his thirties and could know little of the bloodstained culture of his ministry.

Semichastny shrugged and spread his hands in an invitation to speak.

"I seek permission to pass state secrets to a foreign power, in fact an enemy state, the fascist West German regime."

"And you're asking my permission to do so?" Semichastny shook his head.

Sakharovsky immediately replied, "Very well" and began to turn round.

"Where are you going, comrade?"

"Sir, you said no. That is the end of the matter."

Semichastny smiled. "I was shaking my head at the idea that you people are still bringing operational matters to the minister for approval. I'm sure you have a good reason to divulge a secret if you need to. You don't need my approval."

"With respect, sir. No one beneath me was willing to take responsibility. If it goes wrong, it's their career, pension, or worse. Everyone else up the line to me passed it on...sir."

"And now you're passing it along." He shrugged. "Very well, tell me. But you must sit down. Looking up is hurting my neck." The minister put his hand to the nape of his neck.

He was silent as Sakharovsky outlined the problem. The intelligence problem was draining local resources in New York. Not a serious issue, especially when the other side was expending resources on the same matter. But they just couldn't figure out why the woman was of any importance at all.

By the time the older man had finished, the minster understood perfectly well why he was being asked. This was a fishing expedition with an expensive lure in a lake that might lack fish. It could reveal the KGB and *Stasi*'s penetration of the German security service even if the woman was of no value or interest. "So, you want to lead the Germans to this woman, just to find out why they want her so badly?" Sakharovsky nodded. His minister went on. "I can see why no one wanted to authorize this plan. If it fails, the responsible party can easily be made to look like the agent of the German BfV...but if we tell them how to find her, where she is, then what?"

"We hope that the BfV will do something, anything, that may explain her importance to them."

"And why should we care?"

"Minister." He cleared his throat, and gathered his thoughts.

"The German BfV have been working too long on this matter for it to be of no importance. They are more suspicious of us than the Americans or the English. They work harder at penetration than their patron powers. And they don't even share what they do with the other anti-Soviet regimes." He stopped. Had he convinced the minister? "We must find out what they want with her. We can't think of another way to proceed."

"Very well. Proceed." Semichastny waved his hand in dismissal. The man stood there, unmoved. "What?" said the minister.

The older man pulled a flimsy from his coat pocket. "Can you sign the authorization personally?"

So they needed him to implicate himself in this wild goose chase. "Covering your ass, are you, Aleksandr Michaelovitch" The younger man smiled. It was not a friendly smile.

* * *

Selling Gil Romero to the Brits wasn't hard. Once they found out he'd run their nuclear debris back to Moscow's people in Italy, they'd be only too glad to interest themselves in his whereabouts. The only question was whether Romero's name would work its way back to the Germans and be enough to lead them first to Rita Romero and then to Margareta Trushenko and Rita Guildenstern. More than that the KGB was not willing to risk.

So, first Big Jim Healy, head of the Waterside Workers Federation, was told to hint some knowledge of the nuclear tests the English had conducted in the outback to someone in the Australian Labour Party. This friend of Healy's had a word with someone in the British Labour party, who had a word with its deeply patriotic leader, Hugh Gaitskell, who had a word with the UK Ministry of Defense. Back to Healy came the discreet inquiry of how he might have learned a secret so closely kept only the Australian prime minister knew of it. "Just a guess from the medical man at the union clinic. Is it true?" This was all Jim Healy was told to say, but it was enough.

* * *

Gil had just come out of the Sydney Bridge Club, heading to his now ancient Holden, parked a hundred yards from the club, when he saw the figures coming towards him. It was late on a Friday evening and Gil had stayed longer than usual. The other players had been particularly strong, but cards had fallen right for him all evening. He'd won a few.

The men wore hats and coats, badges of middle-class membership. Still they looked vaguely threatening, and Gil didn't really breathe a sigh of relief till they had passed him along the footpath. As he exhaled, he felt a strong hand close down on each of his forearms. An English voice spoke quietly. "Please come with us, Mr Romero."

Gil had no choice, he immediately recognized. The men were larger and evidently stronger, perhaps armed, and certainly persistent, as they frog-marched him past his car. They slipped into an alleyway that widened into an open space behind a building where another Holden, much newer than Gil's, was parked. He was bundled inside but not before being patted down — as if they expected him to be carrying a weapon. The fear that had gripped him from the moment he'd been taken was momentarily broken. *These people don't know me very well, do they? Thinking I might be armed. They've mistaken me for someone else.* Then the fright returned, making Gil shiver visibly. It was too dark in the back seat and the gloom of the alleyway to make out anything of his captors. The driver pulled into the street. Then each of the men grasped one of Gil's hands and a black hood was pulled over his head.

After what seemed an eternity, he was pulled from the car,

still hooded, and walked to a door, then told to mount a rickety wooden stair, floor after floor, till he lost count. Out of breath, now wet with the perspiration of fear and exertion, he stumbled across a threshold, was caught by the same strong hands that had been holding him, and pushed down into a chair. "If you leave your hands in your lap we won't be forced to handcuff you, Dr Romero." The voice was new and very English. Gil calculated immediately and with relief, *Not Russian. You'll be fine.*

Gil had every intention of complying. "Yes, of course." He placed his hands squarely before him. "Can you remove the hood?"

"I regret, no." He could hear the noise of a match striking, and then smelled tobacco smoke. Unusual. Foreign? American? No. Egyptian? If only they'd give him one.

"Dr. Romero, did you know what you were doing when you took those cruises to Trieste five years ago?"

"I was the ship's doctor, acting as *locum* for the regular medical officer."

"We really don't want to beat you, Doctor, but palpable untruths will provoke us." The register remained preternaturally calm.

There was, Gil decided immediately, no reason to test the limits of this man's patience. "I suspected I was carrying something radioactive for Soviet espionage agents."

"So you were. Who organized the task?"

"I have no idea. I was asked merely to carry something handed to me as I boarded and surrender it to a customs agent when I landed." He sincerely wanted to be as helpful as possible. "I was asked to do it by a man who called himself Macintosh, but was obviously central European, probably Russian. The first time we met he had a bodyguard with him, someone he introduced as Armstrong."

"No need to describe him, Doctor. or his henchman. But why did they ask you, or even know you?"

"No idea, sir."

"If you are going to convince us of that, you'll have to tell us all about yourself, so we can piece it out."

"Please, I'll be glad to help. But couldn't you take the hood off? I'm dying for a smoke."

"Impossible." Gil could feel the cigarette smoke come through the blindfold. It had been directed at him. "Get on with it."

"With what, my life history? How far do I need to go back?" He knew already. "I was in the Russians' pocket even before I got to Australia in 1950."

"Explain."

"I was in Moscow during the war. Left as soon as I could afterwards. Got married. Had kids. When we decided to emigrate to Australia I went back to France for my medical certificates." *Do I need to tell them the certificates were fakes?* "Then I tried to get into Spain for some other documents I needed. Didn't have a passport the Franco government would accept. I suspect the people who smuggled me across turned me in to the Spanish and sent word back to Moscow." Gil leaned back and raised an arm. The hood was annoying and he needed to scratch. The arm was quickly forced down and then clamped with a handcuff. "I only wanted to scratch my nose."

"Carry on."

"Not much more. I was a physician at one of those vast mental hospitals, north of Melbourne, for a couple of years. Then I got an offer to come here and work for the maritime workers' union." *Might as well tell them.* "Looking back, I don't think it was by accident. Probably arranged by the Russians and Jim Healy, head of the union."

"I am sorry, Dr Romero, but we know all that. I am afraid we will have to beat you." Gil could hear the man rise and move away, while another set of footsteps located another man behind him.

"What more can I tell you? I've told you everything." *Can I make up something?* It would have to be something that would distract them, something they'd have to spend time checking on. *Something about Rita perhaps?* Nothing serious, nothing that could get her into trouble, of course. Just something that would stop them beating him. "Wait." The sound of footsteps behind him stopped. "There's my wife. She might be involved with them too, with the Russians." He paused. *Would it work?*

"Pray continue, Doctor Romero."

"Well, I never quite understood how she survived the war. Lived in Germany for most of it. Don't know how she did it. Had to have had help—identity papers, ration books, work. She might have been a Soviet agent. I don't know." Then suddenly Gil knew how to continue. "When we got here she suddenly became interested in languages. Eastern European ones, ones she spoke already, don't you see? Why do that? Did a university course with lots of Aussies, government types, even spies I suspect." He had to convince them. "Why would a woman want to do that?" He paused, hoping for some sign of interest. None. He had to up the stakes. "Anyway, she ended up in the Foreign Ministry, moved to Canberra. Then she went to New York, United Nations."

"Why?"

"I don't know. Maybe she had a hand in the Soviets tracking me all the way from Poland after the war ended." Gil stopped. He'd gone too far, embroidering much more than he had wanted to, carried away by fear of being beaten and the plausibility of his fairy tale. *If you get out of this alive, you'll have to warn her.*

"Speculation is really not good enough, Doctor." The coolness in the voice, its almost conversational tone, gave Gil a momentary hope. And then it came. A whoosh, then the crash of something heavy against his face, so heavy it toppled his chair and his head hit the wooden floor. While the pain waxed and waned in his head, two, three four times, the chair and Gil still handcuffed to it were picked up. He was sitting again, with his free hand rubbing his temple, feeling for damage through the hood. Then it too was grasped, brought down and handcuffed to the chair. The voice came again, still without emotion. "Is there anything else you can tell us, anything it would be worth carrying to our superiors, besides the news that we found a Soviet agent?"

And then Gil remembered. Something Rita had said, one night, in the dark, in bed, as they lay there, smoking after making love, soon after they'd arrived in Australia. It was one of the few times he'd been able to listen as she spoke of Karpathyn and the Ghetto. She'd told Gil what made her leave. Someone, he couldn't recall now who, had told her a secret, or something she thought was a secret, one she'd kept, never telling anyone. It was about the Poles breaking the Germans' encryption codes. Only it couldn't have been right, what she'd been told. In his discernment, he'd realized, it had to have been concocted, something made up, just to give Rita the courage she would need. Otherwise it would have come out, after the war, when secrecy was no longer needed. Still, it was worth trying. He was almost surprised he could still speak after the blow to his head. "My wife...she had a secret, that she passed on to me." He paused. *How to make them believe you?* "She swore me never to tell anyone."

"Carry on." The clipped, restrained, very British voice was still without emotion.

He had to make it convincing. "She told me that just before the war began in '39, the Poles had broken the German codes... their military codes."

"And..." The single word showed more interest than anything his interrogator had said before.

"And they'd given it to the Brits, to your lot." Gil coughed.

There was a silence in the room. Then he heard the man in front of him, the one who'd been asking the questions, rise and walk away. A door closed. A few minutes later what sounded like the same door opened. There was the sound of two sets of shoes. Gil's interrogator had returned with another man. "Dr.

Romero," the voice sounded emollient, encouraging, almost importuning. "Please repeat what you just told me."

It must have worked, what he had conjured up. Gil was relieved. He'd repeat it, even embellish it if he could think of how. He'd be able after all to give them something they wanted, enough to get him off the hook for his rather low-level espionage. "I think it was in '50 or '51, before we moved to Victoria State, out in Ararat..."

"Get on with it." It was another voice, impatient and more imperious.

Apparently this interlocutor wasn't interested in a narrative, even one that would enhance the credibility of his story. "My wife told me that the Poles had deciphered the German military code before the war. And they'd passed the method on to the British." He paused. Would it be enough?

"You're quite certain of this?"

"Yes. I'm sure...that's what she said."

"And do you think she's ever told anyone else?"

"Can't be certain, but I don't think so." He paused to think. "There's no one she's close to." Then he thought, *How would you know, anymore, Gil?*

"And have you ever mentioned it to anyone, anyone at all?"

"No...I swear. Never." He hadn't even thought of it, not once in all those years. *Should I say so?* Gil was still wearing the infernal hood over his head, and he had not grown any more used to it. Only the fear had distracted him from the terrible claustrophobia, stale air, and disequilibrium. Now he'd satisfied them, he was sufficiently reassured to ask again. "Please, can you remove the hood now?"

There was no response at all. Instead he heard one of the two say to the other, "Can't be helped. No choice, really. You know the drill."

"Very well. I suppose you're right." The two men sighed and then there was the sound of one of them walking away, and the creaky door closed behind him. Now Gil heard and felt the remaining man walk around him, brushing past his arm, still held fast to the chair by a handcuff, until he was directly behind the chair Gil was *fixed* to. *Good, he's going to take off the hood.* It was the very last thought that passed through Guillermo Romero's head. Then, the last sounds—the hammer of a Webley Mk IV .38 mm revolver as it struck the firing pin, igniting the primer of a round already in its chamber, and last of all the terrific report of exploding propellant as its bullet penetrated his cranium three inches from his ear.

Chapter Twenty-Five

"When one's been followed round for a month, you begin to notice." Rita was lying back on her pillow, exhaling cigarette smoke into the dark, watching the taxi headlights along Lexington Avenue slide across the ceiling. It was a Friday evening towards 11 in early November. Things had settled down at the UN. Rita's boys were out of the house, somewhere with Phil's daughter. Rita had gone to Phil's for an evening with him. They'd kept things very discreet. Romances were frowned upon at the United Nations. In fact nepotism rules even made marriages secret. It wasn't just the people at work who were in the dark about Rita and Phil Morton. His daughter and her boys knew them for one another's parents.

"Following you?" Phil responded. "Who's following you?"

They turned towards each other. "No idea. But it's two of them, taking turns, several days a week."

"Are you sure?"

"Yes. It's a sense, a habit I picked up in the war, looking into strangers' faces. These men turn away too quickly." Rita shivered slightly, thinking about the past.

Phil noticed and reached his arm across her waist. "Worried?"

"Well, I can't think what they want." A bitter laugh came. "Secrets from the interpretation service of the Security Council? What secrets? We have none." She thought for a moment. "Why is this starting to happen to me now?" She almost said *again*.

But Phil didn't catch her drift. He was focusing on the men she'd spotted. "Tell me what you know, anything you've noticed, what they look like, when and where they pick you up." Phil suddenly was sounding professionally concerned.

"Don't know anything really, except one reads the *Daily News* and the other reads the *Post* when they're with me on the subway. Both wear hats they don't take off, ever, so I never get a decent look at their faces. Neither really knows how to wear a necktie. They pick me up near Lexington Avenue or on 84th Street." This was where Rita and the boys lived, a few blocks from Phil Morton's apartment. "They drop me at the UN Plaza. I haven't tried to lose them yet. Maybe they don't realize I'm on to them."

Phil was impressed by the coolness of her report.

"There's something else…" He was silent. Rita reached over for his cigarette and put it into her mouth. She needed to show him a mark of intimacy before continuing. "I told you about my ex- back in Sydney…Gil."

He nodded. "Not exactly your ex—?"

"Yes. We never married, but he's the boys' father and we were together for almost fifteen years…Well, he's missing. Left his job…That's how I found out. They called me, his clinic, all the way from Sydney. No one can seem to find him. Been gone almost three weeks."

"Are you worried about him?"

"Part of me, yes. He might have taken a cruise. Used to go as a ship's doctor. But he'd always clear it with the clinic. They've even gone to the Sydney police. No trace."

"Could he be coming here, to visit the boys maybe?"

"It's possible, I suppose. But I'd have heard from him, if he was coming."

"What are you going to do?"

"I've decided to tell someone in UN security."

Phil raised his eyebrows. Suddenly he was preoccupied. "Who?"

Rita saw the look. "I was going to ask you who I should talk to. That's why I mentioned it."

Phil's smile was sardonic. "Well, you already have told UN security, at least unofficially. Care to make it official?" His torso rose as he leaned on his elbow in bed.

"I don't follow, Phil."

"Head of documentation at the UN, that's me...well, also head of security, but we don't advertise. Bad for the UN image to have a security service. Raises doubts. Who are we serving? " He paused, lay down again and blew a long purple shaft of cigarette smoke across the ceiling. "So, want to make your inquiry official?" Then he smiled. "Here in bed with the director?"

She moved closer to him and draped her body across his. He could feel the smile flicker across her face. "Best place for confidentiality, no?"

He put his arm over her shoulder in a gesture they both recognized as comforting. "Seriously, do you want me to do anything?"

"No, not about Gil. Not yet. But if you can find out why I'm being followed. I can't help feeling there's a connection to Gil's disappearance."

* * *

Three days later, Phil reported. "We tailed your tails for a few days, Rita. They're just a couple of private investigator gumshoes...usually spend their time following cheating wives and husbands for people with too much money." It was Phil trying to sound reassuring.

"But why follow me then?"

"We're going to try to find that out without turning over any hornet's nests." He paused. "Any word from your ex—?"

"Nothing."

* * *

No names were exchanged. It was always like that when MI6—intelligence service, the spies—talked to MI5—counterintelligence, the spy catchers. The two parties of the British Secret Service hated each other, always had, never knew why. But Rennie, at MI6, knew perfectly well that it was Merlin Jones on the MI5 end of the dedicated line. "Your information was correct. Romero was the courier who got the bomb-blast fall-out signatures back to Moscow." He paused. "But they had to terminate him."

"Why?"

"No choice. The standing order." MI5 and MI6 had adopted this rule a decade before. The risk of any disclosure of Enigma was too high. It was a matter of unspoken but continuing amazement in the services that still, seventeen years after the war, the hundreds, the thousands who'd worked at Bletchley Park had never spoken a word. Was it loyalty or the Official Secrets Act? No one in MI5 or MI6 could say. Would any of them have been killed to stop a leak? Of course. It hadn't yet been necessary. But a half-dozen others, outsiders, had gotten close enough to the secret to be silenced. Gil Romero was only the latest. "He knew...or at least said the right... uh, wrong things." The silence bid MI6 continue. "They'd had no idea he knew when they picked him up. Worst of all, he blurted it. Didn't even have to force it out of him. He just spilled the beans first chance he got."

"Well then, right decision for certain." He thought for a moment. "How long ago?"

"Ten days?"

"Why the delay in sending word?"

"Not near secure communications. Spent time disposing of the body completely. Concerned about questions and leaks." Both knew MI6's chief in Australia well enough to give him latitude.

"There's something else...serious little complication. He got the secret off his wife. She knows."

"Why didn't they take her out?"

"That's the complication." There was silence as he waited for more. He knew he'd be told if he had a need to know. "She's not in country. Left for the USA in '60. Works at UN as an interpreter...international civil servant."

"I see." They both knew that the Americans didn't tolerate wet operations on their soil. "UN counts as American jurisdiction, then?"

"'Fraid so. CIA was asked for permission to terminate. It was refused at highest level."

"Why?"

There was an audible sigh on the other end. "Kennedy's people won't sign off on terminations just now. Spooked by the Castro fiasco last year. Worried about leaks. Now they've faced down Khrushchev on the Cuban missiles, trying to preserve their standing in the UN. International civil servant, loud noises if the Secretary General finds out, chilling effect, that sort of rubbish."

"Preposterous. Letting a nobody run round with a secret like that. Just to preserve a reputation they don't even have." He thought for a moment. "Americans have got the same protocol on this sort of leak, don't they?"

"Yes."

"Well, what's the trouble then?"

"My chief doesn't want to tell them why she needs to... go. Tell them why, and then too many people begin asking. Whole pitch queered. " He knew they couldn't let matters stand.

"Can you do it quietly?"

"Not likely to get away with it. If the cousins will find out, it will cost..."

"I see."

"Here's a thought. Let's tell the BfV. The Germans won't have our qualms."

"Good idea."

* * *

Stefan Sajac was clearing out his desk, deciding what to toss and what to put in the briefcase he'd take to his next assignment. He was looking forward to another desk in another corner of the Cologne headquarters. It had to be a more interesting assignment than what he'd dealt with for too long now. *And maybe the boss won't be a lizard trying hard not to molt back into a full-fledged Nazi.* Stefan smiled at his image, letting it loop through his mind's eye a few times.

There was nothing on his boss's desk, nothing but a few scraps of paper, a receipt, a pay-envelope, a creased and dog-eared sporting newspaper, flotsam. His boss was gone.

Otto Schulke's demand for more resources had been denied. He'd been given the choice of continuing at the fixed level of investment in this project or terminating it and moving to another assignment. Stefan had "helped" his boss work up the resentment, suspicion, indignation, to call their bluff. Now he hadn't seen Schulke for days. *A bender? Blind drunk? Will he blame me? It would be worth it.* Stefan knew he could recover from whatever rating Schulke might give him in his next assignment.

He'd slid the central drawer of the desk closed and snapped the clasps on his briefcase when he heard the key in the door. It could only be Schulke. Why had he returned?

The door opened. "Ah, Sajac. Still here? Excellent." Schulke had never looked so...so professional. Clean-shaven, his pate shiny, almost conservatively dressed, a belt tight across his girth, holding it in. He slapped down a file, opened it and, smiling broadly, passed a sheet to Stefan. "Travel orders." He looked like he wanted to hug someone he was so happy.

Stefan gulped. "Where? Why?"

"They found her...in America." In his thrill of incredulity he repeated, "They found her."

"Who?"

"Guildenstern, Trushenko..."

Stefan shook his head. "No. I know whom you're talking about. That's not what I meant. Who found her?" The professional in

Stefan was already alert to the coincidence.

"No idea. Probably the Amis, since she's there, in New York."

"But why would they be looking for her? Do they suspect she knows? I thought it was only us who knew about her..." *You dumb cop, Schulke. You're not thinking things through. This is a counterintelligence problem. Why should she turn up now, just as the* BfV *is forcing us to shut the case down?* It was obviously a question Schulke hadn't raised.

"We're going after her. Both of us." Schulke was aglow. It was more than vindication, it was the relish of the hunter sighting the trail of his prey.

"When do we leave?" They could fly direct from Frankfurt, a short train ride away, Stefan knew. But if they left immediately he wouldn't be able find out how this information was dropped into their laps. Then he thought, *Doesn't matter. You don't have the right to ask anyway.*

"First sailing from Hamburg two days' time." Schulke grimaced. "Winter crossing. Can't be helped."

Stefan was almost irate. "An ocean crossing? We're not going to fly?"

Schulke looked at him with the menace of a drill sergeant addressing a recruit. "I don't fly, Sajac. And you won't either, not so long as you're my subordinate." He began to rummage in his desk. Then he pulled out a small black book. "Got one of these, Sajac? You'll need it." It was the standard BfV expense ledger book.

"Where do I get one?"

Schulke replied but Stefan didn't absorb what he said. He was beginning to calculate. Did the BfV-*Vizepräsident*'s office know Schulke was afraid of flying? Had they approved a crossing instead of a flight? Did they care about the delay? Did someone want to give Schulke's quarry a chance to escape? Could he answer these questions? Almost certainly not. Just asking would cause him some serious professional trouble. Could he work out what was really going on from first principles of intelligence and counter-intelligence trade-craft? He would venture just one question to Schulke. "Look, Boss. Why are we doing it? Can't the Amis do it for us? They're on the spot."

"All I've been told is that they won't. We've got to do it. I have it from the *Vizepräsident* himself. Maybe the Amis are just too squeamish."

Stefan had to risk the question. "Does he know we're going by ship and it'll take a week?"

"No, he doesn't." Schulke sounded cross. "That's operational detail and doesn't concern him." Then he looked at Stefan. "And it'll take ten days in winter."

* * *

"Vladimir Yefimovich." Even standing at attention, General Aleksandr Michaelovitch Sakharovsky felt he could use the name and patronymic today. "I am pleased to report that the mission you approved worked perfectly."

The minister of state security frowned at the familiarity, even from one a generation his elder. He looked quizzically at the older man, the head of his KGB first directorate, the foreign intelligence department. The minister's desk was littered with documents and there was a fountain pen in his hand. He'd evidently been annotating, commenting, approving and reproving. He was too busy for operational detail. When would they learn? "Which mission is that, General Michaelovitch?"

"The plan to give one of our agents to the English so they'd find his wife." He paused. "You will recall giving permission to do so."

"Worked perfectly, you say?" He smiled, put down the pen and in an act of forced patience, folded his hands. "Well, well, there is a first time for everything. What are the chances you succeeded by accident, comrade?" He waited for the sarcasm to sink in and then continued. "As it happens, I do remember the matter. So, you've discovered why the Western security services are so interested in the woman? Please tell me."

Suddenly General Aleksandr Michaelovitch Sakharovsky was perspiring. He wouldn't mop his brow. The minister would certainly notice. "We haven't learned that yet. But the Germans are closing in on her. They're sending agents to New York, where she is working for the UN. It must be very important, whatever she knows. The English have already killed her husband, told the Germans, who immediately took action."

"Why didn't the English do the job?"

"We haven't learned that yet."

"So, your plan worked perfectly? But instead of enabling us to find out why the Western intelligence agencies are interested in this woman, you have made it possible for them to kill her. Very good." He paused to allow his annoyance to sink in. "Carry on, General." Semichastny dismissed the man with a wave of his hand.

Chapter Twenty-Six

Why would the KGB *rezident* in the Soviet consulate be prepared to blow his cover, Phil Morton wondered? It was 8:30 and he had a fine view of a cold gray morning. From the window he could see the steam rising out of tall stacks rising from the dirty crust of snow covering the wharves across the East River. *Too early for diplomacy, or even security*, Morton chortled to himself. He'd arrived early and was sitting in his office, waiting for the man to be announced. The intercom phone buzzed. "Counselor Yakushkin, sir."

"Send him in, please." Involuntarily Morton straightened himself in his chair. He rose as the visitor was ushered in. The man's taut posture, his three-piece brown suit fully buttoned, the narrow tie with the wide knot, hair closely trimmed in gray, the wide shoulders showing musculature above a pronounced paunch, all suggested a military bearing. It forced Morton almost to attention, as though he were reporting for orders. Yakushkin proffered his hand and attempted a smile, something between a grimace and a grin.

Shaking it once firmly, Morton pointed to a pair of seats before his desk. He didn't want to put a desk between them. Relations between international civil servants and the officers of member nations were not to be adversarial.

"Thank you for seeing me so quickly, Mr Morton."

"Your delegation chief said it was urgent." It was extremely unusual for a nation's representative to speak to anyone below the rank of assistant secretary general. For an Eastern European to do so was unheard of.

"We had to get to you quickly, sir."

"Very well. Shoot." Suddenly Yakushkin looked puzzled. *Stupid me*, Morton almost said it out loud. "I mean, go ahead. 'Shoot' is a kind of slang expression. It means speak freely."

"Yes, I know." The voice was gruffer perhaps than Yakushkin wanted it to be. Then he shrugged his wide shoulders, knowing where he had to start and not wanting to start where he had to. "Well, perhaps you know, I am the KGB rezident at the consulate." This fact, that Yakushkin was the KGB's top dog at the UN, was one a few people in New York had guessed at, but no one could know for certain. Making it plain could not be a gaffe. It had to be an announcement that what was coming would be most important. Morton was not quite able to hide the effect of the statement on his face. "And just as I am the KGB rezident in New York, we know you're the head of United Nations security." He waved a hand as if Morton's denial might have been a fly buzzing round his ear on a warm summer day. "It has come to our knowledge that Western security services are a danger, a serious danger, to one of your employees, a person on the interpretation/translation staff."

"Who is that, Mr Yakushkin?"

"Mrs Rita Romero."

"I beg your pardon." Morton needed not to know this name. "Who? Please repeat what you said." Yakushkin repeated it. So, Rita was being followed by Western services? The Brits, the Americans, who? Why? Morton put his hands on his knees palm down and gripped his legs, hoping to suppress the tremor in his fingers. He couldn't stop the flush that rose in his face and the Russian couldn't fail to notice it. *How much can this man read from my face?* Morton could only say, "Go on."

Yakushkin was all business, seeming not to have noticed anything. "It came to our attention first that her husband was taken, almost certainly by British security services about three weeks ago. He was immediately...eliminated."

Phil Morton said nothing. He couldn't add what he knew— that Gil Romero was missing. That would reveal a personal acquaintance with Rita. *Unless you already have revealed it, what with your uncontrolled reaction*, he damned himself. Keeping a tone he hoped would sound disinterested, he asked, "Do your people know why he was...killed?" He said the word. *No euphemisms, Phil.*

"The man Romero was a low level courier for our intelligence services. He'd carried radioactive debris back from English nuclear tests in Australia some years ago, in the '50s. But we don't think they would have killed him for that. We don't know why they did so."

"And now the Brits are after his wife?"

"We don't know whether they are or not. What we know is that the West Germans are. Their BfV is sending two men to New York. We presume they have authority to take her away or worse." The Brits, the Yanks, and now the Germans? Morton rose, went to his desk and reached for the telephone.

Yakushkin followed and placed his hand on Morton's, preventing him from lifting the receiver. "Haste is not necessary, sir." Morton's face asked the question *Why?* Yakushkin went on. "They won't be here for a week at least." He shook his head in mock disbelief. "They are traveling by ship, *TS Hanseatic*, German American Line, docking next Friday evening at the earliest."

"You're certain they're on that crossing?" Yakushkin nodded and Morton relaxed his hold on the receiver. "Any idea why they didn't fly? Seems odd, no?"

"We have no idea. But my belief is that they are afraid of flying. It's not unknown, Mr Morton." It was the most reasonable hypothesis, Morton had to agree. He moved back to the chairs. Both men sat again.

Now, as Morton realized, there was time to decide what to do for Rita. He began to think like the professional he was. *Why are they revealing this intelligence? Why is the life of a low level UN interpreter worth blowing all this cover, handing out all this information, exposing their networks to discovery?* He used Yakushkin's cover title: "Counselor, why are you telling me all this?"

Yakushkin did not reply immediately. Morton realized he was trying to decide how to do so. "Ah, yes, why?" But still he said nothing.

Morton waited a further time for an answer. Hearing none, he spoke. "Can it be a disinterested concern for United Nations staff?" Morton shook his head slowly, emphasizing the sarcasm.

Yakushkin wouldn't be provoked. Blandly, he spoke. "Mrs Romero is still a Soviet citizen. We are prepared to offer her complete protection."

"Soviet citizen?" Gil knew perfectly well that technically she had been one, but he feigned ignorance.

"In 1939 she was a Polish national living in the section absorbed by the Ukrainian SSR. As such she became a Soviet citizen."

Morton suppressed an undiplomatic laugh. "Few Poles who were able to leave the Ukraine have ever sought the protection of the Soviet state, Counselor Yakushkin." He used the title again, to make the gulf between them clear.

"Nevertheless. We are prepared to offer protection, provide a passport and airline tickets, ongoing support."

"You are very interested in keeping this lady from the clutches of Western intelligence services, sir. Any reason you brought the matter to me?"

"I'm very sorry, Mr Morton. We don't want to interfere in your affairs"—he realized it might have been an impolitic word—"but we do know about Mrs Romero and you."

The penny dropped instantly. It wasn't the Brits or the Yanks. It was the Russians who'd been following Rita for weeks now, perhaps even before her ex was killed. *So, Phil, now you know something they don't want you to know. But why do both the Russians and the Brits want her? And now the Germans too? And why didn't the Russians just take her?* Morton needed to get rid of his guest, to talk to Rita, to think out what all this added up to, besides a lethal threat. "So, you're inviting me to communicate your offer to her? Why don't you try talking to her yourself?"

"She will trust the communication if it comes through you, sir. We are reluctant to make contact with her directly."

You mean you don't want anyone to know you're doing it, or find out you're following her either. Why not? There were too many questions here. Phil Morton rose, signaling that the meeting was over.

Yakushkin looked anxious. "We would wish at least to speak with her, with Mrs Romero, to convey our offer personally. Will you permit that? Will you arrange it?"

"I suppose I can do that. Where and when?"

"Not here at the UN or at the consulate. A neutral place."

Morton again understood immediately. Neutrality wasn't the issue. It was clandestinity. The UN buildings were under constant surveillance. So was the Soviet consulate. Evidently the Soviets didn't want anyone to know of their interest in Rita.

The Russian looked hopeful. "Tomorrow?"

"I will arrange it."

"Alone?"

"I'll ask her." *But not before I frisk you*, Morton thought to himself.

Yakushkin rose, pulled at his tight suit coat and offered his hand once more. They pumped hands, this time a little more warmly, and he was gone. Morton turned to his desk and the telephone.

He didn't wait for her answer. There was no preamble from him. "I know who's been following you."

"Yes," was all Rita said. She waited.

"Meet me at Larre's" This was a restaurant on 56th they'd often used, before or after the theater—semicircular banquettes, comfort food for Frenchmen stranded in New York, an unpretentious wine list, inexpensive, but with surly waiters.

Not waiting for a reply, Phil went on. "Don't bother losing your tail. It doesn't matter." Then he hung up, his abruptness burning in his throat. He wanted to tell her everything immediately. He knew he couldn't, not on the phone.

*　*　*

Phil was sitting in the rear, already sipping a rare mid-day martini, when she arrived. He looked like he needed it, ashen, his mouth a sliver tightened by a clenched jaw. The inch-long ash of a forgotten cigarette hung precariously over the lip of the ashtray, its thin line of smoke iridescent in the dim light.

She pecked him on the cheek and sat down. Immediately he covered her hand in a gesture she recognized as his apology for the curt phone call. "It's the Russians. Been following you for a month, or rather having you followed. And before you ask, they don't know why."

"I don't understand. They're following me for no reason at all?"

Phil shook his head. He had begun badly. "I'm sorry. Let me start over. I'll tell you what I know and then we can try to figure out what's going on."

"Very well." A waiter arrived. Rita looked up, then pointed at Phil's martini. "I'll have one of those." Then she lit a cigarette and settled back in the banquette.

Why did she look so damned relaxed, so distractingly good, damn it! He pushed aside the thought, cleared his throat and began. "Yakushkin, head of intelligence at the Soviet UN mission, came to me this morning. Blew his cover completely. We suspected he wasn't just some dogsbody, but there's this tacit agreement to pretend otherwise all sides respect. Anyway, first he told me that"—he had to reach for her hand again, and look her in the eye—"that your ex, Gil, is dead. Killed by the Brits. He was involved in some kind of espionage for the Soviets." There was no more than a flicker in her face. Did she know? "You're not surprised."

"Not entirely." She inhaled deeply and blew the smoke through her nostrils, repeating the word 'dead,' drawing out the one syllable. Rita had somehow been prepared for this news. Now it was confirmed, she had to think. How she was going to tell the boys, and what she would tell them? All the years, Gil had lived a don't ask-don't tell relationship with her, refusing to share what was really going on in his life, refusing to learn what was going on in her head. It had emptied her not just of love or concern, but even interest. Would she need to show mourning to her boys?

Phil gave her no chance to answer the question for herself. Without interruption, he told her the rest.

After a silence, Rita spoke. "So, the Brits killed Gil, but it's the Germans after me?" She paused. "And the Russians don't know why...even though they've been following me for months now, even before Gil was killed. Why?" Phil shrugged. "Let's work it out." She thought for a moment. "How did the Brits find out about Gil? You say it had to be years ago he smuggled radioactive material out of Australia."

"Must have been...what, five, ten years ago the Brits were testing bombs in Australia? There's been no atmospheric testing by anyone but the Russians for years."

"Well then, knowing the Russians, they may have given Gil to the Brits when he was no more use to them. But why?"

Phil suggested, "Because they didn't need him anymore?"

"Maybe, but why would they have killed him immediately? That's the sort of thing we're told Russians do."

Phil was rueful now. "What I just said was wrong, that they gave Gil away because they didn't need him anymore. That's silly. To begin with, he could have revealed things about Soviet operations in Australia. No. They had to have had a good reason to give up even a small asset like Gil. They were sending a message, a signal...but to whom?"

Rita nodded. "So, question, why would the Soviets follow me around for weeks, and then give Gil up to Western intelligence?"

"Because they knew where you were, and Western intelligence didn't. The Russians wanted them to find you—without leaving any fingerprints."

Rita covered his hand with both of hers. "That makes sense." Phil nodded. Then she went on. "But that still leaves bigger questions. Why kill Gil if they were just looking for me?"

"And why are they looking for you anyway?" Phil was struck by Rita's dispassion. "The Russian didn't tell me why."

"Phil, I've got to find out why." She swallowed. "When can I meet with this man, Yakushkin?"

"It's too dangerous, Rita. We've got to get you away, before the Germans get here, and without the Russians knowing." Rita was shaking her head, but Phil went on. "I think I've figured out how."

She was still shaking her head. "No. I...need to know why." She looked at him, her face hardened by the threat. "I've got to know why. I'll never be safe...and now it's the boys, too, if I don't find out!"

"No. It's too dangerous. Look, I'm going to get you documents that will get you out of the country. We've done it before once or twice...asylum for defectors from the East Bloc." He stopped. "And I can take care of the boys, as long as they need me to."

Rita was still shaking her head. "If the Russians want something from me, we've got to figure out what it is. Maybe I can give it to them."

Phil was shaking his head. "It's too dangerous."

"Look, they could have picked me up anytime the last six weeks." She paused. "Even today, coming here, they could have taken me." Then it came to her clearly. "Don't you see, Phil? They knew the Germans were interested in me. But they don't know *why* the Germans are interested. That's why they have staked me out for so long, like some sort of bait."

"I guess it does make sense of the situation," Phil conceded.

"Now they know the Germans are coming to"—she gulped—"for me, they don't have much more time to find out why. That's why they want to talk to me. That's why they're offering 'protection'." The last word was coated with sarcasm. "I've got to find out if they know anything more, anything at all."

"Very well." Phil could almost feel her *sangfroid*. Where was it coming from?

"One more thing, Phil. I have to meet him alone, if I am to learn anything more than he's already told you."

Morton raised his hand in protest, but he could see immediately that she was right.

Chapter Twenty-Seven

Yakushkin and Morton walked quickly down 42nd Street from the UN buildings. Each had reason to wonder if they were being followed, but neither betrayed any interest in the matter to the other. It was blustery but bright as they walked into a steady west wind coming down the broad avenue from the Hudson. It was late enough in the afternoon to wear sunglasses against the glare from a low sun descending in the sky between the high buildings on either side of the street. Morton stopped them at Lexington Avenue, raised his hand for a cab, and then as a bus passed them, obscuring any observation from across the street, he tugged at Yakushkin, and led him down the stairway, through turnstiles into which he dropped tokens, and into a warren of subway corridors. There were trains in several directions to choose from, at least six by Morton's calculation.

The stairs descended to the deepest line, the Independent or IND trains. These plied a route between Times Square and obscure stations in the hinterlands of Queens, ones that might not be familiar even to most New Yorkers. There they stood waiting for a Queens-bound train, which arrived at the same moment as one coming in from Queens, headed to Times Square. Just before the latter's doors closed, Morton pulled the Russian across the platform and into it. Anyone following would have to be very nimble indeed to stay with them. Morton detected no one. At Times Square there was another warren of corridors and stairways up to the IRT running north and south on Broadway. There they waited, well hidden in what was now the rush hour crowd on the northbound platform, again until an express and a local train came in together. There Morton moved to the local train and Yakushkin followed. Only two stops later they came to Columbus Circle.

As they descended once more, Morton turned to the Russian.

"Do you know the tune? You take the A Train to get to Sugar Hill way up in Harlem?" At the bottom of the stair, the platform was largely Negroes, a few Puerto Ricans among them and almost no one who'd call themselves 'white'. A Russian or even a New York private detective would be easy to identify in this crowd. Despite the rush hour they had to stand a long while waiting for the 8th Avenue express. Long enough to learn if they were being followed by anyone at all.

From here on 59th Street the A train ran seventy-five blocks without stopping, the longest run in Manhattan, sweeping past seven local stations to arrive at 125th Street and Lenox Avenue, at the epicenter of Negro America.

Together Morton and Yakushkin ascended to the street. No other Caucasian was visible moving up the stair, or behind them for that matter. Now at last the Russian grew impatient. "How much further, Mr Morton?"

"Just a short walk." He wanted to reassure. "We'll meet Mrs Romero on St Nicholas Terrace, above the park. Do you know it?"

Already visibly out of his element, Yakushkin grimaced with distaste. "Not at all." By now they were climbing through short narrow streets, six-story walkup tenements on each side, fire escapes draped with laundry flapping in the cold twilight wind. Suddenly there was an open space to their right, a city park. They continued until shortness of breath made Yakushkin pause, and ask again plaintively, "How much farther?" Then, before Morton could answer, he added, "This was not necessary. None of my people is following."

"We'll meet Mrs Romero in front of that high school up there." He pointed at a square, mock gothic building. It was her son Thomas' school.

* * *

The three figures stood facing one another in silence for a moment. Looking from one face to the other Phil spoke. "May I frisk you, Mr Yakushkin?"

"If you think you are in a Hollywood movie. Go ahead." He raised his arms. "But as we could have taken Mrs Romero any time in the last month or so, there isn't any reason for you to worry now."

Morton looked sheepish, shrugged and spoke. "Well, I'll leave you both to it..." His glance towards Rita expressed the thought, *If I must...*, then he turned and walked west downhill on the long blocks towards Broadway.

"Shall we walk along the park, Mr Yakushkin?" She'd remembered his name and though she couldn't see why, she felt that she was in control. They wanted something from her. Something that they didn't think they could get by force. What was it? Rita would be listening for hints or slips, some new piece of information that might help. She knew he'd be guarded in the presence of Phil, that he'd underestimate a woman, that he might not repeat exactly what he'd said to Morton the day before. They began to walk along the park.

"How much time do you think I will have before the Germans arrive?"

"Four or five days, perhaps a few days more."

"And you wish to provide me with protection? Here?"

"The Soviet government will welcome you in Russia. There you will be beyond the reach of the Fascist German authorities."

"So Mr Morton told me." She turned to the man, put a question — "Why did you want to meet now?" — and resumed walking.

"I was hoping you could tell me something about why the Germans are coming for you, something that could help us protect you."

"But I don't have the slightest idea." As she spoke, an unvoiced thought formed itself: *But your people must have some idea, or you wouldn't have had me followed for so long.* "My work at the UN is perfectly above board. Nothing crosses my desk that isn't public information."

He shook his head. "It can't have anything to do with your work, Mrs Romero."

He was going to tell her something now, something new, Rita could sense it. Casually she replied, "It can't have? Why not?"

"Because the Germans have been looking for you since long before you came to New York."

"And how do you know this?"

Yakushkin shrugged and did not immediately reply. Then he spoke again. "We don't think the Brits killed your ex-husband because he was working for us." Now he stopped and turned towards her. "It must have had something to do with you, Mrs Romero. If we can figure this out, it may help you a great deal."

Help me? Poker face, Rita! There was nothing she could tell him, no bait or lure to make him reveal anything. "Perhaps if you could tell me how long the Germans have been looking for me, or how they found me. That might help."

"All I have been told is that finding you has been something of an obsession for one particular officer in the West German BfV—that's their counterintelligence department—for years." It was Yakushkin's turn to show a poker face. "I don't know how they finally found you, unless the Brits shared what they knew about your ex—."

Because your lot gave them Gil so they could find me! Rita was on the point of blurting it out. "Do your people know anything about this German officer?"

"De-Nazified policeman from Mannheim, middle fifties. I don't have the name but I can find it."

Mannheim, a few kilometers from Heidelberg, where Rita had spent the last years of the war...Mannheim, where she'd meet her friend Dani on a rare afternoon or evening...Mannheim, where they'd been arrested by the Gestapo, in the winter of '44, and released…And then everything fell into place. The pieces of the jigsaw she was trying to piece together all sorted themselves into a pattern that interlocked perfectly…Now, suddenly, she understood. It had only required her to find one little piece to assemble all the others into the right picture. She didn't need to ask Yakushkin any more questions. Now she knew everything. She knew she was in mortal danger, from the Germans and from the Russians. The Germans already knew, or at least suspected strongly. And if the Russians had as much access to the German service—what did Yakushkin call it, the BfV?—then they knew or would soon know as well.

She needed to break off this conversation before it went any further. But she needed to do it without arousing suspicion that she now knew what it was about her that so interested the BfV and the KGB. *Change the subject…but not too abruptly.* "If my ex, Gil, was working for you, would that have come to the attention of the Germans? Would this German policeman think, perhaps, that I am working for you too? And try to make a name for himself somehow by finding out?"

The Russian replied, "I doubt it." Had she distracted him, Rita wondered? He went on. "No, the Germans didn't learn anything about your husband, ex-husband, until"—he paused, and Rita silently finished his sentence, *until you told them about him*—"until after he was dead. The Brits almost certainly would have told the Americans and the West Germans about the Australian business. They all work pretty closely together." The last observation was surely as close as Yakushkin would come to admitting it was the KGB who put the Brits on to Gil. But, given what she now knew, it was enough to confirm Rita's worst fears. Somehow the Russians suspected she knew something big, suspected the Germans wanted to know what it was, expected to learn what it was and hadn't. That was the only reason she was still alive.

Again Rita stopped, looked at Yakushkin hard, and spoke. "There is only one secret I know." He raised his eyebrows, waiting. "It has nothing to do with Russia or the British, or the UN. It's about an Australian politician, someone who is now in the government in Canberra, a junior minister in the foreign office, maybe responsible for their espionage service." Still no response from the Russian. "What I know about him could destroy him." She stopped. Would Yakushkin ask for it? Would it distract him sufficiently? Could he even convince himself it was relevant?

Yakushkin raised his eyebrow. "Well?"

"It's a man named Mallory, Robert Mallory. He's a Country Party member of the Australian parliament, and undersecretary at External Affairs—their foreign ministry."

"And what do you know about this man?" There was little interest in Yakushkin's tone.

"He's probably a homosexual, and so can be blackmailed, and his academic credentials are quite fraudulent. Exposure would force him out of office."

"This is very interesting, Mrs Romero, but it doesn't explain why the West Germans might be interested in you...interested enough to want to kill you."

It's not working. Think of something, anything. "He was a prisoner of war in Germany, for a long time. Maybe he's a Nazi-sympathizer?" She shrugged. "That's all I know that could be of interest to anyone..." Her voice tailed off in resignation.

"I am sorry, Mrs Romero. Just walking along and talking like this is not going to help us. We need to sit down somewhere, quiet, and work back through your past until we find something that explains why the Germans are targeting you."

"What do you mean?" She tried to sound sincerely quizzical, though Rita knew exactly what Yakushkin was thinking and exactly what he was looking for. He was right and she couldn't acknowledge it, not for a moment and not even slightly.

"It's like this. You know something, or they think you know something. But you don't know that you know it. You don't realize its significance. They do. If we can debrief you—ask you enough questions—we may be able to figure it out." He tried to smile a reassurance. "...And save you." The look failed completely and he knew it. "Will you come with me now? I have an apartment we can use." He put a hand to her arm, pressing more strongly than he meant to.

"Mr Yakushkin." As Rita spoke, she tried to remove his hand. "My friend, Mr Morton, is waiting for me at a café down on 135th Street and Broadway." She gestured down towards the Hudson and looked at her wristwatch. "If I am not there in ten minutes, he will call the New York police, and the American FBI." She paused. "Look, you said we have a few days till the Germans arrive. Let's arrange another meeting, where we can do what you suggest."

Yakushkin released her. "Very well. Tomorrow at the latest. Have Mr Morton call me."

Chapter Twenty-Eight

The fall evening was already dark. It would be at least ten minutes' walk down from Saint Nicholas Terrace to Broadway. A lifetime, in her heels, listening as they clicked one after the other on the downward sloping pavement. Needing to show confidence, assurance, the bearing of someone who couldn't be touched, she had turned and began to stride down the hill. But behind the bravura the fear was rising into her chest. She had a secret, had it for years, without knowing its importance. And now suddenly she'd been shown how it could destroy her. The thought came, *This is what killed Gil. He was always so smart. He must have figured things out.* Rita knew her husband well enough. He would have confessed the knowledge the moment the British started on him. *Yes, and that's why they eliminated him the moment they realized he knew. It must be.*

A hundred paces down the street, Rita froze. *If you tell Phil, he'll be in the same danger as you, the same danger Gil was in.* She gulped. Anyone suspected of knowing what she knew would forfeit his life, like Gil. Phil and probably her boys' lives, too, were already at fatal risk. Telling Phil was inoculating him with a deadly bacillus. Not telling probably wouldn't work either. They'd assume he knew, that he was infected, too, just because he was helping her, protecting her. *Either way, you have to tell him.* She'd decided by the time she came in sight of the small Puerto Rican café where they'd arranged to meet.

Coming out of the night, it was so bright, Rita had to squint. The chrome beneath the counter gleamed. The wide edges of the bar stools were fish-eye mirrors, reflecting the colorful signs framing the ceiling like a frieze. Eyes adjusting, she found Phil sitting at the back end of the counter, his body angled towards the door. *Was he watching for danger?* There was a large mug before him. As she sat he looked at the woman behind the counter, pointed to his cup and to Rita. The woman nodded. Soon a second cup steamed before her.

As though he were reading her mind, Phil began. "Rita, I called the boys at your apartment. Told them to head over to my place, have dinner with my daughter." Then he looked left and right. "Look, it's safe to talk. I don't think anyone here speaks English, not well enough to follow."

"Are you sure? It's critical." She waited till he nodded before continuing. "Phil, I understand everything now. We're in great danger, me, you, the boys..." She paused. Would he tell her to stop, to wait till they were completely alone? He said nothing. "Something Yakushkin said made me realize what this is all about." She took the cigarettes from her purse, offered him one, then saw Phil was already smoking. He lit hers and she began again. "Soon after the war began I was told something, by someone. He was certain the Germans would lose the war. Told me why he knew. Said I could survive till they lost. He got me the documents I needed to escape the ghetto in Karpathyn." Phil waited. "What he told me was that the Poles had broken the German secret military code, and that they had gotten it to the Brits before they were defeated by the Germans."

"Did you believe him?"

"I didn't know what to think. He could have made up a dozen stories. Why that one? He'd been a mathematician before the war and he said he knew the people who did it."

"What happened to him?"

"Killed fighting with the partisans." Rita didn't name him to Phil, but she remembered everything about Erich. How could she avoid it, every time she thought of the son she'd secretly named for him? Now Rita couldn't be distracted. "Anyway, he said he was sure the secret would enable the Allies to win the war." Phil nodded. "But once the war ended, you'd imagine the secret would have come out, if there was a secret. Think about it, the atom bomb didn't remain a secret, the V-2 rocket didn't.

So many secrets about the war came out. But there was nothing about breaking the German codes."

"So?"

"Well, when no one revealed it, I decided he'd just been wrong about 'the secret'." She looked at him. "But what if I was mistaken? What if the Allies were reading German code, but the Russians never found out they were?"

Phil saw what she was driving at immediately. "They took every bit of technology from the Germans they could. So did our side—rockets, jets, snorkel submarines! But if the Soviets thought the German codes were unbreakable, they'd start using them." He smiled ruefully. "That means the Brits, the Americans, maybe even the Germans now, could have been reading Russian radio traffic all this time since '45. And the Russians wouldn't know it." It would, Phil also realized, explain a lot about the repeated tactical success of Western strategy against the Soviets in the Cold War.

Rita broke into these thoughts. "If they are still using the German code, then anyone who knows it was broken is in terrible danger. The Brits must have killed my husband just for knowing. Afraid he might tell the Russians he was working for."

"I see that. But that doesn't explain why the Germans are looking for you?"

"Because they've been looking for me since 1942. They must have learned about Erich, what he knew, and who he could have told. He lived with me for almost a year in the ghetto, in the same flat, the same room, on the same **mattress** ." Phil looked at her. "No, it wasn't like that." She paused. "There was only one mattress."

"Rita, I don't get it. If the Western intelligence agencies are looking for you, why would Russians lead them to you?"

"That's it! The Russians don't know. They don't have the slightest idea what this is about. If they did, they'd just stop using the German codes. They wouldn't come after me at all.

Not worth their time."

"Now you've lost me, Rita." He stubbed out the cigarette in a gesture of annoyance.

"Look, either the Russians or the East Germans have penetrated the BfV, the West German security service. They found out the West Germans have been looking for me, maybe for years. But they don't know why. That secret they haven't stumbled on to yet, for some reason. Perhaps it's too closely guarded. But they must have been asking themselves why are the Germans looking for me. "

"So, they got tired of waiting for the West Germans to find you and decided to help?" Phil shook his head. "Too complicated, Rita."

"Yakushkin clearly doesn't know why the Germans are after me. But he does know whom they've sent...to kill me now. It's the same man who arrested me in Mannheim in December of 1944. I can remember what that Nazi said, to this day. He had a sheaf of documents about me that went all the way up to the RSHA." Phil frowned. Rita clarified. "The Reich Main Security Headquarters. They'd been looking for me for more than two years. That's what he told his boss. At that moment I decided Erich had to have been telling me the truth. I was so scared I'd spill Erich's secret I looked for a way of killing myself then and there."

"What happened? How'd you escape?"

"I didn't. They just let me go. The man in charge, the senior policeman in the office, just told the one who arrested me, who'd put the paperwork together, to let me go. In fact his boss drove me home that night. He knew the Germans were going to lose. The US Army was only a 100 kilometers away. Everyone thought they'd be in Germany by Christmas, things were moving so fast. The other man, who had arrested me, he was livid. But the boss said they couldn't afford to be arresting Jews this late in the war if they wanted to survive themselves."

There was still disbelief in Phil's voice. "But that was, what? Eighteen years ago. Are you telling me they've been looking for you all this time? You're not that important, Rita."

"No, of course not." She nodded in agreement. "But suppose right up to the end of the war the Gestapo was looking for anybody who might have known Erich, because they suspected he might have told them about the code. And the Germans kept records. You know how meticulous they are." She stopped. "Now bear with me, last link in the chain." Phil nodded. "What if this Nazi cop who arrested me got himself de-Nazified and only then, a few years ago, was told the Western intelligence services had broken the German code during the war, and had been listening to Russian military messages ever since they adopted it."

"He'd start to move heaven and earth to find you," Phil said. "He'd get the credit for stopping a huge threat to western intelligence."

"Yes, and if he was a Nazi, he'd still be after the Jewess who got away, no matter how long it took."

They fell silent, each seeking evidence or argument against this complex construction of surmises. Phil spoke first. "Whatever reason Yakushkin had for seeing me, it had to be overwhelmingly important for him to just blow his cover completely like that. And then when he practically admitted they'd given your ex away to the British, that raised the stakes." He paused. "But here's the thing. Yakushkin said your ex was 'immediately eliminated.' The Brits wouldn't have killed Gil on the spot, without getting prior approval from London…unless there was some protocol in place, some rule about who was to be eliminated immediately." He glanced at her. "Your story would certainly explain why they killed Gil the moment he told them what he knew." Then he bit his lip. "And it means you're in extraordinary danger, and not just from the Germans."

"So are you, if our relationship comes out."

"What about the boys?" Before she could answer Phil rose.

Chapter Twenty-Eight

"Rita, we can't wait. And we'll have to sort things out on the fly."
There was a firmness in his voice she'd never heard. He put his
hand beneath her arm, making her rise.

Rita resisted. "Where are we going?"

"To my office. We're going to get you some travel documents
and get you out of here before the Germans come, before the
Russians try to debrief you again."

Her voice was quiet but strident. "Phil, what about my boys?"

His reply was ready. "They'll be with me. I've got ways to
protect them."

Chapter Twenty-Nine

They were standing at the conference table in Phil's office, papers spread out before them. An electric typewriter Phil had rolled from the side of his desk was humming on its steel support next to the table. "The first thing we'll need is a name, and then an identity to go with it. Any ideas, any preferences?"

"I went through that once before, Phil. In the war." He nodded knowingly, but Rita continued. "It's got to be something that'll sound natural when I say it."

Phil brightened. "What name did you use in the war?"

"Trushenko, Rita Trushenko..." She paused. "But that's the last name I could use now. It's a name I had when I was arrested, back in '44. They've got that name!" Rita thought for a moment. Then her sudden smile surprised Phil. Before he could say anything, she began. "Look, Phil, my name isn't Romero at all. The boys' father and I never married. My name is Feuerstahl. And the Germans have no record of it at all. In the Karpathyn ghetto I was Guildenstern—my husband's name." She wanted that name again, Feuerstahl, the one she'd been able to take back for the brief time after the war, before the boys were born. It had been her passport to a certain kind of freedom.

"OK." He smiled and sat down at the typewriter. "Makes things easy. Hand me the passport." It was a booklet covered in the light blue of the United Nations. "You're...Rita Feuerstahl, UN interpreter/translator, transferred from headquarters New York to UN Europe, in Geneva. Spell the name for me." He began to type out the details onto the passport, smiling at the neatness of it. "Let's see, what's next? Hand me that letterhead from the Interpretation division."

Rita looked at the light blue cover of the passport, then slowly laid it on the table. "Look, Phil, thanks...but this isn't going to work. Even if I could get out of New York on a UN passport without anyone noticing, how long can I last in Geneva before the Germans, the Russians find me again? A week, two weeks?"

Phil smiled. "Thought that through already. All I think you really need is a week or ten days. We'll just have to hope you've got that much time."

Rita looked at him quizzically. "Explain, please."

"It'll take a week or so, but I am going to get you a Canadian passport, in my wife's name." Morton frowned briefly, thinking about her death. Then he brightened. "You'll have to age five years, I'm afraid." Rita laughed at the irony but did not explain that she had taken five years from her age in her first false identity, five years she'd never given back. "Somebody from the embassy in Berne will get that passport to you in Geneva. Then it's only a question of where we go."

"We?" She looked at him. "Phil, what was it Humphrey Bogart said to that French police captain in *Casablanca*? 'Louie, I think this is the beginning of a beautiful friendship'?" They'd seen the movie just a few weeks before at a ratty little theater tucked into a side street off Broadway on the Upper West Side.

He covered her hand with his. "My secondment here ends in six months. When we met I asked for a renewal. But now I think I'll make other plans. Where would you like to live? I think I can probably have my pick of embassies anywhere Canada's got one."

"Anyplace but Argentina." She laughed. "Too many Nazis." Then she leaned over and let Phil hug her close and for a long time.

* * *

Together they worked for an hour and a half, creating a collection of documents that described a German lady of a certain age, single, fluent in three of the official languages, seconded from New York to Geneva at the request of the Secretary General's office. It was nearly ten in the evening when they finished. "I'll call security in Geneva when they open in the morning. Then I'll have travel orders and plane tickets for you in the morning." She nodded. "You'll fly out tomorrow late afternoon. I'll hold off the Russians till your flight leaves."

"What about the boys, Phil?"

"They'll stay with me till things are settled."

"That could be a long time." *Could it be forever?* The look on her face conveyed the fear voicing itself in her thoughts.

"It doesn't matter," he said. "And I'm about the only one in a position to protect them, anyway. Certainly you're not." *Does she understand?* "Anyone who threatens them to find you will have to deal with me. And I've got some resources."

Rita sat before Phil, silent for a long time, her eyes closed. He could not know the memory that had flooded unbidden into her mind, the sharp pain of losing her first child, twice. Now she would lose two more. The new feeling of loss resolved itself into a thought. *I won't do it.* "Phil, this isn't going to work. I can't leave. I can't give up the boys." To herself she silently said, *I did that once before.* The emptiness she'd felt before was too much to experience anything like it again. She'd never told him, or anyone, about seeing her boy that day in the park in Salzburg back in '47. How had it haunted her, the memory suddenly intruding, completely at random, day or night, months, seasons, even years apart, with force undiminished by the years? She wouldn't suffer it again. She had to convince him, and convince herself, it was futile. "Besides, how long will it take the Russians, or the Germans for that matter, to get back on my trail? A week, two weeks?"

"I don't know, Rita. If you don't leave now, you will give your boys up...for certain." He paused. "Give them up with your life." He let the thought take hold of her and then drummed it in. "What's more, not going—or taking them with you, even if you could—you'll put them at greater risk...if anyone ever suspects they know what you do." He sighed. "I don't know how long a lead this will give you. But it's the only chance you've got."

Suddenly she saw the difference between Salzburg and now, terrible in its stark outlines. Then she'd given up her child so he might have a life with the mother he knew. Now she would have to give up two more children so that she might someday return to have a life with them. There was no obvious return route, back to her boys. But she would have to be selfish, have to survive, if she was ever to have them in her life, if she was ever to find a way back. The first time, giving up Stefan, it had been an act of selfishness, too, despite its torture. What she had wanted then, most of all, for herself, was that her child be happy, and she knew what reclaiming him would do to him. This time it was selfish love of her boys making her escape. *Why can't my life just be ordinary, commonplace, boringly normal? Why am I fated to this endless nightmare, forever in the wrong place at the wrong time? It can't be just because I have the stamina for it.* Rita recognized these questions. They had preoccupied her, vexed her, daunted her throughout the years in hiding, and she'd answered them then. *Can you remember the answers still?* "Of course, you're right, Phil." She could think it, but she could not yet feel it.

* * *

They choreographed the next day carefully. Phil would call Yakushkin to set up her rendezvous for the evening, after her flight had already left Idlewild. Would the Russian call off the gumshoes he had following her? They had to assume he wouldn't. Yakushkin might even substitute his own people. So everything had to look entirely normal. She'd have to send the boys off to school as though it were simply another day. It had to look like that to them, too, Phil warned her. "You'll leave for work as usual. Don't even give the boys an extra hug at the subway. Assume the Russians will be watching. Just tell them to go to my place after school."

Rita shook her head. "No. That would be suspicious. If they come home, it will be a signal they're expecting me. I'll call them from the airport then, and tell them to go to your place."

"Good idea. If the Russians are following you and lose the tail, they'll go back to your place. If they follow the boys to my apartment, they'll assume you're there too."

* * *

Eric, Tom and their mother all left home together, the boys' books and notebooks bound by the elastic straps that were the fashion that year. Rita's briefcase carried only the documents she'd need to board the flight and present to the UN Geneva office. She'd managed to steel herself to a sort of mute normality with the boys as the local train rumbled its way down the five stops to 42nd Street. There they would have to separate. She would leave the subway to walk to the East River and the UN. Tom would take the shuttle across to Times Square and then north. Eric would shift to the express down to Union Square. Rita felt the dread of that moment rising in her. *Think about the alternative!* She bit her tongue, grateful that in the rush hour crush, standing so close, no one looked anyone else in the face. On the platform she tried to draw each under an arm to hug them both and saw for the first time that they'd grown beyond the reach of her arms. *Big enough, old enough, to survive without me?* She gave each a hug in turn, from which both struggled in a mannish show of independence and a frown as if to say 'I'm too old for this sort of thing.' An express train pulled in. Eric smiled and waved briefly as he entered. Tom looked at his watch and ran up the stairs, glanced back towards his mother as he reached the top, and then he, too, was gone. *Forever?* Rita found a wooden bench, folded herself into it and began to sob. After a moment the admonitory voice came into her head. *And what if someone is following you?* She took a tissue from her pocket and made as if to sneeze. Would it fool anyone?

A day of routine, translating documents, reports, letters, stretched out endlessly. There would be no word from Phil, no contact, nothing to punctuate the quotidian order. At lunch she would go to the canteen with the usual noonday company, and in the afternoon share a tea break, drinking coffee with her fellow interpreters, switching languages indifferently as each joined or parted from the brief conversations. There would be an evening session of the Security Council, for which a few of them would be needed. Only when Rita's voice was missed in simultaneous translation did anyone begin to wonder why she wasn't in the booths above the council chamber. But by that time she had slipped away.

Following a map Phil had drawn from memory the night before, she had found her way down to basements and sub-basements in the Secretariat building she'd no idea existed. There she moved through a warren of gray-walled corridors, and out a series of white, unmarked, unnumbered doors she'd had to carefully count off. Then suddenly a fire door closed behind her with a lock, and she was walking down a dark, unheated, rough-hewn tunnel, along the middle of which a rivulet of muddy water flowed visibly enough to confirm that she was walking slightly downhill. After a dozen yards the tunnel's mouth began to grow in her view, a black arch around ambient light off street lamps filtered by rain. Rita came out of the tunnel at 39th Street and the East River. She could see the East River Drive to her left and in the other direction the pre-war Tudor City apartment on First Avenue. She was in the right place. Two double headlamps came on and a checker cab pulled up. Phil opened the door and she climbed in.

* * *

They were at Idlewild in the new TWA terminal, waiting at the gate for the 707 to Geneva. Silent all the way from Manhattan, Phil and Rita had been too tense to note the newness of the structure as their cab drove up to the gleaming white buttresses holding down the flying saucer terminal. The dramatic brightness of the inverted bowl-roof reflected Hollywood klieg lights into the winter night, making the sky entirely starless. Rita noticed the garish glare. It reminded her of how the blinding glow above the Karpathyn ghetto had obliterated the stars on a night almost twenty years before, the night she'd also escaped her fate.

Sitting side by side, Rita and Phil watched the clocks facing them on the departure lounge wall, each second hand sweeping in synchrony across a different hour—New York in the center with San Francisco to the left and London to the right. The boys would be home by now. She was making herself wait for the boarding announcement before calling to speak to them one more time, to tell them to go to Phil's apartment. Meanwhile Phil was slouched in his seat, hat over his eyes but underneath it scanning faces and watching men come and go from the lounge.

The voice came over the loudspeakers. "TWA flight 800 departing for Geneva 7:30 PM, boarding commenced at gate 16."

Rita looked at Phil, who nodded. She rose and fished in her purse for a quarter. The call from Queens to Manhattan would cost more than the usual ten cents, she knew. The phone rang three times before anyone picked it up. "Hello, Romero residence." It was Tom.

"Ah, Tom, put your brother on the extension in the bedroom, I have to talk to you both."

There was impatience in his voice as he called out, "Eric, get on the other phone. It's Mom." Then into the phone, "Make it quick, Mom, we're watching *The Untouchables*."

The sound of another handset lifting from its cradle came. It was her other boy. "Aw, Mom, you always call at the worst time."

Rita knew she couldn't stop to admonish. "Listen very

carefully, both of you. I'm on my way back to Australia. Something has happened...to your father."

After a silence, both boys spoke. "What...happened?"

Rita gulped. "I don't know. No one has heard from him for days. The police have asked me to come back. I'm not sure why." She let them absorb her words. Then she went on. "I don't know how long I'll be gone. Phil Morton will take care of you. You're to pack a week's worth of clothes and go over to his house right away. Alice will be expecting you." Again she stopped. There was no sound on the line. "Boys, do you hear me?"

The voices came back strong. "Yes. Of course." They hadn't asked about their father at all, taking her word there was nothing more to tell them. Rita's relief was tinged. Then Eric spoke. "Where are you, Mom?"

Rita ignored the question. "Do you understand, both of you?" *You don't, you can't, I can't let you.* She stabbed a fingernail into her palm, the pain distracting her enough to go on. "You're to stay with Philip Morton. I may be away some time." Then she blurted, "But you're not to worry. Everything will be alright."

It was the wrong thing to say. Suddenly, her sons were taking her seriously. "What do you mean?" came Tom's urgent voice as Eric repeated plaintively, "Where are you?"

"On the way to Sydney. I'll call, I promise, as soon as I know anything." Rita commanded herself, *You're not to be drawn out, just from a desire to hear their voices a minute longer.* The more they asked, the more they would know. It could endanger her...and them. The loudspeaker began again, "Final call TWA flight..." They couldn't be allowed to hear the number. They'd be smart enough to figure it out. She covered the receiver. When the voice ceased, she spoke. "I've got to go boys...be good." Firmly she cradled the receiver at the side of the pay phone, turned and, refusing to cry, joined Phil holding her place in the embarkation line. They waited to the last minute to embrace. Then, wordlessly, he walked away.

* * *

Rita turned from her reflection in the blackness of the fuselage window, looked at the martini glass on the tray table, already warm, watching the condensation droplets glide down the outside towards the stem, wishing she'd asked for smoking and a blanket. It would be ten hours to Geneva in the roar of a Boeing 707. She'd arrive sleepless, climb down the stair onto the tarmac on a morning as wintery as the evening chill she'd left, then she'd climb up the stairs into the terminal. The inner dialogue repeated itself. *You need to remember, Rita, you've been through worse. Yes, but I was twenty then. No, twenty-five, don't tell yourself the lie about your age everyone else seems to believe. You're twenty years older now. Can you do this all over again?* She sipped the dry martini. *No choice, Rita. And you're a lot smarter now.* She was convincing herself. It was the only way she'd ever stand a chance of seeing her boys again, though when and where, and how, she wouldn't even think about.

* * *

Rita was shaken awake by a stewardess in a blue serge suit, looking fresh and bright. "This is Geneva." She smiled. "We let you sleep through breakfast"—she looked at her clipboard— "Miss Feuerstahl."

Rita rose and looked about her at the almost empty plane. *Well, you've made it this far.*

Passing through passport control, she headed for the baggage hall and customs. Only then did she remember she had no bag; she had nothing but the briefcase in her hand. It was a new life, another one. *How many lives have you lived? Three, four?* In the taxi from the airport, she kept losing count.

Part V

End Game

Chapter Thirty

Four days after Rita landed in Geneva the Norddeutscher Lloyd liner *Bremen* docked at Pier 88 on the Hudson. At 22 knots plowing through a winter storm, it had arrived 24 hours early. Disembarking was still a matter of half a day. Other German government officials on board were armed with expedited landing rights, and whisked through customs into the arms of the local consular officials. Schulke and Sajac couldn't do anything like that without breaking a deep cover they would need to remain untraceable. Stefan was anxious about carrying the small Walther pistols Schulke had required them to bring along, but no one searched them. Indeed, none of the officials dockside even looked up into their faces as they quickly processed their papers and stamped their virgin passports.

The passports and everything else they carried bore cover names. "Jewish-sounding names" Schulke had complained, before Stefan could point out that most people speaking German in New York would probably be Jewish. Bags chalked by customs, passports stamped, they found themselves in a cold wind under a gray sky, beneath an elevated highway, facing a broad cobblestoned boulevard on which large cars were passing at speed. Schulke pointed to a VW beetle moving past as fast as the behemoth vehicles surrounding it. Both smiled at this slightly comforting sign of home. Schulke shouted over the din. "Well, Sajac, you've got the language. Get us a cab."

Stefan looked each way and found the taxi rank behind him a dozen meters away. By the time he'd raised his hand, a large yellow checker pulled up. The driver didn't get out, but indicated the trunk, which slowly sprung open. Each man dropped his bag into the large space and then both clambering over the jump seats they hadn't expected as they opened the doors on each side. The cabbie still said nothing, so Stefan leaned forward.

"Hotel Commodore…42nd and Lex—"

"I know where it is, buddy," the cab driver interrupted, without turning around. The car's sudden acceleration sent both their heads back on the rear deck behind the seats. Stefan could see the cabbie smiling. Both looked at the driver's hack-license, displayed on the sun visor about the windscreen. *Weinstein, Abe.* Both passengers immediately understood and by mutual agreement refrained from speaking.

The cab turned onto 42nd Street. Within blocks they were surrounded by movie theater marquees, their lights bright enough to compete with the midday glare. Suddenly the amusements gave way to the quiet dignity of a vast marble palace, whose large lions at its entryway on a broad avenue both men studied as the cab waited through a light. Then the cab moved off. Soon it came to a halt again, just beyond an overpass at what had to be a vast railway station, from its look and the crowds surging in and out. The trunk of the cab rose up behind them and the driver turned with a palm up. They could see the fare on the meter but he repeated it with a glare of evident hatred. Schulke put a two-dollar bill into his hand. "Receipt please." Stefan smiled. This *would* be the one English sentence Schulke knew.

The man looked at the bill and back to Schulke, almost startled. "Where'd you get that, kraut?"

Stefan understood the words, but not why anyone would seek the provenance of a piece of US currency. He leaned forward and asked, "Is it not right?"

The man shrugged and began looking for a receipt pad. He muttered to himself, "No one's asked me for a receipt in a month."

Schulke waited patiently as the cabby wrote ponderously with a pencil stub. Stefan got out of the cab and began manhandling their bags on to the curb.

They wedged themselves into successive compartments of a revolving door and moved across a carpet thick enough to muffle every footfall. Within moments, and with no need to present passports or fill out police forms, the two men were hurtling up to the 16th floor beside a young, liveried, Negro elevator operator. He was chewing gum and entirely focused on making his car come to a perfect alignment with each floor at which it had to stop.

Once in their room, Schulke dropped his case and without doffing his hat or winter coat went to the night table between their twin beds and pulled out a very fat telephone book. He opened it and began leafing through the pages. "Ja so..." There it was, in plain sight on page 510 of the Manhattan directory, the one and only entry for Rita Romero: 49 East 84th, MU9-6865. He scribbled the address on a notepad by the phone on the table and handed it to Stefan. "Sajac. You'll go stake out the place, now. I'll relieve you"—he looked at his watch—"in four hours, at 18:00."

Coming out of the revolving door, Stefan was about to hail a cab. Then he stopped. Would he risk missing her if he walked? Middle of the day, probably at work in the UN. He didn't think he'd miss her. Turning left toward the East River, he walked down to the end of the block, complimented himself on his memory of the map and sense of direction, then headed up Lexington Avenue. It was as close to tourism as he could expect to get. Stefan was glad he'd been sent off immediately. Seven days in a stateroom with Schulke had taught him much more about the man than he'd ever cared to know, confirmed the stereotype, and added to his etching from Grosz. Stefan needed to get away, even for just a few hours on a chilly winter's day.

Long strides took him across short blocks. Every ten streets or so the pavement gave way to strips of steel mesh over dark spaces, from which rose warm breezes he didn't expect, along with the loud rumbles of underground trains. Stores were doing brisk business. Many sported opened canopies shading steel mesh grates folded back from shop windows. They were crowded with women's clothes, costume jewelry, or European salamis. There were flags, far more than one would see on a German street. Men, mainly black and swarthy Hispanics were swiveling handcarts over pavements or moving pushcarts along the curbs. Women pulled wire mesh shopping carts out of stores, followed by children, the boys in caps with earflaps and the girls in flamboyantly colored tights under short winter coats. He counted the intersections with covered stairways leading down to subway stations. At each such stairway, the same combination of coffee shop, newsstand and telephone bank was repeated. The few men on Lexington who looked anything like him were wearing hats and overcoats. Stefan wore neither and was beginning to feel conspicuous and not a little cold.

More than a half hour since he'd begun, Stefan reached 84th Street. He turned right and was surprised that the blocks east to the river had suddenly become much longer after ones he'd become used to going north. On either side of the narrow streets the buildings were much shorter than in midtown, some narrow and only three stories up with wide brown stone stairways, others wider and six or seven storeys, only a few larger and grander. 409 East 84th Street, when he got there, proved to be a modest apartment house of medium size. There was a healthy tree directly across the street from the entrance. He would be able stand behind it without being noticed by anyone entering or exiting the building. Stefan stepped inside and scanned the push buttons—17 of them, numbered, each above a slotted brass mailbox door. Romero was apartment 15. That would be the fifth floor, he estimated.

Then he wrapped his wool scarf a little tighter and retreated to the tree on the other side. There were cars parked on both sides of the narrow street. Stefan took out a packet of *Peter Stuyvesants*. Lighting up, he realized his mistake. These cigs had an aroma completely different from the Virginias that Americans smoked. Someone coming along would notice and remember. He knew he'd notice. Reluctantly he ground the smoke out. *Can I walk back to the avenue and buy an American brand?* He wouldn't know which, and the accent, the indecision, the fumbling with the change, they would all mark him out if anyone asked. It wasn't that he was worried. It was more a matter of professionalism. Leave the smallest trace you can, no matter what the job. But then he realized there was little need for concern. Twice in the next three hours a uniformed policeman passed. His greatcoat was a naval blue with a row of brass buttons climbing each side of his chest. A blue-visored officer's hat hooded the man's eyes. Without breaking stride he moved passed Stefan, twirling a nightstick, but with no evident interest in a man who'd been lurking on the same spot for ninety minutes or more. *What is it that makes you invisible, Stefan? Your white skin and open countenance?*

Keeping the vigil, there wasn't much to think about except the job. Stefan perfectly well understood the necessity, the urgency, of silencing this woman. *Silence her? We'll have to kill her.* He knew it, though he'd not yet said the words silently in thought. The knowledge she carried was too dangerous for any other course. Reading East German *Stasi* was the only way to keep covert control over the hundreds of perfectly schooled authentically German agents the East had planted throughout the West German government. If this woman's knowledge came to the attention of the Russians or the *Stasi*, every source they'd been reading would go dark. It would be like turning off a deep sea diver's air passage, quick asphyxiation for the very state itself. It mattered to Stefan who would win this grueling, quiet but very real war with the east. It made his task important, very important. Convincing himself he muttered the words out loud, making them real. "Yes, you'll have to kill her."

When darkness finally came Stefan allowed himself to look at his watch. It was 18:00 and there, with military precision, was a yellow cab coming to a stop before him. Schulke stepped out. "Take this cab back. Pay the man. Get the receipt, both ways. Have some schnapps with your supper." Schulke's smile was at once ingratiating and conspiratorial. He'd brought a duty free bottle from the ship. "Come back at 22:00."

Stefan looked up at the building. "I think it's fifth floor. No lights, none since I got here." Then he got in the cab.

This time, coming back, Stefan took the subway up Lexington and he took his winter coat. Noisy, dirty but fast, the train brought Stefan quickly to the wide boulevard of 86th Street, two streets north of the stakeout. He had a few minutes to wander round. His eyes searched beneath the bright street lamps for any signs of the pre-war Little Germany neighborhood mentioned by the ancient *Baedeker* he'd brought along. He could see no sign of it beyond a pastry shop proudly selling Bavarian Crèmes in its sidewalk display case. The same bottle of Schnapps Schulke had brought from the ship was sitting in the window of a liquor store. He smiled to himself. *Well, someone shares the Boss' taste here, anyway.*

Schulke was not visible as Stefan walked down 84th Street. Where was the man? The professional taking hold of him, he began to look round, listen for footfalls behind him, seek out the small forecourts before some of the brownstone stairways. Three meters from the building, Schulke's head poked out the door, hat pushed back. He hissed at Stefan. "No one's in the place at all. No Frau Romero, no kids, nobody."

Stefan entered the warmth of the vestibule. "No one? It's got to be the right place." He looked towards the row of buttons and mailboxes. "Her name's there."

"Yeah, and the box is full of several days' mail. You might have noticed."

"Ach, stupid of me. Sorry, Chief." Stefan shook his head in mock despair. "What'll we do?"

"Let's go. We'll come back tomorrow in the daylight and search the place."

Chapter Thirty-One

They buzzed a third floor apartment's entry bell and got an immediate response. Letting themselves in, they descended the stairway to the basement and then listened for anyone who might have been suspicious of an unexpected visitor. After five minutes of silence, they mounted the stair to the fifth floor, where Schulke extracted a lock-picking kit. Within a few moments he had the entry door of apartment 15 open. They closed and double-locked it behind them, then surveyed the apartment. Schulke gave the orders. "Go through the bedrooms. I'll do the living room. Keep things in order. We don't want to give ourselves away."

An hour later the two men sat down in the living room, emptyhanded. Stefan spoke. "Let's switch. You have a look through the bedrooms; I'll take the rest of the flat. There must be something that can help us."

Don't look for the obvious, Stefan ordered himself. *How do you do that, not look for the obvious?* Then he mumbled out loud: "Look for what's missing." He wandered back into the bathroom between the two bedrooms, and stood before the sink. Then he noticed the water glasses, standing in chrome holders on either side of the shelf below the mirror. Both were white from toothpaste dribbled off toothbrushes. But there were no toothbrushes in them. *Of course.* He smiled. *They're gone.*

Behind him stood a white rattan laundry hamper with a wooden top. He opened it. Empty. No boys' clothing, no socks, no underclothes, no towels or handkerchiefs, empty. He swung open the mirrored door of the medicine cabinet. Brylcreem, men's hairstyling cream, but no hairbrush or comb. Now he was certain. Stefan walked into the boys' bedroom. The twin beds were made. He pulled the drawers out of the two bureaus. The upper ones were almost empty, the lower ones full, crowded with summer clothes, short-sleeved shirts and shorts. Then it came to Stefan: *Her kids had time to pack up and leave. Someone had warned her.*

Back in the master bedroom, Schulke was on his knees, feeling round the bottom of a night table next to an unmade double bed. Stefan stood above him and spoke. "Don't worry about anyone barging in on us, Boss. They're gone and not coming back."

Schulke nodded and rose. He was perspiring in his topcoat and hat. "I guess I can take these off."

Stefan walked into the master bath. There in the glass on the side of the medicine cabinet mirror was a toothbrush and a tube of toothpaste. He opened the cabinet. The shelves were crowded with no gaps. Nothing had been taken from them. There was a towel thrown over the shower curtain rod, as if to dry after use. The seat was down, and there was the wrapping of a pair of nylon stockings in the trash next to it, as well as a tissue blotted with lipstick. Stefan closed the door. There on the back a wire hanger hung from a hook, covered with a drycleaner's clear plastic bag and a tag for a woman's suit. Stefan pulled the bag towards him and looked at the date. It was a week old, the day after they'd sailed for New York. He opened the door, found the laundry hamper at the foot of the double bed and opened it—half full of woman's underclothes, some towels and a bathrobe. Stefan came out of the bedroom and moved to the bureau. Schulke's eyes were following him. The small upper drawers were relatively full of woman's underclothes—panties, brassieres, a garter belt, slips, and scarves. Then he went to the closet, pushed the clothing aside to look behind. Nothing but a row of shoes, with an empty place where one pair had been taken. Stefan pulled the light chain that hung before him in the closet and looked up. There, above him, were three suitcases entirely filling the space between the closet hanger rail and the ceiling. He turned to Schulke. "You've looked in these?"

"No, but I shifted them. They're empty." Stefan turned away so the man wouldn't see his reproachful look, then pulled each of them down. Schulke dutifully opened them, vindicated by their lack of any content at all.

Both men sat on the bed. "Look, Chief, there is something odd here." Stefan waited for Schulke to invite him to continue. "Well, the boys packed up and cleared out, even made their beds. But she didn't."

"What do you mean?"

"There's no sign she packed up anything when she left. It was just another workday morning for her." He began to enumerate the evidence. "She put on a pair of stockings, took a suit from a drycleaner bag, even blotted her lipstick. There's no space in the closet where a missing bag might have been taken from. Didn't make her bed...something you'd do if you were going to pack a suitcase on it."

"So?"

Stefan wanted to shout, *Don't you see?* but instead he spoke deliberately. Leading Schulke through his reasoning would test its logic. "Look, her children were not in a hurry when they left. They took clothes, maybe even dirty clothes, toothbrushes. She left for a day's work and never came back. What does that mean to you?" Schulke was silent. "It means they were warned we were coming." He thought again. "But that's not all it means."

"Well?" Schulke's face showed impatience and incomprehension by turns.

"She was warned we were coming. But then why would she have the boys pack up clothes and not pack up herself?" Still the other man was silent and now Stefan was thinking aloud. "Because they came back and packed up after she left! And for some reason she couldn't come back for anything...or maybe she wanted to make it look like she wasn't getting out before we got here?"

Now Schulke was thoroughly confused, but Stefan continued to try to reason things out. "If the kids came back and packed after she'd gone, she must have known they had time before our arrival, maybe even known we were coming by ship." Would Schulke rise to the implied criticism? Stefan went on. "Maybe the day she left, she didn't want her kids to know what was going on, so she couldn't pack anything. Then, when she'd gotten out, the kids were brought back to get their stuff."

Now Schulke interrupted. "And who told her we were coming, and coming by ship?"

"Yes, that is the question. And it raises a lot more questions, Boss." Would Schulke get it? Would he catch up?

He did. "Like, where is the leak back in BfV Cologne?" Stefan nodded. "And who are they leaking to?" Schulke glared at the world. "It could only be to the Stasi or the Russians. My God in heaven, is it too late? Have they found out?"

"There's no secure way we can find out here in New York, Boss." Schulke was shaking his head, trying to disbelieve the facts. Stefan continued. "If she's gone, we can't waste any time, Chief. We'll have to fly back right away." Schulke's face suddenly took on the rictus of a drowning man. Fearing he would resist out of his fear of flying, Stefan sought to cushion the blow. "But let's see if we can find anything else. Maybe we can test this reasoning a little more." The older man went out of the room looking relieved.

Stefan lifted one of the suitcases to replace on the closet shelf. It was a Scottish tartan cloth-sided, zipper-closed bag, and as he twisted it up, a weight slipped from one side to the other. Stefan rotated the bag in the other direction, and there it was again. He turned the bag over. There was a hidden zipper on the underside, closing what must have been an outside pouch or space for soiled clothes. What came out was an ancient manila file, cracking and crumbling as he withdrew it. There was a rubber band round it so old, dry and fragile that it broke as he removed it. But the paper the file held was still strong. It was onionskin, very thin, almost translucent, but damaged by age. Everything about this file announced that it was old and forgotten. It was written out in a still dark fountain-pen ink, closely and with little correction, but the letters carried accents, tails, and strokes, diacritics he instantly recognized. This was a manuscript in...Polish. The cover sheet had the title, *Memoir of the War, 1939-1945*. Stefan turned to the first page and read a few lines. It was the correct, educated Polish prose his mother had made him learn at home during his years of German school. Then he riffled through the pages, all covered in a closely written but perfectly legible hand, blotted here and there with a drop of fountain-pen ink. The last page was numbered 258. He closed it up, and carried it into the living room. Schulke was in the kitchen looking beneath the shelf paper in the drawers.

Stefan went back to the drop-leaf desk through which he had already searched. But now he had an idea of what to look for. On the top was a large business envelope, unsealed, empty, with no address and the return address *Document Office, UN Secretariat, New York, 17, New York, USA.* Why an empty, unsealed envelope? What had it held? He pulled out the right side desk drawer. There was the Australian passport he'd already leafed through. *She won't get far without that...* He looked at the envelope on the desk. *Unless she's using a brand new UN passport she brought home the night before she left.*

Beneath the Australian passport there were other documents. Her children's passports, some school reports, yellow smallpox certificates everyone needed for travel...one for each boy, but none for Rita Romero. So, she was planning to travel internationally. Beneath that there was another legal-size envelope he'd checked before, also old, brittle, and sealed. But now he noticed the upper left, where the return address should go. Two faint letters, *M.T.* and beneath it, in equally faint German words, *Ausweis, Kennkart,* Baptismal Certificate. Stefan laughed out loud. "M.T?" Then he spoke the words. "Margarita Trushenko."

"What did you say?" Schulke spoke from the kitchen.

"If you had any doubts, Boss, you can drop them now." He

handed the older man the envelope. Schulke had no qualms about ripping it open. "Margarita Trushenko, in the flesh. And she left her Australian passport, in the name of Romero. Now the only question is what names she is using and where she went."

Schulke nodded. Then he smiled. "Her kids must know. Wouldn't take much to squeeze it out of them. If they know what she knows, we'll have to terminate anyway."

Stefan was shaking his head. "Too dangerous now. Whoever warned her we were coming for her, they'll find out if anything happens to her kids, and so will she. If it's the Russians, we'll drive her right into their arms." He stopped. "We've got to find her and silence her before she knows what's happening."

"And without the Ruskies finding out either? How do we do that?"

"I don't know, but we can't do it here, can we?" Schulke would have to face the need to fly. "We're going to have to get back to Cologne—fast." All he got from his chief was a grim nod.

Chapter Thirty-Two

By midnight they were on Lufthansa flight 403 from Idlewild to Frankfurt, sitting in *Senator* class. Schulke had begun drinking himself into a numbing stupor well before takeoff at 21:00. The stewardesses knew the syndrome and had made allowances from the start. One leaned over and whispered in Stefan's ear, "We'll keep him calm till we land. But you'll have to get him off the plane." Now Schulke was snoring into Stefan's ear.

Stefan rose, pulled his briefcase from under his seat and took out the file he'd taken from Rita Romero's apartment. He signaled the stewardess. "Bitte, can you take these plates and bring me a brandy?" In a moment the white damask of his small table was clear and there was a globe of amber liquid sitting before him. Stretching his legs, Stefan loosened his tie, pulled out a *Stuyvesant*. Before he could light it the stewardess had a Dunhill lighter in front of him. She'd been standing in the aisle, smiling an invitation to conversation. He nodded in appreciation, then held up the file, and trying to look sheepish, he shrugged the plea of work.

Opening the file, he turned the title page and began to read. The flowing, cursive woman's hand took a little getting used to, but as he worked at it, Stefan found himself adjusting, guessing, and then reading fluently, gripped by a narrative it was impossible to stop reading. This woman had plied a course through six years of war he'd never read or heard the likes of.

* * *

Now, almost eighteen years after the war, there was still a lot of complicit reticence about what had happened. Germans needed to pretend to ignorance. Those who suffered at their hands seemed to need to turn away from their victimhood. Still, Stefan had read about more than one Jew who'd survived the worst of Nazi atrocities. Here was another. They were an infinitesimal sampling from millions, he knew. The numbers just numbed you. That's why he had to read the narratives. He had his own private, secret drive to do so, knowing he too was a survivor, a child rescued and raised by a heroic foster-mother. Neither mother nor son had so much as mentioned the fact of his rescue. So, he needed to read this manuscript, and not just on the chance of a clue to this woman's mind that might help them find her. In these pages he might find out a little more about the past that had formed him.

The narrative began with a name he didn't recognize, her maiden name—Feuerstahl—her marriage to a physician named Guildenstern, and her child, just before the war. The boy's name was Stefan. The coincidence that gave him a shiver. Their town, Karpathyn, was too small to matter. Stefan had never heard of it, at any rate. But he knew the name Guildenstern well enough from the endless lists he'd been forced for weeks to walk his finger down, sitting in a windowless, airless Cologne cubicle.

When the Germans attacked, she'd made her husband leave. She thought him too weak, a burden she couldn't deal with if she were to try to preserve herself and her child. She'd taken a lodger in her home, named Erich, who continued to live with them in the ghetto to which the Jews had been consigned before extermination. The man was a mathematician. Stefan's smile was knowing as he read the sentence. Here was one of the Polish code breakers. But there was nothing more about whether he passed a secret to the woman.

As conditions worsened, Erich had helped her send her child out of the ghetto to her parents, living in the west of the country, now absorbed into the Reich, beyond the military occupation. But then she'd lost track of the boy. As the SS finished its liquidation of the ghetto, sending its last workers to the gas chambers at Belzec, Erich had secured her the false identity of a Pole named

Margarita Trushenko—the other name Stefan knew too well by now.

So, she'd escaped the burning ghetto. Page after page narrated her grim ingenuity in the face of threats lurking everywhere— Germans, Poles, even other Jews—ready to snare anyone hiding in occupied Poland. Brazening the false Polish identity into the German papers of a *Volksdeutsche*—an almost-Aryan—Rita Feuerstahl escaped Poland's ninth circle of hell for Germany's first circle, first in Warsaw, then Krakow and finally Heidelberg, hiding in plain sight of the Reich. He read and reread the chapter in which she risked everything in a final forlorn hunt through the Warsaw ghetto for her lost child and then bitterly accepted his death.

Lighting up smoke after smoke, Stefan followed her course obsessively through the night, lost in Rita Feuerstahl's defiance, luck, and resistance in a war of attrition waged against her by the whole German nation. Eyes smarting, he closed and rubbed them, then looked across to Schulke, snoring under the boom of the four 707 jet engines. Down the aisle all the overhead lights but his were out. Even the stewardess who had tried to flirt was asleep, mouth agape, in the crew seat facing him under the dim lights illuminating the galley. He looked at his watch. He'd been reading for two and a half hours and was on page 198. Stefan glanced at the number on the last page—258. *Sixty pages to go. You'll finish before we land*. He recognized that an admiration for this woman had been building since soon after the beginning of her narrative. She was smart, resourceful, and strongly willed to survive. *Knowing the secret that now makes her your target, that would have given her the will*. He had to know how the story ended.

No, you already know how this story ends. You'll be ending it. He sighed slightly at the task he had to discharge. Then he turned back to the manuscript.

Stefan read on, willing Rita Feuerstahl to greater safety, first in Warsaw, then in Krakow. Finally, he found himself breathing sighs of relief as she crossed the border from occupied Poland into the Reich, where she could be a little safer. Now the manuscript took on a lighter tone—the story of someone who knew she was going to survive. It even recorded vignettes at the expense of the Nazi family of seven in whose home she served as the single servant. The family's certainty of the Führer's invincibility was quickly overcome by their fear of the Russians. By the winter of '44 they were hoping for a rapid American-British advance from the west. And then came a passage that made sense of all the chafing that Stefan had suffered under the yolk of Otto Schulke, something that explained the man's unbounded obsession with this case, with the need to find this woman, the very vindication of his being, apparently the only thing that could make his life matter to anyone.

Rita had been in Mannheim, a few kilometers from Heidelberg, on a November night in 1944, with a friend, a girl from the ghetto in Karpathyn. The girl, named Dani, had meant much to Rita evidently. She'd risked her safety repeatedly through the war to harbor this woman. Dani had been the only one of Rita's friends to have escaped the *Aktion* that cleared the Karpathyn ghetto for final transport to the extermination camp at Belzec. It was in the bombed out tenements of Mannheim that they'd been arrested by a policeman who had been suspicious of Rita once before. He'd caught her, a supposedly uneducated domestic, trying to slip out of a university lecture hall where the policeman had set up an identity check. He'd set up the check not for any reason beyond annoying upper class students who'd managed to avoid even the home-front dislocations and privations of the war. Evidently, Rita wrote, the man had taken her name and begun to run checks on women of her description in the RSHA—the Reich Main Security Headquarters. Spotting Rita again, in Mannheim with her friend Dani, the policeman had brought both of them before his superior, flaunting documents he'd gathered from Berlin, from Krakow, even from Warsaw, all suggesting that Rita

Guildenstern and Margarita Trushenko were names of interest to the SS and military intelligence.

Stefan looked up from the page. *So, someone had suspected something about Rita even back then.* But how could suspicions raised by an *SS-Unterscharfsfurher*—a low-ranking Nazi policeman—have been communicated to Otto Schulke of the BfV fifteen years later? The question answered itself. *The cop who arrested Rita all those years ago in Mannheim? It must have been Schulke!* Involuntarily Stefan hit his forehead with his hand. *Dummkopf.* He was avid as he turned back to the manuscript.

Instead of confirming the arrest and congratulating the arresting officer, his superior ordered the policeman to release both Rita and her friend Dani, even knowing they were Jewish women using false identities. To the fury of the arresting officer—if only the memoirist had remembered his name—the superior had even driven them both home. He had done this not out of any anti-Nazi zeal, the manuscript averred, but because, as he said, the war was about to be lost and policemen would need to show that they did no more than their duty, and perhaps sometimes a little less. Now at last he understood Schulke's pathological obsession with the woman who wrecked his future.

Stefan came to the last chapters, as Rita Feuerstahl was liberated by the US Army, worked in the USO canteens for American servicemen, and then in the tracing services. These sprang up everywhere in Germany to bring refugees—Jews from the extermination camps, political prisoners from the concentration camps, forced laborers from the east—together with any family that might have survived the war.

The sky out the plane window was still midnight black but now there were a few cabin lights on as passengers were beginning to stir. Ahead of Stefan the stewardess was passing among them offering morning coffee. He gratefully took a cup, then looked over at the still sleeping Schulke, his head now resting on his chest, with a fine line of spittle descending from the right side of his mouth. *What does he need to know about this manuscript?* Then came the subversive thought: *Why does he need to know about this manuscript at all?* Stefan was glad it was in Polish, and he would be able to control what if anything Schulke might take from it for their mission. Still, he had to finish it and put it way before the older man awoke.

Quickly he skimmed through the last few pages. Margarita Trushenko became again Rita Feuerstahl. She had returned to Poland seeking to learn what had become of her parents in the west, but not risking a visit across the Soviet border to Karpathyn. There, in Poland, she found her husband—now a medical officer in the Red Army, "married" to a Soviet woman with a child, and utterly uncomprehending about even the possibility of her survival. It was soon after that she met the man Romero, whose twin sons Rita Feuerstahl had conceived, the man whose name she would eventually take. But there as they prepared to smuggle themselves west, out of Soviet-occupied Poland, the manuscript broke off.

It came to the end of a page with no summing up, no conclusion, no moral, no peroration, no backward glance at the years of horror, tragedy of loss, adversity and danger, nothing that suggested Rita Feuerstahl had finished her narrative, told her story, was ready to let it go, put it to rest. Page 258, Stefan knew, was not meant to be the last page of this memoir. She'd been interrupted, had suddenly been required to put it aside. Then, inexplicably, she'd never returned to it. *But she kept it with her all these years. One more mystery...why and how did her war story end? You'll never know.* Stefan closed the file, rose from his seat and replaced the pages in his bag. No need Schulke ever knowing what had kept Stefan awake all night.

Rita Feuerstahl had broken off her memoir, she hadn't come to a conclusion. Could Stefan say the same for himself? He'd been shaped, he knew only too well, by the same terrible events, his life's course fated by the malevolence of the Third Reich.

Like Rita he'd suffered, but had been luckier, lucky not to have been able to carry from his infancy any of the wartime history he shared with her and millions of others. He'd been a young child with no real memory of any father at all, only the inchoate early image of being held closely against cold winds, warmed by the body of the woman who'd raised him. Was it his mother or was it already his foster mother in the remembered image? He couldn't really say. Growing up in the Germany that had sought to kill his kind, he had been ardent to become someone else. He had needed to be someone Germans wouldn't have sought to annihilate. Indeed he needed to become a German himself, albeit one ready to face the awful historical responsibility of the country he had become a part of. It would be much harder now to be a German, now that he'd read this woman's account, one that turned history he knew into tragedy he could feel.

* * *

The speaker directly over their heads crackled, announcing the time to landing in Frankfurt. Breaking through the jet engine roar, the noise finally woke Schulke. He had not traveled well— pasty skin, disheveled pate of stringy hair, stains on the shirt below a collar askew. A too-wide cravat, pushed to one side, revealed the top button of a collar over which a lizard's gullet shivered from side to side. Sitting so close, Stefan could see the tracery of veins wandering around the yellow of his now open eyeballs, and smell the rank odor of someone who'd sweated through his clothes in fear before finally succumbing to alcoholic oblivion.

Now that Schulke was awake, the reality of air travel immediately reasserted itself. He tugged at his seat belt, sought the sight of land below them, and then gripped each armrest with quickly whitening hands. It was, Stefan thought, a model lesson in fear of flying. There were at least another twenty or thirty minutes, an eternity for Schulke, during which he said nothing, looking straight ahead, allowing the perspiration to trickle down his forehead where it was absorbed by thick eyebrows. Only once did he let go of the right armrest, just long enough to reach for a *Lufthansa* airsickness bag. The bag remained between his fist and the chair divider for the remainder of the flight. It was the sort of manifest discomfort that would draw anyone's sympathy. Stefan felt the urge almost to pat his hand, but he knew any expression of sympathy, or even notice of Schulke's distress, would be repaid later by abuse. Instead he spoke as if to no one in particular, "Almost there now." He made a show of tugging at his seatbelt and adopted a pose of quiet confidence that he hoped might be contagious.

As the 707 shuddered to a roaring stop and then in sudden quiet turned off the runway, Schulke sought an urgent, officious demeanor. "We've got to get to Cologne as quickly as we can. Find out if they're still able to read the Russian signals. If the Russians haven't changed their code, that means they haven't found her. We may still have a chance." Stefan only nodded. They'd head for the Frankfurt main railway station and then it would be three hours by the fastest train. *Should I suggest we fly?* Stefan smiled to himself. *He'll treat it like a provocation.*

Seeing the mobile stairway brought to the side of the airplane, Schulke was practically clambering over Stefan in his haste to rush off the plane. Stefan had noticed the Lufthansa bus a little further off, and realized that being first off wouldn't get them to Cologne, or even to the passport control and customs inspectors, any faster. Schulke was brandishing what looked like a policeman's warrant disk as he spoke out loud to the few other first class passengers in seats ahead of theirs. "Out of the way, official police business." Startled and docile, the other passengers collapsed back into their seats. Standing at the cabin door, almost crowding the stewardess trying to open it, he looked back at Stefan, gesturing at his hat, coat, in the overhead shelf. A cold blast of early morning wind swept in out of the still, sunless morning as the door swung away. Schulke suddenly shivered. But after his peremptory rush, he could hardly return for the coat and hat in Stefan's hands. He rushed down the stairs and tried to hurry directly to the terminal 200 meters away. The others waited as Stefan followed him, smiling sheepishly. Exiting the plane, he could see a female ground attendant with a clipboard, pointing to the bus, as Schulke started walking directly towards the terminal, waving his disk in her direction as he passed. Still standing at the top of the stairs, Stefan had a clear view. A baggage handler bigger than Schulke managed to tackle him as he began walking towards the path of a smaller plane, it's righthand propeller on a collision course with Schulke's skull.

* * *

Even jumping every queue between the terminal entrance and the S-bahn to Frankfurt main station, it was still two hours before they were settled at the breakfast bar of an express train to Cologne. "Boss, what if the Russians have changed codes? We abort the mission, right?"

Schulke looked at him with frank hostility. "Not necessarily. In fact not at all. She's broken German Federal Republic law, she's revealed a state secret." He growled. "The most well-kept secret we have."

"Can we be sure she told them? They might have figured it out themselves. What about the leak to Russians that we were looking for her? It certainly came from inside the BfV." He stopped, hoping for a change in Schulke's angry look. "Someone in the *Vizepräsident*'s office? The *Vizepräsident* knows about this mission, doesn't he? And his adjutant, what's his name, Schelling? That's where the leak is, someone in his office, no?"

"No, Sajac. The leak could be anywhere. Some flunky in the travel department, for example. They knew where we were going, and which ship we'd take." He glared again. "For all I know, you could be the source of the leak." Stefan was silent, refusing to be drawn into this argument. Schulke calmed. "No, we're going to keep looking…till we find her…no matter what."

In the silence that followed, Stefan wondered aloud, "Yes, but how do we look for her without tipping off the Russians again?"

Schulke hadn't heard or wasn't listening. He'd pulled a fountain pen and his expense ledger from his coat pocket and then spread a half-dozen receipts on his lap.

* * *

They were at the taxi rank, backs to the station, facing the Cologne cathedral. When a cab pulled up, Schulke put up his hand to prevent Stefan's joining him. "I'm going to see the *Vizepräsident*. I'll find out whether the Soviet radio traffic has changed codes." He evidently didn't want Stefan tagging along. Why not? Schulke would have to report the failure of their mission. Had he hidden the fact that they had travelled by ship, that it had turned out to be a costly handicap? "Meet me at the office at 17:00 this afternoon."

Chapter Thirty-Three

The morning Schulke and Sajac landed in Frankfurt, Rita was on the tram from her bed-sit in the Paquis quarter of Geneva up to the old Palace of Nations. The vast pile had been built for the League of Nations in the '20s and ceded to the United Nations in 1946. Now it served a dozen of the UN's departments with an insatiable need for document-translators and negotiation-interpreters. Mme. Feuerstahl's arrival had been therefore welcome, even routine, though it didn't feel like it to her.

* * *

With nothing but the briefcase she'd carried on to her flight, Rita had gone directly from the customs barrier to a *Bureau de Change* where she'd acquired over a thousand Swiss francs for most of the money Phil had put into her hand at Idlewild. The teller's acceptance of her French was reassuring after years not using it at all. Then she'd hailed a cab directly to the Palace of Nations, and flashing her UN passport quickly found her way to the Translation/Interpretation Bureau. It was there, standing before the Directress of the bureau, that Rita began to feel anxiety. The woman was wide, thick, dressed in a drab gray suit over a yellowing nylon blouse, hair a gray to match the suit, pulled back so tightly from her forehead it looked painful to Rita. There was no ornamentation on her body or her desk, just a nameplate—Dr Ludmilla Sholokhov—in Cyrillic letters. Was this international civil servant also a loyal Soviet person, or for that matter, a KGB agent? Had Rita walked directly into the hands of one of her two pursuers?

The unsmiling Russian looked at the personnel file Rita and Phil had crafted in New York, and immediately began speaking to her in native Russian. "What did you do exactly in New York?"

Rita responded in Russian, "Mostly Security Council simultaneous interpretation."

The woman immediately switched to Polish. "And why were you transferred?"

Is she suspicious? Rita pointed to the transfer-orders in her packet and replied in Polish. "I assume because you need more staff here. They asked me because I have no family and can move."

Now Sholokhov switched to an almost accentless British English. "When can you report for duty?"

Very well, English then, Rita thought in annoyance. "As soon as I am settled. I just got off the airplane and came right here."

The woman looked behind Rita. "Where did you leave your bags, with the concessionaires at the *vestiaire*?" This was French. *Is she testing my languages or showing off?* The English thought came, *Time for your first lie, Rita.* She gulped and answered in French. "They missed my connection in Paris." Would the woman look at the travel orders and see Rita had flown direct from New York?

A slight smile of approval briefly glimmered on Sholokhov's face. Back in Russian now, she pointed to a chair. "Sit. Any other languages?"

Rita decided to be silent about German and Ukrainian. "Only dead ones," she replied.

"Nationality?"

No point dissembling. It was in the paperwork and on the passport. "Australian, but I was born in Poland." *Will she ask which part?* There were three possible answers to this question—the part that used to be Germany and had been given to Poland, the part that used to be Poland and been taken for the Ukraine, and the sliver that had stayed Polish. Surprisingly, the woman wasn't interested in this politically charged matter. Perhaps she was neutral enough to be trusted.

Sholokhov took a notepad and pen from a central drawer.

Then she wrote out a note and passed it to Rita. "Take this to the accommodations bureau. They'll find you something close by." *Something you can easily find, to keep tabs on me?* Rita rose. Only now was there a bit of informality in the woman's voice. "You must be tired from your journey. Start tomorrow, Wednesday. Understood?" This time English again. She smiled a little less wanly and flicked her wrist in the direction of the door.

As Rita left the inner office the receptionist who had gate-kept Rita on the way into Sholokhov's office detected Rita's anxious frown. She rose to close the door behind Rita. Once closed, she held Rita's arm for a moment. "Don't worry, Mademoiselle Feuerstahl. She's quite all right. Interrogates everyone that way the first time, even the men." With a warm smile, she released her. "See you tomorrow?"

Rita nodded. *The woman must have had the intercom on the whole time. Why?*

* * *

The rest of the day would give Rita enough time at least to purchase a change of clothing and toiletries, if she could find a place to stay quickly enough. She would have time to contemplate, to calculate how much danger she was in. Rita was a few days ahead of the Germans but the Russians would already be looking for her too. She knew that from the moment she left this building she would need to be vigilant about surveillance. Here in Geneva it would be much harder to distinguish a new tail—German or Russian—from just another UN employee, moving along with her in synch back and forth from work to a flat in the town.

Clutching a list of available bed-sits, one-room studios, and spare rooms, Rita spent the morning inspecting a half-dozen places between the open plaza before the main train station and the lake. Closer to the train station would be better—cheaper, on the tram line to *Nations*, the old League of Nations stop. It would be easier to melt into the crowds surging in and out of the station if she needed to lose someone she might suspect of following her. As she walked Rita found herself sizing up every person who passed, and automatically glancing behind her every few minutes. Would others notice too? She made herself walk along, until her imagination and her anxiety forced her head to snap round, searching out the pedestrians behind her for a pair of eyes following her. *Stop, Rita. You're making yourself even more conspicuous.* Again, she reassured herself she had at least a few days grace, perhaps a week, before anyone could pick up her trail and organize surveillance...or interception. *But then what will you do? Run again?*

Rita realized she'd done all this before, twenty years ago, done it in Warsaw and Krakow, seeking shelter from the cat-and-mouse game that Germans, mercenary Poles, even a few desperate Jews played, stalking prey on every street—catch, extort, release, repeat. *This is going to be easier, Rita,* she commanded herself, but without effect.

By early afternoon she had a small, furnished studio at the end of the Rue de Berne, just beyond the red light district between the train station and the lake. Of this she was reassured by the landlady. An hour or so after that she'd returned from the large *Manor* department store with enough new clothes and a pair of sensible shoes to begin to walk like a European. Walking back to the flat she reflected on how un-European she looked after a dozen years away—hairstyle, clothes, shoes, purse, hat, even the little makeup she wore, was giving her away. Then there was the stride, adapted to the speed of pedestrian traffic in New York. She'd only noticed the differences because once upon a time she'd been European. Everything would have to be toned down.

By late afternoon the jet lag she'd never experienced before completely overcame her. Throwing herself down on the narrow bed and its sagging mattress, she woke four hours later in the dark, still dressed and suddenly unaware even of where she was. Looking round she saw in the window the flashing lights of a small hotel across the narrow street. This located her. Rita undressed and crawled under the eiderdown in the unheated room. And then the time zone change she hadn't bargained on kept her asleep until long after she was due at work the next morning.

Rita woke with a start, pulled the wristwatch on the night table to her face and then sprang from the bed. *Late your first day!* In a panic she dressed—no time for shower or makeup or a bite. She was at the tram stop on the Rue de Lausanne in twelve minutes, by her watch, combing through her hair, at first oblivious to the stares from matrons and the mothers of schoolchildren. Only when she noticed did she stop and begin to search the few men's faces, memorizing them to match with future encounters.

* * *

"Sorry, got slightly lost on the way here." It was a lie, believable for her first day, but not even required by the receptionist she'd met the day before.

The woman smiled. "Your secret is safe with me...today." Then she rose. "Let me show you to your desk. There's a sheaf of reports and documents waiting for translation from English into Russian." As she walked along, Rita trailing behind her, she spoke. "I'm Nadine, by the way. Can I call you Rita?"

"Of course."

They walked into an open area at which a dozen men and women were seated before pamphlets, booklets, stapled reports and loose sheets on their desks, some writing in longhand, using impressive fountain pens, others shifting between their desks and attached typing tables.

Nadine went on. "There are no meetings in the next few days, so no call for interpreters. It will be pretty much desk-bound work. If you fall behind, you can take some of it home." Soon they were standing before an unoccupied desk, with 'Mme. Feuerstahl' on a nameplate visible at its edge. "There's a coffee break" —she looked at her watch—"in forty-five minutes. Staff canteen for lunch, 1:00 downstairs. Everyone goes there. I'll let you get on with it." Nadine turned to go back to her desk. "There's some paperwork for your paycheck, and other forms I should have given you yesterday. I'll bring them round."

Sitting down, Rita surveyed the stack before her. Then she turned each item in the stack over on a fresh pile, hoping for something that might hold her interest, distract her, make her feel some semblance of normality, security. It was a random assortment of material from a half-dozen agencies—meteorology, telecommunications, health, the High Commission for Refugees. All of it what the Aussies would have called 'bumf' —protocols, data, pro-forma reports—nothing with much real importance to the great mission of the organization. Rita pushed it all aside, and pulling her own fountain pen from her purse, pulled a piece of UN Geneva letterhead from the drawer on the left side of the desk.

My dear boys,

Just a line to say I am fine and that I love you and miss you and hope to be back with you someday. I am...

She stopped. She couldn't say where she was...she couldn't use this letterhead. She shouldn't be writing to them at all, or to Phil. Certainly a letter with a UN stamp or even a Swiss one and a Geneva postmark would be an announcement to anyone monitoring their mailbox in New York. And a letter with Phil's New York address would be a tip-off to anyone monitoring the outgoing post here.

Rita's heart sank. The weight of what she was bearing became too great. The certainty of discovery, almost immediate discovery, overwhelmed her for a long moment. The hopelessness of what she faced settled over her like a heavy blanket of wet snow.

Hiding was pointless. It merely postponed the unavoidable end for a brief time, just toying with her emotions. She felt the strength to resist drain out of her. She was suddenly exhausted by the relentless, implacable, anonymous malevolence that for almost twenty-five years now had, time and time again, marked her out for a kind of torture invisible to others. She didn't want to struggle on. She wanted it to end, now. She wasn't going to be her own personal, invisible, resolute hero anymore.

Then the voice in her head barked harshly. *No, you won't give in. They will have to destroy you. You won't do their work for them. It will never be as bad as what you've already been through.*

Rita drew in a long breath. Pretending to scan the first document before her, she forced herself to think things through. She wouldn't be able to contact anyone, not immediately. She couldn't really do much of anything safely until she knew she hadn't been located. So, the first problem was how to make surveillance by the Russians, or a threat by Germans, reveal itself? It could be weeks or months till either of the two found her, or it could be days. More likely it would be just days. The name change would help cover some tracks, but the job was too similar and the relocation glaringly obvious. Someone would begin looking for her here and soon. They might already be on their way from Moscow if Sholokhov was a loyal enough comrade to report back everything that crossed her desk.

One step at a time, Rita cautioned herself. At first every face would be new and unfamiliar. Geneva was a smaller city, in which the UN was the largest employer. She was bound to see faces over and over. It would be much harder to tell whether the same face was coincidence or surveillance. It was near a certainty the Germans and the Russians would place agents in the building. *Or they were here already. Why did Phil think you'd be safer here? He didn't. There was no alternative.*

* * *

All the rest of that week Rita watched, coming and going to work, learning the faces around her on the trams, in her street, at the Palace. She'd need to spot new ones the second time they showed up. Friday that week was a slack day, the diplomats all taking a long weekend. Fewer people showed up at work, and none of the absences were remarked upon. It would be easier to spot strange faces. She spent the weekend in her flat, hidden and safe at least for 48 hours. The next week, she knew, would be more dangerous.

* * *

Rita heard the sound of the snack cart rolling through the large workroom and the scrape of chairs as people rose to follow it out into the corridor for the morning coffee break. The white-coated attendant stopped the chrome pushcart before a wide window through which the bright sun shone unfiltered by any drape or gauze curtain. As her place in the queue came near the cart she looked through the window across the lake that lay beneath the Palace. There, dominating the eastern horizon, was the vast, shaded purple mass of Mont Blanc. Suddenly she had a plan, not a very good one, but at least it was something.

"Nadine?" The receptionist still in the queue behind her looked up. Rita gave up her place and moved back to stand with her. "Is there a staff outing club?"

"Oh, yes. Someone or other's going to Chamonix nearly every weekend till the snow covers the trails. After that it's skiing of course. The staff club even lends out gear."

"How do I find out about it?"

"There's a posting on the bulletin board in the staff lounge." She smiled appreciatively. "My, but you're keen. You haven't been settled into town a week."

Yes, a weekend in the Alps, walking the trails, if they were still open now in early December. Every station stop from Geneva to

Chamonix would pare down the passengers, every kilometer from Chamonix up into the mountains would shake off all but the serious walkers. By the time she was high enough above the town, the only people behind her would almost certainly be ones she should suspect, to begin with. And she wouldn't be alone. The whole weekend she'd be with people who knew her, even if only slightly. It would be more protection than she'd have in Geneva on a weekend.

Chapter Thirty-Four

Stefan came back to the BfV in the winter darkness of a late afternoon, as ordered. The office was dark. He was alone. After ten minutes of respectful waiting he leaned back on the two rear legs of the chair, swung his feet onto the small desk and lit up a smoke. He'd figured out what he didn't want Schulke to tell him when he came back from higher authority—that the Russians hadn't twigged, that they were still transmitting in a cypher that could be decoded, and he and Schulke still had to find their target and silence her. Stefan wanted the game to be up. He wanted to hear that the Russians had found their target and figured things out. He wanted very much that it not matter anymore that they find this Romero, or Trushenko, or...Feuerstahl—a name only Stefan could connect with her.

Through the course of the afternoon back in his flat, unpacking, showering, shaving, killing time, the recognition grew in Stefan that he wanted nothing to do with apprehending this woman. If it were a matter of national security, well, he'd do his duty, of course. The matter was too consequential for personal feelings to intervene. But he knew his feelings. Rita Feuerstahl's narrative had affected him. Stefan couldn't help seeing the parallels. There were hundreds or thousands of men and woman who had lived lives like hers in the war. The horrors these men and women had experienced were not so different from his own mother's. Stefan would not deny Rita Feuerstahl her suffering. And like thousands of others, like the unknown woman who bore him, she too had given up a child, sent him away, into hiding, a hiding so complete she'd lost him, just as Stefan had been lost. Child of the same fate, Stefan would hate himself for what he was going to have to do. *But you will do it!* It was a categorical imperative he had legislated for himself.

It was after 6:00 when Schulke came in, almost aglow,

carrying a bottle of schnapps wrapped in brown paper, to escape detection at the office door. His flushed face and breath revealed he'd already cracked the bottle open. He dropped it onto his desk with a decided thud, pulled a cheap cigar from the shirt pocket beneath his coat and proffered its end for Stefan to light. With the cigar still in his mouth, Schulke announced, "So, we are still in business, Sajac...Have a belt!" It sounded like an order as Schulke pushed the bottle towards him.

Stefan quietly put the brown bag aside. "What are we to do, Boss?"

"Well, how do you find someone who's gone to ground with a week's lead?" He didn't wait for an answer. "We'll send a signal to every intelligence bureau in every embassy and consulate where we have a secure contact." He began searching through the material on his desk. "Here....I took this picture from her apartment." It was the Romero woman with her two sons at her left, and a lake behind, in rather garish colors. It was obviously recent, from the size of the boys, taller than her shoulders. He tore the two boys out of the photo. "We'll have this sent out with a description." Stefan was shaking his head even before the older man had stopped. "What else can we do, Sajac? Just give up?"

"Look, Chief." He knew Schulke liked being addressed that way. "It won't work, and it's too dangerous anyway." Stefan watched his shoulders sag. Slumping into his chair, Schulke took another drink. His silence bid Stefan continue. "She could be anywhere in the world and our network is too small. Besides—"

"We can't do nothing, Sajac. There's a woman running around with the security of the West in her head."

"Look, Boss." Stefan was suddenly peremptory. "We know there's a leak here in the bureau, but we don't know where. If we send out all this information, we'll probably alert the Soviets, and they've got the biggest network...all over the world." The silence persisted. "We'll just end up making it easier for them to find her."

"And do you have a better suggestion, *Subalternoffizier* Sajac?" There was irony and contempt in his use of the lowest officer rank in the military.

Stefan hesitated. He wanted so badly not to proceed, but he had to. It was his calling. "Yes, I think I have an idea, sir."

"Well, out with it."

"It may take a little time." He paused. "Have the Vice-Präsident's office ask the Amis to look through all the departures from New York for the last ten days or so, and send us the names on all the UN passports who left in that period, and where they went."

"How do we do that without the leak here tipping off the Russians?"

Stefan had to hide the exasperation. "We know there is no leak in the Vice-Präsident's office." Stefan had to go on before Schulke could ask why and look foolish. "Otherwise, the Russians would have changed their codes, right?" The older man nodded curtly. "Vice-Präsident can just pick up a secure phone and talk to the CIA in Bonn. If we go through the communications channels, what are the chances the Russians will get word of what we want?"

"Very good, Sajac." He rose, pulled his shirt tail back in his trousers and straightened his tie. "I'm going back upstairs to get things going."

"Boss, it'll probably take a few days. Can I have some time off? Just 36 hours? Haven't seen my family in some time."

Schulke looked at his watch as if it could tell him how long 36 hours were. "Be back day after tomorrow." Then he left the office.

Get out of here before he comes back and changes his mind. Within ten seconds Stefan had grabbed his hat and coat, turned off the lights, pulled the door closed and locked it behind him.

* * *

Three hours later Stefan was riding the last tram from the Dortmund central *Bahnhof* to the neighborhood where he'd grown up. He'd called from the station to alert his mother he was in town. It would be a short walk from the ring road streetcar stop to his mother's home. The elderly building was one of the very few that had survived the devastating daylight bombing raids of 1945. It was already surrounded by new construction when Frania Sajac and her nine-year-old boy arrived four years later. Assigned to the old building as refugees from the German lands handed over to Poland after the war, they'd remained as the gray stucco building was reconstructed around them. His mother lived there still.

Stefan was in no hurry for the streetcar to arrive at his stop. He was thinking about how to broach a subject he'd hardly ever talked about with his mother. He'd been thinking about it all the way from Cologne. He couldn't deny to himself it was why he had to come home. Reading Rita Feuerstahl's memoir had kindled in him a curiosity about himself and his mother Frania he'd managed long to suppress. He'd known that they were refugees from the slice of eastern Germany given to the Poles after the war. He could bring to mind those photographic flashes of memory—the pram loaded with bags, his mother hurrying him down a railway track whose sleepers were too far apart for his stride, vast halls and long tables on which bowls steamed with a hot but thin soup—but he didn't know and he'd never asked her the details of her war, or his. That she hadn't borne him, that she had saved him, these things were rarely acknowledged between them. There was no father to miss, to blame, to be ashamed of, still less to return after the Soviets released the last of their prisoners of war, when Stefan was already a boy of fifteen. His ignorance of the details wasn't unique. None of his fellow schoolboys knew much about the war. They'd been too young. It was a subject no one talked about with one's parents, for fear of finding out too much. Whether victim or victimizer, it was best to leave dying embers unstirred. *Not anymore, not for me.* The voice in Stefan's mind was insistent.

* * *

The light from the ground floor window signaled that Frania Sajac was still up at midnight. He buzzed the building's entry and found the door to the flat open. His mother was standing there, in a flannel robe, still tall and strong-looking at fifty-eight, a grin lifting one side of her mouth higher than the other. He stepped into her hug, then she held him away from her and looked him over. Satisfied, she took his hand and led him to the kitchen table, where a plate of cold cuts, Muenster cheese and a Dortmund beer stood, glistening with condensation.

"Eat up. Then to bed." Frania Sajac's head turned towards her son's room. "It's late."

"Are you going to work tomorrow, Mutti?"

"No." His mother had left the Intelligence Service and now worked for a judge, sometimes even on Saturdays. "Court's recessed for a week." Frania Sajac knew well enough not to ask her son about his work.

"Then we can have breakfast, yes, and spend the day." He smiled.

"Only the day? How long do you have, dear?"

"Just the day, I am afraid."

* * *

It was a good time to ask. Her back was turned to the small kitchen table, as she washed the breakfast dishes. She wouldn't have to face him as she answered. She wouldn't have to control her expression if she decided to deny or deflect or dissimulate. *Sound casual!* The command came to him. "How exactly did we manage to survive the war, Mum, in Poland?"

"We were very lucky, Son." She turned around, facing him. "We almost didn't." It was an invitation to ask more questions. He could feel it.

"What do you mean?"

"Well, I'd been a secret courier for the resistance, the Polish Home Army. The Gestapo arrested me, just before the Polish Home Army uprising in the summer of 1944. Kept me for ten days before they released me." She looked down at her fingernails, remembering how the interrogator had taken one each day until he'd given up. "You were almost five when they took me. Were you old enough to remember?" He shook his head. "I was so frightened for you, alone, a toddler in that little flat. I'd gone out for a moment, across the road for some milk. They arrested me in the street. I couldn't tell anyone about you. Certainly not the Germans. They'd have killed you on the spot." They both understood why well enough.

"What happened? Who took care of me?"

"That's just it. I never knew. When I got back, there you were, safe and sound, not even hungry, clean clothes...it was a miracle." She shook her head. "You told me a man came and told you I'd sent him and you were to come to the country for an adventure. You told me about sleeping in a tent and cooking food on a fire, like red Indians, you said. Nothing comes back, nothing at all?"

"Well, sometimes a flash of green and woods and summer sky come to me. But I can't tell if it's a memory or my imagination. What I can remember is later, leaving that flat, pushing the pram loaded with everything we could carry."

She prompted him. "That was in Radom. We went from there to Bratislava. It was before Czechoslovakia was taken over."

"We weren't Germans. Why did we leave when the Germans had to get out of Poland?"

"After what the Nazis did, the Germans weren't welcome to stay. And we left with them because I knew that there'd be no future for you in a Communist state, not with a mother who was Polish Home Army. The Russians treated us as though we were Fascists, and the Poles had to follow their lead. It wasn't hard to claim to be German. No one was going to check up." She smiled.

Stefan thought for a moment. "You were a courier, carrying messages for the underground?"

"Yes, that's right. It was easier for women. We weren't really suspected till late in the war."

"But if you were a courier, how exactly did you end up with me?"

"Well, it was early in 1942. I'd been doing it for almost two and a half years, from the end of '39. I was in the east, coming back from Romania, where some of the pre-war government had been interned and then imprisoned. I stopped in this town at a safe-house and someone from the ghetto asked me to help get you to your grandparents south of Krakow." She paused. "I was headed in that direction, so I agreed."

"But wasn't it terribly dangerous—traveling with a little Jewish boy?" Stefan's question answered itself. As he spoke, the thought came to him again: *There must be a thousand stories like mine.*

Frania Sajac shrugged. "Everything we did back then was dangerous." Then she turned back to the sink.

Now, you'll ask the question. It will be some different town and that'll be the end of this eerie coincidence. Stefan had to keep the tremulousness out of his voice. "Mom, do you remember the name of the place you took me away from?

She hadn't heard the question. She was far away in time and space, reliving another day. "I was twenty kilometers from the town I was to bring you to, when I was told not to bother. Everyone, all the Jews in the town, had been rounded up and sent to the extermination camp at Auschwitz. You'd been with me a couple of weeks by then. I'd asked you to call me Mummy. You did." She smiled at him.

"What was the name of that town, the one you took me from?" He had to keep the tone bland curiosity.

"Big town east of Lemberg, L'vov, we called it before the war." Then it came to her. "Karpathyn."

Now he knew the answer to his next question. "And the town you were to take me to, where my grandparents lived?"

"Small town south of Krakow. Near Nowy Saz. Can't remember."

Stefan's tone became urgent. "Was it called Gorlice?"

His mother noticed the squint of tension in Stefan's eyes. "Yes, that's it."

"Are you sure?" The question was peremptory.

"Look, dear, what's this about? I'm not a suspect to be cross-questioned."

"You've got to be sure, Mother."

"I'm certain. Now what's this all about?"

You can't tell her. She's your mother, no one else is. He couldn't bear it if she knew that all these years the woman who bore him still lived. How would she feel? What might she do? Now she was adamant. "What's this about, Stefan! Answer me."

"Sorry, Mom. Didn't mean to upset you." The lie came to him, the excuse so natural she wouldn't question it. "I need to fill out the forms for *Weidergutmachung* that's all." They both smiled at the wonderful word, one only a German could construct. It had been coined after the fact of the Holocaust, literally it meant 'making it all good again,' as though a monetary payment might restore the *status quo ante*. The West German government was paying substantial amounts to those few who survived the ghettos, the fewer still who emerged from the camps, along with people who worked in forced labor or lost their property to the Third Reich. Frania Sajac had been a combatant and was proud that she didn't qualify for restitution. His mother wouldn't know about the process. Stefan added, "The forms, they have to be exactly right, or the claims will be invalidated."

She dried her hands, put down the dish towel and drew a chair out from the table and sat, reaching out to cover Stefan's hands with her own. "What else do you need to know, Son?"

"I think that's it. I'll need to sign under oath that no one else is making claims on my behalf."

"Well, I wouldn't worry about that. The Nazis cleaned out the Karpathyn ghetto, burned it down, sent everyone left to the gas chamber. That's what I was told anyway, when I asked." She stopped. "After the war, the Amis handed the SS commandant in Karpathyn over to the Poles. There was a lot of talk against it. They hanged him." Then she thought a moment. "Stefan, don't use your birthdate, the one we made up for school. There won't be a record for such a birth in Poland—I guess it's the Soviet Union now—and your claim may be denied. Just leave it blank and explain you were too young to know. I never had any trouble when I explained why we didn't know."

Chapter Thirty-Five

There was too much time to think on the train back to Cologne. First came the outrage against his orders. *You can't kill your mother!* The thought was swamped by another, just as forceful. *She's not my mother. Frania Sajac is my mother, not Rita Feuerstahl.* Then the pendulum in his head swung back. *She bore you, brought you into this world, gave you up to survive, knowing she had almost no chance herself. No, no, no*, the silent voice shouted, *It's Frania's sacrifice, her stalwart courage under torture you owe your life to.* Too many conflicting thoughts were rushing through his consciousness. Stefan rose, excused himself as he brushed past the others in the compartment and sought the corridor. There he lit one of the smokes he'd brought back from the States. *Dispassion, Sajac, think this out.* He forced himself to walk through the alternatives. *If you don't put an end to her life, the Russians will find her, and they'll do it, but only after extracting knowledge she might resist giving them. Even if she doesn't resist she'll be disposed of quickly.* He saw where dispassion was taking him. *So, you have no choice, Sajac. You'll do your duty. You will hate yourself for doing it. The imperative is categorical!* Then the resolve unraveled and the original train of thought returned. *She's your mother, God damn it!* He staggered back into the compartment and sat heavily.

* * *

All that Sunday afternoon after his return, sitting by his telephone he waited for a call from Schulke. Nothing. Monday morning Stefan went in. Once the sun rose at 8:30 the cold brightness of the day seemed ominous. There was nothing in his pigeonhole at the staff entry, and nothing but the normal Monday morning bustle in the hallways. A few perfunctory 'good mornings' and he was at the door of their office. It was ajar. Schulke was already there, winter coat on the hook behind the door, under a Bavarian hat with a paintbrush feather Stefan hadn't seen before. Stefan looked him over, freshly shaven with two little plasters covering razor nicks, but the beard already visible again in the pores on his cheeks.

Schulke was on the phone. He ushered Stefan in with his free hand. Then he put the receiver down. "Nothing yet from New York about boardings at Idyllwild. They told me they sent out the request on Friday, but the Yanks take weekends off."

Stefan nodded. "Time zone difference is six hours this time of year. They won't even open till 3:00 our time."

"Nothing to do but kill time. Policeman's curse, waiting around, eh, Sajac?"

There was a sporting paper on the desk—soccer news and cheesecake photos. Stefan picked it up without much interest. He couldn't sit there. The man across the desk was going to kill his mother, and his duty would be to assist. Worse, the man would do it without a moment's hesitation, with gleeful vindication, as soon as he found her. Stefan allowed himself to glare in Schulke's direction. "Going to the canteen for some breakfast, OK?"

"Just stay in the building, now you're here."

Sitting alone at a long table, nursing his coffee, Stefan felt like a relative in the hospital, waiting for a surgery to end. The doctor would come out with the prognosis he knew was coming: patient in serious condition, likely to worsen. Chances of pulling through small.

Suddenly he saw Schulke at the entry, smiling broadly and searching the tables for him. With resignation, Stefan waved him over. There was a piece of Teletype paper in the man's hand. He sat down across the table and handed the sheet across. Stefan glanced at it and asked, "How'd it get here so fast?"

"They did it Friday and it sat here all weekend waiting for distribution this morning. We could have been on it all weekend." Then he paused to allow Stefan to read down the list of about a dozen names. "What do you make of it?"

Stefan scanned the list, looking for the name he already suspected would already be there. *Hasn't the man looked already? Is he playing with me?* The sheet was marked, "UN Passports from Idlewild, November 15 1962." There were a dozen names, all male, except for two, a Miss Akai Tanaka, Pan Am via San Francisco to Tokyo, and a Mme. Feuerstahl, TWA to Geneva. Stefan put his finger on the name. Schulke nodded. "Right under our noses."

Stefan tried to sound casual. "Well, 800 kilometers from our noses...but it could have been a lot further."

Schulke rose from the table. "We'll leave tonight. Be there in the morning."

Delay, Stefan, stop him somehow. You need time to think! he told himself. "Can we sort out the travel vouchers and expense money that quickly?"

It was a natural question, but Schulke cut him short. "We can't go through channels, waiting for the Russians to find her. And there's the leaks in this building. If we ask for all the authorizations we need, something is bound to get to the Soviets or the *Stasi*."

Stefan realized Schulke was right about the Russians, and the East Germans too. Now his hand was being forced. He'd have no choice but to track her down. It was no relief. "What do we do?"

"Buy the tickets ourselves."

Stefan was sheepish. "Don't have that much money on me. I'll have to go the bank." He looked at his watch. The banks were already closed. *Good!* "First thing in the morning, sir."

Schulke growled. "Get enough for several days. We'll put in for expenses when we get back." He rose and reached for his coat. "Meet me at the railway station tomorrow at noon. We'll catch the first train for Geneva we can."

* * *

They met at the long-distance ticket office of the Cologne station. Each paid for an express ticket, 2nd class, departing at 12:45, with an evening arrival in Geneva main station. Stefan forgot to get a receipt and turned back to the ticket window. The man behind the grill stamped and embossed one. "Did your friend want one too?" He gestured towards Schulke, standing a few feet away.

That's a first — the boss, forgetting a receipt. Nerves, or just excited?

"Yes, please." Stefan took the second receipt and handed it to his boss. Schulke took it and slipped it into his trouser pocket.

Schulke was calm, friendly, even a bit conversational as they downed two Pilsners in the station buffet. It was cheaper than a drink on the train, and more choice too. In a compartment with other travelers they wouldn't be able to speak openly.

"What'll we do, Boss, when we get there?"

"Get a couple of hotel rooms." He smiled at his wit.

"No, I mean, how do we find her, and once we do…" Stefan knew the answer to the unvoiced question.

So did Schulke. "Think like a cop for a change, Sajac. It's not hard. She's at the UN in Geneva, no? We find her, wait for the right moment. We rub her out." He used one of the few English expressions he knew. It was the first time Schulke had been explicit. Stefan repeated the words and then translated. Schulke nodded and pulled open his jacket just enough to reveal a small side arm, in a holster under his arm. "Got yours?"

"No, Boss. I turned it in when we got back."

Schulke grimaced. "Too late now. Can't be helped."

"Are we" — Stefan searched for the right word — "authorized to do that? Don't they want us to get her back to Cologne for interrogation?"

"Don't be daft, sonny. Of course we've been tasked to take her out. Only the job can't be traced back to us. The Russians, remember — we got to keep them in the dark." Stefan could only nod. He forced a grim smile. Schulke went on. "It may take a few days." They heard their train announced.

* * *

Wednesday morning Sajac and Schulke were standing at a gate before an entrance of the Palace of Nations. Men and women were passing them on each side. Schulke had already stopped one or two and asked in German whether this was the only entrance. All he got was a look of displeasure and a snarl in French. "Let me try, Boss," Stefan whispered. He walked back away from the gate out of earshot, spoke briefly to a woman and nodded his thanks. "She says there are four. But this and one other are the main entries. The other one's all the way round on the other side of the building."

"Very well. We split up. I'll watch this one." He began looking for an inconspicuous place, away from the gate, to stand. "You take the other entrance. If you spot her, follow...but at a distance, Sajac. Can you do that?" Stefan didn't answer the provocation. "Meet me back at the hotel. You know what she looks like well enough?" He pulled the torn photo from his coat pocket, showed it briefly to Stefan. It was now dog-eared and creased, the photo stock paper separating as though it had been subject to a great deal of handling.

Cold and bored, Stefan felt far too conspicuous, standing at the end of a fifty-meter roadway on the Avenue de la Paix. There was a stairway and some large pine trees on the hill behind the street. How does one blend into the scenery standing on the stairs leading up to the headquarters building of the International Committee of the Red Cross? Stefan stood in the same spot from 9:00 AM morning gloom to the dark of 5:00 PM in the evening. The whole time he was trying to look as though he'd just come down the stairs headed for the tram-stop nearby.

There were only a few men coming and going up and down the street all that long, cold, gray day. A handful of taxis swept past him into the drive. But at 5:10 large numbers, including women, began to emerge, in groups. It was too dark to identify anyone at that distance, so he moved to the tram stop. Just as a tram pulled up, there she was, surrounded by three other women, along with a young man. She was, he thought, too preoccupied by the conversation to notice him. Stefan stood well back. *You're watching your mark, you're watching your mother.* He looked her up and down. She was still tall, blond hair to the shoulders. In the tram, under the lights, the face looked to Stefan far too young for the mother of a grown man. She had to be forty-six or forty-seven at least, yet she looked like a woman in her thirties. *Two pathways, starting together, diverge for twenty-four years. Now they intersect. What does it mean?*

The tram wound its way back down the rue de Lausanne in the direction of the train station as passengers alighted and descended. Then she noticed him, Stefan was certain. She'd been glancing round as she talked, obviously watching for something. *Do I break cover?* He smiled slightly. *Why did you do that,* he asked himself? Would she notice? If she noticed, there was no acknowledgment. She stopped looking and resumed an animated conversation. He remained on the tram when she left, watching her turn down the rue de Mole.

Schulke was in the hotel bar, nursing a schnapps, when Stefan entered. He looked up. "Any luck?"

Stefan shook his head. "Maybe she's not here?"

"We'll start earlier tomorrow, and we'll trade places."

When will she spot you? Then a thought froze him. *When will he shoot her?*

* * *

Stefan hadn't been watching the main entry, on Place de Nation, for more than thirty minutes the next morning when Schulke came up to him. "Let's get out of here. I spotted her, going in by the entrance across from the Red Cross Headquarters." Stefan pretended to shake his head at his poor skills. "We'll come back before quitting time. With both of us on her tail, we won't have much trouble shadowing her right to her door."

* * *

That evening Rita spotted Stefan for the second time. Now she knew someone had found her. Again he had smiled openly, and she'd almost smiled back before realizing that it might be a trap. There might be others on this man's team. It would be better if she somehow could suggest that she hadn't noticed at all. She certainly hadn't made Schulke, who was literally standing next to her, facing away towards the back of the tram. Again she left the tram, this time walking back along the busier rue de Lausanne in the direction from which they'd come.

Knowing this was her stop, Schulke got off ahead of her. Guessing her direction correctly, he maintained contact from in front. Stefan remained on the tram one more stop, then quickly walked back towards their quarry and his chief. A few minutes later he found Schulke, walking back towards him, on the busy street.

"Number 6 rue de Pieure, at the end of the Rue de Berne, third floor. She seems to share a flat with another woman or she's a lodger. Can't tell." He turned back towards the rue de Pieure. "Let's see if she goes anywhere tonight, or the flat mate. Maybe we can finish this job tonight. I'll take the first watch. Relieve me in two hours."

"I better stay close, Boss." *Think of a reason, you fool.* "If she spots you, I'll need to take over."

"Well, I don't mind the company. There's a café back there." He pointed twenty meters down the rue de Berne. "Spell me every thirty minutes." He looked round. "I'll be in that carriageway next door."

Three hours and six shifts later, Stefan saw the lights go out in the apartment they were watching. Stefan was stamping his feet when Schulke came out of the café. "Let's pack it up for the day, Sajac."

* * *

At 7:30 the next morning the two men were waiting for her. Schulke was in the café on the rue de Berne with a good view of the door of number 6, and Stefan at the tram stop on the rue du Lausanne. Suddenly he saw their target walking down the street. She wasn't alone and she wasn't dressed for work. There was another woman with her, both wearing trousers tucked into socks over high-topped boots, carrying small rucksacks. They walked arm in arm right by the tram stop and continued in the direction of the main railway station. A long twenty meters behind them walked Schulke. As he passed Stefan there was a grimace of fury on his face. Stefan fell in five meters behind him as they all marched toward the station plaza.

Instead of entering the main railway station, the two women joined a larger group, men and women at another tram stop. By unspoken coordination Sajac and Schulke made for the main station entrance and lurked there till the group's tram arrived. Then, just before the doors closed on the now crowded tram, they mounted, one through the front and the other in the rear. The tram crossed the Rhone River and then ran along the south side of the vast lake to the last stop. But the crowds remained, shielding the two Germans from their quarry.

Last off the tram, Schulke and Sajac realized they were at another, smaller railway station. Above the entry was a sign, *Eaux Vives*. By the time they had descended, their mark had entered the station and was to be seen along a platform full of people kitted out for sport. There was a three-car train already at the platform, doors closed.

Stefan pulled Schulke to the side of the door. "They're going to Chamonix." The older man's face remained blank. "What's that?"

"It's a mountain resort, about two hours from here. By the looks of it, there's no skiing yet. No one is carrying skis. So, they'll be walking the trails still."

"We need to see where she goes when we get there. Then we can figure out our next step. Go inside and buy a ticket. I'll wait." Schulke was about to walk in when Stefan grabbed him again. "Let's split up, travel in different coaches." He needed to be alone, to think things through, for the thousandth time. The man nodded and went into the station.

Stefan looked over the timetable next to the station entry. This train would leave in three minutes and arrive in Chamonix at 12:49 after three stops. With forty-five seconds to go by the station clock Stefan walked in, bought his ticket—remembering his receipt this time—and went out onto the platform. Schulke was well along towards the back of the train. The doors of the train opened and the crowded platform began emptying into the carriages. Quickly he strode up to the entrance taken by the woman and her group. *The woman? Your mother...* The words came to Stefan like the pulse of a migraine. He needed her to see him again, looking friendly and reassuring. The trouble was he didn't know why he needed it. Stefan had no plan.

Surely she'd notice him, looking conspicuous in a suit and a topcoat amongst all these sportsmen and women. Well, that was to the good. He sat three rows behind her group. They were in facing seats across both sides of the car. Could she feel him watching her? When she looked up from her companions, glancing at the increasingly severe alpine scenery, he tried to catch her eye with a smile. If she noticed him she showed no sign. *By now she must know you're following her.*

* * *

It was only after the station stop at Saint Gervais, the last one before Chamonix, that Rita decided to smile back at him, just once. There was no point pretending she hadn't noticed him. He looked familiar, somehow. Like someone she knew. Rita began to search through her memory for faces. He evidently wanted her to notice him. But why? *What does this young man, this boy want? Is he Russian, is he German? Is he just someone who fancies older women? No. He was there on the tram to the Palace of Nations two days before.*

Rita felt safe among her friends and fellow workers. If he was following her, well, then that vindicated this strategy for smoking out surveillance. She tried to turn her attention back to her companions' conversation. It was hard. Vagrant thoughts of the threat she faced intruded over and over. *Whoever's following you, they didn't lose the trail for long.* "What did you say, dear?" Rita tried to pick up the conversational thread. *If he's German, he's going to kill you.* The woman repeated her remark. All Rita heard was the voice in her head: *If he's Russian, he's going to kidnap you.*

* * *

Fifteen minutes later the train arrived at Chamonix in a rainsquall. Gray clouds were scudding low over the town, hiding the high walls of the narrow valley. At the *Place de Gare* before the station, the crowds spread, some heading to the left, down towards the great gondolas Stefan had seen as the train rumbled into town under their cables. Others went right, up to a trestle pedestrian bridge across the railway tracks. But as the two men came into the waiting room from the platform, they saw Rita's group head across the *place* to a café. Watching from the windows in the darkened waiting room, they saw the group find two tables and sit down.

"It's raining. They're in no rush," Stefan observed. Schulke had lit a cigarette and was looking for a buffet or bar the station was too small to allow for. "Boss, with those rucksacks they're carrying, they're here for the weekend."

Schulke spit a bit of tobacco from his lower lip. "So are we, Sajac. So are we..." He was evidently not happy about the matter. "We've got to separate her from this crowd, to do the job... cleanly."

"Can I scout round a bit, Boss?" Stefan had no idea what he was looking for, but he needed something to construct a plan on. *A plan to do what? To stop Schulke or to stop her?* He looked across the *place* to Rita sitting in the café. *To save you... from the Russians, one way or the other.* He could only address her in his thoughts as *you—whoever you are, whoever you are to me...*

Fifteen minutes later, he was back in the station. "Anything?" Schulke demanded.

"Well, it's a ski town without snow yet, just this rain for the moment." He nodded at the glistening pavement. "Anyway, up there, over the trestle" —he pointed to the right— "there's a rack railway to a glacier and a sort of mountain hotel...a refuge, a Berghütte." Did Schulke understand what that was? Stefan looked at the group working its way through a leisurely lunch. "If they go that direction after their meal, it'll be to spend the night there."

"Very well." Schulke nodded. "We follow."

"Not like this, Boss. We can't go up there dressed for... business."

"What do you suggest, Herr Leutnant? We wait here for them to come down?"

Stefan shook his head. "If they head up the rack railway, we'll know where they're going. By the time they finish their lunch it'll be too late for them to hike today. Besides, it's still raining. So, we've got time to buy some kit and get up to the hut before dark. Tomorrow we'll see where they're going." Schulke frowned. Then he nodded in acquiescence.

The café was closing, chairs were being turned over onto tables. Waiters sweeping up before the afternoon closing. Finally

Rita's group rose and paid. Slinging their rucksacks on their backs, they moved out of the café. As they passed the windows of the station, headed for the trestle footbridge, the two Germans stepped back into the dark. Stefan noticed that most of them carried what looked like collapsed ski poles attached to each side of their packs. When they were gone, Schulke spoke. "Let's get out of here."

Chapter Thirty-Six

"Two pair of socks, sir. Remember," the salesman at the counter of the mountaineering store enjoined them. "Otherwise it's the worst blisters." Stefan translated for Schulke. They'd purchased the cheapest wool pants and anoraks at a military surplus store near the great gondola lift to the Aiguille du Midi. At a similar shop they found a used duffle for their street clothes. The boots would complete their preparations. Stefan was paying for the boots when he noticed the barrel of ski poles. He looked towards the salesman. "You sell those, but not the skis to go with them?"

The salesman leaned over, pulled one from the barrel, collapsed it and twisted it. "Not ski poles, *bâtons de marche*." Then he translated. *"Trekkingstocke."*

"How much?" The man mentioned a figure. Stefan took two from the barrel. "I'll have a pair, please."

The man looked at Schulke. "And you?" He spoke German.

Schulke replied in German. "Not old enough for a cane, thanks." He looked at the receipt for the boots, tossed it in a trashcan by the counter and left the store. Stefan noticed, but this time it did not occur to him how out of character the gesture was for Schulke. He was too preoccupied.

* * *

They were sitting in the almost empty rack-railway car, mounting the side of the valley in a forest of stately pines. Much of the valley below would have been visible had they been sitting on the left side. Instead their view was of the retaining wall where the track had been cut through the hillside to reduce the steepness of the roadbed. There was no conversation. Schulke was growing increasingly anxious as the train mounted. When it stopped halfway up the valley, to allow the downward train to pass and regain the single track, Schulke closed his eyes and with his elbows on his knees covered them with his hands. It was the fear of heights that apparently came with Schulke's fear of flying. Once the clouds beneath them cloaked their altitude, Schulke regained his composure. Then the train broke through to a fierce blue sky above the white tufts of cotton nimbus that still covered the valley floor.

The doors opened onto flat ground at a vast overlook. An attendant called out, "*Mer de Glace,*" and opened the platform gate to allow descending passengers on to the little train. As they stepped across to the retaining wall, the view was sublime, dominated by the sawteeth of the Aguille du Dru across the glacier, already white with new snow. Stefan was drawn towards it. At the barrier wall he turned to his right, looked up the valley to the massifs that dominated the sky and obliterated any horizon. Schulke had meanwhile seen the stone and cement structure set at the brow of the cliff side—the *Hôtel Refuge du Montenvers*. He was already moving towards it steadily, staring directly at the ground before him.

Stefan caught up with him at the door. Entering, they found a wiry Frenchman, dressed in a woodsman's flannel shirt and Tyrolean corduroy trousers, just coming out from behind the small registration desk. Behind the counter were three rows of pigeonholes, none of which seemed to have a key hanging from its hook. Suddenly Stefan was anxious. Could they be booked up for the night? The man returned to the registry desk and opened a ledger. "You'll be wanting to stay the night, messieurs?"

"*Oui.*" Stefan nodded. "Have you space for us?"

"Not in the *dortoire.*" It was a word Stefan didn't know. His face looked blank. The man understood. "The sleeping hall, bunk beds. Full up with a group from Geneva." Stefan translated for Schulke, noticing how the innkeeper grimaced when he heard the German. "Just so happens I have one private room left. One night?" They both nodded. The man went on, smiling.

"Wouldn't have mattered."

Stefan did not understand. "Wouldn't have mattered. Why not?"

"Last train's gone and it's almost dark. I'd have to keep you even if it meant your sleeping on a table. That's the rules binding mountain refuges in France."

"Well, thank you." He turned and translated to the unsmiling Schulke.

"Documents, gentlemen. Payment in advance please." He held out his hand. Schulke paid. Both men produced their German passports. Stefan saw the innkeeper wince again momentarily and then smile. "Dinner at 7:30. No choice. *Raclette*, I'm afraid." It was a simple cheese dish common to alpine farm families in winter. He handed them a long, single-toothed key with a cardboard luggage tag label. "Room 011, down on the ground floor." He pointed to a stairway.

Schulke demanded, "Ask if we can eat in our room." Stefan did so.

The man smiled. "Only the mice eat in the rooms." The receipt was still on the counter. Stefan picked it up. *What's gotten into him, forgetting again? He's never forgotten a receipt in his life.*

* * *

The unheated room had two narrow beds with a small pine table between, open shelves and a few hooks. The space was illuminated by a naked incandescent bulb hanging low enough from the ceiling to graze Stefan's head as he walked by. He dumped the duffle on one bed, while Schulke took off his coat, hung it on a hook, stretched himself on the other, and pushed his hat over his eyes.

Quietly Stefan moved to the coat hooks, moved his hands over Schulke's coat, feeling for his weapon. *Why are you looking anyway? Do you want to pull the trigger?* He had no answer to his own question. Looking out the window, Stefan noticed a trail marker in the deepening gloom. "I'm going out for a reconnoiter."

"Suit yourself," was the only reply from under the hat.

He pulled the trekking poles from the duffle and went out.

* * *

At first the path rose gently but steadily. Then Stefan found himself at a fork with a wooden signpost. On it one arrow pointed to the left, *Signal de Forbes (2143 m.) 1 heure, difficile.* Beneath the arrow pointing to the right path, he read the words, *Plan de Aiguille, 3 heures, moyen* — medium. A small thrill of boyish adventure forced Stefan to go left.

A few minutes later he was huffing and coughing as he pulled each leg up a series of boulders just too large for steps. The footing was wet from rivulets of rainwater and he was glad of the trekking poles. Despite the dropping temperatures he was soon perspiring. *Too much clothing for this much exertion.* By the time he'd gone thirty minutes it was becoming so dark that only the path was still visible. Suddenly he emerged from the trees and found himself on a ledge, rock wall to his left, and nothing but air to his right, with the twinkle of town lights a thousand meters below. How long this narrow walkway carried on he couldn't tell in the gloom. He would have to descend.

* * *

Schulke was still asleep when Stefan returned. Stefan grabbed one of the two small, threadbare towels and went down the corridor to the communal showers. There was no soap and he had brought none. He chose a compartment. There, quite alone, he stood beneath the hot water and thought things through.

* * *

Stefan shook Schulke out of his nap "I think I've figured things out, boss." The older man rose on his elbows, listening. "In the morning we get her to leave the group early and walk by herself, up a trail I found. When she's far enough along on the track it will be easy to take her out without any one observing..."

"Yea, how you going to make her take a walk alone up some mountain track?"

Stefan had an answer ready. Would it work? "Leave that to me. I think I can do it. She's noticed me smiling already...and she's smiled back."

Schulke's grin was knowing. "Sajac, I've been after that woman for almost 20 years. If I'd gotten her the first time..." He paused. "I'd be running the whole BfV, instead of running you." Stefan turned his back. He wanted not to hear. It had no effect on Schulke. His tone became angrier. "She wrecked my plans, made me a nobody," He paused and then began to maunder about his blighted past, indifferent to whether Stefan was listening. A lifetime's self-pity, then bitterness, and finally a murderous anger against this woman seethed from his throat. Singlehanded she'd thwarted his life, Soon it became a screed. Stefan ceased completely to listen to. "But, I'll have my justice, Sajac...in the end, you'll see." What Stefan could see was that all his life Schulke had been alone in his head with the image of a woman, never making a real human attachment to anyone, grudging everyone else, fixated on this one woman. Abruptly the man fell silent.

Stefan had stopped listening. Something had been bothering him for a day or more now, gnawing almost since they'd left Cologne. Now it bit hard enough to draw his full concentration. *The old man's not keeping receipts, not even for large amounts, like rail tickets. Clothes, boots, a hotel bill.* It was totally out of character. Why not? He doesn't care about being reimbursed, he is fixated on killing this woman. *It's all he can think of. Or maybe this mission isn't even authorized anymore.* If it had been cancelled there'd be no travel vouchers. *We had to buy our tickets with our own money. Is Schulke on his own, and carrying me along with him. He's going to kill this woman no matter what, even without authorization. Maybe even against orders?*

Stefan was about to confront Schulke. He opened his mouth and then it froze. What if he was right? Would it make a difference, then and there? Schulke might just decide he had to kill both of them. *You're letting yourself be carried away.* Schulke was a man who'd followed orders all his life. He couldn't stop now. *All this receipt business, Stefan, it's just the excitement of the chase....* It had to be. *He'll be relieved when you hand him the receipts tomorrow.*

Schulke finally ended his rant and Stefan suddenly feared some response would be demanded of him. Instead Schulke rose and asked him "Suppertime?"

* * *

Rita was sitting with half a dozen others at a circular table in the dining room that stretched along the downhill side of the building. It was clear enough to see a few lights twinkling from the mountain huts across the valley. Below them the moonlit clouds still obscured the village below. After their vast lunch, the group had been happy enough with the spartan fare of the hotel. Now there was a small glass of *Marc de Bourgogne*—a liquor, clear but powerful, sitting before each of them.

* * *

Rita's head recoiled at the sight of the men entering the dining room. She'd been certain about the young one tailing her on the train. When they hadn't turned up on the rack railway, the feeling that she was safe for the moment had increased. The group had somehow lost them going up to the *Mer de Glace*. *Foolish you. They didn't need to follow. There was only one place you'd go on that train.* Things had worked pretty much as Rita had wanted, had feared. But at least the tactic had worked. She knew where she was. Then she realized: *No you don't. Are they Russians trying to squeeze a secret out of you they don't know? Or are they Germans here to prevent you from passing that secret along?*

She watched as the two men sat and gave an order to the waiter, who brought two bottles of beer, and then two plates and a table heater for the *Raclette* cheese dish. The younger man began to pat his pockets, obviously searching for a packet of cigarettes. He spoke a word to the older man, one she hadn't noticed before. Then the younger man rose, looked down at his companion staring into his beer. Then he stared straight at Rita, hard, for a long second, till he was certain she'd seen the look. He left the table and walked towards the stairway.

Rita waited a moment and rose. "Back in a minute," she said to no one in particular, and headed for the ladies WC, also down the stair.

Stefan waited in his room for a long minute. His signal hadn't worked. Quietly he opened the door, looked up the hall towards the stair and went out. Just as he passed the pebbled glass of the now dark shower room, a hand reached out, grabbed his shirtsleeve and pulled him in from the corridor. There she was, a step away from him. He exhaled in relief but she didn't notice. The words spat from her mouth. First a few words in Russian that he didn't understand. Then the words he did. *"German or Russian?"*

"German," he responded. "But wait." He reached out to hold her by both arms, then released her to put his finger to his mouth. She understood, or at least she remained silent. "It's the other guy we have to worry about."

"We?" she hissed. "Who are you?"

"It doesn't matter. Now listen. If I were a danger to you, you'd be dead already." He pulled her hands to his waist and then his chest. "See, no weapon." She nodded. "But the other guy has one. And he intends to use it." Stefan gulped, suddenly knowing his plan. "It's not enough to stop him using it. We've got to… get rid of him…permanently." She was silent. "Look, tomorrow morning, after breakfast, go out alone. Tell your friends you're having a smoke or something, anything. Just be alone. Start up the trail to the *Signal de Forbes*. It's the hard one just behind the hotel."

"What? So you can get me alone and kill me?"

"You've got to trust me. It's your only chance. Either that or wait for the Russians to find you, the way we did."

"Your lot, the Russians, what difference does it make?"

"We can't argue. Just do it, will you…please." Stefan held her shoulders. His words were spoken as a plea, not a threat. Then he released her.

Without a word Rita turned and left him alone in the damp darkness of the shower.

Stefan left the shower room, and headed back to the dining room. Schulke had begun spooning the *Raclette* into his plate. He hadn't seemed to notice Rita's return to her companions. Schulke's raised eyebrows spoke his silent question to Stefan. Pulling his chair out, Stefan answered quietly. "I'm not sure. I think so. She didn't refuse." Schulke began to dish out more raclette onto his plate. Stefan wasn't hungry.

Rita sat there, at the table, reeling. She kept her hands under the table and her face from showing any of the emotions that succeeded each other. *What is this young man asking me to do? Walk off alone so I can be killed without anyone witnessing?* She downed the Marc and watched as one of the men at the table immediately refilled the glass. Then she downed another and put her hand up to stop further replenishment.

I can't trust him just because he smiled at me on a tram in Geneva.

He certainly hadn't been smiling a few moments before, down there, in the shower room. And he was steadily avoiding her furtive gaze now.

You must decide, Rita. She'd had to do it before, many times — been forced to decide by gut instinct or the flip of a coin, all the way back to her escape from the Karpathyn ghetto. To trust or not to. *Which side are you on, nameless young man? Are you a Mallory or a St John? An Erich Klein or Phil Morton...or a Gil Romero?* Suddenly, a face she had trusted came to her. It was the face of a policeman, a cop in a trench coat on a train out of Lemberg in 1942. She'd broken down, confessed her real identity to him...and he had told her what to do, sent her on her way to survival. *Very well.* She decided, reached for the bottle of Marc and poured out another. Resolved, she breathed deeply, and suddenly felt strong.

* * *

At the table a few meters away Stefan was trying to decide whether she would do as he'd asked. He'd just had a furtive conversation with his mother. *Will you ever talk with her again?* He looked at her, watched her, saw the three small glasses of Marc she'd taken, one after another. *Was it Dutch courage to do what he'd asked or fear?* Stefan's thoughts shifted. *She thinks you're dead...She's thought so, been certain of it, for those same twenty years you thought she was dead. Will she die that way, not knowing? What might it be like, to have found each other?* And then he stopped himself. He looked at the man opposite, the man who would do the killing, taking a third helping of the now caked and tepid cheese dish. Schulke called over the waiter. Pointing to the other table, to Rita's table, he said to Stefan, "Tell him to bring us whatever they're drinking over there, will you?" Stefan made the request. In a moment two small glasses and a bottle were standing between them on the table. Schulke dismissed the *Raclette* with a gesture and poured two glasses, then raised one in a toast. Under his breath he spoke. "To tomorrow. It will finally belong to us...." It was, Stefan recognized, the refrain of an old Nazi song.

"What do you mean, Boss?"

The older man tapped the hard bulge under his flannel shirt. A distinctive rictus shaped his mouth. He'd kept the holstered pistol on his chest even as he slept.

* * *

There were still people in the dining room, drinking, playing cribbage, talking quietly, a few minutes after ten when Rita's group rose *en masse* and headed for the *dortoire*. Stefan and Schulke could hear the waiter ask them, "When do you want breakfast?" and the reply from several, "8:30." The late autumn sun would just be rising.

When they'd left, Schulke rose, and Stefan followed. "Tell him breakfast for us at 8:15. Don't want to lose track of them tomorrow."

Chapter Thirty-Seven

Stefan woke from a dream. It was one he'd had before, back to his boyhood. He was standing on a shoreline while someone out in the water kept coming to the surface, calling his name, demanding he swim when he couldn't. It was a dream that came to him always before an examination, the day a punishment was due, a dental appointment, when he knew there'd be something to dread, like this morning. Stefan reached for his watch. Suddenly he was hot from the flush of having overslept. It was after 8:00. He had to wake Schulke and get him up to breakfast.

The man didn't want to rise. Stefan had to push again and again. Finally he hissed in Schulke's ear, "They're leaving soon. If you don't get up we'll lose her." This worked. Schulke rose and padded off to the toilet in his underwear. Stefan was dressed by the time he returned. He grabbed his coat and his trekking poles. "I'm going upstairs." Schulke swept his arm towards the door, as if to say get out. Then he began looking round on the floor by his bed for his clothes.

Rita was already at a long table set for the number in her group. But she was alone, and looked as though she'd both not slept at all and slept in her clothes. She was facing the windows, with a cup of coffee before her, and slice of baguette buttered and half eaten. She rose, looked at Stefan and spoke quietly, "Very well…"

Stefan shook his head. "Don't leave yet. Not till he gets up here. Another few minutes." He didn't want her to get too far up the track before they started after her. She shrugged and sat back down, staring blankly at her coffee cup.

They could hear a door close below and heavy footfalls on the stair tread. Schulke arrived. Stefan nodded and Rita got up just in time for Schulke to see her leave the refuge, carrying her trekking poles.

Schulke's head jerked in her direction and Stefan rose from his chair. By the time they were out the front door she was gone from sight. Both knew this meant she'd gone right, towards the trail across the *Grande Balcon Nord* that paralleled the valley floor, a thousand meters above it. Turning, they walked quickly towards the start of the trail. There they saw their quarry, looking briefly at the sign and going to the left, up steeply along the steps of broken boulders into the pine forest.

The two men followed. Over the first several hundred meters Rita lengthened her lead, looking back occasionally, as if signaling that she knew she was being followed. Soon however, the boulder steps grew more difficult and her pace slowed as she had to clamber instead of stride from rock to rock. Her poles proved an encumbrance and she found herself switching them from one hand to the other, unable to use both on the rocks. It was now that the two began to gain on her, Schulke leading, though Stefan could hear his labored breath. In the morning sun their eyes began to sting with perspiration and at almost the same instant both men shed their anoraks, leaving them on the trail. There was no relief to the sustained upward course, though the pines grew smaller and great vistas opened up to their right. Then suddenly they broke out of the tree line altogether and found themselves on a narrow track. This neither rose nor fell as it threaded between an overhang of solid rock on their left, and the kilometer of sheer drop-off to their right. The track was only about fifty meters long, from where the path opened to the rock face to the place it climbed again away from the edge, up the fall line protected by another grove of stunted pines. Stefan recognized it as the spot where he'd turned back in the twilight of the previous evening.

Until that moment at the opening of the narrow path Schulke had been focused on the woman up the trail, calculating with each step whether he was gaining or losing. But now he stopped, looked down, and took a step out onto the exposure beyond the trees and bushes. The vast panorama stretching along the deep valley of Chamonix suddenly came into full view. The town lay below him, windows gleaming in the morning sun, the Arve River running down to rapids they could see but not hear. Far below, a Piper Cub was flying silently up the valley beneath them. The exposure was too much for Schulke. "I can't do it." He turned to Stefan. "Go on...after her, before she gets away." He reached for his pistol to pass it to Stefan.

"Boss, go ahead. I'm right behind you. You can do it. Just twenty steps." He grabbed on to Schulke's belt, tugging at it reassuringly, turning him round. "*Achtung. Vormarsh,*" he ordered. It was what he'd have said to a squad of recruits. Stefan released the belt, but still Schulke hesitated. "She's getting away, Boss." Stefan pointed up with his trekking pole. Again, louder, he commanded, "*Vormarsh.*"

Then, just as Rita turned back to watch, Schulke took a hesitant step forward, a second one and a third. There was already a meter between him and Stefan. Behind him, Stefan couldn't see his face. *Is he conquering his fear?* He caught up, almost too close to Schulke. It was only then that he finally and irrevocably decided. Stefan thrust one of the trekking poles between the older man's legs and pushed with the other one, hard.

Schulke tottered, tried to keep his footing, then pirouetted back towards the cliff face. The words formed on his mouth, *Was hast du gemacht*—What have you done? But as he lost footing, the words were overtaken by a howl that turned into a shriek. Beginning to slip off the ledge, his feet slid away completely. But as he fell Schulke reached out and managed to grab first one and then the other of Stefan's trekking poles.

The sudden weight on both pulled Stefan to the edge of the track. He fell down on his knees against the shards of rock where the narrow path had been cut into the cliffside. Leaning back to save himself, Stefan was holding the older man's weight, keeping him from dropping away. Stefan let go of the poles, and Schulke dropped by a hand span. Instead of falling, though, Schulke was still there, his hands gripping the last ten centimeters of the poles.

It's the straps, damn it. They were taught on Stefan's wrists, pulling his arms down towards the struggling Schulke.

Stefan could see the man's malevolent eyes boring into his face. He would die with Schulke, pulled along by the other man's weight, down a thousand meters.

Then the straps slowly slid over Stefan's hands, gently lowering Schulke till the sticks dropped away, still in Schulke's hands. Stefan watched his face grow smaller as he fell away. After the first hundred meters the whole body bounced like a water bag off an outcropping and fell again in a drop that seemed to last forever. Watching, Stefan finally lost sight of the speck of green against the carpet of trees on the valley floor.

He looked up. The woman had watched, too, her eyes following the same downward path and then turning towards Stefan. He could not make out her expression.

Stefan just stood on the path as she slowly worked her way back down to the far side of the exposed route. She walked steadily across the narrow pathway, showing no sign of anxiety. When she was only a meter from him she spoke, in German: "What now?"

"We will have to return to the *Mer de Glace*, find the police and report this most regrettable accident. You saw how I tried to save him with my trekking poles. But you will have to do the talking, as I speak very little French."

She nodded silently but agreeably. Then, conspiratorially, she said, "Are you certain he is dead?"

"No one can be sure of these things, but it was the best job I could make of it."

* * *

It was late in the afternoon when the deputy chief inspector closed his notebook, stared from one face to the other, and said with a look of sincere regret, "I am sorry you have had to go through this so many times." He turned to Rita. "It must have been painful, mademoiselle." She managed to heighten her somber affect. Then he turned to Stefan. "And for the loss of your friend, my sympathies." Stefan made a Gallic shrug as if to say there was nothing more to do.

Both Rita and Stefan rose. Each smiled wanly to show no resentment at the repeated and sustained questioning. They had been at it all day, separately and together with three different ranks—the gendarme at the desk, his sergeant, and now the detective in a suit and tie, smoking endless Galois. All they could say was that they saw the man lose his footing and spiral off the path downward for a long time before he became a speck above the carpet of treetops far below. Stefan was able to add that his friend had spurned trekking poles, was afraid of flying, but never expressed any acrophobia. Rita told each questioner the same thing: She'd been hiking alone, had seen the two other walkers behind her as the switchbacks turned to give a view of the path behind her. Once across the narrow path, she'd stopped to catch her breath, heard the shriek as the man began to stumble. The other man had tried to save him with the poles. Then she'd watched him go down the precipice. She'd rushed back to the other walker and they'd both gone back to the *Hôtel Montenvers*, hoping to find a telephone to call the *Gendarmerie Nationale* in the village below.

They were reaching for their anoraks when the telephone on the inspector's desk rang. He looked at them, and then at the phone. Putting up a hand to keep them from leaving, he answered, "Oui?" He was silent for some time, nodding and doodling on his blotter. Finally, he said, "*Merci, Monsieur le médicine.*" Then the inspector looked back at them. "Well, someone's found the body, still holding your trekking poles. A forester cutting wood for the winter came upon it. Hauled it onto his lumber cart and drove to the hospital. They've got the body. They say he was probably dead before he hit the ground. Huge wound, and the concussion caved in half the skull. Could only have been caused by hitting rock after a long fall. That's what the doctor said."

Now Stefan had to speak. "I see. What will happen to the body? I'll have to reach his family."

"Don't worry about it for a day or two. They'll send his body to the *pompes funèbres*." Stefan didn't understand the word. He looked at Rita.

In German she said, "'Bestatter'—mortician."

* * *

"Where to now, *Madame* Feuerstahl?" She wasn't young enough for a *Fraulein,* but he couldn't call her *Frau.*

She smiled at the formality. "Up the mountain for my gear. Then I'm going back to Geneva. You?"

"Yes. I'll stay round long enough to collect the body."

They were silent as they ambled into the main square of Chamonix, beginning to glow from the lamps coming on in the tourist shops. Beneath their awnings the cafes were still serving hardy souls on their exterior terraces in the late November twilight. Rita paused, put a hand on Stefan's arm. "Let me buy you a coffee, Mr Sajac."

"That's a good idea." They turned to the nearest *Bar Tabac.*

Stefan went to the counter and purchased a packet of *Stuyvesants* while she chose a table towards the back, screened from the bar by a turn in the wall. *She doesn't want us to be seen, or disturbed, or...* Stefan thought. *Suits me.* He'd said almost nothing from the moment she'd joined him on the trail, beyond the words *You saw me try to save him with those poles, yes?* She had nodded her head. That had been the extent of their conspiracy, one that therefore couldn't be betrayed by a lie. Now he had to speak, and he had no idea of what exactly to say.

* * *

The small cups of *espresso* had arrived. Stefan had taken out a cigarette, then offered the packet to Rita, who took one. They both drew long and exhaled. "So, Mr Sajac. What is this all about?" She was speaking German. Stefan couldn't decide how to begin. She leaned forward. "Why was he going to kill me? Why did you stop him?"

Because I couldn't let you die. You had to know you were my mother, you had to know your child survived. No, That's not enough, that's not even why. It's just what you want to tell her now. Stefan didn't know why he'd done it. There wasn't a reason, a calculation, a motive. It was pure emotion—more than one, that had driven his act. It was a rush of love...and anger that had moved him, a need he could feel that Rita live and Schulke die. He could sense the emotions echo through his body still, hours later... *Just answer her question!* "You had...have a dangerous secret. It's why your husband was killed."

Rita exhaled the cigarette smoke. There was a detachment in her voice, and irony. "He wasn't killed by the Russians. And they wouldn't have come after me either, if your lot hadn't started."

"It wasn't my idea."

"I understand." Then she sighed. "It doesn't matter...now."

Stefan had no immediate reply. "It still does, actually. The Soviets are probably close to finding you ..."

"I know. They found me in New York and wanted to squeeze me. That's why I had to get away."

"Well, they didn't know your secret, and it looks like they still don't."

Rita was losing patience. "How can you be sure?"

"I can't answer that without getting you and me into more trouble."

"I can guess." Rita frowned. "And the Russians are still looking for me?"

"Yes. But now I think I'll be able to put them off."

Rita relaxed slightly. "What about your people? Can you stop them too?" *Can I have a life again?* The thought expressed itself on her face.

"Well, I am going to try to do both." He had figured it all out coming down the trail that morning. "I'll go back and get the BfV to tell itself that we've established you know nothing. That'll get back through leaks to the Russians and the *Stasi* and they'll stop looking for you."

"But you killed your boss. They'll see right through that in the BfV."

"I'm going to tell them that if they don't drop the matter, all the documents that led us to you will be sent to the *Stasi* in Berlin. Then the Russians will know why we were looking for you. I'll give the papers to someone who'll send them the moment anything happens to you...or me." *I won't tell her about Frania. Not now.* "Then I'll just go back to the West German Army, where I came from. They won't touch me there."

Rita sighed. "So, maybe I'll have a life after all?"

Stefan smiled. "I think so, yes. What will you do with it?"

Rita thought a moment. Then a look of contentment came into her face. "Go back to New York, pick up the pieces, live the life I was living...if your plan works."

"I'll make it work." There was confidence in his tone. He needed her to be sure of things.

Rita squared her shoulders. Suddenly she was all business again. "You still haven't answered my other question. Why did you do it? Why did you kill your partner instead of letting him kill me?" He remained silent. She reached across to him. "There's something else, Mr Sajac, isn't there? What is it?" She gripped his forearm.

Stefan gulped. Then in Polish he said, "Call me Stefan."

Chapter Thirty-Seven

"Very well. Stefan." She replied in Polish but did not release her hold.

"I read your memoir, the one you wrote about the war." Before she could ask, he explained. "I found it in your flat in New York."

All she could say was, "So? So what?"

"The other guy, my partner...actually, my boss. His name was Schulke, Otto Schulke. Ring a bell?"

Rita shook her head. "No, why? Should it?"

"He was a low-level policeman in the Third Reich. He arrested you in Mannheim, winter of '44. He'd been investigating you for months, suspicious of your cover story as a domestic."

It was only his name she hadn't been able to recall. "Now I remember. His superior forced him to release me...us. I was with another woman, a friend."

"Well, you became an idée fixe, an obsession for this guy. All his life, he couldn't give up the notion that having to let you go wrecked his life, changed everything for him. He had to find you. In the end it was some kind of pathological revenge, crazed vindication."

She was still impatient. "Get to the point."

"Anyway, I think he might have been ordered to quit looking for you. But he didn't tell me and he wasn't going to quit. He was going to kill you no matter what."

"Well, I owe you my life then." She smiled.

Stefan had to speak. "I owe you mine. That's why I stopped him." Rita looked at him blankly. "I read your memoir. I know about your first child, your son...the one you had to send away. The one you thought was dead."

Rita shook her head. "No. He didn't die in the war, he wasn't killed. I saw him one day, afterward...in '47, with the woman who saved him."

She hasn't been listen to my words, Stefan realized. *How can I tell her?*

Rita was still talking. "He was seven." Then she thought about the woman, her hands, her finger ends, the torture she'd survived. The memory came to Rita. *She said she was from Radom, and I had to lie that I was from Krakow, not Karpathyn.*

Stefan raised his hands to her sides, held both her arms, and gently forced her to look at him. Then, quietly but firmly, he repeated himself. "I owe you my life...you are my mother."

Rita looked at Stefan again, and she knew whom she was talking to.

He spoke again. "You saved my life by giving me to a Home Army courier, who became my mother too." He watched the tears welling in her eyes. Then Rita's words registered with him. "It must have cost you so much. When you saw me again, when you found me, back in '47." There was a kind of awe in his voice. "You made yourself give me up again."

Rita heard it as a question. She had to explain, to herself again, as much as to Stefan for the first time. "I couldn't take you away from her...I couldn't take you from your mother a second time, not after she'd saved your life, protected you, raised you..."

He reached over and held her to him for a long time as they both sobbed.

Afterword

The decryption of the German Enigma code was publicly disclosed only in 1974, even though hints had appeared for the previous five years, in the writings of Polish military historians. The British official history, including the role of Alan Turing, and the invention of the first programmable digital computers, appeared in five volumes after 1979.

Reading German military radio traffic was crucial to British survival during the Battle of the Atlantic in 1940-41, to the defense of Egypt against Rommel in 1942, to monitoring the disposition of Wehrmacht panzer divisions in France before D-day in 1944. The limited success of the Germans in the winter of 1944, during the "Battle of the Bulge," was partly due to the fact that the Wehrmacht was required by Hitler to employ telephone lines and prohibited from using radio communications. Thus Allied reliance on decrypts of Enigma signals led them to complacency about possible German offensives.

No reason has ever been given for the Allied governments' reticence about these matters for over twenty-nine years from the end of the war.

Also by Alex Rosenberg

The Intrigues of Jennie Lee
(Top Hat Books, 2020)
9781789044584

Autumn in Oxford
(Lake Union Publishing, 2016)
9781503939073

The Girl from Krakow
(Lake Union Publishing, 2015)
9781477830819

Top Hat Books

Historical fiction that lives

We publish fiction that captures the contrasts, the achievements, the optimism and the radicalism of ordinary and extraordinary times across the world.

We're open to all time periods and we strive to go beyond the narrow, foggy slums of Victorian London. Where are the tales of the people of fifteenth century Australasia? The stories of eighth century India? The voices from Africa, Arabia, cities and forests, deserts and towns? Our books thrill, excite, delight and inspire. The genres will be broad but clear. Whether we're publishing romance, thrillers, crime, or something else entirely, the unifying themes are timescale and enthusiasm. These books will be a celebration of the chaotic power of the human spirit in difficult times. The reader, when they finish, will snap the book closed with a satisfied smile.

If you have enjoyed this book, why not tell other readers by posting a review on your preferred book site.

Readers of ebooks can buy or view any of these bestsellers by clicking on the live link in the title. Most titles are published in paperback and as an ebook. Paperbacks are available in traditional bookshops. Both print and ebook formats are available online.
Find more titles and sign up to our readers' newsletter at
http://www.johnhuntpublishing.com/fiction

Follow us on Facebook at https://www.facebook.com/JHPfiction
and Twitter at https://twitter.com/JHPFiction